Treasured Love Series

Book One

◊◊◊◊◊

Emerald Flame

◊◊◊◊◊

Katrina Shelley

Treasured Love Series – Book One – *Emerald Flame*
3rd Edition
Copyright 2009
ISBN1448667674
EAN-139781448667673

Editor: Heather Frederickson

Available titles by Katrina Shelley

Treasured Love Series
Book One - Emerald Flame
Book Two – Forbidden Amber
Book Three – Golden Confessions
Book Four – Sapphire Storm

Treasured Love Series - The Ancestors Collection:
Book One – Emerald Flame, Book Two – Forbidden Amber, Book Three – Golden Confessions

Treasured Love Series Friendship Connection - Timeless Melody

Forever Fan Trilogy
Second Time Around
Second Chances
Second to None

Embraced

~~~

Children's Titles
Written as Shelley Nakopoulos:
(Illustrated by Emma Nakopoulos)

How Big?

Twelve Months Make One Year:
An Encouraging Artwork and Creativity Book

Emmy Ponak Series
Imagination Overload

Dedications:

Mom,

Thank you for instilling in me a love of history and always taking me on those day trips to Harper's Ferry, Gettysburg, Antietam . . . Thank you for allowing me to read my first historical romance—and my second and my third . . . Thank you most for loving and supporting me in my dreams and endeavors to write (and everything else, too). I love you.

Dad,

Thanks for working so hard. Your commitment to your job allowed us to take those day-trips, which fed my knowledge and growing dreams of becoming an author . . . Thank you for being a reader and therefore giving me the desire to do the same (even if you do only like non-fiction). I love you, too.

For Mom and Dad Both,

It is a blessing to have parents who, even from a young start, were strong examples. You built a family and home for us filled with love. I never noticed your age or the struggles you likely had or how hard you must have worked to learn to be the wonderful parents you are . . . I saw love—only, only love.

For my editor, Heather Frederickson –
My continued thanks.

Prologue

1842
McClaran House ~ Dublin, Ireland

Brianna McClaran sat in the dim light the bedroom windows allowed and watched her mother's labored breathing. Leila was peaceful during sleep. It was when she was conscious that pain and nightmares plagued her.

It was now six months since Brianna's father had lost his life to the sea he loved so dearly. Adjusting to life void of Patrick McClaran's exuberant personality was difficult for all who had known and loved him; for his wife Leila, it was impossible.

The doctor deemed Leila McClaran healthy and capable of living a normal life, she simply chose not to. She had given up and there was nothing more that could be done to save her.

Brianna forced a smile to her lips as her mother's eyes fluttered weakly open. Leila attempted to talk and her dehydrated throat cracked. After she took a sip of the water Brianna offered her, she spoke softly. "Bria," she held Brianna's hand limply. "How horrible all this must be for you. Will you ever be able to forgive my selfishness?"

"Mama, sure and you know there is nothing to be forgiving. I'm doing naught but what any other child would do for the mother they love so dear, as I do you." They had revisited this conversation many times. Brianna was unsure whether its repetition was Leila's need of reassurance or the effects of her voluntary illness.

A look of surprise lit Leila's listless blue eyes, "No, you are wrong. You have always done the bidding of your mother and father, just as the Holy Bible instructs. You should never take such an accomplishment lightly."

"It's glad I am that I please you, Mama as it means more to me than the greatest riches." Though sincere, it was the reply Brianna had trained herself to give. She no longer begged her mother to try to return to the happy life they had once shared. Those scenes only proved emotionally draining for them both and never resulted in change.

Her mother's gaunt hand rubbed the soft skin of Brianna's wrist tenderly. "Your father and I are truly blessed to have you." Body-racking coughs ravaged Leila's shape.

The latest visit from Dr. Cobb had been grim; pneumonia had set upon Leila's bedridden body. Her self-induced illness was now alarmingly real and becoming increasingly worse.

Brianna rubbed her mother's back until the powerful coughing-fit was subdued. Rearranging the pillows behind Leila, Brianna asked, "Would you have a mind for me to read aloud?" After Leila nodded, Brianna reached for the Bible on the bedside stand.

As her daughter began reading, Leila's mind wandered. The Irish lilt in Brianna's words was music to Leila's ears and the older woman's lips slid into a serene smile as she recalled a time in her life—a time that didn't seem all that long ago—when she had been strong and beautiful like Bria.

Once upon a time, Patrick McClaran had traveled to America in search of a partner for his fledgling business. His dream had been to own a shipping company and through that endeavor, he befriended William Chase and Thomas Elliott. Together the threesome began Chase-Elliott-McClaran Shipping Line and with it a bond of life-long friendships.

As William's younger sister, Leila was in the midst of this relationship and with her warm smile and welcoming manner, endeared Patrick to her quickly. Using his own buoyant Irish charm, Patrick soon won Leila's heart amid a flurry of blushes and smiles. The couple was married just two years later and blessed with Brianna three years after their wedding.

Now seventeen years old, the childish characteristics of their little girl had transformed faster than seemed possible.

Brianna's once wiry orange hair had deepened to a hue that reflected both Leila's chestnut and Patrick's burnt-orange tresses. Gone were the freckles and awkward features of an adolescent redhead. The brown sprinkles had faded away, replaced by creamy white skin and glowing cheeks that would rival the fairest complexion.

There was no doubt that in part, Leila wanted to go on living for her daughter's sake, but the other side—the side that was winning—wanted to be with Patrick. An unearthly certainty told Leila that her remaining time was short. But there were matters that needed her attention before she could go. Leila would see her only child settled—surrounded by love.

Brianna would suffer at first, but only because she didn't know her own strength. Soon enough she would learn, for what greater lesson of fortitude was there, than surviving the loss of those closest to one's heart? It was a sorry moral, but everyone endured its teaching.

Close family friends, Jonathan and Lauren Gordon, would gladly take Brianna in. Their daughter, Deirdre was Brianna's cherished friend, so it seemed like the perfect solution; but not the one Leila had planned—not the one her dreams told her Patrick wished. So often now, she dreamed of when they were young, in Virginia with their old friends, laughing, dancing, and talking as though that special time had come again.

Jonathan had—albeit reluctantly—agreed to help Leila finalize Brianna's future and Leila was secure in her choice.

Comforted by that though, Leila sunk deeper into the pillows and concentrated on her daughter's soft tones. The words from one of Leila's favorite passages slid over Brianna's lips, seeming a perfect fit to Brianna's future, "Your people shall be my people, and your God my God . . .."

The words lulled Leila until she drifted off into a sleep from which she would never wake again.

Chapter One

Misty Heights ~ Bolivar, Virginia

Devon Elliott firmly pulled on the reins of the large black stallion and dismounted even before the animal came to a complete stop. When the young stable hand came to offer his assistance, Devon excused the boy with a smile and subtle shake of his head. Caring for Leviathan was something Devon enjoyed doing when he had the time. It eased his mind.

And, today his mind most definitely needed easing.

Sometime before the day was over, Devon had to stop putting off the inevitable and inform his ward, Larissah Chase, of his upcoming trip to Ireland.

Larissah would be displeased, to say the least but that had much more to do with their relationship as lovers than it did Devon's responsibility as her financial guardian. With a mental shrug, Devon reasoned that the tiresome—though physically pleasing—woman would simply have to accept his decision.

Continuing the busywork of brushing over Leviathan's silky black mane, Devon felt good about finally shirking some of his weakness where Larissah was concerned. After all, she was not the kind of woman around whom a man could safely let down his defenses. It was dangerous enough that she continued to believe that he would one day offer her a marriage proposal.

For a brief time that had been Devon's plan; their families were connected as neighbors, friends and business partners. They had been raised together. Still, the day their physical re-

lationship began was the same day all chance of a lifelong union died.

Devon's disappointment had not been enough to keep him
from returning time and again to the honey-sweet tones of her
pleasure or the warm willingness of her supple body. Their
newfound relationship was built on a mutual understanding of
simple convenience—while neither was faithful, both were sat-
ed, Larissah's social reputation remained more or less unblem-
ished and Devon's life as a bachelor was secure.

Larissah rarely kept anything simple, however, and this relationship was proving no different.

In recent weeks, she had changed from a carefree lover to a
jealous annoyance. Devon figured that at least some of the
blame lay in her age. At twenty-three, she had little time left
before she was considered a spinster—a social outcast. No
matter the reason, Devon was through dealing with Larissah's
self-indulgent attitude. She had finally become far more of a
burden than her pleasures merited.

When he returned from Ireland, Devon intended to focus on
his new ward and break off his affair with Larissah.

From all reliable information, Devon assumed Brianna
McClaran had led a sheltered life. Coming to a new country,
establishing old relationships and making new friends was certainly going to set that pattern tilting. At least they weren't
complete strangers. Devon and Brianna's parents had been
lifelong friends. Drawing the connection even tighter, Larissah
and Brianna were first cousins. Still, Devon was uncertain if
the distance that kept his two wards more strangers than family
was a blessing or a curse. Without parents or close family,
Devon was the reasonable choice to see the Brianna married to
a suitable man. Devon planned to bring the young woman to
America, find her a suitable man willing to take over the responsibility of her care and promptly return to the bachelor-life
he so thoroughly enjoyed.

The last time Devon remembered Brianna McClaran
visiting America, she had been in the midst of a clumsy
transition into womanhood. Based on those memories, Devon
did not hold out much hope for a favorable result.

Brianna's hair had been long and not being the proper age
to wear it upswept, the endless strands of orange were con-

stantly in a tangle or bound together with childish braids. When she spent too much time in the Virginia sun, her freckles multiplied rampantly. That minor affliction was often accented with bright splotches of red sunburn. With the straight figure of pre-womanhood, Brianna looked like a beet-red stick, capped by wisps of orange hair.

With a pat on his groomed horse's rump, Devon silently amended that no matter what she looked like now, Brianna was Devon's responsibility. The time had come for a change in his life and if nothing else, bringing Brianna McClaran to live with him would do precisely that.

At least—if memory served him well—Devon could finally find solace in the anticipation of a purely platonic relationship with his unattractive new ward.

◊◊◊◊◊

McClaran House
Dublin, Ireland

Even knowing her mother's life was floundering, the first grief filled days had been the worst of Brianna's life. Unlike the loss of her father, Brianna had no family to console her and—in her mournful mind—friends, no matter how dear, could not truly understand the loss she was feeling.

She cried until her eyes could stand the scratching, burning pain no longer and then she rested. Curtains drawn, covers over her head, Brianna slept and rested, secluding herself from the rest of the world and their barrage of condolences.

When she emerged from her room, it was with a straight back and head held high. Sorrow would continue, she knew, but it was time to begin picking up the pieces. Neither of her parents would want her to linger in such a state as she was allowing herself.

Slowly at first, time passed. February rolled into March and March rained into April. Just as she'd imagined, the tears came less often. Memories became happier, rather than visions of her mother's frail form wasting away. Tears no longer threatened from every corner of the house. The steadiness of normalcy slowly began to seep back into Brianna's life.

Keeping busy helped Brianna's and so Brianna threw herself into the role of Lady of the House. She had mostly taken over the job before Lelia's passing, but now, she learned the full extent managing a household—organizing servants, keeping inventory of food and cleaning supplies, accepting and declining visitors and invitations.

This week she chose the difficult task of cleaning out her parents' belongings. What could no longer be used would be donated to a local orphanage. Though it brought more tears than she'd allowed in more than ten days, Brianna persevered. She liked the idea that their possessions would be useful to others, rather than remaining stored in trunks in their bedroom or on the attic, to become nothing more than a feast for the moths.

This morning she would finish sorting through the last two trunks. Needing a break, she wiped an errant tear and headed to the kitchen for something cool to drink, Brianna met her dear friend Jonathan Gordon as he entered her home.

"Good morning to you, Brianna. I hope this day finds you in good spirits." Urging the servant girl away with a shake of his head, Jonathan hung his coat and hat by the door and waited for Brianna's reply. She looked good; healthy and pink cheeked. Not at all the sallow eyed young woman she had been weeks before. Her auburn hair was pulled up with an array of straw-like wisps sticking out from its haphazard style. The dress she wore had seen better days, but considering the rummaging work she had been doing of late, the worn blue-gray attire was more than appropriate.

"Truly, I feel better than I have in months," Brianna answered sincerely. "And how are you this day, Jon?"

Sliding his arm around her shoulders and hugging her gently, Jon changed Brianna's original path and steered her into the study while replying, "It's glad I am to hear of your mood, Bria. You've worried us."

At her questioning look, he merely motioned her to take one of the leather back seats at the far side of the study, but Brianna could not hold back from teasing, "Jon, I've noticed that when you are nervous, you tend to sound a wee bit more

Irish than normal." She raised a quizzical eyebrow and at his
sheepish expression prodded, "So unless you've had a dram too
much for the early hour of day, would you care to be telling me
the truth of your visit?"

Holding a sheet of folded paper out toward her, he answered simply, "This."

Brianna reached for the document and unfolded the page
somewhat hesitantly.

Mrs. McClaran,

*Let me begin by extending my heartfelt condolences for the
loss of your husband. Patrick was a fine man and I am blessed
to have known and done business with him.*

*I must admit that your request was unexpected, though not
one that I am entirely against and after some deliberation, I feel
it is a great honor to be chosen to take your daughter into my
household and care as my ward.*

Brianna paused and would have spoken, but Jonathan urged
her, "Finish the letter, Brianna. Then I will answer your questions."

Cautiously she did as he suggested and resumed reading.

*As you know, I live within minutes of Larissah's home.
We do socialize often, which will give the cousins plenty of
opportunity to know each other better*

*The only reservation I have about taking Brianna into my
custody is my expectation of her obedience and respect as she
obeyed and respected her parents.*

*If, after some discussion, Brianna finds this agreeable,
then I wholeheartedly consent to help such a trusted and true
friend of my family.*

My Prayers and Respect,
Captain Devon Elliott

Folded within the first letter was a shorter communication:

Mr. Gordon,

As I predict my terms will be accepted, I will be leaving Maryland within the week. "Sea Enchantress" should dock at Dublin near the second week of April. I will send word as soon as we arrive.

Respectfully,
Captain D. Elliott

The sheet of paper shook in her hand as Brianna looked up accusingly, her tone angry. "Jon, you *knew* about this? You knew that my mother was making plans to send me across the sea for *America* and you kept the truth of it hidden *from* me?"

Jonathan held his hands up in a futile attempt to ward off her anger. "This is the way your mother was wanting it, Bria. She dreamed of you seeing more of the world than Dublin's swarming streets and Ireland's farmed out fields, especially with the state of our homeland in dire straits. The famine seems to be touching all parts of society, even us. You are intelligent; you know these things. You also know how hard it was to thwart your mother, once that mind of hers was made up." Warm brown eyes pleading, Jonathan implored, "What else would you have me to do?"

"You'll *not* be acting the victim in this, Jonathan. *Someone* should have told me. After all, 'tis *my* life we are discussing. Now I find I'll be expected to live with a man who is mostly a stranger to me. To top this joyous news, I'll be in a place I know nothing of, to be near a cousin of whom I have no recollection . . . ." Taking a breath, she added at a new loss, "And sure, I *love* Dublin's swarming streets and rolling green farmlands. 'Tis no matter to me what its economic situation." Discarding the unwanted letter on the edge of the desk, Brianna gripped the arms of her chair so tightly that her knuckles splotched red and white. "How long am I to be forced away from home?"

Jonathan could not allow his eyes to meet hers. He answered softly. "Until your twenty-fifth year or marriage." Looking up then he finalized, "'Tis best for you to be thinking on America as your home now, Brianna."

Her back was ramrod straight and her chin rose. "Never will that be. *Ireland* is my home."

Jon yearned to take this girl, so like a daughter to him, into his arms and console her. How dearly he wished to tell her she could live with his family, but it was not to be. Looking out the window, he gathered his thoughts and softly pointed out, "Brianna, 'tis the second week of April now."

"Meaning *he* will be here any day now."

"I'll speak to Captain Elliott. I'll see to arrangements for you to remain here a bit, learn something about one another, until you're ready—" The look on her face had Jonathan backtracking his words. "At least until you're better adjusted to the circumstances."

Brianna's green s narrowed and with certainty, she scathingly assumed, "He'll never allow *that* much time."

"You can't be knowing that," Jonathan reasoned.

That steely gaze flashed stubbornly. "But, I do, for 'twould take *years* for me to become adjusted to this farce I'll be living."

Jonathan sighed. "At least try to be positive about this, Brianna. You'd be wise to give the man a chance." His next words delivered the jab he expected, "*Trust* your mother."

Brianna didn't reply to his comment but followed the spinning within her mind by asking, "Why didn't Mama just let me stay with you, Jon?" She pleaded for understanding. Trust or not, Brianna felt betrayed by her mother's choice.

The dam holding back her flood of tears was precariously close to breaking, so Jonathan gave her the only explanation that he could. "'Tis a question I've asked myself many times in past weeks, Bria. Sure, I would have you, but I must do what she asked of me." Leaning forward, he took her hand and waited until her heartbroken eyes met his. "Do not be forgetting, no matter how far or how long you're away, you always have a home and family with us, if you're needing it when the time comes."

His tender reminder pushed her over the edge and with a choked sob, Brianna raced from the study and to the sanctuary of her bedroom.

◊◊◊◊◊

Devon pushed through the overpowering throng of people crowding the wharf. Everywhere he looked, merchants sold every imaginable type of ware, and he was anxious to be free of their harping. He was not familiar with this particular port and that was something that made Devon especially uncomfortable. Often enough, his father had spoken well of Dublin and those who dwelled there, but Devon still preferred firsthand knowledge.

He stopped walking and turned in a complete circle. The First Mate of his ship had disembarked only minutes before Devon. Certainly, in this crowded environment, it was easy for Drake to disappear, but Devon was still stunned at how quickly he had done so.

Just about to give up his search, Devon spotted the man through the window of a questionable looking establishment. Moving forward, Devon ignored the swarm of foul smelling people and tried not to lose sight of Drake again.

The tavern door was propped open by a blind man in rags. The pitiful beggar held out a tin cup expectantly. Devon obliged by reaching into his breast pocket, retrieving a single coin, and plopping it into the dish as he passed over the threshold.

Even at midday, the interior of the pub was crammed with men puffing tobacco smoke into the air almost as quickly as they uttered profanities. There were very few high-ranking seamen in the crowd; higher pay meant entertainment at an establishment a step above the one Devon had just entered.

Devon chuckled as he approached his first mate. With admirable precision, Drake was presently attempting to balance his mug of dark ale in one hand, an overflowing spoonful of stew in the other hand and a buxom wench upon his knee.

Drake Fraser was a long time sailor on the *Sea Enchantress*. Devon was uncertain of Drake's age but knew the man had been a teen when he'd started as a cabin boy for Devon's father's schooner. Therefore, a close estimation made Drake about forty-five years old and nearly twenty years Devon's senior. Drake's time of service entitled him to master his own ship, but despite Devon's offers, Drake always declined. He was content to be second in command, as long as he could remain aboard the *Sea Enchantress*. His sunbaked and wind-wrinkled skin proved his love for sailing.

The well-endowed woman with Drake eyed Devon with open admiration. "If ye 'ave a mind to it, there'll plenty of me left o'er when I'm through with this one, Cap'n." Feigning the need for air, the comely brunette leaned forward and fanned herself in a manner that offered Devon—and several other patrons—an abundant view of her attributes, as they strained against the worn, white material of her blouse.

Grinning, Devon replied, "As tempting as that is, I've more pressing business to see to this night." Then, laughing in his friend's direction added, "I'm sure Drake's more than willing to have a second romp in my place, though." Devon tossed a coin to the girl, offering substantial payment in advance.

As the girl quickly stuffed the coin down the front of her bodice, Drake squeezed her backside and bounced her slightly. His mouth full of cabbage, he agreed, "Ye speak the truth, Cap'n." Then with a huge gulp of ale, he forced the remainder of the bite into his stomach. "And I thank ye kindly for yer generosity."

Devon nodded, smiling wider when the girl pressed, "Just the same, I'll be 'ere tomorro' night too." Smiling in a way that made her seem much more attractive than she had before, the young woman slid from Drake's lap and warned him, "Don't ye be findin' no other girlie while I'm away, ye hear?" With a suggestive rub on his inner thigh, she walked away, swaying her hips seductively.

"Are you sure you're up to that, Drake?" Devon asked with an admiring glance toward the smooth motion of the woman's hips. "Seems to me she's but a quarter your age." Devon taunted, returning his gaze to his companion.

Playfully, Drake offered Devon a crude hand gesture that expressed precisely how much he valued this particular opinion. "I kin still hold me own, Pup. Don't be worrying yerself o'er that."

Pulling out a chair and sitting, Devon laughed. "Yes, I'm sure you can." Another willing lady offered Devon a mug of ale, which he swilled immediately. The dark brew washed through him, slowly melting away the tension of running the *Sea Enchantress* safely into port.

Refreshed, Devon informed Drake, "I plan to meet the McClarans early this evening. I sent Josh out to notify Jonathan Gordon of my arrival."

Drake eyed the younger man closely and asked, "Ye sure ye want to be doin' this? God knows the kind of burden this young lass might turn out to be."

Devon had already asked himself this question a thousand times since replying to Leila McClaran's letter. Still, as Devon saw it, he was past the point of no return now. All he could do was pray for the best. "Burden or not, Drake, I owe my father the honor of helping his friends."

"Your father and his friends are all gone now," Drake reminded him bluntly.

Devon nodded. "Which solidifies the matter. You know what close friends our families were. I really have no choice." Devon downed another swift drink of his ale and averted the knowledge that the connection of which he spoke was truthfully all that was keeping him in Ireland at the moment—he motioned for a refill.

Looking up from his empty bowl, Drake pondered. "What does Miss Chase think of the new addition to your *family*?" Drake watched the struggle of emotions on Devon's features.

Just the mention of Larissah's name caused the recently relieved tension to fill Devon's body again. "She's not happy, that's for sure."

Drake expelled a breathy-bark of a laugh, "Is that woman *ever* happy?"

Devon sniffed, allowing the only humor he could manage considering the current topic. "Aye, when she's getting her way," meeting Drake's sympathetic gaze, Devon finished, "but this time, Larissah has even less choice in the matter than I do." With that, Devon finished his refill of ale in one gulp and bid his friend farewell.

Chapter Two

Soft, warm, luxurious.

Brianna sat straight up in bed. "Dear Heavens, I've fallen asleep!"

Though not at all thrilled by the notion of being reacquainted with Devon Elliott, Brianna had still wanted to greet him politely when he arrived. Following afternoon tea, she had come to her room, intending to take a soothing bath, hoping to alleviate the headache her nerves had caused. Instead, she had fallen asleep and most certainly missed her new guardian's arrival.

"Could you be more absentminded?" Brianna questioned herself while grabbing her ladies-watch off of the bedside table. She read the time, and with a groan of frustration, yanked on the pull cord summoning Molly. The dratted servant girl should have been there thirty minutes earlier.

Brianna had no time to wait. Throwing off the towel she had snuggled in during sleep, she snatched the hairbrush from her vanity and dragged the grooming tool through her still damp hair. With the assistance of a dozen hairpins, Brianna managed to twist her curls up into some semblance of a lazy chignon.

The click of the door behind her heralded Molly's timid arrival and without a word, the young maid set to helping her irritated mistress dress. Spinning in an agitated circle, Brianna commanded, "Don't bother with my hoop, or corset. I'll just be wearing my chemise, drawers and petticoat." Molly grabbed for the clothing as her mistress rattled off the list. In a rushed tone, Brianna added, "I'll not be bothering with stock-ings or slippers either." When her maid did not move, but stared at her in shock, Brianna threw out, "I haven't the *time* to be worrying with them, Molly, and I see no reason that Captain Elliott will be inspecting my undergarments."

Molly immediately clamped her mouth shut—though her beet-red expression spoke scandalized volumes.

The servant-girl held up a black gown, but Brianna shook her head. "Fetch mother's dark gray one. The hem is shorter and it will work better without my hoop." Molly nodded and dashed from Brianna's room. She was back in less than a mi-nute and quickly helped Brianna into the specified dress.

Looking at her reflection in the full-length mirror, Brianna muttered with mild approval, "Not bad for such hasty work." Smoothing an errant wrinkle from the skirt, she swept from the room, calling back, "Wish me luck, Molly." Then she padded barefoot down the hallway and stairs to greet her future.

Jonathan Gordon begrudgingly found himself liking Cap-tain Elliott. He was a levelheaded man—especially consider-ing his youth. Jonathan's wife, Lauren, had added her approval in a quick whisper to her husband, declaring the Captain was a good choice for Brianna. Jonathan let that comment slide— Lauren was constantly in need of making matches, apparently, even *this* situation was not safe from her scheming. Jonathan would be relieved if Brianna liked the man half as easily as Lauren did.

From his place in the dining room, Jonathan could see the staircase. For the fifth time in a quarter hour, he wondered where Brianna was and what could possibly be keeping her from joining them.

Lauren caught his attention and nodded toward the opposite side of the table where Devon sat in silence. With his eyes, Jonathan begged his wife for help—he couldn't think clearly now, since Brianna's delayed appearance was causing him great distress. It was hard to believe that, even in her frustrated state, Brianna would be so openly rude and expect him to make her excuses.

Smoothly, Lauren took over. "Do you find Dublin to your liking, Captain Elliott?"

Devon finished chewing his mouthful of roast pheasant before replying, "Honestly, this is the first time I have been to port in Ireland, Mrs. Gordon. And—for obvious reasons—I haven't had much time to survey the area."

"Perhaps you'd be allowing Brianna some time to show you our home then, before returning to America?" Lauren was not anxious to see Brianna go, and though she had tried to hide the wheedling motive from her voice, Devon detected it just the same.

With a smile disarming enough to charm an enemy, Devon stated with an undercurrent of humor, "Now, that all depends."

"On what?" Lauren was hopeful."

"On whether or not I get to see *Miss McClaran* before I have to return home."

Lauren flashed her husband a concerned look that he returned ten-fold. Jonathan cringed visibly as he spoke with clear sincerity, "I truly do not know what could be keeping her, Captain Elliott. I'll go and bring her down, if you wish."

Devon shook his head. "No. I am actually curious as to how long she will keep me waiting." Studying the man at his left, Devon pondered, "You're certain she was agreeable to this situation her mother requested for us?"

Jonathan cleared his throat lightly. "*Agreeable* is not exactly the word I would be using to describe Brianna's way of it."

Devon wiped his mouth with a linen napkin and when it rested on his lap again, asked, "Exactly what word *would* you use, Mr. Gordon?"

"At best, tolerant."

Devon raised a dark brow. "And at worst?"

"We only ask you to bear in mind that our Brianna is not overanxious to leave her friends or homeland," Lauren quickly intervened.

"That is to be expected," was Devon's only reply. Internally he could see Brianna's point of view. Devon too enjoyed the Gordon's company, the food was delicious, and the area he *had* been given the opportunity to see was lush and green. The only thing lacking was Devon's newly appointed ward, whose feelings he was trying to keep in consideration. Still, no matter how she was reacting to this change in her life, this rudeness as she was showing Devon was uncalled for and if he were forced to wait much longer, he would likely stride up the stairs and retract her from her hiding place himself.

Lauren attempted to veer Devon's thoughts from present frustrations, "Won't you tell us of your home, Captain Elliott?"

Whether she realized it or not, Lauren Gordon's gentle Irish lilt was calming to Devon and he begrudgingly allowed his mood to ease a bit. After all, his entertaining hosts were not to blame for Brianna's actions—actions he fully intended to deal with separately.

As his tense features eased, Devon inquired softly, "My home?" When the host and hostess nodded, he continued, "My home is Misty Heights, a fair sized farm on the outskirts of Harper's Ferry, Virginia in an area known as Bolivar."

"Misty Heights is a lovely name for a home. Was it given by you?"

Lauren was sincere in her urging and Devon gladly appeased her. "No, my great-grandmother named our home. The story passed down claims her favorite time of day was dawn and she could often be found on the verandah or wandering the grounds during those early morning hours. She named our home for the thick mist that rises from the nearby rivers and covers our lawn each morning." Offering a smile, Devon reminisced. "When we were children, my brother, Daniel, and I would sneak out to play buccaneers. The creaking porch boards made a sturdy schooner and our yard was a stormy sea."

"It sounds as though my new home may be rivaling my current one in beauty." Brianna's entrance took the rooms occupants—so enchanted with Devon's description—by surprise.

The spell was broken.

"I have no doubt that it will," Devon assured her, following his confident remark with a deep swallow of wine. Over the goblet rim, Devon studied Brianna McClaran from head to toe. Outwardly, his gaze seemed disinterested—in reality, it was all Devon could do not to gulp down the remainder of his alcohol and request a refill.

This was not at all the child he recalled. The beauty before him was pure woman and he had the uncanny feeling that he was in dire trouble. Her deep red hair appeared damp, her peaches and cream complexion flushed—likely with anger at being placed in his care. No matter the reason, Devon was instantly irritated by how much he liked the way she looked.

The scoop neckline of her charcoal gray mourning dress was chastely cut, long sleeves ending in a decorative—if outdated—point in the middle of her delicate hands. Rather than wash out her complexion, the drab color enhanced the outlining color in her green-gold eyes and when she moved further into the room, dainty toes peeked out from beneath her swaying hem.

Trying to ignore the blood pounding in his ears, Devon forced his mind clear. He couldn't allow her looks to overpower his senses. From the very beginning, she must realize that he was in charge, or he would end up with another Larissah to handle and *that* chance was an unacceptable one. Brianna McClaran would respect him and his wishes from the start.

Taking her seat, Brianna offered, "I am truly sorry that I'm tardy." After being served her food, Brianna added, "I'm afraid my afternoon nap was a bit longer than I had intended."

"*Rude* is what it was, Miss McClaran." Devon's blunt statement and the manner in which he spoke it, made it clear that Brianna had insulted him.

All that Brianna heard, however, was that the man she would be spending the next eight years of her life with was judgmental and unforgiving. Her lateness had been accidental, her explanation and apology sincere, yet he chose to be boorish and blatantly point out her mistake. Brianna's eyes narrowed and she leveled Devon with a bold stare, assuring her guardian that he had not intimidated her and would be hard pressed to do so in the future.

Jonathan could see the two setting their battle lines. Clearing his throat, he intervened before Brianna could speak again. "You should have told us you were resting, Brianna. Sent Molly to wake you."

Her fierce gaze had yet to leave Devon and—current situation considered—she saw no need in stating that the servant had already failed in that mission. "'Tis no matter, Jonathan. Certainly the wee bit of time the Captain and I lost means nothing since all *too* soon we'll have every day of what seems like *forever* to be spending in each other's company." Brianna smiled with spitefully deliberate sweetness before taking a dainty bite of pheasant.

Devon slowly laid his fork aside and pushed his plate away. "And to think I had somewhat been looking forward to that opportunity."

Not glancing in his direction, Brianna replied, "Because *you* were given a choice in the matter."

Devon laced his fingers tightly together. At the moment, it was the only way he could manage to keep from shaking this ungrateful woman. "Do not mistake choice for duty."

"You owe me no duty, Captain."

"No, but I owe our parents respect and in honoring their requests *I* fulfill that duty." Devon watched, and though she still didn't look in his direction, he caught the barest of flinches as his words hit their mark—her guilt. Offering no reprieve, Devon quickly added, "Possibly—had you been able to control your tongue and show propriety in your choices of attire while your mother was still with us, she would not have felt it necessary to ask me this favor upon her death bed."

Brianna's green eyes narrowed and she had to concentrate on not choking on either the bite of food she was swallowing or the ire he raised in her. "*Propriety* is it? I'll be reminding you, *sir*, I am in mourning. Sure and parading about in a pretty evening gown, just to please your senses, wasn't a high priority to my mind, Captain."

Shaking his head as though he were correcting a wayward child, Devon indicated the space she had occupied while making her entrance. "Obviously, neither were slippers." With more desire to embarrass her than to correct a matter that truly didn't bother him, Devon supplied, "A Virginian lady would never traipse around with bare feet, most especially not in the presence of a man."

"I was hardly *traipsing*." Closing her eyes and taking a steadying breath, Brianna lowered her voice to a dangerous whisper, "And tell me this: *What* kind of gentleman is so bold to point out such personal shortcomings to a lady; *especially* in the presence of others?" Leaning toward him for emphasis she added, "*Virginian* or otherwise, I've not had the misfortune of meeting such an unmannerly rogue . . . *until now*."

Devon nodded slightly at her insulting retaliation. "I think *much* of what I will do will be new to you, Miss McClaran." The bitter tone he used pushed his meaning home. "Bear in mind that no matter what your experiences have been in the past, I am in charge of you now."

Brianna's back went rigid. "I'll not be needing your lessons, Captain. Sure, I'm old enough to know right from wrong."

"If that were true, you wouldn't have insolently kept a guest waiting, nor would you openly disagree with me as you're doing now."

Brianna was incredulous. "You cannot change who I am simply because my mother has given you control over my future." This man was all arrogance; it virtually oozed from his pores.

Domination heavy in his sapphire blue eyes, he informed her, "As I see it, Miss McClaran, I can do absolutely *anything* I want."

"And would you care to wager a guess at just how surprised I am by such a declaration?" Brianna sarcastically returned with a sneer.

A muscle in Devon's jaw jumped twice before he allowed himself to reply. "Miss McClaran, the only guessing I am doing now is at how long it will be before I turn you over my knee." The calmness of his tone merely underlined his anger.

"Are you meaning to frighten me?"

"It is a warning."

Brianna was filled with such fury she could scarcely breathe. "You'll not lay a hand on me. My parents never did and I'll not be permitting the first blow to a stranger."

"A great folly on their part."

"No greater than the one my mother bears having appointed an overbearing fool to be my guardian."

All fell silent in the wake of Brianna's blatant declaration.

Before either Devon or Brianna could think clearly enough to speak through their rage, Lauren spoke softly, her disappointment evident in her tone. "Brianna, why are you behaving like this?"

"This is not at all like you," Jonathan added.

Turning as though she had completely forgotten their

presence, she replied, "I'll not be treated as though I have no value."

Drawing everyone's attention back to him, Devon stated, "And I did not travel so far and offer my hospitality only to be shown nothing but disrespect."

"Respect is an honor earned, *not* demanded, Captain."

With a nod of agreement, Devon replied, "You would do well to keep that in mind, Miss McClaran." Standing, Devon offered a polite glance at Jonathan and Lauren before excusing himself and striding from the dining room, slamming his way out of the house.

Devon's first meeting with Brianna McClaran was finished and he seriously wondered if there would be a second one.

Brianna tossed one final time before throwing the covers aside and climbing from bed. Arms crossed over her chest, she paced the floor, her mind continuing its ongoing debate.

By all that's holy, how *am I to endure living with a man so stubborn as Devon Elliott?*

And sure, by being just *as stubborn.*

If he'd only not open that spewing mouth of his, he'd not be nearly so hard to bear.

Because he's handsome? The giddiness within her came in reply, so her cynical side badgered, *"You'd fair better to remember his arrogant sneer. A*ppearance *has little to do with a person's true heart.*

Sure and with that *fine an appearance his heart is easy to forget!*

With a wit's end roll of her green eyes, Brianna groaned aloud and threw her hands in the air with frustration. She truly wanted to hate the man who'd caused this humiliation and anger to swell within her. Such a feeling was difficult, however, since each time she closed her eyes to sleep, she saw his charming smile—the one she had witnessed when she first stood in the dining room doorway and encountered him describing his ancestral home.

Brianna returned to the comfort of her bed, wondering aloud, "Mama, *what* were you thinking?"

No ready answer came to mind, though the reprimanding she had received from the Gordon's did.

After Jonathan and Lauren took the opportunity to assure Brianna of precisely how disappointed they were with her treatment of Devon, Jonathan had gone to call the carriage around.

That was when Lauren seized her opening and the resulting motherly revelation had not been helpful to Brianna's state of mind, though it certainly had given Brianna much to consider.

"Bria, your mother was as dear as my own sister. Even before your father passed—God rest his soul—she spoke of her young life in America. Heed my words—'tis *grateful* you should be that all your mother did is place you in the *temporary* care of Captain Elliott."

"*How* can I be grateful when she just as easily could have left me with you and Jon?" Brianna's features were still flushed from her argument with Devon and the following reprimands.

Lauren grinned the knowing way a woman can only do after years of motherhood. "Because when you were young, there was talk—*serious* talk—of a marriage arrangement for the two of you."

Brianna's eyes could not have gone any wider. "Between Devon Elliott and me? Saints be praised, such foolishness wasn't seen through to the end."

Again, Lauren smiled. "'Tis not the end of it, yet." Before Brianna could find her tongue to reply, Lauren suggested, "Two people, with such strong minds as you and the Captain, are like dynamite waiting to be lit. Sure and if wick is lit, the explosion'll be out of your control."

Brianna rolled her eyes disdainfully. "We've already *seen* that, Lauren. *I'm* confident there will be more such arguing to come."

With clear purpose, Lauren stated, "*Conversation* is *not* the explosion I was meaning."

Brianna's face flamed. She had spent enough time at the docks with her father to piece together the happenings between a man and a woman. "I'd rather lose an eye than let that man touch me."

Her words, laced with a harsh determination, brought a hearty laugh to Lauren's lips. "I'd be more concerned with losing my heart than my sight if I were you, Brianna McClaran." Making her way toward the entrance, Lauren offered the younger woman a last bit of parting advice. "Don't close yourself off to Devon. You may not see it yet, but I think Leila knew *exactly* what she was about, in her decision. You have an opportunity to start afresh. No past, no pain—just future and hope. Give the Captain a chance. Give yourself a chance too—at friendship, for the very least." Lauren chuckled lightly at Brianna's confused expression, leaned in to kiss her daughter figure on the cheek, and then turned to leave.

Even as these words of sincere hope faded from the forefront of Brianna's mind, she couldn't help but wonder what her mother would make of Devon Elliott *now*. How would Leila feel about the way the evening had evolved?

No matter—*Brianna's* opinion of the man was forged. Captain Elliott was a controlling brute and a bully and she did not care if she ever saw him again.

Well, you could see him again. 'Tis not the sight of him that's so displeasing. Brianna swatted her forehead—that was as close as she could come to reprimanding her traitorous mind and its wayward thoughts. Still, whether she wished it or not, seeing Devon again was inevitable, just as changing the path of her future was.

Moving back to the comfort of her pillows, she rested her head and reconsidered all she had thought and said that evening. No matter what *she* wanted, Brianna's mother's wishes had been clear and above all, that was most important. Brianna had never defied her parents during their lives and she certainly didn't aim to do so since they were gone. If anything, she needed to honor them more now than before—just as Captain Elliott had so cunningly pointed out earlier.

Perhaps tomorrow would be better. Brianna would try harder and if need be, bite her spiteful tongue. After all, she had the make-up of an Irishman and a southern American woman—a challenge was something she craved daily.

Chapter Three

It took twenty-four hours and several unhelpful and negative, conversations with his first mate, before Devon's temper
cooled enough to even consider returning to Brianna's home.
Once that obstacle was crossed however, Devon's decision was
firm and final—the time to take on his responsibility was at
hand.

He had given his word to a dying woman, and he would not
disrespect her, or his family, by backing down from that duty
now—even if the young woman in his care were utterly incorrigible.

Giving word to a disappointed and suddenly tight-lipped
Drake, Devon went to his cabin and changed into some suitable, but comfortable attire. He needed to feel refreshed before
facing that woman again. Truth be told, her blatant disregard
for him was not the only thing about Brianna McClaran that
caused Devon's senses to reel.

Unlike their first meeting, Devon would this time be prepared for her attractive appearance and—if need be—offer a bit
of his own charm to warm Brianna to him. Something had to
work, otherwise, the next years of their lives would be excruci-
ating.

◊◊◊◊◊

Brianna sat at her dining room table, blessedly alone. Jonathan and Lauren had sent word that they were going to the
theater for the evening but would come around the next day to

see her. Brianna was relieved and welcomed the silent solitude.

Turbulent thoughts still kept her from sleeping well and her anxiety had grown as the time passed without word from Captain Elliott. Perhaps she had pushed too far and he had seen the error of his previous agreement. Brianna could hardly fault him such a choice, though he had not been the most delightful individual of the evening either.

Maybe it would be better for everyone involved if Devon *did* decide to return to America without her. Then Brianna could remain in Ireland, in the home she adored and near the friends that she loved without feeling any guilt—or at least much—over the entire matter.

Halfway through her early-evening meal, Brianna's worries were put to rest when the butler entered to announce Devon's arrival.

Stubbornly, she unsuccessfully tried to ignore the relief that flooded her, while assuming the most welcoming expression she could manage. Simultaneously, her mind, which had been taunting her relentlessly for nearly twenty-four hours, realized the futility of discounting his handsomeness—Captain Elliott was absolutely striking.

There was nothing exceptional about his attire—black breeches and jacket with a white shirt beneath, no cravat or necktie to enhance the plain clothing. His wavy black hair reached to his collar, long enough to tie back, but not a length that made him appear unkempt.

Were it possible for Devon to refrain from speaking, Brianna felt that she would undoubtedly enjoy living under the same roof with this man.

Shattering that possibility, Devon greeted, "Miss McClaran, forgive my intrusion. I did not know you would be dining so early."

Wiping the corners of her mouth with a napkin, Brianna replied, "'Tis no bother, Captain. I often take my meal early if I've no outings or company planned."

A light grin of good humor danced at the corners of Devon's mouth. "Are you reprimanding me for calling unannounced?"

Brianna's eyes widened in surprise. "It hadn't occurred to me."

"Otherwise, you would have reprimanded me?"

For a moment, Brianna wondered if Devon was teasing playfully or egging her on toward a fight. His smile gave him away, however and she relaxed somewhat. "No reprimands here, Captain. Only hospitality." Motioning to the seat beside her, she invited, "Would you care to join me for a bit of lamb stew?"

"Do you have biscuits?"

Brianna's expression became curious. "Yes."

"Then I would love to join you." Taking the seat she had indicated, Devon waited as a bowl of steaming soup was placed before him and a plate stacked with two large biscuits to the side.

Grateful and willing to use any topic to show him her truer, calmer self, Brianna questioned amicably, "You've a fondness for biscuits, Captain?"

Nodding, Devon slathered butter on the crumbling bread. "Don't you know that southern boys are raised on them?"

She laughed lightly. "No, 'tis new knowledge for me."

"Well, we are." Dipping his spoon into the stew, Devon took a healthy bite before adding, "I must tell you that we are also raised to be far more polite than I was the other evening."

Brianna had the grace to blush. "I could be saying the same for myself."

Devon accepted the wine from the servant and sipped before offering, "Perhaps we could begin again?"

"Perhaps."

With slow deliberation, Devon replaced his wine glass to the table while lifting his gaze to meet Brianna's. "You still have reservations?"

"Tell me, Captain, if you were without family and written off to a stranger who is charged to take you across the ocean to start a new life would you be eager?"

Devon's answer seemed to come easily. "In truth, I would be, but I am a lover of adventure."

"It's not the adventure that concerns me."

"All life is an adventure, Miss McClaran." She watched him in silence. When she offered no response, Devon continued. "I understand your hesitation having to leave your home, but this is not a simple decision for me, either."

It was the first time Brianna had considered that possibility. "And I suppose my attitude has done little to make ease your concerns."

Devon merely grinned and took another drink before asking, "What can I do to make this *adventure* more appealing to you?"

Brianna immediately understood the unspoken part of that desire—if she was happier, more compliant to this situation neither of them had asked to be part of, then Devon's life would be less complicated as well. Lowering some of her guard, Brianna informed him, "To start, call me Brianna. The way you say Miss McClaran makes me feel as though I have done something wrong."

The silent humor returned to Devon's expression. Holding back a chuckle, he conceded, "That is an easy enough fix."

"I'm not finished," Brianna assured him.

"I have no doubt," Devon teased.

Taking no offense at his fun, Brianna smiled while she added another wish to her list, "Hold your patience with me. Bear in mind, 'tis *your* home and familiars we're going to, not mine."

"I *do* bear that in mind, Brianna."

For a second, Brianna reconsidered her request that he call her by her given name. The way he said it was somehow more distracting than the authoritative sound of his *Miss McClaran*. Shaking off the silly thought and feeling, she reminded him, "Even so, you still have the advantage. I'm a stranger, even to my cousin. Surely she's more your relation than mine."

Devon's hearty appetite vanished. Setting aside his bowl and spoon, he replied, "Larissah is my ward, but she is also extremely independent. I help her with financial decisions. Other than that, she does as she wishes."

Brianna's heart leapt with hope. "Is there some unknown reason that *we* could not also come to such an arrangement?"

Quick images flashed through Devon's mind, most of which were entirely inappropriate for the place, time and lady before him. "There are *many* reasons I can think of that make me want to have a different relationship with you than the one I have with Larissah." Before Brianna could comment, he stated, "Not the least of which being that my father was a friend to your parents and shirking this responsibility would surely bring him shame."

"Responsibility means a great deal to you?"

"*Honor* means a great deal to me," Devon corrected. "As does *bearing in mind*," he borrowed and emphasized her earlier phrase, "how difficult it is for you to leave the Gordon's, your home and be *advised* by me, a stranger to you in my own right."

Her surprise registered and her words sprang forth without thought. "You've been thinking a great deal about this."

"As I said, this is not a responsibility I take lightly."

And with that comment, Brianna felt the tide within her shift. This man might seem overbearing and pompous, when in truth, he wanted the same thing she did—to live life with meaning and to show those they cared about that their love was worthy of respect. Meeting his gaze with newfound understanding and bravery, she promised, "I will do my best from now on."

"As will I," Devon assured her, raising a glass in silent toast to their amiable future.

Happily, Brianna returned the gesture.

◊◊◊◊◊

Their truce opened a floodgate of meaningless conversation that continued throughout the meal. When Brianna suggested they retire to the parlor, Devon offered his arm like the gentleman he claimed to be.

Again, Brianna felt a girlish giddiness as he escorted her down the hall to the next room. Deciding she'd had too much wine, Brianna stated, "If you'd care for a brandy and cigar, I can fetch one from the study."

Appreciating the gesture, Devon shook his head, "Thank you, no. Your hospitality has been kind enough already." Leading her to the ladies chair in front of the low burning fireplace, Devon sat on the nearby settee. "Such charm, certainly you have more than just dear friends you are leaving behind, Brianna."

An innocent flush colored her cheeks. "Are you asking if I have a gentleman caller?"

Enjoying her sweet discomfort, Devon taunted, "Have you?"

A sudden sadness entered Brianna's gaze. "Unfortunately, this past year has seen me locked away as a nurse to my mother, rather than attending parties where a lady might meet a gentleman worthy of calling."

Sympathy filled Devon. "I'm sorry. It must have been difficult."

With a melancholy grin, Brianna reminded him, "As you said, Captain, honor is everything and who better to honor my parents with care than myself?"

"Well said," Devon complimented. He liked what he was learning about Brianna McClaran. So far, she was night and day different from her cousin—enough on its own to make him enjoy her company. Add to that her pleasant conversation, beliefs equal to his own; her flashing green eyes, fiery tendrils dangling against the fair skin of her neck . . . .

Devon shook his wondering mind back to attention. It was a good thing he *had* declined the brandy. The ale with Drake and the wine with Brianna had clearly been enough spirits for the evening.

Accenting his thoughts, the mantle clock struck nine.

"Oh, I had not realized so much time had passed," Brianna stated, glancing from the clock to Devon again.

"Merely a sign of good company," Devon admired aloud. "However, it is late enough that I *should* take my leave."

Brianna nodded and stood to walk Devon to the door.

Apparently the wine had finally and fully taken hold of her senses and the room tilted as walked into the foyer. Praying she would not embarrass herself in front of this man more than she had already, Brianna veered from the front of the entry to place a steadying hand against the staircase balustrade. "You're welcome to stay the night here, rather than hail a cab for cross-town at this late hour, Devon."

Devon had the strong inclination that her suggestion was as pure as she was. He could also see that her head was swimming from the surprising amount of wine she had taken during supper. Still, the flush on her cheeks and the dilated darkness of her deep green eyes, Devon could not stop he wayward imagination. He had heard the same silkiness in a woman's voice often enough to know what caused such invitation—alcohol was not the *only* culprit.

Brianna didn't understand why Devon was looking at her with such an odd expression. Feeling the need to fill the space with sound, she said, "Dublin can be dangerous at night, especially the wharf." A twinkle came into his unbelievable blue eyes and Brianna blushed. "I imagine you know that already."

"Aye," Devon commented softly.

Brianna felt the odd flush of warmth pour through her again—just as her name on his lips and his hand on her arm had caused earlier. Quickly, she rambled, "I assure you that staying is entirely proper. My maid, Molly, and the house manager, Mr. Doyle will be here with us."

A charming grin broke Devon's full lips. She was very innocent indeed. The fact that she felt the need to tell him they were not alone hinted of her concern for reputation. The fact that she thought the staff's presence would stop him from seducing her if he so wished, solidly proved her naïveté.

Brianna's warmth doubled. Devon's grin, his gleaming blue eyes, his heady scent, his broad shoulders . . . . She felt heavy, as though she was on the brink of sleep; every sound in the room seemed magnified, even her breathing.

Then with his answer, her breathing ceased altogether. "Aye, I'll stay, thank you."

Brianna tried to overlook her reactions. Licking her dry lips with the tip of her tongue, she murmured, "The guest room is just at the top of the stairs and to the left."

He made no reply, simply stared at her with those hypnotic blue eyes and Brianna felt the need to flee. When she tried to move however, her limbs wouldn't respond. She parted her lips in an effort to take in more air.

Devon could feel the tension between them, knew that her pulse was racing, just as his was. Experience told him that this woman was his for the taking, but he was determined to act differently with Brianna than he had with other women. "Goodnight, then." Devon prompted in a husky whisper—the sound seeming to caress Brianna inside and out, sending an unexpected chill over her spine.

Brianna had subconsciously backed up the first two stairs toward the upper landing while the uncertain feelings scrambled within her body. When she attempted the third, the hem of her petticoat caught under her heel and her wine-induced mind lost control of its balance.

Brianna had nowhere to go but forward.

In three strides, Devon ended her tumble with one hand around her waist and the other cradling her head; the mass of Brianna's auburn curls twisting around his fingers, snaring him in an inviting tug-of-war and pulling him beyond reason. With a soft curse, Devon gave in to the curiosity lighting her emerald eyes and claimed the full lips she so willingly presented.

It took no more than the briefest touch of Devon's mouth for Brianna to sigh into his teachings. Encouraged by her timid kiss, he teased her wine-flavored lips tenderly with his own.

She was a quick and avid learner and as the remaining strength slipped from her liquid limbs, Brianna allowed her sense of touch-and-feel to overtake her entirely. Cautiously, she slid her hands over Devon's shoulders and along the taut muscles beneath his jacket.

Devon clung to his small reserve of rational thought—an almost impossible feat, since what he truly wanted was to scoop Brianna into his arms, stride swiftly up the stairs to her bedchamber and teach her much more than this comparatively chaste kiss.

Fighting the urge to do as his body wished, he managed to break their kiss. Gazing down at her was nearly his undoing.

What he saw within the murky green depths of her searching eyes declared that Brianna wanted him just as much as he wanted her—even if she was too pure to understand her emotions.

Yet it was due to that same innocence that Devon realized he must be the one with the strength to end this scene before it continued any farther. Gently, he rebalanced Brianna on her own two feet. In the same instant, his eye caught and held to the perfect support he needed during this moment of weakness. Halfway up the staircase wall hung a portrait of Brianna's, his and Larissah's parents.

Nothing could have better doused Devon's desire for Brianna than the guilt brought on by that picture. He was responsible for this temptingly innocent woman. Perhaps he should act as though he was worthy of that honor.

Though his actions confused her, Brianna was both relieved and wounded by his sudden rejection. Over lips already swollen from his kisses, she asked nervously, "Devon, have I done something wrong?"

Devon closed his eyes and breathed deeply—the scent of her overwhelmed him and he exhaled quickly before insisting, "Go to bed, Brianna."

When Devon opened his eyes, what Brianna saw in those blue depths made her quiver with fear and excitement. The longer she returned his stare, however, the greater the fear became until she instinctively knew that she would be much safer alone in her bedroom than to spend another second within the circle of this man's powerful arms.

Not trusting herself to speak, Brianna offered him a shaky smile, turned, and moved quickly up the stairs and into the safety of her bedroom.

Once the lock on her door slid into place, Brianna allowed her lungs to release the breath she had been holding for what seemed like eternity.

Still at the stair landing, Devon waited, giving Brianna ample time to settle securely in her room before he too walked up the stairs.

Once in the guestroom, Devon realized that it was going to be a very long night and wondered exactly what he had done to deserve the temptations his wards continuously and inexplicably offered him.

Chapter Four

Brianna woke the morning to the sound of a distant thumping. It took only five muddled seconds for her to realize that the noise was coming from inside her head. With a groan that sounded much louder than it actually was, she grabbed for her pillow to cover her eyes and ears. The movement caused her stomach to roll and she tried to swallow in order to alleviate the nausea but there was absolutely no moisture on her tongue.

Behind closed lids, the previous evening rolled through her mind. Devon's arrival, the wine, supper, the wine, conversation, the wine, the parlor, the foyer . . . .

Her head throbbed harder.

How was she to go downstairs and greet Devon this morning? How as she to travel to America with him? She had literally thrown herself into his arms!

The thumping her head was replaced with the sound of Lauren Gordon's laughter and Brianna set forth and explicative that—mingled with her behavior the night before—guaranteed her a spot in Hell.

Silently promising five Hail Mary's, Brianna tossed aside the pillow and her blankets and sat on the edge of her bed. First things first, she reached for the water pitcher and glass and promptly rehydrated her body. In actuality, it took two refills to accomplish the task. Cautiously, she placed her feet on the floor, found that she was far steadier than the evening before and walked toward the armoire across the room.

She was halfway there when she realized the heel of her foot was directly connected to the pounding in her head. She leaned against her goal for three minutes before attempting movement again.

Turning her head, she gazed longingly at the pull cord that would summon Molly to assist her. It, however, was five steps away and made Brianna want to cry.

Deciding not to waste her already achieved steps, Brianna yanked clothing from the wardrobe—she didn't care what she took out, only that she would be able to cover herself with the garments.

Heading back toward the stability of her bed, Brianna tugged on the cord for Molly and tossed the clothing on the foot of the bed as she unceremoniously flopped face down beside them.

Instantly pressure was placed on her bladder and the wine and water forced her to move again. With each step toward the chamber pot behind the silk room-divider, Brianna came more and more to despise wine and anyone who might ever again offer it to her.

Just as her business was finished, she heard Molly enter. Shuffling around the divider, Brianna found that not lifting her feet from the floor somewhat helped to keep her head from aching quite so much.

One look at her mistress and Molly offered a quick curtsy and without a word helped Brianna from her night trail. After stepping into her chemise, Brianna questioned, "Is Captain Elliott awake yet?"

"Awake and gone some three hours, Miss Brianna."

"Gone?" Brianna gaped, instantly regretting the sharp reaction.

"Yes."

"Did he leave word or a note?" Brianna turned to face Molly.

The young maid looked as though she feared giving any answer at all, let alone the one she *had* to give. "He said to tell you he will be back in three days and that you should be ready to leave for America then."

"Oh, he *did*, did he?"

Molly could only stare at Brianna. Clearly no matter what reply she offered her employer would not be pleased. "He dressed, gave me the message at the door and left." In after-thought she added, "He didn't eat a bite, either."

Brianna wasn't listening. She'd heard enough. Her head was pounding, her shame was taunting and now her pride was stinging. What kind of man kissed a woman that way and then left without so much as a by your leave? Brianna's only relief was that she would have more time before facing him—but now she wondered if that was a good thing or not. Delaying the inevitable certainly didn't make the thought facing him any easier.

Crawling back into bed, Brianna ordered, "Put those clothes away, Molly. I won't be taking any callers today and don't fix any food until I ask for it."

Curious to the point of bursting, Molly could do no more than Brianna ordered. However, there was no stopping her imagination as she went about her day wondering what had occurred to cause Captain Elliott to stay the night and leave before the break of day and Brianna to be so irritable in the morning.

The possibilities were endless.

◊◊◊◊◊

As luck—or some evil little wood sprite—would have it, Brianna was not left to wallow in her misery and self-deprivation from sunrise to sunrise as she had desired.

Following a light tap on the door, Lauren entered with the swish of satin and leaned against the edge of Brianna's bed. Softly she informed her, "Molly tried to tell me you were too ill to dine out this evening."

"Then why didn't you listen to her?" Brianna griped from beneath the pillow.

Lauren chuckled and took the blockade away. "Because Captain Elliott was kind enough to inform us that he was allowing you three more days to say your goodbyes before leaving." When Brianna's eyes narrowly opened, Lauren smiled and stated, "I intend to take full advantage of the time he has so graciously offered us."

"I'm ill," Brianna stubbornly hedged.

"Hmm."

Brianna's narrowed eyes flashed. "What?"

"Does your illness have anything to do with the meal you shared with Captain Elliott last night?"

"If you *must* know, it has *everything* to do with it," Brianna snapped. "Now, if you'd be so kind as to leave me to my suffering."

Lauren laughed again.

"Faith and Begora!" Brianna fired, realizing with a bit of relief that her headache was almost entirely gone. "What is so amusing?"

"You are," Lauren informed the younger woman. "I only wish you were staying here longer so I could enjoy the entire show."

"There is no *show* to enjoy," Brianna assured her friend's mother who merely continued to smile smugly in her direction. "Perhaps you should tell me what Captain Elliott's note said."

"Over supper," Lauren enticed.

"I don't want to know that badly."

Lauren laughed again.

Brianna glared.

Turning from the bed, Lauren called back, "I'll meet you in the parlor in fifteen minutes."

◇◇◇◇◇

Brianna sat in the carriage beside Lauren twenty minutes later. "I do wish Jonathan was joining us," Brianna grumbled, though the statement was entirely sincere.

"As do I, but Deidre's head mistress does not allow the young ladies to travel home on holiday without parental escort."

"But you didn't go," Brianna pointed out unnecessarily.

Reaching over to squeeze Brianna's hand, Lauren informed her, "Someone had to be here to share your last days."

Some of Brianna's foul mood slipped away. "Thank you."

Lauren smiled. "No need for thanks. We love you as our own."

Tears sprung to Brianna's green gaze.

"Now, tell me about your evening with Captain Elliott. Dare I hope it went better than the evening we shared with you?"

Brianna scoffed. "A bit."

Lauren's eyes twinkled. "Do tell."

Finally, Brianna laughed. "Lauren Gordon, do you realize that you are precisely the busy body your husband accuses you of being?"

With a look of surprise, Lauren replied, "Why, of course I do, my dear."

Shaking her head and retaining her smile, Brianna inquired, "What did the note say?"

"We are not at supper, yet," Lauren stalled.

Brianna's gaze grew shrewd. "Which means you intend to keep me talking until then."

"You know me well."

"He kissed me."

Just as desired, Brianna managed the seemingly impossible—she shocked Lauren into momentary silence.

But momentary only.

With a fair amount of awe in her voice, Lauren admitted, "That's even a wee bit sooner than I imagined."

"There was a good deal of wine involved."

Lauren's blonde brows shot upward. "Was he trying to seduce you?"

Brianna's face flamed and she was thankful for the dim interior of the carriage. "Would I know if he were?"

A vision of Devon Elliott flashed into Lauren's mind. "Oh, my, yes, dear, you would know."

"Then I believe it may have crossed his mind but he thought better of it."

"Good." Lauren bit her lower lip. "Good for now."

"For now?" Brianna gasped.

"'Tis too soon for the seduction," Lauren advised. "It would make the traveling very difficult."

"That's your concern in this conversation?"

Lauren laughed. "You needn't sound so appalled, Bria. Love is a beautiful and pleasurable thing."

"To be shared between a husband and wife and *not* openly in conversation."

"You are a woman, Brianna, about to embark on the adventure of a lifetime. There are matters about which you should not be so innocent."

"I *know* of matters," Brianna informed Lauren, unable to hide the embarrassment from her voice.

"The way of it is entirely different than the *feeling* of it."

"As I do not intend to be having *any* of it, I do not see that this conversation is necessary or proper."

"Pish, Posh. A man as virile as Captain Elliott will have you eating from the palm of his hand while wearing your virtue like a medal on his chest before you even hear the words, 'welcome to America' if you don't heed my advice."

Brianna groaned in embarrassment. "It was only a kiss."

Lauren laughed. "That's the start of it."

"You are confusing me more."

"More than what?"

Tossing caution to the wind, Brianna gushed, "More than the way he makes me feel and the things he makes me want to do."

Lauren's laughter faded. "It was only a kiss?"

"A very, very good kiss," Brianna amended.

"What did he say after?"

"That he would spend the night."

"What?"

It was Brianna's turn to laugh. "Only after I invited him and assured him that Molly and Mr. Doyle were there. He stayed in the guest room and I slept in my room."

"How did he act this morning?"

All humor fled. "Like his usual imperious self."

"And how do you know that is usual and not simply the character *you* bring out in him?"

"Why else would a man kiss a woman like that and leave without a note or speaking to her?" Shame filling her words, Brianna told Lauren, "He left word with Molly. There is nothing personal or romantic about that."

"Romance is fleeting," Lauren quickly assured her. "It is a moment that comes and goes upon occasion. Reality is excitement and propriety and guilt."

The last word hung in the air between them.

"You think he feels guilty for kissing me?"

"I would wager money on it."

Narrowing her eyes, Brianna inquired, "Does Jonathan know how flip you are with his finances?"

Lauren smiled again. "Who do you think taught me everything that I know?"

Brianna caught the double meaning in Lauren's words and with a sigh of relief, she admitted, "The thought of Devon leaving because he feels guilty does make me feel better."

"Why else would he leave without word?"

"Because my behavior disgusts him and he is overwhelmed with the responsibility of taking me into his life."

Lauren contemplated Brianna's suggestions before replying, "I think if that were the case, he would not have come to your house seeking amends, nor would he have stayed the night."

Brianna nodded slowly. "I'm glad you forced me to supper with you."

"I thought you might be," Lauren replied.

Watching her mother-figure a few moments more, Brianna guessed, "There was nothing more to the note than Devon telling you I was leaving, was there?"

"Not so much as the time of day you are to depart."

The carriage stopped and Lauren leaned over and sweetly kissed Brianna's cheek.

◊◊◊◊◊

Lauren scarcely left Brianna's side during the next days. The evening before, she treated Brianna to dinner at her favorite restaurant, Daugherty's, before bidding her a tearful goodbye.

Brianna cried herself to sleep like she had not done since her mother's passing.

Today was a new day, however, and with Lauren's advice ringing through her mind, Brianna intended to set out for America with optimism as her guide.

At half past nine, Devon arrived to escort Brianna to his schooner. Her trunks and bags were being loaded atop the cab and she gave her bedroom one final glance.

Turning away before the tears could fall, she found Devon standing behind her at the top of the sunlit staircase. "Whenever you are ready, we can leave?"

Trying to hide her tears, Brianna laughed shortly. "I'm assuming you do not mean a year or two?"

Devon smiled kindly. "Do you have everything?"

Taking a deep breathe, Brianna nodded.

Devon took her hand in his. "It will be easiest if we leave quickly."

She nodded again.

Devon squeezed her hand and then led her down the stairs and out the door to the rented cab, weighed down with her trunks and waiting to transfer them to the harbor.

Outside the carriage, the day was an unnaturally clear and bright one for Ireland. Inside the ride, Brianna was quiet.

Thankful she had not dissolved into a feminine fit of tears, Devon generously allowed Brianna her silence. She would need time to heal and he took the opportunity to clear his jumbled mind and emotions.

Not that the short trip to the harbor would accomplish what the last three days had not eased. Brianna had frustrated him at first but after their truce she had shown him a different side of herself—a kind and honorable young lady; a tempting woman. Today she showed a strength he hadn't expected. Every time he was in her company, Devon found himself more intrigued by Brianna and now he wanted to learn more about the woman she was, not merely the girl she appeared to be.

Devon's thoughts returned to the present when the cab stopped at Dublin Wharf. While Brianna waited, Devon left the carriage and briefly conversed with two men who returned to the coach with the Captain. The men promptly unloaded Brianna's belongings and Devon helped Brianna down. "I have much to do."

Seeing no good in arguing, Brianna simply nodded her understanding and allowed her new guardian to lead her across the wharf and aboard the waiting *Sea Enchantress*.

◊◊◊◊◊

Amid the rush of pre-departure, Devon quickly introduced Brianna to a few members of the crew. Josh, the cabin boy appointed to the needs of all passengers for the duration of the trip, squeaked out a hearty, blush-filled welcome. Martin, a man closer to Devon's age, was the cook onboard. From the looks of his tidy appearance, Brianna surmised that he prided himself on cleanliness, a fact her father had taught her to look for and appreciate onboard a sea bound vessel.

Finally, she met Drake. The first make was just an inch or two taller than Brianna with a yellowed beard and mustache that hinted of red hair in his youth. His eyebrows were bushy, his cheeks round and rosy and his smile easy.

Brianna liked him instantly.

Excusing himself to ready the ship, Devon left Brianna in Drake's care and the First Mate offered her a short tour of the schooner, *Sea Enchantress.*

Having already seen the upper decks, Brianna followed Drake down the stairway—which to Brianna's way of thinking was better described as a four rung ladder—and discovered two doors to her immediate left. The first opened to Drake's cabin and the second was a passenger cabin, which she was to share with Meghan Callear—a young woman traveling with her brother and his new wife.

To the right of the stairs was a large, open space. Two rows of hammocks, stacked one above and one below, were strung from the center support beam to the wall. Brianna guessed there were seven sets of bunks, which Drake informed her would comfortably sleep all of the crewmembers. Two other cabins sat across from the open space of the bunkrooms. Brianna was told that the smaller of the two rooms was to be occupied by the newlyweds, Caleb and Katherine Callear, and the other was the Captain's quarters.

Drake finished the tour near the hold, a large open area on the lowest level of the schooner. Here was stored any cargo the *Sea Enchantress* might transport during a voyage. Various goods were often shipped and traded between countries and continents. Merchandises such as lumber, grain, and tobacco were popular exports of America. Silks, sugar, and other luxuries were brought back home from exotic ports all around the world.

Curiously, Drake stated, "I should'na be surprised about such a yearnin' to learn." With respectful admiration he praised, "Ye're a McClaran, after all."

Brianna felt tears prick her eyes. Drake's pride was aimed at her father and the good name he had made for his family along with their mutual love for the sea and sailing. "Da loved talking to me of the sea and the ships that he loved so dearly."

Drake nodded. "And sure, he wanted his loves together."

Captain Elliott called to ready the ship and raise anchor. "Ye'll excuse me?"

Brianna nodded and watched Drake hurry away. Left to her own devices, she stepped into her small cabin and lay down. She'd made one new friend today, soon her cabin mate would arrive and with any luck, Brianna would have someone else to help drive away the sadness and escort her toward this new life she was undertaking.

◊◊◊◊◊

Their departure had gone smoothly and now, Drake leaned against a barrel of ale, watching Devon guide them to sea. The younger man was the embodiment of seafaring masculinity in its prime. Tall and strong, eyes keen on the horizon, hands steady on the helm.

Feeling Drake's stare, Devon looked to the First Mate. "For all your blushing and stuttering, I assume your opinion of my guarding Miss McClaran has changed?"

Drake was a man who took everything in stride. Devon's taunting was no different. "She's a fine lass."

"If only you'd have thought so during the weeks we traveled here. My ears would have been saved a great burden of negativity."

"You'd rather I tossed ye to the winds without a care for yer wellbein'?"

Devon chuckled, returning his gaze to the sea. "I'm a grown man, Drake. Tossed or otherwise, I can care for myself."

Drake's eyes narrowed in thought, but he kept those wanderings to himself. "She'll be a sight easier to handle than Larissah."

Devon recalled their first meeting while replying, "I believe so, too. Though our relationships will be entirely different."

Drake laughed.

Devon looked back at the humored man. "What?"

"She's knowin' a schooner nearly as well as me, she's got a natural likin' to the sea and she's a darlin' to look upon."

"It's not going to happen, Drake."

The older man laughed again. "At least I'm glad to see ye fightin' it. Makes it more worth the while and lastin' when 'tis harder to come by."

It was Devon's turn to laugh. "Perhaps not so much harder than you'd hope."

Drake's humor fled. "What've ye done?"

"Ha! A fine way to regard me and my intentions," Devon defended.

"I've plenty o' chances to regard yer intentions."

"My intentions are pure, I assure you."

Drake stared at Devon in silent argument.

"There was a kiss—"

"An' that'll be yer downfall."

"I thought you said she was a *fine* lass," Devon countered quickly.

Standing straight, Drake shrugged. "Then it'll be *her* downfall."

Devon's eyes narrowed. "Haven't you some work to see about?"

"I'm headed that way, now," Drake assured his Captain. "But I'll be keepin' an eye on you as I go, too."

Watching the older man amble away, Devon cursed into the wind. Realizing a part of his conscience was glad for the extra supervision that Drake intended to offer, Devon cursed again and set his mind on the task at hand—guiding *Sea Enchantress* home.

It felt so good to be off land and back on sea that Devon was able to hold to his primarily lighthearted mood. The sea was where he belonged, where he longed to be since his first trip to sea. Appropriately enough, he had been aboard the *Sea Enchantress* and as soon as Devon's young feet touched the planking, his thirst for knowledge had been unquenchable.

Devon had learned the skill of seafaring in the same order any other sailor employed by his father. In vast difference, Devon's younger brother, Daniel, found an immediate attachment to the railing of the schooner, rather than the helm, on that first voyage. It didn't take the younger Elliott long to decide that he would much rather handle the paperwork end of the company, gladly sacrificing the high-sea adventures to Devon.

Therefore, when the brothers began managing their inheritance of Chase-Elliott-McClaran Shipping all worked out well. Daniel managed the offices in Fells Point, Maryland on the outskirts of Baltimore and was bequeathed the family's townhouse which placed the city-loving brother exactly where he wanted to be. Furthermore, at the green age of twenty-one Devon proudly earned the rank of Captain and claimed the title of Master of Misty Heights—the home built and lived in by his ancestor's for close to one hundred years. The manor house was no more than a hard day's ride west of Baltimore and mere hours by the luxury of train, away from the hustle and bustle of the city, just as Devon liked it.

In the past, Misty Heights' rural location had never posed a problem for Devon's lifestyle. However, with Brianna's part in his life, Devon was forced to question the suitability of such solitude. Bolivar and Harper's Ferry were not the ends of the earth, but compared to Dublin and Baltimore's continuous parties, the rural setting was quite tame. In addition, ladies required ladies—feminine companions with which to share their time and experiences with—someone to learn from.

An education different than that you *could provide*, his mind ridiculed, flashing forth the memory of his kiss shared with Brianna.

Urging his nagging, guilt ridden and tempting thoughts away, Devon considered the only other permanent residence of Misty Heights—his household staff. Abram, his wife, Hesper, and their daughter, Tansey, were three freed slaves who had been with the Elliott family as long as Devon could remember. Though Tansey was near Brianna's age, she was a woman of color and therefore not a proper social companion for Brianna.

Still, Devon would rather Brianna was influenced by Tansey than Larissah. Beyond all doubt, Larissah Chase was far from the shining example Devon preferred for Brianna's company.

There was the possibility of Brianna visiting Baltimore, at least for the social season, but then Devon had to consider the propriety of Brianna living under the same roof with Daniel, a bachelor. Also, much of Daniel's time was focused on the shipping company and therefore would limit his ability to escort Brianna to the desired outings, anyway.

With dread lining his gut, Devon reasoned that perhaps it was time he reconsider *his* options for feminine companionship—the appropriate kind, the permanent kind.

Even in the security of his most private thoughts, Devon pondered the possibility of marriage with great caution. There were a few young ladies whose company he enjoyed— Samantha Bartlett in Shepherdstown and Celia Smythe of Martinsburg readily came to mind. However, was a moment's recollection enough to consider marriage—a *lifetime* commitment?

Devon felt perspiration bead his brow and knew full well that it had nothing to do with the heat of the sun. How could he possibly be willing to sacrifice *all* of his freedom for Brianna's comfort—even if her virtue *was* a possible sacrifice of that decision?

Still, something had to give—there was no denying that fact.

Solemnly, Devon decided to hold off on his worries a while longer. After Brianna was settled in her new environment, he would take time to sort out his possible prospects, no matter whom they might include, after all, nothing was permanent until he said, 'I do.'

With the look of a man whose conscience had just served him a death sentence rather than endless possibilities, Devon turned back to the task of guiding his ship along the endless expanse of blue water.

Chapter Five

The time spent aboard the *Sea Enchantress* was a soothing balm for Brianna—her embarrassment and frustration with Devon and their life path slowly fading as her grief melted to an occasional pang rather than a constant sorrow. It felt good to be so close to nature and God. Surrounded by His majestic creations, it was hard to focus on anything else—so long as Devon was out of sight.

Brianna had no trouble obtaining her sea legs. In fact, she found that she enjoyed the feel of the waves beneath her. She also found a fun companion in her cabin mate. Now, more than a week into their voyage, Meghan and Brianna had settled into the routine of spending the afternoon strolling the deck together.

Neither of the young women carried a parasol or had bothered with a bonnet to shield them from the sun and the breeze felt glorious on their sunpinkened faces. Since Meghan's overly proper sister-in-law/chaperone, Katherine, was stuck in her cabin with seasickness, Brianna and Meghan chose to leave behind many accoutrements of proper dress. To Brianna's personal satisfaction, that included replacing their laced boots and stockings with dainty thin silk slippers.

Presently, they rested on a bench fastened to the planking outside the galley. Amid their bouts of girlish chatter, Brianna occasionally caught Devon's gaze resting on her. When he discovered her watching him in return, he lazily returned his attention to the rope in his hands.

It was not long before Meghan noticed the stolen glances. In conspiratorial whisper, she remarked, "Captain Elliott is quite pleasing to the eye." Brianna continued, as though Meghan never spoke. Not one to be so easily put off, Meghan pushed, "How will you contain yourself sharing a home with such a man?"

The mixture of her Irish accent and American drawl amused Brianna. Meghan had resided with her older brother in Baltimore, since the age of fourteen. With him, she had recently returned to Ireland, for Caleb to marry his longtime sweetheart. All were returning home to America now.

Sufficiently coerced, Brianna peeked at Devon, who was currently helping Josh secure a figure eight knot in one of the lines. Trying to convince her own mind, as much as her companion, Brianna offered, "I'm thinking it'll not be so hard to manage."

Meghan sniffed with doubt.

Exasperation tinged Brianna's tone. "I am a lady of proper morals, after all." At Meghan's continued expression of doubt, Brianna added, "*Looks* are not *everything*, Meghan." Even as she spoke, she forced aside the image of him up close, his sultry eyes looking down at her, his full lips giving burning kisses.

"With such as *that*?" The other woman sounded as though she was speaking to a blind woman. "Even if he were the Devil himself, *I* could stand to be in *his* company." Meghan wiggled her eyebrows, causing laughter to bubble forth from Brianna.

"I'm near to convinced he's not quite as bad as all that, though I doubt Lucifer himself could be any more stubborn."

From the look in her new companion's eyes, Brianna knew that any cautions she offered would go unheeded. Meghan was hopelessly smitten, and Brianna forcefully ignored the uneasy feeling that caused in her.

"Even as stubborn as you claim, I'd wager our handsome captain has an eye for you. And I'm not too proud to admit a sting of jealously over the fact."

Brianna hadn't thought that she and Devon's mutual attraction would have been so easily noticeable to others and was taken aback by Meghan's statement. Trying to warn her friend—and her own giddy feelings—away from such a possibility, Brianna offered, "He is a man of honor. Perhaps he simply enjoys the charitable deed of helping me and my family."

Meghan studied Brianna. "And, sure, 'tis only duty that has him checking with me about your well-being every day since the voyage began?"

"With the stars in your eyes and music in your ears, I'm certain you've misunderstood something."

Happily, Meghan retorted, "The fine Captain wants to be sure that you are not left alone to grieve for your parents or your homeland, that you are eating well, getting enough rest, enough fresh air . . ."

If Brianna had been taken off guard before, she was positively stunned now. Here was a side of Devon she had not expected. He had been kind when their truce was arranged, but that made sense. No one wanted to spend day in and day out with a person they constantly disagreed with. There was no doubt he desired her physically, but actual concern, compassion, *feelings*?

Was it possible that Meghan was wrong? Maybe infatuation had clouded the woman's perception of what Devon had been asking and why.

Yet, to be fair, she must allow that Devon was a kind man, or at least that she had seen *some* hints of that characteristic within him. After all, it was part of the reason she had come to reasonably deal with—if not accept—her new living arrangements.

In the time since their travels began, Brianna had witnessed his gentleness in the help and teachings he offered the crew. Also, in the way he had assisted Katherine and Caleb back to their cabin after the new bride's continuous bouts with seasickness. At the time, she had considered those actions to be part of the Captain's duty, but now . . .

"Looks aside," Meghan continued, interrupting Brianna's thoughts. "He's inherited one of the most lucrative shipping lines in the country." Nodding her head as though she were giving her new friend a priceless gem of social gossip, Meghan finished, "Meaning, my dear Brianna, if you ignore his attentions, you're a fool of the largest kind. Captain Elliott is by far one of the most sought after bachelors in both Maryland *and* Virginia."

Brianna ground her teeth and refrained from pointing out the obvious—of *course* she knew what he had inherited since part of it was hers. Instead, she suggested, "'Twould seem you're a wealth of wisdom where Devon Elliott is concerned, Meghan. Maybe *you* should be setting your sights on him, instead of pointing all of his qualities out to me."

Meghan didn't bother to reply. Even if she had harbored such an inclination toward Devon, Meghan knew it was useless. The way the Captain looked at Brianna, he wasn't likely to glance in any other direction.

Brianna wasn't sure how to react to Meghan's continued silence and she quickly regretted her hasty and foolish suggestion. An unease that had nothing to do with the motion of the *Sea Enchantress* settled in the pit of Brianna's stomach.

Looking from her cabin mate to the Captain, there was no denying what a handsome couple the pair would make. Meghan was petite, her curves well-rounded and laughter often graced her dancing blue eyes and adorable smile. Wavy, yellow-blonde hair and a sweet, confident demeanor crowned each of these fine attributes. Alongside Devon's dark hair and tanned skin, Meghan would positively shine.

Try as she might Brianna could not dispel the image of her new friend's reaction to the same kisses she had tasted weeks earlier.

With more emotion in her voice than she cared to show, Brianna huffed, "Never you mind my business, Meghan Callear." Curtly she excused herself, "I've tired of this conversation and will seek rest from it and any wishing to continue it."

The only acknowledgment Meghan offered was the soft sound of mocking laughter following Brianna's retreating form.

◊◊◊◊◊

Late afternoon the following day, Brianna enjoyed her time on deck alone. Meghan had volunteered to sit with her sister-in-law so that her brother could rest and—especially after their conversation the day before—Brianna welcomed the chance to be alone and away from Meghan's glowing opinion of Devon.

A sudden gust of wind caught her light skirts and swept the hem upward—the whipping breeze carrying a deep chuckle with it. Brianna found it difficult to hide her chagrinned expression when she looked toward Devon's approach.

"I see I've caught you without proper footwear again, Brianna. However am I to tame such scandalous behavior?"

Setting her skirts right, Brianna accepted his arm and they began an easy stroll along the deck. "Captain, if you're thinking this is the *worst* of my actions, you'd do well to turn this schooner about and sail me home for Ireland."

Devon gave her a pointed look. "And shirk my responsibilities? Why, that would make me as scandalous as you." Seeming to give the situation serious thought, he conceded, "I suppose I will simply have to bear my lot in life and accept the challenge of retaining your reputation and mine, to the best of my ability." As though taking her into a clandestine camaraderie, he leaned close to promise, "Meanwhile, your shocking secret is safe with me."

With mock relief, Brianna assured him, "'Tis forever in your debt, I am, good sir."

"Not at all." He waved her faux gratitude aside. "Bear in mind, however, that on windy days such as this, you should take care that some creature of the sea doesn't gobble up those delectable little toes of yours."

Brianna swatted his arm playfully. "Devon, these toes are hardly delectable."

"Would you care to wager on that?"

She carried on while trying to ignore the feelings he was igniting in her core. This man was a puzzle—tempting and teasing one moment, proper and condescending the next. Brianna struggled to keep up, though, as she found she enjoyed the heady mix. With a certain air of her own, Brianna guaranteed the handsome Captain, "The only wager I'll be winning is that *you* are the monster for mentioning such things in my presence."

Her attempted prim and proper comment only set Devon laughing louder. "I'll wager further that I am the monster you should fear most." Wiggling his brows in an attempt to look villainous, Devon finished, "I am, after all, a great connoisseur of dainty, sweet-tasting toes."

A blush—as well as an unwanted deluge of sense-teasing memories and imaginings—flooded Brianna's features. Trying to reroute their conversation, Brianna scolded, "Have you left your post only to torment me, then?"

"The *Enchantress* is in good hands," Devon assured her, before continuing, "However, there *is* another reason that I wanted to talk to you. Teasing you was only an added pleasure." At her admonishing look, Devon grinned and offered, "I wanted to let you know that the men have decided they would like to have some music on the fore of the ship tonight. They will gather after the evening meal and you are welcome to join us."

"Oh, yes, that would be wonderful. It seems ages since I've heard any music. Do you play?"

Devon shook his head negatively before answering. "I was always too busy learning about schooners and sailing to worry over music. Do you?"

"No, though I do enjoy a bit of singing." When he scrunched his face up in mock agony, she indignantly defended, "I'll have you know, 'tis been said, I sing a lovely ballad."

"Hmm, and does *it* sound like a leprechaun, too?" He couldn't hold back his laughter and it spilled forth even before his question was finished.

The look on her face spoke volumes on what she thought of that particular comment, so with the strongest Irish brogue she could manage, Brianna returned, "Perhaps a *wee* bit."

It felt good to laugh together and Devon was reaping the benefits of their jovial behavior. It was a marked step in Brianna's growing trust and acceptance of their relationship. The brightness of her smile was almost as intoxicating as the richness of her laughter and her green eyes danced lively, causing the golden specks within them to seem animated.

As was becoming customary when he was near her, Devon felt the warmth of his reaction as it slowly began to burn in his body.

Brianna's breathing slowed dramatically. The darkness she saw seeping into Devon's blue eyes churned recent memories and emotions that warned if she were to escape—both Devon and herself—it would have to be now.

Averting her gaze from his dangerous eyes, Brianna patted Devon's arm lightly and admitted, "If I am to share in the evening entertainment, I'll excuse myself to ready."

Though Devon doubted her appearance needed any improvement, he graciously stepped to the side and broadly swept his arm in the direction of the hatchway. "By all means, Flame."

Brianna forced distance between them, seeking isolation from the warmth kindled by the tender name. But at the top of the stair she turned to him and with a brilliant smile that made Devon weak and offered, "Until this evening, Captain."

◊◊◊◊◊

In his private quarters, Devon lit the lantern hanging over his davenport and dispensed a dim light into the room. Walking to a small chest at the foot of his bunk, he flipped back the lid and removed a bottle of brandy and a small snifter. Devon poured the rich liquid until it reached nearly to the brim of his glass. Tipping the snifter back, he allowed the familiar relaxing heat to swirl through him, and then dragged his fingers through his thick waves of hair as though he could physically push the thoughts of Brianna away.

In the next breath, he sat and gave up his constant battle, allowing those same spinning, hovering, *tormenting* thoughts, to move unhindered through his mind.

He had been relatively unable to stop thinking about her over the last days—talking with her today had only added to his unwanted attraction toward her. Brianna's determination to remain independent was unnerving and quite possibly the most seductive quality Devon had ever encountered in a woman.

His desire for her was quickly being replaced with burning need. She was nothing like Larissah who used any means to make her life pleasurable—Brianna didn't even use what was offered to her.

Devon felt that it was this very difference that warmed his heart to her favor most of all. Second to that was his unexplainable impulse to help her.

And therein lay Devon's problem.

At present, *he* was the one from whom she needed the most protection.

Devon shook his head and groaned aloud with misery. The women fate had tossed his way would be the death of him. Larissah was the kind of woman he needed—one who gave him his pleasure and expected little in return. But in the time since he met Brianna, Devon discovered that she was the kind of woman he *wanted*. With every instinct, Devon realized that Brianna was the one who would give him passion unlike he had yet experienced, who was capable of loving him with all of her being.

Devon knew that Brianna McClaran was the kind of woman a man wanted to spend his life with.

That thought had Devon reaching for his liquor glass again. He had always thought Larissah was dangerous, but apparently, a woman such as Brianna was far more perilous than any he had met before. No other woman caused him to think *seriously* of lifetime commitments.

Cursing, Devon wished now he would never have allowed his thoughts to wander. It wasn't enough that life onboard the schooner's close quarters during the next few weeks would be a trial for all of the passengers, his raging hormones and her intriguing innocence were poor additions to the fray.

Devon downed the remainder of his drink and allowed a final thought to intercede, "Whatever will be, will be. I won't force or stall the issue." As he replaced the brandy and glass back in the trunk, Devon ignored the shaking of his large hands and the unnerving thought that such control was in fact, *not* his to control.

Looking for something familiar to calm his racing mind, Devon returned to his davenport, opened the desktop and began the task of writing in the ships log for the evening.

◊◊◊◊◊

The evening was bright and clear; every star in the sky a twinkling decoration for those in the middle of the sea. The *Sea Enchantress* would make land tomorrow, her two week voyage finally at an end. Brianna had mixed feelings about reaching their destination. She was excited and nervous, melancholy and hopeful.

For tonight, though, she would set aside her worries and enjoy nature's beauty and the music the crew promised. Urging the festivities one, Brianna looked to the man holding a harmonica in his hands and called out, "How about a song, Drake?"

"Gladly, Lass." Nodding to Randall, who toted a fiddle, Drake put the harmonica to his lips and together they struck up a lively tune. Brianna grabbed Josh's hands and began swinging around the deck with him. The rest of the crew clapped, keeping time with the music, while several of the men traded Brianna around as a dance partner.

Soon she was out of breath and begging for a rest. "I had no idea I'd be the only lady in attendance this evening." Looking around the group of people, she asked, "Where is Meghan?"

Stepping into the lantern lit circle, Devon answered, "I just saw her heading below decks. She claimed to be too tired and chose to retire to her quarters."

Brianna made a face of mock misery. "Sure and my feet will never be the same."

Smiling with unequaled charm, he requested, "Before you seek refuge from our company and the abuse it is bringing your dainty feet, might I have a turn around the deck?"

Brianna laughed breathlessly, but couldn't seem to manage speech while anticipating the feel of being held in Devon's arms again.

Mistaking her silence for lack of enthusiasm, one of the crew encouraged, "Go on then, the Cap'n can dance quite a smooth waltz, Missy." Nudging the shipmate closest to him with a bony elbow, he added with zeal, "Remember that night we seen him in tha' dance hall with tha' pretty lassie in the red dress tha' barely covered her . . ."

"Ahem . . . I believe the lady can do without the *exact* details of the entire evening, thank you, Tim." Devon quieted his crewmember with a pointed look, causing a spattering round of guffaws to circulate amongst the men.

"Sorry, Cap'n," Tim offered humbly, and then prodded with an apologetic tone, "Jus' go on and show her how ye can dance so smooth."

Taking pity on Tim, the rest of the crew began to goad the Captain, too.

Devon nodded and amended, "Soon enough, men, but first, let's give her a rest." Glancing toward Brianna, he continued, "I understand the lady can sing and I would truly love to hear her do so."

With a smile, Brianna looked to their makeshift band and asked, "Do you know 'Galway Bay'?" Nodding their heads simultaneously in the affirmative, the twosome played the first strains of the song and Brianna turned to her audience.

Her throaty alto traveled smoothly through the air and by the final chorus, most of the men were trying to hide the tears in their eyes.

And if there's to be a life hereafter,
And somehow I'm sure there's going to be,
I will ask my God to let me make my heaven,
In that dear land across the Irish Sea.

The last strains died away and the only sound heard was that of the waves around them. All members of the crew understood that what Brianna sang so sweetly was true to her hear. It had been evident in her voice and in her eyes with each note she'd crooned for them.

Devon's raspy tone broke the silence. "Aye, a lovely voice you do have, Brianna."

"Thank you, Captain." She cleared her throat softly, then offered Devon a curtsy, her hand, and a question, "Shall we dance?"

With a nod, Devon accepted and looked to the musicians. The sound of the harmonica and fiddle began again, this time with a three-quarter rhythm.

Randall and Drake's tune was nearly drowned out by the catcalls and rousing laughter of the men. Before long, though, they hushed as the song moved through them like a lullaby, the smooth movements of the schooner on the water rocking them like infants in a cradle.

As they moved around the deck, Devon's deep blue eyes held Brianna in a trance. Her stomach filled with fluttering sensations and she felt the urge to loose herself in the intensity of those murky depths forever.

Devon enveloped one of her hands in his, Brianna's other hand rested on his shoulder, the muscles beneath her touch warm and solid. She could feel the strength of him engulf her as they spun in slow circles.

Breathe, she reminded herself and closed her eyes, inhaling deeply. *Seawater, brandy, musky-masculinity*—the cleansing breath had not helped in the least.

Brianna felt giddy. Her senses were alive, taking in the twinkle of millions of stars and the flapping of the sails above them. The sound of the waves against the pitching schooner, the tension and the scent of his body, the heat of his eyes—all of it engulfed her.

Several moments passed before she realized that they had stopped moving.

When Drake cleared his throat, only then did she notice that the music had stopped, too. "Beggin' yer pardon, Cap'n. Do ye think I might have a go?"

It took everything within Devon to pull his gaze from Brianna's and even more for him to relinquish his hold on her to Drake. "I suppose that's only fair." Bowing to Brianna, Devon announced, "I believe that I will now retire, seeing as the highlight of my evening is now over."

Even after the sound of new lively music began and Drake held her hands, Brianna's eyes continued to follow Devon's retreating form.

The remaining crew was privy to her expression and it was obvious to them precisely what Brianna was feeling for their highly regarded Captain, even if she had yet to realize it herself.

Chapter Six

Daniel Elliott waited on the wharf for his older brother's schooner to dock in Fells Point, Maryland. The fresh air provided him with a much needed break and, in addition to missing his brother's company, Daniel was anxious to see Brianna McClaran. Like Devon, it had been years since Daniel had seen the young woman and he could not wait to see precisely what his brother had gotten himself into. Attractive or not, meeting Brianna would provide Daniel with enough brotherly ammunition to torment Devon for several weeks, at least.

Guessing his only sibling already had him figured out, Daniel did not intend to wait for Devon to bring Brianna around to the office to meet him. The ship was still a dot on the harbor horizon when the dock loaders had done as requested and let Daniel know the *Sea Enchantress* was making her way inland. Thirty minutes later, Daniel donned his jacket and strolled happily to the docks where he watched—with dozens of curious bystanders—the crew work together, diligently bringing the schooner safely into port. Men called out to one another. Devon's voice carried on the wind and Daniel imagined his brother was in his seafaring glory.

Two crewmen disembarked quickly, tying the massive ropes that would hold the ship to harbor. Their task complete, the scanned the gathered crowd, spotted Daniel and threw their hands high in friendly greeting. Daniel returned the gesture and then turned his attention to the set gangplank—a young couple made their way down, followed by a woman whose face was shadowed by a brown parasol. After the trio came Devon escorting a fair skinned, auburn haired beauty.

Daniel forgot all his plans to torment his brother.

Adding to Brianna's beauty, she moved as though floating on air. When Devon said something that caused her to laugh, the sound carried to Daniel like a song in the breeze.

The trill also delivered two rather strong assumptions to the younger Elliott—Brianna McClaran's smile outshone all of her other physical qualities and no man in the world would stand a chance to win her heart, so long as his brother was nearby.

Daniel's disappointment was short lived, however, as the woman walking in front of Devon and Brianna lowered her parasol. The wind caught the blonde wisps of hair decorating her adorable face and her dancing blue eyes caught and held Daniel's with unabashed interest.

Forgetting all else,—including his waylaid interest in Brianna—Daniel stepped forward, boldly took her hand and lightly brushed his lips against it. Straightening once more, he looked to his obviously amused brother and remarked, "Devon, I don't know how you kept your senses during the voyage. So much beauty would surely drive a lesser man insane."

All of the women blushed prettily.

Devon rolled his eyes in response to his brother's blatant charm and replied dryly, "By the grace of God, I suppose." Devon avoided his brother's prying gaze by introducing the group, indicating each person as he named them. "Daniel, this is Brianna McClaran. Our other travelers for this journey are the Callear's; Caleb and his new wife, Kathleen, and Caleb's sister, Meghan."

Without hesitation, Daniel sought Caleb's attention. "Mr. Callear, please allow me to celebrate your marriage at my home this evening. I won't accept no for an answer."

Judging from the look on his sister's face, Caleb knew Daniel Elliott was not alone in that esteem. "If Katherine is feeling up to it?" He replied, speaking in his wife's direction.

Katherine, still a bit pale from her seasick journey, softly reassured her husband, "So long as my feet remain on solid ground."

Caleb offered an appreciative bow to Daniel and accepted. "We would be honored, sir."

With a final glance of fascination in Miss Meghan Callear's direction, Daniel stated, "Then I look forward to our evening."

◊◊◊◊◊

Rather than travel immediately to Bolivar as Brianna had expected, Devon took the next few days in Baltimore and Fell's Point to oversee minor repairs and the restocking of the *Sea Enchantress*. Though,—now that she was in America— Brianna was anxious to see her new home, she enjoyed spending more time with Meghan.

Daniel enjoyed Brianna's friendship with Meghan as well and blatantly used it as an excuse to spend time with the young Irishwoman he was so taken with.

Anyone could see that the feeling was mutual, too. Apparently, Devon was not the only Elliott male abounding in charisma. Daniel's smile was easy and contagious, his brown eyes warm and quite often teasing. Watching him with Meghan caused Brianna a small pang of jealousy—what might it be like to have someone look at you like all else failed to matter?

Rather than dwell on childish wishes, however, Brianna enjoyed Daniel and Meghan's guide to the city's sights.

Unfortunately, Devon kept himself far too busy to join Brianna and the blossoming couple on their daily outings. He'd briefly explained that his intent was to spend all of his time at the docks and finish his business there, so that he could take Brianna to Misty Heights as soon as possible.

On their last night in the city, however, he surprised the trio by treating them to a lovely supper out together. They returned to Daniel's townhouse and spent the remainder of the evening chatting in his parlor.

Not for the first time, Meghan sweetly coaxed, "Devon, it would be so nice if the two of you could stay for at least part of the social season. It's just beginning and Brianna will miss all the fun."

Devon considered her words for a moment. The height of the season had rarely been of any interest to him, and so he had given it no thought at all. Perhaps they should stay a while, though, for Brianna's sake.

Nevertheless, before Devon could say as much, Brianna intervened with her own opinion. "Parties have never been one of my great priorities, Meghan. They are fun, but dressing up and being surrounded by people every night for months isn't something I would enjoy very much. I am more at ease in the country, where I can run through the grass in my bare feet"— she deliberately kept her gaze from straying to Devon—"and gallop across the field as fast as a horse can carry me."

Meghan shuddered. "Brianna McClaran, sometimes I find you very odd."

Daniel and Devon both chuckled at Meghan's brash reply. It was exactly the sort of comment they had come to expect of her and none took offense to her words.

"*I*, however, find you refreshing, Miss McClaran," Devon declared with an easy smile.

Brianna smiled in return before appeasing Meghan. "Perhaps Devon will allow me to return later in the season. I do like *some* festivities, after all."

Meghan looked relieved.

"I would be glad to see to her care if you cannot return with her, Devon." Daniel offered easily.

Eyeing his brother with a skeptical expression, Devon asked, "And escort her from party to party?"

Daniel nodded. "She and Meghan would have great fun together."

Immediately Devon understood why Daniel was so willing to welcome Brianna's return visit. With mock sympathy, Devon protested, "But I thought you detested such functions, dear brother."

Daniel took the teasing good-naturedly. "All things are subject to change, if one has the right incentive."

Instantly, Devon's eyes found Brianna's. "I know precisely what you mean."

Brianna's stomach fluttered. She had missed spending time with Devon. During their voyage she had come to enjoy his teasing. This was the most time they had spent together since dancing aboard the *Sea Enchantress* and the way he looked at her now made her mind shift back even further to their kiss in Ireland.

While Brianna's thoughts tumbled, Daniel caught the look she shared with his brother and was able to read between the lines—not that it took much effort to do so. Daniel guessed that a blind man could have detected the chemistry between Devon and Brianna.

Briefly, he wondered if Devon had any idea how evident his desire for Brianna was. He also wondered what Devon intended to do about that desire.

Daniel enjoyed Brianna's lighthearted company and his siblings interest in her caused Daniel some worry. It wasn't that Daniel didn't want Devon to find happiness. On the contrary, it was simply that Daniel knew too well Devon's record with women.

Larissah had never been one of Daniel's favorite people; it was hard to imagine anyone sincerely liking her personality. Even so, what Devon did with her was little concern to him. But Brianna was a different story. Daniel did not want to see her hurt and a man like Devon—a man of experience—could easily hurt an innocent like Brianna without even being aware of what he was doing.

Returning to the subject at hand, Daniel instigated with lighthearted curiosity, "Does that mean you will be coming to the city, too?" Not really giving Devon time to comment, he added, "The local matriarchs will be abuzz with the chance of ensnaring the unobtainable Captain Devon Elliott for their daughters of marrying age."

Matching his brother's wit, Devon replied dryly, "How dare I miss it when you present the prospect in such an inviting manner?"

Daniel shrugged. "I only consider how busy you will be with *two* charges to care for. I doubt you'll have the opportunity to come, even if you *really* want to."

Devon smirked good-naturedly. "Do not worry yourself, Daniel. I would be bringing Brianna with me and I've never found Larissah incapable of tending for herself in my absence before." Devon paused, before smoothly questioning, "Unless you meant for me to bring *her* along as well?"

Daniel's mild grimace lent evidence to how distasteful he found that suggestion. "I'd just as soon you not, Dev."

While the topic was at hand, Devon inquired, "Have you heard from her while I was away?"

"Mmm," Daniel murmured, affirmatively. "She and a friend of hers."

"Oh?" Devon's eyebrows rose with mild curiosity. "Is her *friend* anyone I know?"

"Larissah and Robert Montgomery spent three days here and left the morning before you arrived."

"Pity we missed them," Devon offered insincerely.

"Larissah is engaged?"

Brianna's question took both men by surprise. Daniel laughed and Devon responded, "No, not Larissah."

"She comes to the city with a man she is not betrothed to?"

"Larissah tends to do as wishes with whomever she wishes," Daniel clarified.

Brianna's brow furrowed. "But you are her guardian."

"I am," Devon confirmed.

"She doesn't answer to you?"

Daniel laughed again until Devon's fierce expression promptly shut his brother's humored mouth. "As I told you in Ireland, Larissah is my ward in financial matters only."

A short laugh from Daniel lasted even less time than the last.

Before Brianna could ask Devon if he'd actually growled at his brother, he asked Daniel, "Was Larissah well behaved?"

Daniel shrugged. "By Larissah's standards, yes. She stayed with me, and Robert boarded at the Admiral Inn."

"Why didn't he stay here, too?"

"She didn't ask and I didn't offer." Chuckling softly, Daniel guessed, "Perhaps she didn't want to sully her reputation by staying with an unmarried man who wasn't her guardian, or at least nearly her guardian."

Devon's expression proved how likely he found that statement to hold true. "I assume she was shopping; how much of my money did she spend?"

Laughing at his brother's expense, Daniel informed Devon, "Enough to fill an empty steamer trunk I had to provide for her return railway passage."

Brianna was silent as she listened to more detail of her cousin. It was clear that Daniel held little regard for Larissah or the company she kept. Devon's opinion seemed only slightly higher.

Drawing Brianna's attention back to the men and away from her curious wanderings, Devon implored, "I do hope this penchant for spending money does not run in the family." Smiling to emphasize his lightheartedness, Devon continued, "Else, before long I will be begging a room from you, Daniel."

All of the occupants chuckled at Devon's exaggeration and Brianna reassured him, "Have no fear, Devon. I am not overly fond of shopping."

Meghan scooted to the edge of her seat as though she had just heard the juiciest tidbit of gossip. "For Heaven's sake, Brianna! You don't like parties, you don't like shopping, and you don't like groups of people! *What* do you do for fun?"

Without intending it, Brianna's eyes dodged to Devon and saw that his sapphire eyes were twinkling with a shared memory—a memory they still had not garnered the opportunity or nerve to discuss. Yet—Brianna surmised—the mutual remembrance was apparently never any farther from Devon's mind than it was hers.

In seemingly perfect gentlemanly form, Devon offered, "I intend to make sure that Brianna is properly entertained, Miss Callear."

Brianna's face flamed to match her hair.

Amazingly, Meghan seemed to miss the expression of embarrassment engulfing Brianna's features. Either that or she didn't feel the need to remark—a possibility Brianna found highly unlikely. Instead, she passed Daniel a sly look and suggested, "Perhaps I can rely on Daniel in a similar fashion."

If possible, Brianna's eyes widened even more and Devon roared with laughter as he assured the unsuspecting lady, "I have no doubt that you may, Meghan. No doubt at all."

◊◊◊◊◊

Bright beams of sunlight filled the rooms, spilling into the bedchamber through two windows, and lending a similar glow to the connected sitting area. Glass paned double-doors exited onto a second story veranda, the balcony running the entire length of Misty Heights and affording a sprawling view of the west side of the Elliott family land, expanding over fields and forest beyond.

The furnishings within the rooms were of pine, covered with sage and champagne hued fabrics.

"Hesper, this is perfect. I couldn't ask for anymore." Smiling broadly, the heavyset Negro woman beamed under Brianna's praise.

"I'm glad to hear that." Each woman turned and laughed at the comment Devon made as he walked into the sitting room to join them.

Giving due credit, Hesper admitted, "All I done was put it right. Mista Devon, he done picked all the colors and such 'fore he leave to fetch ya home to us."

Brianna liked to hear Hessie's broken dialect, and the sense of belonging her words gave. She was also warmed at the news Devon had tried to make a special place in his home for her, even before making the journey to Ireland. His thoughtfulness endeared him to her, His obvious good taste—at least in Brianna's opinion—impressed her as well.

"Don't let Hessie fool you, Brianna. There's not a thing I could do around here without her. She runs a tight ship. In fact, that's the real reason I like spending so much time at sea." When Hesper planted her meaty hands on her apron-clad hips, Devon offered his reasoning. "On board the *Enchantress* I am obeyed, but make no mistake, it's Hessie that in charge here at Misty Heights."

"And don't be lookin' fo' that to change no time soon, neither." Continuing her mock-sternness, Hesper declared, "'Sides, I always had to keep things in order with ya'll two boys runnin' aroun', into all kind a trouble. Miz Lily had her hands full enough to be sure."

Brianna smiled at the image her mind conjured of Devon and Daniel as children, Hessie waddling after them in frustration. When she looked toward him, Brianna found that Devon had been watching her, too, enjoying the expressions her warm thoughts carried to her features.

When their eyes met, the rest of the world faded away and the look that passed between them spoke of a mutual need to discuss what was happening between them and do so soon.

Hesper suddenly had the impression that she was in the way. She had helped raise Devon and in those years, had come to know him, learned to read him by his expressions and actions. She also liked Brianna—had actually adored her parents—and if the attraction she already felt flickering between Devon and Brianna was any indication of what lie ahead for the young couple, Hessie would be the last person to stand in their way. If they needed time alone, then that's what they would get.

Now seemed like the perfect time to continue unpacking Brianna's trunks and almost unnoticed, the heavyset woman excused herself and passed through the adjoining bedchamber door, pointedly leaving the barrier open behind her.

Breaking the temporary silence, Devon inquired, "So you approve? Do you think you will be comfortable here?"

Brianna clasped her hands together to still their excited shaking. "Yes. Thank you, Devon. You have done so much for me and I appreciate it all."

The sincerity of her words touched him. "You are most welcome. Though I really did only what was expected of me."

"I think we both know that is not entirely true."

The never-far thoughts came to the forefront of both their minds and the silence that followed her statement was heavy. The fact that they had spent no time alone since leaving Ireland was taking its toll.

Devon studied her graceful features—her auburn hair, her porcelain like skin, her beguiling green eyes. Unable to resist, he reached forward and brushed her cheek with the backs of his long fingers. "So lovely, so kind."

Brianna blushed but could not pull her gaze from him.

Devon's conscious rebelled. Internally, he knew this was not a safe route. They should talk about propriety, about the rules of their relationship.

Instead, all Devon could think about was the feel of her mouth against his and how much he wanted it again. Softly, his breath barely more than a whisper, he asked, "In Ireland you asked for patience from me."

Unable to form her words, Brianna nodded.

"Is there no more that you require from me?"

Despite her nervousness, Brianna answered with the truth. "Devon, I find it difficult to think about anything *other* than what I want from you."

He couldn't deny the relief that her words caused in him—nor the desire. Trying to lighten the air around them, Devon teased, "Am I so lacking as a guardian already?"

Smiling at his teasing question, Brianna replied smartly, "Thankfully, I have yet to find you lacking in anything that can't be temporarily overlooked."

Surprised by her quick remark, Devon roared with laughter. "I suppose with some effort I may find a compliment within those words."

"*I* suppose with very *little* effort you can find compliments in many situations," she replied wryly.

Devon's dark brows jutted upward. "Where has this sharp tongued snip come from? I thought I brought a sweet young lady from Ireland."

"Perhaps 'tis your influence that has changed my demeanor." With a smirk, Brianna challenged, "Find a compliment in that if you're able."

"Do you truly believe that informing me that I have influenced you so easily is anything other than a compliment?"

With an unladylike roll of her green eyes, an exasperated sigh and a shake of her head—all overruled by her soft laughter, Brianna stated, "Perhaps the true problem is that I already feel as though you've *always* influenced me."

Slowly, Devon's visage changed as she stunned him into silence. Her unexpected quick wit was nothing in comparison to this bold admission. Her gaze wavered, slid to the windowed door as the weight of what she'd just shared with him settled upon her. Realizing it was too late to take it back, she looked back at Devon and added, "Even worse, I *can't* describe the feeling. I am innocent, but not completely naïve. I know *where* such feelings can lead me, but what you've shown me— the *reality* of it, the sensation of it—seems much different."

Devon forced his flabbergasted mind to work. "Believe me, lacking innocence does not make these feelings any easier."

"You feel the same?"

He grinned at the surprise in her voice. "Aye."

A blush crept over her neck and cheeks but she forced her embarrassment aside. Suddenly she wanted to set all her doubts and worries free—more hiding her feelings in shame or fear.

Devon's breathe caught as Brianna advanced the few steps between them. With a conscious effort he tried to calm his racing pulse, his raging fantasies.

With careful precision, Brianna moved until she stood directly in front of Devon—close enough to hear his ragged breathing. "Kiss me, Devon."

He cupped her cheek gently in his hand. Her emerald gaze implored him and Devon caved. He captured her lips with his and gave no more thought to holding back.

Both of them realized that Devon had the ability to control Brianna's desires and in so, her every move. He could lead her as he wanted; yet he held back—his lips patient in their teaching.

Brianna reveled in the knowledge that she was free, that Devon knew her desires. In his embrace, her heart soared, her skin tingled and, still, she wanted more.

Brianna's curiosity tasted like a sweet answer to his desperate longing. *This* is what he had been searching for so many years with Larissah and *she* had proved a poor substitute. Brianna was soft and yearning and when she sighed into him, a purr of contented surrender passing from her mouth into his, Devon closed his eyes against the rush of heat that pulsed through the core of him.

His body demanded he throw caution aside and take her now.

His mind cautioned against repeating past mistakes.

Nevertheless, the chance was gone and the moment lost when the sound of Hesper's singing in the next room penetrated his thoughts, yanking him back to reality and responsibility.

Devon was breathless as he set Brianna slowly away from him. "Brianna, we must stop this," she didn't speak, but looked into his eyes with understanding.

Then the bond was broken and Hesper walked—*seemingly* oblivious—back into the room. The older woman may not have been formally educated, but she was wise and knew right away that she had entered an environment altogether different from the one she had left. She refrained from saying anything, but glanced in Devon's direction. His reaction only solidified what she had already guessed.

Devon spoke tersely; his tone one that he rarely used toward her. "Is there a *reason* you are invading my privacy without announcement, Hesper?"

Hessie's dark eyes narrowed a fraction. She knew the liberties she had with the Elliott's, but she knew her limits too. "I only come to see if'n ya need anythin' else."

"I have everything under control," he ground out deeply.

Hessie threw him a look and sounded a muffled grunt, easily allowing him to assume how much she agreed with his point-of-view. "Jus the same, I thinkin' Miz Brianna need her rest now."

Brianna was humiliated, what had she done? What had she instigated? Why had Devon once again been the one to stop their foolish venture? And worse, this woman whom Brianna had just met must be forming a rather blemished opinion of her.

Not able to make eye contact with either individual, Brianna agreed, "Hesper's right, Devon. I *should* rest awhile." On shaky legs, she started for the door.

Devon could only guess at the shame Brianna was feeling and he wanted to comfort her, to hold her gently until her doubt and humiliation faded. But he wouldn't go to her if it weren't her choice. Softly he called to her, "Brianna?" When she halted her steps, turning toward him in slow question, Devon offered, "Do you need me?"

Her answer struck him deeper than any desire he had known. "Yes, Devon, I'm afraid I do." Rather than coax him to her, those words held him firmly in place.

Before more could be said by anyone, Hesper stepped forward to slip a motherly arm around Brianna's waist, leading her into her bedchamber—away from Devon and certain ruin.

Chapter Seven

Larissah Chase held her dressing gown together with one hand and with the other ushered the reluctant man toward her bedchamber door. "Robert, hurry up. You should never have stayed this long."

Ignoring her frustrated tone, Robert jerked her against him for a passionate kiss. Unfortunately, he failed to notice that the embrace left him more winded than it did Larissah.

Pushing him firmly away, Larissah stated, "Robert, you really *must* go now."

"Why, Rissah? You weren't in such a hurry to be rid of me earlier." His laugh grated on her nerves almost as much as his unwarranted arrogance did.

"Don't be crude," she spat with irritation.

Pulling out of his arms, she readjusted the belt of her robe, an action that gave Robert a teasing glimpse of her body. "Rissah, do you have any idea how you affect me?" His throat was raspy with desire.

Glancing up from her belt, she laughed deeply. "Of course I do. Why else do you think I keep you around?"

Grabbing a fistful of golden hair, he bruised her lips with another kiss. "Minx," he murmured, his mouth just a breath from hers.

"Your sweet compliments won't change my mind today." Biting his bottom lip, she purred, "Now go before you *really* upset me." With no more warning, Larissah shoved Robert out the door, soundly bolting the door behind him.

Rid of her stunned lover, Larissah impatiently awaited the bath her slaves automatically knew was to be delivered the very moment Robert departed her home.

To pass the time, she averted her mind to the next matter in need of handling. Devon was home and Larissah wanted—no, *needed*—to see him.

A week earlier, Daniel had told her of his brother's imminent return. For the last three mornings she'd sent one of her slaves, Bess, to Misty Heights to check for his arrival. Larissah had hoped he would send word of his return to her at her home, Reverie, but there had been none, yet.

Then, just this morning, Bess reported he was home.

With a flash of jealousy, she assumed that the reason was due to the extra attention he was forced to give her cousin. Larissah remembered that Brianna had been a cute child—annoying but cute—and it irritated her to assume the girl had therefore grown in to an equally attractive woman. Yes, she'd been rough around the edges, but everyone with eyes could see she'd grow into a beauty.

Plus, she was a relative of Larissah's—how could any less truly be expected?

Sitting on the edge of her bed, Larissah peered into the looking glass on the other side of her room. Holding back her hair, she grimaced at the silver strands she *believed* were beginning to show at her roots. Imagined or otherwise, the tell-tale signs of age became more prominent on Larissah's pretty face each year. Powder and paint were now adding to, rather than disguising, the marks she had previously been able to hide. There were the slightest indications of wrinkles at the corners of her mouth and eyes and recently, she had been forced to curb her appetite. It was apparent that her corset could no longer camouflage everything.

Now Larissah had to compete with a younger woman, which only added to the constant strain on her physical attributes.

It didn't help that she had already sensed a negative change in Devon during the weeks before his voyage. Larissah was confident in her capability as a lover. Devon was certainly satisfied. Still, she was no fool. Like any man, Devon Elliott would leave her the instant he found someone better suited to his needs. She *had* to obtain a proposal and *soon*.

It had been nearly three months since they were last intimate, which only confirmed Larissah's suspicion that she was in danger of losing Devon. He was a man who lived for pleasure and would go where it was best offered to him. Now he was tiring of her. Larissah had hoped that Devon would not want to waste his time with a lover he would have to teach, but now, the longer she waited for word from him, the more Larissah doubted her instincts.

Therefore, she had sent a note requesting he call on her today.

According to his reply, he would be here within the hour.

As the last bucket of water was added to the tub, Bess announced Devon's arrival. With a smile, Larissah ordered, "Send him up, Bess. I've been expecting him." Sliding beneath the satiny, lavender-scented water, she watched the door and waited for Devon to stride through it so that she could welcome him home properly.

◊◊◊◊◊

Brianna watched through the reflection of her vanity mirror while Hesper's daughter, Tansey, arranged her hair. The lovely girl did her job well and Brianna relaxed as the other woman's agile hands pulled the brush through the layers of her thick auburn mane.

Studying Tansey's working features offered Brianna a clear vantage point of Tansey's white lineage. The light amber tone of her brow furrowed slightly in concentration, ebony hair, straight and silky in texture. Her strongest African feature was her almond shaped eyes the shade of dark coal with endless warmth emanating from their depths.

Though she had no proof, Brianna strongly assumed that Abram was not Tansey's biological father.

It was little concern to her, however and since Tansey seemed comfortable with her position at Misty Heights, Brianna found it easy to be around her. "Tell me, Tansey, how long have you lived here with the Elliott's?"

Not missing a twirl of her fingers, the darker woman replied, "Mama say we came jus' after I was born, almost twenty years ago this past winter."

Which Brianna instantly calculated, made Tansey just two or three years older than her. It also meant that Tansey would likely know a great deal about Devon's life—a realization that caused fluttering in Brianna's stomach.

"So you grew up with Devon and Daniel, then?" Brianna knew her question was not unusual but couldn't help the quickening in her chest as she awaited the answer.

"I did." Tansey stuck another hairpin in Brianna's curls and then started on the other side of her head. "I spent a lot of time learnin' to be a proper lady's maid with their Mama, Miz Lily, too."

"I don't remember her very well. Is Devon much like her?"

Tansey nodded, her smile coming easily. "She was a fine woman. She cared about everyone she knew, but nobody more than her boys."

The conversation lulled between them for a while, each woman lost in thoughts of her own. Brianna's curiosity had been sparked, though, and it wasn't long before she prodded, "Were they the devilish lads, I'm guessing? Have they grown to the men their parents aimed them to be?"

Tansey didn't meet Brianna's gaze in the mirror but continued to focus on the task at hand. Her mother had insinuated that there was something working between this new lady of the house and Devon—surely that was the reason for Brianna's questions. Since Tansey knew well what it was like to fall under the Elliott spell, she sympathized with her new mistress immediately.

"They mama would be proud, but they sure could be rascals when we was young." Coaxing forth some memories, Tansey offered, "Lots of times Mista Daniel and Mista Devon and me would play together, if I weren't too busy with chores. I always been closer to Dan—Mista Daniel than Mista Devon. I think that mostly 'cause we closer to the same age. That and 'cause Mista Devon always off on one of them ships whenever him pappy give him the chance." Brianna noted the glimmer that flashed in Tansey's dark eyes at the mention—and blunder—of Daniel's name and her curiosity was further piqued.

Something told her more than Devon's frequent absences had caused Tansey to be closer to Daniel.

Thanks to time spent around her father and his workers in Dublin, Brianna had heard stories of slaveholders taking the women they bought and using them as mistresses. Was it possible that Daniel had taken advantage of Tansey that way? Or was there more to it than that? From the look in Tansey's eyes and the history she and Daniel shared, Brianna surmised that either situation seemed quite possible.

Another indicator that Tansey was favored by at least one of the Elliott's was her speech, more refined than Brianna had expected. Though Brianna's knowledge of slave-master relationships was limited, she understood enough to know that education in slaves or servants was frowned upon. Yet, this young Negro girl's speech and manner was almost as cultured as Brianna's own heavily Irish-laced American-English—a social taboo in its own right.

For the present time, Brianna set aside that particular prejudice to concentrate on the great deal of time and effort it must have taken Tansey to polish her behaviors. Brianna was impressed, both that Tansey had struggled for self-improvement and that the Elliotts had given and allowed her tutelage. There were still some cultural wordings that Brianna surmised would never completely go away, but otherwise Tansey spoke exceptionally well for her station.

In hopes of gaining further evidence to her assumption, Brianna inquired, "Who taught you?"

"Taught me, Miz?"

Brianna was cautious. She didn't want to insult Tansey, but her curiosity was a force to be reckoned with. "Your speech, 'tis better than I expected."

Understanding lighting her pretty face, Tansey still hesitated—her words more controlled and thought through when next she spoke. "No, the way I talk mostly Miz Lily's doing. She say there no sense havin' a house slave that can't serve guests proper."

Realizing with mild disappointment that she wasn't going to be able to corner Tansey into mistakenly offering gossip about Daniel—unless she were much more obvious—Brianna veered from the topic. "What about my cousin? Did Larissah help with your learning too?"

Brianna caught the mix of disgust and amusement that passed over the other woman's face before Tansey remembered she could be seen through the looking glass. Clearing her expression, she answered, "Miz Lily ask her to, but Miz Larissah always busy into somethin' for herself."

Tansey said no more and Brianna could sense a wall of protection sliding between them. Clearly, Tansey was recalling that one wrong word about Larissah, to the wrong person, could certainly bring a lot of pain and trouble down upon a Negress—freed or not.

Meanwhile, Brianna skimmed through the repetitious remarks about her cousin. With a roll of her green eyes, Brianna declared, "Faith and Begora, is the woman really so selfish and uncaring as everyone is leading me to believe?"

When Tansey didn't speak, Brianna glanced at her through the mirror. It was obvious that she didn't intend to reply, so Brianna prompted, "You can speak freely with me, Tansey. I'll not betray your confidence."

Even with this promise, there was still no way Tansey was going to answer such a question straight out. She may be a freed-woman—not bound to the master-family by more than a need for security—but that security was something she had learned to treasure. In her world, such an opportunity was one that most of her people never really knew. She refused to let loose her guarded tongue just for the relief of telling Brianna that Larissah was mean and vicious, a viper of the worst kind. It also wasn't her place to inform Brianna that her cousin was an easy woman who threw herself at Daniel and used many men for physical pleasure as well as financial gratitude—Devon included.

With a tone indicating she wasn't ready to be so trusting, Tansey stated, "Miz Larissah will likely be around soon as she knows Mista Devon home. You can judge for yourself then."

"If she is so anxious to welcome him, then Larissah and Devon must be very close."

"Yes'm, they are." Tansey said no more but laid aside the remaining pins she had been using to style Brianna's hair. "Now, all done." Tansey finished Brianna's appearance with a broach of pearls, and the uncomfortable conversation came to an end. Surveying her handiwork, Tansey praised, "You sure make a fine lady of the house, Miz Brianna."

Brianna allowed Tansey's compliment and its ultimate meaning to wash over her. Until that instant, she hadn't realized just how much she would treasure that title. Her feelings for Devon were in constant turmoil—had been from the beginning—but each day she came closer to understanding what it was she wanted from him, and it was more than stolen kisses and tormenting, teasing touches.

Brianna's eyes shifted from her own contemplative reflection to meet Tansey's dark gaze and was certain Tansey had guessed at her thoughts. When an easy grin curved Tansey's peach-tinted lips upward, Brianna also gathered she had gained a new friend and confidant in the process.

◊◊◊◊◊

Not caring that he sloshed water over the sides of the tub, Devon vigorously scrubbed soap over his body. He had a desperate need to wash away his foolish weaknesses and the affects they might have on his immediate future.

Earlier that day, he walked directly into Larissah's trap. It was foolish of him. He should have guessed at her plan beforehand. Then again, maybe subconsciously he had, and so made it easy for Larissah to ensnare him. Probably as easy as it had been for him to give in to the temptation of her body and the release he had found there.

If only he'd had the strength to end their relationship instead.

Silently, Devon attempted to assuage his guilt—a new and seemingly persistent feeling he didn't like at all. He and Larissah understood each other and their needs; they always had. Devon was aware that Larissah had other lovers and he'd never much cared. Whomever else she shared her time or her bed with was of no consequence to him, so long as she was available for Devon's pleasure whenever he wanted her.

Moreover, the fact that he had bedded her that afternoon was nothing to be worried about, either. They had used each other for pleasure many times in the past, with no one the wiser, no one hurt by complicated feelings.

However, that was before *Brianna.*

Devon cursed and scrubbed his flesh harder. He was tiring of how often that phrase had come to the forefront of his mind of late. He had offered this new woman in his life no commitment. He owed her nothing except security, yet he felt as if he had betrayed her somehow—and himself in the process. All for naught more than a romp with a woman whom he had intended to break all intimate ties with anyway.

Now, Devon was paying for his uncontrollable lust and Larissah's easy ability to entrap and please him.

The smell of lavender still burned in his nostrils as he remembered the way she had welcomed him. Despite her state of dress—or *undress*—Larissah used customary pleasantries, as though welcoming a guest into the parlor of her home for afternoon tea.

Then she had made her move—a simple one, which Devon *now* understood as her well-planned and perfectly executed strategy.

Continuing to engage him in congenial discussion, Larissah stood from her bath and asked Devon to hand her the drying-towel, which she had conveniently left on the opposite side of her bedroom.

Even now, Devon's mind clearly recalled the way the water ran down the length of her bare form and just as fluidly, his gaze had trailed each droplet along its scintillating journey. When he looked back to Larissah's blue eyes, they'd both known she was victorious.

Their coupling had come fast and furious. Each fulfilled their basest of needs, while secretly harboring deeper, more personal reasons for the tryst.

Devon had closed his eyes in the midst of his passion, visions of a fiery-haired innocent filling his mind rather than the golden seductress who lay beneath him.

Larissah gave all in her attempt to win Devon completely— to bring him fully around to her once more.

Neither cared or even considered what the other wanted.

Devon's thoughts were lost in the realization that even if his weakness was revealed to Larissah and she knew that his desire for another woman had fueled his passion that afternoon, he didn't care. He focused on how good it felt to lose all reason within the arms of a woman. At that point, just about any woman would have sufficed, so long as Brianna was safe and her virtue still intact.

When Devon left Larissah, she rested amid the folds of her coverlets, still damp from their exertions. She had pouted that he was leaving so soon, but her expression and words had no effect on him. At least not the one she anticipated. In hopes of easily escaping her company and along with it, the feeling of nagging guilt already descending upon him, Devon had distractedly accepted her invitation for an upcoming social event she was hosting.

He then departed her home as quickly as his legs would carry him.

Every thought since his exit had centered on his blunder and how it would change Brianna's new trust in him and to what extremes he might go to ensure that she never learn of his quick deception. It was something that would never happen again and for her to discover it would only bring unnecessary heartache to them both.

This brought his thoughts around to Larissah once more and the idea that she would again believe that she held the key to his passion and therefore his fortune.

When she learned that she was wrong, there would be Hell to pay and Devon had the uneasy feeling that he would pay dearly, indeed.

◊◊◊◊◊

The evening air carried a chill as Brianna strolled through Misty Heights' modest flower and herb garden. The coolness was refreshing but the beauty of the star-filled sky sparkling above did little to distract her mind. As silly as it seemed, every time she was alone with Devon, some small detail of a conversation or a glance embedded itself on her memory for later torment.

So much about Devon drew Brianna closer.

Even when she tried to remember how angry she had been at their first meeting, it wasn't possible. It seemed that every kind word or action, heated glance or touch that he had given her since, banned any of her long-lasting negative feelings toward him.

Lost in thought, Brianna failed to hear the very man of her musing approach, and she walked directly into his hard chest, letting out a squeal of surprise. Together they laughed and tried to ignore the tiny sparks of heat caused by the contact.

Brianna was the first to step back and away from the intimate contact.

"I came to let you know that dinner is about to be served," Devon informed with laughter still echoing in his tone.

Brianna grinned. "Thank you."

Her smiled filled Devon with a warmth and serenity he'd not expected and without exaggeration, he replied, "It is my pleasure." Offering her his arm, Brianna accepted the escort with ease, relieving Devon's mood even more. The tension he had expected in consideration of their earlier conduct was not present. On the contrary, Brianna was at ease, her unhurried steps allowing them to linger on the walking path in quiet comfort.

Casually, Brianna remarked, "I looked for you this afternoon." He glanced down and Brianna continued, "Hesper said you were away."

Devon nodded, tried to ignore the returned sting of guilt and informed her, "I went to visit Larissah while you were resting."

If Brianna noticed the edge in his tone, she didn't mention it. Instead she inquired with her endearing Irish lilt, "And how is my cousin, then?" Releasing his arm, she plucked a yellow tulip from the flowerbed and sniffed its sweet scent.

Devon was thankful for her action as it hid the slight start her words caused him.

Twirling the flower stem between her fingers, she glanced up at him with patient curiosity.

Realizing he needed to make some sort of reply, Devon remarked cautiously, "Larissah is well."

Brianna smiled and took his arm again. "Good."

She took his arm again and without thought, Devon moved them forward again. Entering the dining room through the rear verandah doors, Devon clung to the momentary lull in their conversation. He was irritated by his hovering guilt and the awkwardness it brought with it.

The silence was short lived. "Will I meet her soon?"

The later the better, Devon wanted to say, a sense of dread overriding both guilt and awkwardness as he considered the possibility of that meeting and its consequences for him. Trying not to think of the exact state in which her invitation was given, Devon instead informed Brianna, "Larissah is planning a small gathering the middle of next month." Pulling out her chair, he promised, "That should be enough time for us to get you settled in our home before the social season sweeps you away from me."

Accepting the seat, Brianna smiled up at Devon with an unabashed pleasure that warmed him. "Come with me and they'll be no sweeping away," she sweetly suggested. Watching as he moved to his seat across the table, Brianna noticed his furrowed brow and laughed lightly. "You needn't brood. 'Twas only a suggestion."

Grasping her misconception of his expression, Devon forced his facial features to relax. "I'm sorry."

With easy forgiveness, she reminded him, "Social events are not a favorite event of mine, either."

Nodding in agreement, Devon shared some truth with her. "Having just been away and spoiled by my time at sea, the prospect of being trapped in a roomful of gossip mongers is rather depressing."

"Then we'll manage it together," she promised, turning her attention to Hesper as the older woman delivered a platter of fish and potatoes for their dining pleasure and completely missing the new look of longing that filled her companions expression.

◊◊◊◊◊

Devon's night was worse than his afternoon had been. Sleep alluded him and he paced the confines of his bedroom like a caged animal. Finally, he opened the balcony doors and stepped into the night air. Its briskness was exactly what his arduous thoughts needed though a part of him still wished he'd have given in to temptation and brought Brianna to his bed rather than have spent the evening locked in a chaste gave of chess playing.

If nothing else, he now could toss aside all pretenses of believing that his desire for her was only physical. Deep in his soul, Devon knew that it was more. Worse, he had the distinct inclination that he wasn't alone in those feelings. He and Brianna *both* wanted more and the knowledge left a bitter taste in his mouth—the taste of unadulterated fear.

You are falling in love with her.

The words echoed softly in Devon's thoughts. Even as close as he was to completely admitting the truth of that statement to himself, he was still extremely leery of the emotion and all the responsibilities that came with it.

On cue, his mind began tossing negative reasons and excuses as to why a union between he and Brianna wouldn't work—not the least of which being his relationship with her cousin. Many people would find Devon's transition from Brianna's guardian to her romantic prospect, utterly scandalous. While Devon rarely cared what others thought, for Brianna, the sneers might be harder to handle. There was also his livelihood to consider. With him so often at sea, Brianna would be lonely, their relationship tested and strained by distance.

Devon was not willing to sacrifice her happiness by making Brianna into the typical waiting-wife of a sailor. She deserved better.

Better than what? Better than your parents had? Better than her *parents had?*

Devon did not like the direction his mind was headed. Trying to do the right thing, he conjured visions of other women he had courted, other lovers he'd had. Every one of their faces faded to Brianna's.

With a growl of aggravation, he returned to the warmth of his bedroom as his mind charged once more, *Stop fooling yourself and make Brianna yours in all ways. Not just body and heart, but in name as well.*

The last words echoed in his mind with more chill than the outside air. *Marry Brianna?*

The prospect certainly gave him a better feeling than imagining life tied to any other woman he knew. Still, there were all the arguments he'd considered before.

Glancing toward his bed, Devon went to it, climbed into its warmth and closing his eyes, prayed for sleep and a dream that would provide him with all the right answers for his dilemma and his future.

Chapter Eight

The next morning, Brianna stayed in her room longer than normal, enjoying the view from her verandah. The Elliott's had more than one hundred-fifty acres upon which Misty Heights stood. Tansey had explained that since the start of the shipping company, they had farmed out their land, rather than maintain the crops themselves.

Brianna had just awoken when she heard Devon's voice calling out from below, followed by the sound of horse hooves beating against the ground. Sliding from beneath the covers, she had donned her robe and walked to the verandah door. From there she'd watched Devon race across the field, stop and dismount to shake the hand of a lone man working in the field.

Curious, she'd moved out the doors and into the fresh air. She wasn't sure how long she stood watching him converse with the sharecropper before Tansey found her. The freed woman passed along word that Devon would be gone until early evening.

Brianna was disappointed but understood that he needed the time to deal with the farmers using his land, making sure the crops were yielding well and that everyone's needs were being met.

Rather than sit and wait for him to return, though, she would do some exploring of her own and learn her new home inside and out. She may even employ Tansey to show her some of the land if the day lasted long enough.

Her plans firmly in mind, Brianna looked forward to her day with happy curiosity and made her way downstairs.

Just as she stepped foot on the lower landing, the front door
flew wide and, unannounced, a woman entered amid a flurry of
pink satin. Her eyes scanned Brianna from head to toe and
then, with an enthusiasm that didn't quite reach her cool blue
eyes, introduced herself. "Dear little Bria, here you are, returned to us at last." Turning her cheek upward and extending
her white gloved hand in anticipation, she urged, "Come give
your cousin a welcome kiss."

Dumbly, Brianna did as requested, though she wasn't quite
sure why.

"There's a good girl," Larissah gushed. "Now I insist you
come with me today. I'll show you the proper places to shop in
this pitiful little town." Tugging at her already perfectly placed
lace trimmed sleeves, the unabashed blonde added, "And you
must remember a lady *never* choses to shop *here* if she has the
opportunity to do so in the city instead."

Not sure if the enthusiastic greeting and shopping lesson
was finished, Brianna waited in silence.

Finished with her sleeves, Larissah looked toward Brianna
sharply. "Well?"

"Well, what?" Brianna inquired, not certain which comment she was meant to reply to first.

"Are you *ready*?"

"Have I any choice?"

Larissah smiled. "I see you're not just a pretty face."
Turning with a swirl of skirts, Brianna's cousin walked back
out the door, leaving it open in clear indication that her dumb-
struck relative was meant to follow behind without question.

With a shake of her head, Brianna decided that unless she
planned to close and bolt the door, her first instinct to decline
the outing was not an option. As her conscience stepped forward, Brianna took her wrap from the coat rack and passed
through the door, closing it behind her as she rearranged her
day to revolve around reacquainting herself with Larissah
Chase.

◊◊◊◊◊

Close on the heels of her instinct to avoid the outing, Brianna became curious about her cousin. Truth be told, she'd

been curious about her since Ireland, even more when she'd heard the various offhand and often insulting remarks about the woman. How else was Brianna to draw her own conclusions without interacting with Larissah? Add to that the fact that Larissah had been kind enough to come to her and invite her out for the day.

Unfortunately, her final instinct—aversion—did not set in until they were already in the midst of their shopping spree. Brianna had been ushered from one store to another. Colors of all varieties flashed in front of her eyes until Brianna saw blurring rainbows at every turn.

Larissah made sure that Brianna didn't miss any opportunity to buy something and all but forced business owners to treat her as a prize customer at every location.

Rather than endear Larissah to her, these actions sent further danger signals ringing in Brianna's mind. Larissah wanted something more than familial kinship—she was trying too hard for the case to be otherwise. The truth was there, just under her thin façade of camaraderie; Brianna simply couldn't quite put her finger on it yet.

Even now, Larissah's overenthusiastic compliments rang false. "That emerald is the *perfect* color for you, Brianna."

"Do you think so? I would hate to pay such a fee for the wrong shade." Brianna stated, studying the bolt of satin in hand.

"It's just the thing," Larissah looked toward Ruth Donnellson, the shop-owner/seamstress, with raised brows. Obviously Larissah's impatient expectations knew no bounds.

Biting her bottom lip in thought, Brianna nodded when her mind was made up. "I'll take it, then, along with the sapphire blue." Working with Ruth, Brianna finalized her order. "Now that's it, Larissah. I'll not buy another thing today."

Perusing some casual knit collars, Larissah commented dryly, "Whatever you like." Over her shoulder, she suggested, "I believe you should wear that emerald shade to my gathering. You'll look simply lovely." Giving her a girl-to-girl look, she added slyly, "I'll introduce you to a friend of mine, Robert Montgomery. He's in the market for a bride." Stealing a quick glance at Ruth, she added, "Or so I hear."

Brianna rolled her eyes. "It's a pity then that I am not currently up for sale, Rissah. Perhaps you could offer *your* assistance in my place?"

With quick laughter, Larissah informed, "Oh no, Bria, I have *my* sights set on a much bigger catch."

And so was revealed the true reason for today's outing.

Brianna knew immediately to whom Larissah referred and she desperately wished she had listened to her first instinct of the day and remained at Misty Heights.

Cool as she could manage, Brianna questioned, "Surely you're not suggesting I settle for your castaways? Daniel told Devon and me of your visit to Baltimore, and I daresay he left the impression that you and Mr. Montgomery were more than friends."

With venom, Larissah spat, "Which only proves that Daniel Elliott shouldn't waste his time assuming anything about *my* relationships." Closing her eyes and taking a deep breath for composure, Larissah explained, "Furthermore, Brianna, trust me when I say that one can hardly deem a man like Robert Montgomery as *settling*. Especially when *one* is . . . how might I put this delicately?" Feigning the need to search for words, Larissah cleared her throat lightly and shrugged, then allowed her insult to hit home, "Well, let's just say that an *Irish* woman is hardly the best catch these days. We know of all the turmoil and poverty over there—*very* distasteful." Larissah shuddered and spoke as though the entire Irish famine was Brianna's doing. However, even with that, her abuse hadn't reached its summit, as she felt the need to illustrate, "In most cases, your womenfolk have no dowry to sweeten the offer of their hand. Since we have no reason to think differently of *you*, with no more than fair looks and a good name to fall back on, settle is *exactly* what you should do."

Larissah's indication that Brianna was homely and left penniless and alone by her family seared Brianna's ego deeply. Making matters worse, Brianna knew that the other store occupants would spread the gossip at the speed of wildfire.

Brianna could not—would not—stand by and take such treatment. With a tone deliberately forced with an Irish accent, Brianna feigned sincerity. "*Now* I understand, Rissah. Saints be praised, what would I be doin' wi' you an' yer help? Ta be

sure an' true, yer maturity an' experience has done me a good
deed this day." Brianna had the distinct pleasure of watching
Larissah's face transform from peaches and cream to violet and
red. It was evident that a clash of wills was not something Larissah was accustomed to or happy about.

Through clenched teeth, Larissah ground out, "Make certain, then, that you heed my advice."

"Since it is Devon who was appointed my guardian, I believe I'll follow his lead and *not* yours, Larissah."

Before Larissah could reply, the door to the shop opened
and the very man just mentioned strode purposefully through it.

Larissah wavered shortly but not enough that anyone noticed her falter. She wanted to curse at the top of her lungs—
now she would have to wait for another opportunity to inform
Brianna of how her *precious* Devon had betrayed her.

Stepping directly to Brianna, Devon stated evenly, "I've
come to bring you home."

Dutifully enough to make Larissah cringe in disgust, Brianna replied, "I'm sorry to have inconvenienced you, Devon. I
was headed home just now."

He nodded in acceptance of her apology but was glad he
had come just the same. He wasn't quite sure what he had interrupted, but from the tension around him and the looks of the
other people in the store, there had certainly been a show in
progress. Wanting to rescue Brianna and allow both of them to
escape before further harm could be done, he replied, "At least
I have saved Larissah the bother of coming to Misty Heights."

Larissah joined the conversation with ease. "And when
have I *ever* considered a visit to you a bother, Devon?" Not
expecting an answer, she turned to Brianna and with forced
comedy issued a warning, "Take care, cousin, as you can see
from his arrival to return you home safely, Devon takes his role
as guardian quiet seriously. Just wait until you receive gentlemen callers. He'll be positively unbearable."

Devon was quick to reply, though he kept his gaze from
meeting Larissah's. "Brianna need not be warned; as I said,
my concern was to keep you from needing to bring her home.
There was no reason for her to be with *you* any longer."

Larissah's jaw set—apparently, the innocent Brianna was going to pose an even greater threat than she had originally guessed.

Blue eyes flashing dangerously, Larissah's strike was swift and pointed. "Somehow I doubt that my inconvenience was your *only* concern, Devon."

Firmly, Devon suggested, "Take care that you do not go too far in this, Larissah."

Larissah threw her head back with a brash laugh and stated, "My, my, Devon. I *do* believe I've *finally* found your weakness. Or at least a more meaningful one than I've discovered in the past."

Devon's skin crawled with her familiar words. When he had returned from handling his business dealings for the day and found Brianna's note informing him of where she was and, even worse, whom she was with, Devon had watched the time pass slowly. With each movement of the clock hand, his dread grew considerably. His imaginations filled with pictures of Larissah exposing each detail of their past—particularly yesterday's fiasco.

Finally, Devon had no choice but to go retrieve Brianna.

In the same room with Brianna now, he was able to deduce that she was still blissfully unaware of his great mistake. She was still able to look at him without disgust and that was enough to appease his worry for the moment.

Sensing Devon's need to flee, the shopkeeper aided, "Mr. Elliott, Miss McClaran's items are ready. Is there anything else I might be assistance with?"

Devon nodded. "Thank you, Mrs. Donnellson. Just see that the goods are delivered tomorrow and put the bill for Miss McClaran's purchases on my account." Then he announced in a voice almost loud enough to be heard outside, "Send Miss Chase her own bill. I think it's time she start tending to her own matters." He threw Larissah a meaningful look with steel blue eyes and declared, "In *all* affairs."

Bristling with indignation, Larissah watched as Devon took Brianna's hand and led her out of the shop, onto bustling Shenandoah Street and into the carriage awaiting them.

◊◊◊◊◊

Larissah left Ruth's shop fuming but kept her head held high. The closed carriage door had scarcely closed before she hurtled newly purchased packages at the opposite seat and hissed obscenities that would singe a God fearing person's ears.

When her rampage was over and her anger at a simmer, she slumped back against the bumping seat and calmed her mind by formulating plans.

Previously, Larissah had only wanted to make Devon's life unnerving for disrupting their relationship with Brianna's presence. After the public humiliation her cousin and guardian had caused her today—and the screaming instincts that her time with Devon was at an end—Larissah was after more than just aggravation. She wanted embarrassment and pain reined upon them—she wanted revenge.

There were many options open to Larissah. Some involved help, others involved timing but each resulted in the same outcome—Devon Elliott would belong to her, one way or another and Brianna McClaran would be shipped back to Ireland and out of their lives permanently.

◊◊◊◊◊

Brianna sat quietly looking out the window at the scenery of Harper's Ferry. Her concentration was on what she had just experienced more than what she saw, however.

Drawing her attention to him, Devon asked, "How in God's name did you get tangled with her today?"

"When I woke, you were gone. She came and insisted that I join her shopping."

Dark brows shot upward. "I thought you did not enjoy such frivolity."

"No more, it seems, than Larissah takes no for an answer." With a wry expression, she added, "If she even waits for the answer to begin with."

Sighing, Devon informed his ward. "Brianna, there is a great deal about Larissah that you do not understand. She is not the same as you."

"So I've gathered." Studying Devon's face, she inquired, "What makes her that way?"

With a shrug, Devon replied, "I suppose being spoiled by her father and every other man she digs her claws into."

"I fear people with judge me by her reputation."

Devon's expression softened. "They have only to give you a chance and five minutes of their time to realize you and Larissah share no more than ancestors."

Blushing sweetly, Brianna whispered, "Thank you; for your words, your support and rescuing me from a very uncomfortable situation."

Smiling broadly—and causing Brianna's heart to skip a beat—Devon assured her, "That's what I am here for." And the tension slipped away with his heartfelt words.

◊◊◊◊◊

Upon entering the dining room for breakfast the next morning, Devon laughed at Brianna as she impatiently eyed the stack of hot cakes, sausage and gravy, lining the center of the table in front of her.

Ignoring his greeting, she snapped, "It's about time, Captain Elliott. I was beginning to think you intended to make me sit here half the day in torment."

"Good morning to you, *too.*"

Her only reply was a deep grumbling noise from the pit of her stomach. Offering a timid grin, she turned three different shades of pink.

"Hungry?" Devon pondered.

She wrinkled her nose at him cutely. "No, I'm *famished.*"

The evening before, when she discovered that he had already eaten before her return, she had only nibbled on cheese and crackers rather than have Hesper bother to reheat a plate of food for her. She was now feeling the result of that folly.

"By all means, Brianna, *eat.*" Laughing at the way she ferociously jabbed at the stack of sausage patties, Devon advised, "In fact, eat your fill. I want you to have plenty of energy for the day ahead."

Brianna eyed him skeptically. "What do you have planned for us?" She had filled her fork with a bite of gravy-covered hot cake before Devon even had a chance to reply.

"I thought I would show you some of the countryside. I imagine that Larissah already offered you an extended tour of the shopping district."

Brianna rolled her eyes skyward at the thought of her nasty cousin. "Devon, I have never in my *life* seen someone with such a talent for spending money. I think even Meghan would have been outdone."

Devon offered a wry expression. "I'd wager you're correct in that. At any rate,"—he picked up a hot cake and lathered it with fresh butter—"I would like to show you some of the areas best seen by horseback."

Making a sound of excitement that nearly caused Devon to choke on the bite of food in his mouth, Brianna squealed, "How glorious! Do you realize that I have not been on a horse since before my father passed away? Oh, Devon, how wonderful you are!"

"I am glad that you are pleased with my plans." Her genuine thrill invigorated him. With a smile he continued, "I also had Hesper pack us a basket lunch so that we don't have to return until supper."

"I'm sure she was none too happy with the notion of us spending the day together without a proper chaperone." As soon as the words were spoken, Brianna realized their forward meaning and chose to concentrate on the food in front of her rather than Devon's gaze.

Chucking at her reddened cheeks, Devon stated, "Remember, I *am* the chaperone." At her dubious expression, he added, "But you are right and I received the worst warning-filled lecture of all my twenty-five years and that means something considering some of the reprimands I've earned."

"Yes, I can somehow imagine that," Brianna responded with a lighthearted smile.

Devon huffed playfully. "Let's not waste time on that particular topic."

Brianna laughed. "Because I am anxious for the day to start, I'll agree—for now." Still chewing her last bite of breakfast, Brianna headed off to change into her riding habit.

◊◊◊◊◊

Devon's quilt flapped in the breeze as Brianna spread the fabric out on the ground. After tethering the mounts to a near-by tree, Devon made his way back to the spot she had chosen. Relaxing, he was able to watch Brianna work from the incon-spicuous shelter of his drooped eyelids.

If not for the sunlight enhancing the shimmering red strands of her hair, the thick plait hanging over her shoulder would have appeared brown against the butternut of her dress. The matching hat, its point tilted becomingly to the center of her forehead, drew attention to the glowing gold within her jade eyes. When she turned away and bent to empty the bas-ket, the material of her riding habit pulled tight against her hips and backside and Devon's entire form jerked involuntarily. He itched to touch her but refrained. When she turned back to him, he averted his eyes quickly. He had no wish to allow her to see his rampant desire. One of them had to control the sparks flying between them and surely, she was far too inno-cent to handle that responsibility.

Seating herself next to him gingerly, Brianna sighed. "As anxious as I was to ride, I admit I hadn't remembered how ex-erting it is." Rather than comment, Devon pulled on a chicken drumstick with his teeth.

Not very hungry after her huge breakfast, Brianna stood again and walked to a clump of boulders embedded near the edge of a steep embankment. Without looking at him, she commented, "I think this view is beautiful enough to rival the emerald greens of Ireland." Devon caught a slight twinge of homesickness in her voice.

Knowing what her reaction would be, he baited, "There is a romantic legend to go with that view. Would you care to hear it?"

His assumption was right. "I've not known an Irish soul that could ever resist a legend." Leveling him with a gaze full of curiosity, she prodded, "Do tell."

Standing, Devon brushed crumbs off his hands and walked to her side. "Just there." He pointed in the direction of a bend in the rock-clustered water of the rushing river. "That's where the Potomac and Shenandoah Rivers merge; it's called 'The Point'." Indicating the far bank of the Potomac, Devon further enlightened her, "That is Maryland." Directing her attention first to the ground beneath them, then directly across the river from them, he added, "Here, and there, is Virginia."

He was so near that his breath tickled her cheek as he began his tale and Brianna had to force her mind to stay focused on the words of the story. "The legend passed down says that when this territory was occupied by Indians, two warring tribes met and battled here. In the aftermath of the fight, a warrior from one of the tribes fell in love with the princess of his enemy. When the Chieftain learned of the feelings his daughter, Shenandoah, had for the enemy brave, Potomac, he banished the princess to the surrounding hills. Broken hearted beyond repair, the girl grieved the separation—in the end dying of the anguish."

"How tragic," Brianna whispered while turning her gaze from the rivers to Devon's face.

"Learning the fate of his love," Devon continued softly, "Potomac went to find her body. With her held in his arms, he ended his life in the same way that she had. The tears of the separated lovers ran down the hillsides, creating the Shenandoah and Potomac Rivers. Here they are joined together, for all time."

"As they should be," Brianna murmured, not at all sure that she spoke only of the couple in the legend.

There was huskiness in her voice that both startled Devon and immediately drew him to her. Pulling her close he whispered, "Destiny, Flame. It is all part of a greater scheme than we could fathom." He kissed her then, a slow, tender kiss that made Brianna tingle from the top of her head to the tips of her toes and on every spot in between.

This was the moment that each of them had known would come sometime during their day. Denying that they wanted it was futile. They were as powerless against the force, as Shenandoah and Potomac had been and realizing that, Brianna allowed her feelings a brief freedom. She needed to give to receive, and she *desperately* wanted to receive.

Devon felt the intensity surging through her innocent embrace and what once would have pushed him away from a woman now lured him dangerously in. Completely out of character, Devon was not at all threatened by the understanding that his beloved bachelorhood no longer seemed enticing. What he wanted out of life now was more . . . *deeper*—what he wanted was Brianna.

Still holding her close, he gently pressed his lips to her forehead. Breathing deeply, he swam in the scent of her. "Lord, give me strength. Brianna, you affect me to distraction."

Her voice quivered with heavy emotion and light laughter. "I think I comprehend."

Devon surprised her by stepping back. Their embrace ended sooner than Brianna expected, and she was unable to hide the resulting disappointment that filled her eyes.

Pointedly choosing to ignore that look and what it was prompting him to do, Devon clasped their hands together and smiled. "Aye, but what are we going to do about it?"

It was a good question, and one that made her a little uneasy. What *would* happen now? It was obvious that they must get past this point or they would simply keep reliving it each time they were alone. What was next?

Wistfully, she voiced her first thought aloud, though even before she spoke, she knew it was impossible. "Run off into the hills and forget about the rest of the world and what is right or wrong."

Devon smiled. "If only we could give in to that temptation." Brianna looked up at him with eyes so trusting. Whatever he asked of her, she would do, and at that moment, they were both achingly aware of the fact. "Slowly, Brianna. Let's take things one day at a time. We will see where these new feelings lead us."

"That sounds perfect," she agreed, and then pulled his head back down toward her, initiating another kiss.

They spent the remainder of the afternoon there on the blanket, sharing nothing but sweet kisses, chaste handholding and easy conversation about their lives.

Devon began his courtship of her, and Brianna willingly obliged.

Chapter Nine

The following weeks at Misty Heights were filled with bliss as Devon and Brianna allowed their hearts to lead the way. Devon took Brianna on new adventures and outings nearly every day. They started out early, enjoying the fresh morning as they tore across the countryside on horseback. Returning home, they shared sunlit lunches on the verandah. Some evenings they dined out, but they both preferred staying in for a quiet supper of Hesper's delicious cooking.

Afterward, they spent quiet time together in the parlor. Cuddled together on the settee, they shared dreams and traded stories about their lives. Sometimes Devon read a book of seafaring sonnets aloud or Brianna enlightened him with passages from his family's Bible.

If Devon needed to work, he invited Brianna to join him. In the study, she was content to sit on the cushioned chair in the corner, legs curled under her, as she read silently. During these times, she frequently stole quick peeks at his handsome face, caught deep in concentration. She had not felt so secure or happy since before her father had passed away.

Time spent with Devon was heavenly; just being in the same room with him made her giddy. He was a complete gentleman, never touching her more intimately than to offer a chaste kiss—even when her conniving senses wanted more. Brianna knew that he was trying to woo her and she loved every exquisite moment of it.

The only blemish during their time together was Larissah's repeated requests for their company. Devon's response only pleased Brianna further—each time declining with the excuse of adjusting Brianna to her new home.

Still, there were times when doubt crept over Brianna. Though she had no details, neither was she a fool. Devon was not being entirely honest in regards to Larissah, and though Brianna realized it should not make a bit of difference to her what Devon did with her cousin, it did.

Often she would silently wonder, *How am I to compete with Larissah?* Her cousin may be troublesome, but there was no ignoring her beauty. Taller and thinner than Brianna, Larissah was blessed with thick blonde waves that curled naturally. Her mannerisms—though practiced—were graceful, and her explosive blue eyes shone gloriously.

Yet—for some reason beyond Brianna's comprehension—Devon continued to share his time with her instead.

◊◊◊◊◊

Devon could have easily quieted Brianna's worries. However, doing so would have brought his own concerns forward.

He was amazed—stunned even—to find he truly enjoyed the simple things he shared with Brianna. He wanted more than to seduce her; that would be an effortless task, had he chosen it. Devon wanted to know her on all levels, not just the feel of her alluring body and the pleasure he could bring both of them.

At least that was what he told himself each night in bed, when he was most achingly aware of just how much he wanted his needs met.

At times, he wondered how his world had existed before Brianna. They were both falling in love and neither cared to stop the exhilarating whirlwind of emotions that carried them through the passing days.

Together they laughed and teased. Both reveling in the special memories they were creating—even Hessie was unable to ignore their happiness and begrudgingly offered Devon the trust he had been waiting for.

◊◊◊◊◊

Brianna felt carefree and refreshed as the soft summer morning air brushed over her pink cheeks. She had shared a hurried but sufficient breakfast with Devon and now they were headed into Harper's Ferry so that she could pick up her finished gown and dress from Mrs. Donnellson. Enthusiastically, she took in the myriad of views while looking forward to another day spent with Devon.

She was coming to love her new home of Bolivar and Harper's Ferry. The town was busy and the streets bustled with its many occupants. Sights, sounds and smells abounded here. Before experiencing her prosperous new home, Brianna had never dreamed any place could exhaust her senses more than a cluttered seaport—she had been mistaken.

The open carriage bumped along the upper portion of High Street, offering its occupants an extended view of the area.

To the far right was Lower town, where just on the other side of Hamilton Street and the Shenandoah Canal, Virginus Island rested in the river. Devon had explained during one of their previous outings that the island was a large piece of Harper's Ferry's industrious wealth, housing Herr's Mill—a huge stone flourmill—and the iron foundry. Even from this distance, Brianna could faintly hear the sound of screeching metal as wagon boxes and saws, cast iron railings and coal stoves were produced within the sweltering heat of the factory.

The Shenandoah Canal and Baltimore and Ohio Railroad—or B&O as it was often referred—also provided a tour for the senses. The smell of heated coal—caused by the steam-powered machinery traveling upon water and tracks—rose over the quaint city, enveloping its residents with the bitter scent of iron and heat.

As their vehicle moved carefully over the crowded cobblestone streets, carrying them closer to the riverside, Brianna could see anglers lining the banks of the Shenandoah. Other workers loaded factory goods and natural shale—provided by the rivers and Maryland Heights—to be shipped to Baltimore for use as building materials.

Soaking up all of the activities around her, Brianna glowed like a happy child and Devon was compelled to ask, "What's that smile for?"

Her expression grew as she faced her guardian. "The day is glorious and everything around us is in motion. I find it invigorating. I am anxious to see my new clothes too. What *else* do I need to make me smile?"

"*That* is precisely what I am trying to learn," Devon stated sincerely.

Brianna laughed and the sound of it was enough to melt Devon's already weak heart. "Then it should please you to know that my smile seems to come easy these days, Captain."

As their carriage came to a halt before Mistress Donnellson's dry good store, Devon helped her down from the perch. With a brilliant smile of his own that left her already light-hearted senses reeling, Devon had the final word. "Aye, it does indeed, Flame."

◊◊◊◊◊

Devon left Brianna with Ruth and set out to complete the purchase he had been planning for weeks now, perhaps even since the moment he had first tasted Brianna's innocent touch in Ireland. It was useless to argue that from that time on, he had been rendered senseless and unable to turn away from her bewitching charm. The heated moments in recent weeks had only underscored the chain of events leading him to Larson's Jewelry, halfway up Potomac Street.

It had been far too long since Devon had felt such pure joy. He had heard many men declare that one woman satisfied them, but he'd scoffed at their claims. On more than one occasion, he had blatantly informed them of their idiocy or cursed their lying. Now he was humbled and forced to see the truth of those words. As such, Devon decided that it no longer mattered what anyone else thought of his relationship with Brianna. It felt strangely right to him, and that—as well as Brianna's feelings—were all that concerned him now.

The accomplished bachelor Devon Elliott was at long last in love and nearly ready to announce it to the world like a besotted youngster.

As soon as he entered the jewelry shop, James Larson welcomed him with a hearty handshake. "Captain Elliott, so nice to see you." Adjusting his circular eyeglasses on the bridge of his nose, James continued, "How can I assist you today?"

Predicting the reaction he would receive, Devon smiled. "I am in need of an engagement ring. I had emerald and diamond in mind." Devon was not disappointed; the older man looked positively stunned. Chuckling, Devon questioned, "Is that a *problem*, Mr. Larson?"

The elder man shook his head negatively. "Not unless you ask my wife. Martha will have a fit when she learns our Julia no longer stands a chance at winning your favor."

"If only I had known of her intentions sooner," Devon offered with mock consideration, bringing out laughter between the men. Devon patted the jeweler on the back as they walked toward the display case on the opposite side of the room.

Devon knew the ring he wanted at first glance. The emerald was approximately a half-carat in size and cut into an oval shape. It was circled by a single row of ten small diamonds that imitated the shape of the green stone. "That one will do, Mr. Larson." Devon indicated the gem of his choice with a pointed finger.

"I do believe that Miss Chase will be thrilled with your choice."

Without hesitation, Devon informed him, "I doubt that, since the ring is not for her."

The jeweler was unable to hide his surprise. Whistling softly, he commented, "This must be some lady to have drawn you away from one of the loveliest in the area—and quickly, too—if you don't mind my saying so." After placing the ring in a box, curiosity overruled propriety and the shop owner probed, "Might I ask who the lucky young woman is?"

Devon was amused by the way the older man tried desperately to control his interest. The moment he learned the truth and Devon was out of the store, he would certainly be spreading the news throughout the surrounding area. "I'm afraid that I cannot yet divulge that information, Mr. Larson. In fact, I would ask that even this purchase remain confidential, as the lady in question has yet to know of my intentions. That, *and* I still need to work up the courage to ask her."

James nodded and with a chuckle slid the box across the counter to the younger man. "Understood. I suppose you are hoping that the ring will force you to the reality of it?"

Devon smiled. "You, sir, are very perceptive."

"It's not much of a talent. I see many men with the same expression you are wearing now, Captain Elliott, and I boosted my own bravery the same way many years ago." In the moment of common support, Devon paid Mr. Larson for his purchase and exited the store with purpose in his step.

◊◊◊◊◊

Ruth Donnellson was finishing a sale when Brianna entered her shop. Not wanting to hover, Brianna browsed through the small store, examining the wares within while she waited for the business woman.

There was a shelf filled with bolts of cloth. The many textures and colors represented lured in return customers and good business. Ruth was fortunate to live in a town with such a close link to the city. Her fine satin, velvet or brocade materials normally had to be shipped in by special order, but Mrs. Donnellson had the advantage of the railroad and was able to offer her customers a large selection of the scarce items at all times.

Running her hand over a bolt of white cotton material, Brianna considered the price of twelve and one-half cents a yard. Deciding she could do without a new petticoat for a time, she turned to look over some other items.

Next to the many bundles of cloth were wooden and metal sewing and knitting needles, with spools of thread priced at ten cents each. White lace accessories were displayed in a glass top case with gloves of cotton—one dollar a pair—neatly fanned out in presentation of the different shades offered.

The wall boasted sketched advertisement posters of women dressed in the newest styles from Paris. On the opposite wall were some gentlemen's clothing ranging from shirts and jackets to dress shoes with a polished shine, work boots and Brogans. There was also an array of hats for any occasion. At the other end of the mercantile were some household items.

"Miss McClaran, I'm sorry to have kept you waiting," the slightly plump shopkeeper welcomed Brianna.

"Not at all, Mrs. Donnellson. I've enjoyed the chance to shop here again." Brianna followed Ruth to the rear of the store and slipped into the back room through a curtain-covered door. Ruth kept her shop tidy and Brianna immediately noticed the new sewing machine in the corner. "I see you have taken on some help."

Noting what Brianna spoke of, Ruth beamed proudly. "Yes, and you wouldn't believe how much faster my work is because of it. I should be able to serve at least double the customers in the same amount of time."

"That's wonderful, but is the stitching as neat as sewing by hand?" Brianna looked uncertainly at the contraption, her Irish skepticism showing.

Ruth smiled and offered, "See for yourself." Pulling out the first of Brianna's new gowns, she held out the hemline for her approval.

"Very nice," Brianna agreed, running the material through her fingers.

The ladies made quick work of the first gown, deciding that the fit was perfect. Then the exquisite green creation was slipped over Brianna's head and the hook and eyes were fastened in the front of her top. "You do look breathtaking, Miss McClaran." The shopkeeper complemented sincerely. Brianna smiled at her own reflection and silently agreed that the gown graced her entire form superbly.

The store-dividing curtain was pushed aside without warning and Larissah's rude words filled the small room. "Mmm, green, how appropriate for our little leprechaun."

Both Brianna and Ruth turned hard eyes on the unwelcome woman. "If there is something you need, Miss Chase, please wait in front while I finish with Miss McClaran."

With her naturally haughty air, Larissah informed, "What I *need* is to speak with my cousin."

Brianna did not attempt to hide her distaste at this suggestion. "About?"

"What you have been doing *alone* with Devon at Misty Heights for nearly two weeks."

Brianna gave her answer confidently. "I don't see how you are owed that explanation, Larissah."

Brianna's sharp answer only inflated Larissah's resentful assumptions. "Just you remember that *I* was accustomed to him long before you, Brianna."

Exasperated by the presence of this woman—not to mention her petty arguments—Brianna said nothing. Straightening her skirt, she would have brushed past Larissah and into the main room of the store, but the older woman sashayed, effectively blocking Brianna's path.

Larissah didn't like Brianna's precise calm—it made her want to slap the confidence from her face. "You expect me to believe that you have been secluded with Devon and nothing has happened between the two of you?"

Brianna bristled at this publicized insinuation. "It matters little to me *what* you believe, Larissah."

All resolve snapped, and Larissah's words struck with force. "You are a fool, Brianna. You will fall in love with Devon but he will never leave me, least of all for an innocent like you."

Tossing propriety to the wind, Brianna clung to her pride and whirling toward her so suddenly that Larissah took a subconscious step backward, Brianna sneered, "His actions suggest otherwise."

Narrowing her icy blue gaze dangerously, a slow smirk touched the corners of Larissah's full lips—then she began to laugh. "We shall see, Brianna." Larissah stated through her odd mirth, "We shall see, indeed." Without another word, Larissah turned and sailed smoothly from the shop.

◊◊◊◊◊

Brianna wanted to get away. She completed her business with Ruth as quickly as possible and left word that Devon should meet her at the nearby St. Peter's Church.

It had been far too long since she had stepped inside the calming environment of religion and—after her encounter with Larissah—was exactly what she needed.

The church overlooked Harper's Ferry and its surrounding landscape of mountains and rushing water. Its brick structure was lovely—a stone entranceway inset by heavy wooden doors. Two long, pointed-cap windows adorned each side of the doorway, and the steeple overhead reached so high that when Brianna looked up, she felt dizzy. Walking to the doors, she pulled on the iron handle allowing her entrance.

Inside, all was dim save for a few candles. To the left and the right of the entryway were burgundy-curtained confessionals. Advancing to the beginning row of pews, Brianna knelt and made the sign of the cross over her chest. Stepping into the closest pew, she knelt again and prayed.

She prayed for forgiveness of her sins, for strength when Devon tempted her. She asked for comfort and the knowledge to make the right decisions in her life. She prayed for the well-being of Devon and Daniel as well as the Gordons in Ireland.

Finally, she prayed for Larissah. She asked that her cousin know peace within herself and learn that life offers more than material goods and finding satisfaction in the misery of others.

Finished, she stood, repeated the sign of the cross and left the serenity of the church to find Devon and Abram patiently awaiting her return.

Devon offered his hand to help her into the carriage and reading her expression suggested, "What do you say we spend the afternoon riding?"

With a smile of pure relief, Brianna replied, "I say that sounds perfect."

Devon nodded, signaled Abram to take them home and silently cursed Larissah Chase and all the strain she was causing Brianna.

◊◊◊◊◊

If her church visit and the afternoon of horseback riding and shared kisses with Devon was not enough to raise Brianna's spirits, returning to Misty Height to find Daniel had arrived for an unexpected visit did the deed.

Supper was complimented with laughter and in the parlor, Daniel regaled Brianna with tales of Devon tormenting young girls during their school years. "I was a *most* well behaved lad," Devon currently self-defended.

"*Including* the time you hid a snake in Mae Colbert's lunch pail? The poor girl was so frightened; her parents had to come see her home from school." Looking to Brianna, Daniel assured, "He certainly got the hickory switch for that prank."

"I should hope so." Brianna gave a visible shudder, making her opinion of the offensive reptile clear. "Devon Elliott, I do believe that is the most horrible trick a boy could play on someone."

Brianna's indignant response sent the men into a new round of laughter.

"Just wait until I reach his teenage years." Daniel sputtered through the final lapses of his laughter.

Standing, Brianna held her hands in front of her to ward him away. "No and thank you. I'll be having enough trouble sleeping as 'tis. I'm certain I've learned all that I'm safely able for this one day."

When Devon raised a brow, recalling exactly how much she had been willing to learn during their ride that afternoon, Brianna read his ornery look and ducked her head, hiding her reddened cheeks.

"You *behave*," she demanded as softly as she could in Daniel's presence.

After she was gone from the room and the brothers could face one another again without erupting into fits of childish hilarity, Daniel turned serious. "I'm leaving in the morning."

Devon nodded, "This was a fast visit."

"You could come back with me if you'd like more time," Daniel suggested.

"You could stay longer so we'd have more time," Devon parried.

"No, I really can't."

Devon waited, hoping that something else would be revealed.

Daniel waited, not ready to tell all that had transpired during his visit.

When the quiet tension became too strong, Daniel asked, "Will you come to the city with me?"

"Do you truly want me to?" Devon asked, wanting to help his brother who was so clearly struggling. Still, he was loath to leave Brianna at such an opportune time in their budding relationship.

Daniel squelched his brother's romantic thoughts and plans for the next few days. "Yes, Dev, I do."

When Daniel raised his eyes to meet his brother's gaze, the pain within startled Devon. Without additional hesitation, he allowed, "I'll be ready by daybreak."

Chapter Ten

Brianna was having the kind of day anyone would dread. She'd overslept, and in her hurry to dress, tore the hem of her petticoat. She attempted to style her hair but gave up when her fingers caused more tangles than her entire night's sleep had. Frustrated, she dragged the hairbrush through the mess she had created and simply pulled the sides up and back, letting the majority of her thick tresses loose to lay against her back.

By the time she made it downstairs, breakfast was cold and Devon was gone, headed to Baltimore with Daniel. Though Devon had stopped by her room the night before to invite her along, Brianna declined—a decision she was already regretting since she lacked their company.

For solace, Brianna reminded herself of her reasons for opting to remain at Misty Heights.

For one, Devon and Daniel would make far better time on horseback—a means of travel they would likely not have permitted her to join in. Also, without her constant company, the siblings would have an opportunity for "boyish bonding". Finally, once they were in Baltimore, Devon planned to check in on Drake and *Sea Enchantress*, which would have left Brianna to spend her time watching Daniel and Meghan grow closer, while Devon was off at work.

Somehow, those reasons didn't seem so negative now as the prospect of two days without Devon's companionship loomed before her. Childish as it seemed, she missed him already and he was likely still in Bolivar.

But now, on top of her being alone and the way her morning had started, Brianna realized that she wouldn't see Devon for two days. That meant they would have no time together before Larissah's gathering—an event that Brianna wasn't particularly looking forward to anyway, but Devon informed her they were socially obligated to attend.

Therefore, it was with these thoughts floating through her mind and the last of her cold breakfast landing heavily in the pit of her stomach, that Brianna's frustrated mood of the morning was pushed headlong into positively foul for at *least* the remainder of his first day away.

◊◊◊◊◊

As Brianna had guessed, the Elliott brothers were just reaching the outskirts of Bolivar—a fact brought on by Devon's reluctance to leave before Brianna rose. Finally, he had given in to time and now the brothers rode side by side, enjoying the coolness of the morning that would switch to summer's humid heat within the next few hours.

Their pace was relaxed and their mood light as Daniel casually commented, "I enjoyed Brianna's company during my visit."

"Aye?" Devon kept his eyes forward, therefore missing Daniel's understanding and amused smile.

"I also noticed things seem to be progressing well between the two of you."

Devon faced his brother with a sheepish grin—a feat in and of itself for the elder Elliott. "That obvious, is it?"

Daniel released a chuckle and let the answer slide. "Does she know how you feel?"

After a brief pause, Devon divulged, "We are figuring out our feelings as we go. We shared a cozy afternoon at Jefferson Rock recently—just the two of us. In fact, it's one of our favorite spots to spend time together now."

"I can just imagine that it is, heathen," Daniel teased, earning a broad smile from Devon.

"Sorry to disappoint your sordid imagination, little brother, but I have yet to *fully* sully or savor my tempting Irish

Flame. Therefore, you may wipe all those disgraceful thoughts from your mind."

Daniel was not completely convinced. Any other time—any other *woman*—he would have been certain of Devon's conquest. But now, as strange as it seemed, Daniel could *almost* believe that Brianna had transformed his rogue of a brother into some semblance of a true gentleman.

Still teasing, with a mild dose of awe added in, Daniel returned, "Devon, you must understand how hard it is for me to believe that *you* could spend so much time with a beautiful woman and not have your way with her. Not to mention what effect this is having on my respect for your womanizing ways."

Devon smiled at Daniel's exaggerated faith in his gifts with the fairer sex. "Alas, 'tis true." Then he consoled, "Don't lose all faith in me, Dan. Brianna and I have done our fair share of teasing."

"Ah, now you've put my mind at ease," Daniel replied with dramatic relief.

It was Devon's turn to pry. He didn't mind his brother's baiting but fully intended to give some in return. "And how goes it with the lovely Miss Callear?"

Gruffly, Daniel stated, "I believe we were discussing *your* problems, *not* mine." He gave Devon a glance that shouted they would not be continuing that particular vein of conversation and veered, "Which begs the question, have you ended things with Larissah yet?"

Devon allowed his brother the space he needed. He knew that eventually he would come to him, when he deemed it necessary to talk. "I plan to formally let her go Friday evening. We had a mild altercation at C & R Dry Goods the other day, which *should* have made my intentions clear to her."

Daniel raised a brow curiously, indicating he wanted more details, but Devon waved his questioning glance aside, "I'll tell you about *that* another time."

"Understood, but, considering that it is *Larissah* you are dealing with, you'd best be certain there is *no* miscommunication."

Devon nodded. "Agreed, but as yet the opportunity to reassure myself hasn't arisen."

Daniel knew Devon better than that. If his brother had been back in Bolivar for the weeks that he had and not taken the time to perform such a major task, there had to be more of a reason than the weak excuse Daniel had just been offered. "Hasn't arisen, or hasn't been *taken*?"

Devon did not like this topic, it was bad enough that his conscious had been eating at him—he didn't need lectures from his younger brother too. "Perhaps a bit of both."

Daniel simply stared at his brother from across the dirt path, his look indicating that he was not nearly satisfied with that response.

Reading the other man clearly, Devon stated, "Why not simply ask me *exactly* what it is that you wish to know, Daniel? The sooner this subject is ended, the better I will feel."

"Come now, Dev, you're an educated man, you know what it is I'm asking."

"Humor me."

"Did you go to *see* Larissah?"

"Yes." Devon growled.

"When?"

Brusquely Devon offered, "The same day that Brianna and I returned from Ireland."

"And you didn't end your relationship then—why?"

Devon looked straight ahead, grumbling, "It didn't seem like the best time to take the opportunity."

"What *did* it seem like the best time to take?" Daniel pried further.

Devon finally swung his self-disgusted gaze back toward Daniel and admitted heatedly, "*Exactly* what you *think* I did." When Daniel looked at him with eyes full of scorn, Devon added, "If it makes you feel better, look on it as saving Brianna's virtue. It would surely have been lost by now had I not romped with Larissah instead."

Nodding and offering Devon some sympathy, Daniel offered, "Just the same, I am glad to be returning to Baltimore. I wouldn't want to be anywhere in the vicinity of Larissah on Friday night."

"Thanks for your encouragement, Dan," Devon replied dryly.

"Not at all, Devon. Not at all." Their laughter faded and silence loomed. The longer the speechless ride continued, the more certain Daniel became that Devon was searching for an opening. Helping his brother, Daniel prompted, "What's on your mind, Dev?"

Devon readjusted his posture in the saddle, pulled on his glove to tighten it against his hand and then looked up to meet Daniel's curious—yet expectant—gaze. "Daniel, you are a grown man now, but it's my duty to let you know that Hesper had a talk with me and asked that I speak to you."

"About?"

Devon cursed solidly. "Don't play stupid with me. I can't ignore the issue since Hesper brought it directly to my attention. Father promised their security."

Daniel's eyes turned angry with insult. "And you think my bedding Tansey takes *away* that security somehow?"

Devon ignored the cynical question, inquiring, "What did you expect, Daniel, that you could continue to bed the girl and nothing would come of it?"

Daniel scoffed. "Don't talk down to me, Devon. Tansey and I were not the *only* curious young lovers in the area."

Devon's eyes blazed at the truth of his brother's words. "You are right, and look how much trouble my foolishness is causing me now."

"We both acted on our feelings, Devon, but mine are *not* foolishness. What you had with Larissah was lust—Tansey and I share more than that."

"Not to the world outside Misty Heights." Softening his tone, Devon added with sympathy, "I saw the way you and Meghan looked at each other—you have a future. I know you share feelings with Tansey, but that is an entirely different circumstance. What will happen to her when it ends? And end it must. The girl has always loved you. Hesper and her family are part of ours, which only complicates matters for everyone involved."

"Which is exactly why it should be acceptable, Devon."

"Perhaps, but that is an unchangeable point." Devon did not like the role he was being forced to play, but since he was honor-bound to do so, his best option seemed to help Daniel fully weigh his choices.

Shaking his head, Daniel quietly sorted, "Meghan is the wife I require, but I don't love her. I care about her as a friend, but Tansey is the one I love. Do those feelings count for nothing?"

Lightening his own tone a bit, Devon informed, "No, Dan, not where a freed woman and a white businessman are concerned."

"You are ruthless, Devon."

"I am truly sorry that I have to be. You know that if I could change things for you, I would. I am only a man, though."

"What would you do in my place, Dev?"

Sighing, Devon replied, "I cannot say for certain. What I do know is that if you want to continue your relationship with Tansey, you must bring her to Baltimore. I will not permit you to come home only to have your way with her and then leave her behind so that you can return to the city and the *proper* woman when you've finished."

"It's not like that, Devon."

"Maybe not to you, but to all others involved, it most certainly is." After a short break, Devon added, "Abram must agree to Tansey leaving Misty Heights and he must know the truth of the arrangement. I will also expect a replacement for Brianna's maid."

"I truly don't know what to do, Devon." Daniel ran his fingers through his dark hair, imitating the nervous action of his older brother.

"You have to make a decision."

"You think I don't realize that? Even before you broached the subject, I knew that." Daniel was desperate and looked it. "What can I do about Meghan?" He was on the verge of beginning a potentially lifelong commitment with her and by the same action would lose his best friend—the love of his life.

Devon's tone was compassionate, but his words offered little relief. "I wish I could tell you what to do, Daniel. I have enough of my own decisions to make, however." Pausing, he advised, "Above all, remember the importance of a faithful relationship. If you can't end things with Tansey, then you must consider Meghan's situation if you were to marry her. How could continuing with Tansey possibly be fair to her? Also remember that Tansey may love you, but you will lose her as soon as you bring another woman here. I will not matter what color her skin is. It is simply the way of life."

"If only everyone agreed that skin color does not matter," Daniel stated wistfully, wishing for something that would likely never be.

They sat quietly then, each of them contemplating the choices fate threw their way.

◊◊◊◊

Brianna sat on the second-floor verandah directly off her bedchamber and attempted to mend her damaged petticoat. So far, she had succeeded in jabbing her finger and thumb more times than the material she was trying to sew. After the most recent prick, she stuck her finger in her mouth and sucked gingerly on the sore digit.

She could hear the rustling sounds of Hesper and Tansey as they tended herbs in the garden below. The morning was warm and they likely wanted to get out of the sun before the midday heat was upon them and therefore concentrated more on the job at hand than any conversation that came to mind.

When Brianna heard Tansey call out a greeting, she stood for a better view of who was approaching. The slave woman walking toward the summer-kitchen garden was not someone Brianna recognized, but from the vantage point Brianna had, she guessed the visitor was around her own age and quite obviously in the end stages impending motherhood.

The woman leaned heavily against the outside of the white picket fence surrounding the herb garden and declared, "My, but that sun sho' is warmin' up early today."

Hesper sat the basket in her hand aside and wiped her brow with her sleeve. "I reckon now'd be a good time fo' fetchin' the cold tea I brewed up this mornin'." She got no argument from the younger two women as she turned to go through the kitchen door.

Tansey stood up from her haunches with a groan. "Oh, I'll be movin' slower than Mama by the time I thirty."

"Sooner than that if'n your man gets ya in my shape." The other woman gave Tansey a knowing smile and teased

more, "I hear'd he home again. Don't take much wonderin' to
fig're what bringin' him here fo' a visit."

Above, Brianna took a step back from the railing. This was
not a conversation she wanted to be caught overhearing. Despite the warning voice urging her inside and chastising her for
eavesdropping, her strong curiosity won out and she—for better or for worse—remained unseen on the verandah.

The scene below continued with friendly banter. "Never
you mind, Bess." Indicating the woman's growing mid-
section, Tansey added, "Looks like you got plenty else ta keep
you busy." Leaning back to stretch her spine, Tansey inquired,
"How that Jonas? He ready ta be a Pappy?"

"Way I sees it, don't matter if'n he ready or not." Bess
smiled serenely and added, "He do seem proud though. Only
thing make us happier now was if'n we had a good home like
ya do. Miz Larissah sho' don't make life easy fo' me now.
She don't care how big I is, she jus' want what she want when
she want it."

Tansey made a face of disgust. "Larissah don't make life
easy for no one, don't matter if they live with her or not."

"'Ceptin' your Mista Devon," Bess taunted with humor in
her tone. "Miz Rissah do seem to have a way of makin' him
mighty happy when he come aroun'."

Tansey's eyes narrowed. "Girl, you don't know wha'cha
talkin' 'bout. Mista Devon only got eyes for our Miz Brianna
now."

"Maybe so, but when he come back from his long trip, it
ain't his *eyes* that make Miz Rissah holler out like she do."

Brianna felt sick. She should have listened to her self-
warning and gone back inside when she'd had the chance.
Now, she wanted to flee, to hide from what she was learning,
but she had to hear the truth. Nothing could make her leaden
feet move, anyway.

"I don't believe that, Bess. He been with Miz Brianna most
everyday an' he been treatin' her good too."

"Yeah? Well from what I hear, he treatin' Miz Larissah real good."

"What about Mista Montgomery? You sure it weren't him
pleasin' her?"

Bess laughed loudly. "Oh, you know that easy woman; she had Mr. Montgomery, shooed him out an' barely had time to bath 'fore Cap'n Elliott climb on."

"She's disgustin'," Tansey spat with fierce sincerity.

Bess shrugged, "Can't argue that. And now I hear she done with Mr. Montgomery. She movin' on to his indentured man. He a fine man. Fact, Miz Larissah can't seem to choose 'tween Nate Carter and Mista Devon."

Tansey made a sound mixed with distaste and disbelief. "Oh, that answer easy enough ta fig're out. That high an' mighty Larissah ain't never goin' give up the chance at money. Ain't no matter how good a man lovin' up on her."

"Too bad that lily-white lady in Balt'mo don't look away so's Mista Daniel kin keep on lovin' his high-yella gal here, too."

Tansey couldn't speak at first, so she allowed the words to sink in—words she had waited for and dreaded hearing most of her life. "Wha'cha talkin' 'bout, Bess?"

"Miz Rissah gossip on Mista Daniel marryin' some Baltimo' lady." With narrowed eyes, Bess added firmly, "An' don'cha be cryin' to me gal. Long as we been friends and I know'd what you got goin', I been warnin' ya 'bout gettin' hurt."

Bess' holier than thou attitude wasn't helping and Tansey's reply was quick—too quick. "Daniel didn't say nothin' 'bout it. There ain't nobody else yet. He'd tell me."

Bess laughed shortly. "Ya think so? Why he go and' do such a fool thing as tellin' ya? That man know he got a good life, just the way it is—one here an', soon 'nough, one there, too."

Tansey had heard enough. This conversation had gone as far as she was going to allow. "Jus' mind your business, Bess, an' tell me what you really come about?"

Bess took her cue. She had only wanted to warn her friend, not hurt her more than the necessary news naturally would. "Miz Larissah wantin' me ta find out if'n Mista Devon gonna be at her big party end o' the week. He stayin' away more than she like an' she startin' to worry some."

Tansey huffed. "Sound ta me like he been aroun' more than he should." The anger in Tansey's voice was not reserved for the eldest Elliott alone. "Still, I ain't heard no plans 'bout them goin' away. You tell your Miz Rissah, Devon an' Brianna like bein' here alone, just fine."

Bess smiled her easy grin again. "That oughta set her jus' about right."

"Set who right 'bout what?" Hesper asked, returning with cold tea for each of them.

"Nothin' worth talking 'bout no more, Mama." Tansey told her mother while shooting Bess a warning glance.

When Tansey looked back toward her mother, she inadvertently raised her eyes toward her mistresses' verandah. Her heart sank as she saw Brianna retreating into her sitting room. Surely, her new friend was burdened with more information than Tansey would have knowingly given her.

◊◊◊◊◊

Brianna felt like a fool. Worse than that, she felt betrayed, hurt, and angry. The most important things she had asked Devon for were honesty and patience. He had apparently not even made it through an entire day before breaking his word.

Moreover, what of the weeks since their romantic relationship began? Each time he claimed the day for business, was he actually spending the time with Larissah? Was he with her even now?

The questions continued to bombard Brianna and she replayed every conversation they had recently shared. Where before she had heard hope and happiness, she now found emptiness and excuses—she heard only lies.

Brianna could only imagine that Devon anticipated a life with all he desired—a lucrative business, an obedient ward, washing his hands of Larissah's responsibilities and gaining *two* mistresses from his duties—both readily available and waiting anxiously to please the wonderful Captain Devon Elliott.

Well, he was sadly mistaken in that illusion.

But what if it were Brianna who was mistaken? What if— as Tansey had suggested to Bess—Larissah had been with someone else? Brianna was quickly learning that her cousin was an easy conquest, so the possibility for error was certainly present. Besides, Devon had given Brianna no reason to doubt him. She had learned already what her quick temper and premature beliefs about Devon would bring her. Perhaps she should remain calm and listen without judging.

With only mild relief, Brianna decided that was the best route. She would wait to find out the truth after his return from Baltimore.

And if need be, she would resort to simply asking him for the answer—all the while praying that the one he would give was the one she wanted to hear.

Chapter Eleven

The room was bright with overhanging lights, abuzz with voices and Brianna wanted nothing more than to find Devon among Larissah's guests and go home. The sound of her cousin's throaty laughter caught Brianna's attention and she turned in the direction it had come from.

To anyone else, the lovely couple conversing in a far corner of the room would have been a pleasure to watch—to Brianna it brought nothing but immediate jealously.

Larissah was ravishing in her gown—a dark shade of burgundy wine. Shimmering sequins of the same color enhanced the enticingly low cut bodice. And as she watched Devon, her bright blue eyes danced temptingly.

Brianna certainly could not fault her cousin *that*, considering every woman in attendance had glanced at Devon appreciatively at least once since his arrival. The crisp white shirt he wore contrasted and set off his dark features and black evening suit. The silver of his cravat gave his eyes the illusion of being black rather than blue.

Devon leaned close to whisper something in Larissah's ear. With glittering eyes and an inviting smile, Larissah responded with some clever remark that made Devon laugh. Taking her hand in his, Devon led Larissah toward the entrance, but her eyes were not focused on the destination. Larissah scanned the guests, her cold crystal gaze halting on Brianna and sending a triumphant message of victory across the room.

Still following his lead, Larissah moved closer to Devon and they turned into one of Reverie's private rooms. The last thing Brianna saw before the door closed was the lovers locked in the midst of a heated embrace—one that caused Brianna's insides to curl up in a nauseating heap.

It was all the proof she needed.

Brianna left the house and Devon without another glance.

◊◊◊◊◊

Devon had requested a private moment with Larissah so that he could end their relationship. Unfortunately, he had also been forced to charm her for the opportunity. Even worse was the last-second glance he had given toward the main room and the accusing stare Brianna had given him.

Caught off guard by the hurt in her eyes, Larissah's kiss had come completely by surprise. This assured Devon of two things: Larissah had also seen Brianna's expression and—in the conniving woman's mind—the timing could not have been better.

Devon pushed Larissah away forcefully, but in the split second it had taken his stunned mind to react, Brianna was gone. Infuriated, Devon rounded on the woman in front of him. "I have no desire for your body, Larissah. Don't degrade yourself further by trying to force it on me."

She laughed, knowing full well why he was angry. "I am confident that I can change your mind if I want to. I have before."

"You won't have another opportunity. As soon as I've had my say I will leave."

"*Leave*? There is no need to leave, Devon. We'll have Abram take Brianna home and Raemus can return you to Misty Heights in the morning." She reached for the buttons of his shirtfront as though all of her problems were solved by her simple declaration.

Gripping her wrists roughly, Devon halted her attempts at arousing him. "Enough, Rissah."

She glared up at him, her icy eyes throwing shards of anger. "Devon, *what* is the matter with you? You haven't been to my bed since the day you returned home. All of your extra time has been spent with *her*. Do you really believe that I don't know what the two of you are doing?" Attempting to free her wrists—to no avail—Larissah further accused, "What is it about her that could make you turn *me* away?"

"Many things," he intoned rudely, before realizing the folly of giving her too much information.

Her eyes narrowed even more, her tone full of disdain. "You've spoiled her so soon, then? That's awfully fast, even by *your* standards. Is she even now waiting for you to whisk her home and into your bed?" Recalling the look in the younger woman's eyes just minutes prior, she exalted insensitively, "I would venture to say you'll find her door locked to you tonight. Does the prospect of dealing with such childish jealousy and having to answer to someone for your actions bode well with you?" With cold laughter, she taunted his situation, challenging him to admit that her words were true.

"I've dealt with *you* all these years, haven't I?" Then he remembered to rein in his anger. He must keep in mind that every word he spoke, every look he gave from this point on could decide Brianna's reputation. Like it or not, Larissah Chase had the social power to ruin anyone she chose.

Apparently thinking along the same lines as he, Larissah goaded, "I daresay your precious virgin will expect more from you than the pleasure of your body."

"You say that as though *you* do not scheme for the financial security I could give you, along with the physical pleasure. Do not add hypocrite to your long list of sins, Rissah." His voice was deep and rasping, full of disgust and menace.

"You call *me* a hypocrite? Let us not forget that my father trusted *you* to see to my well-being after he was gone and we both know just how thoroughly you took on the task. You didn't even wait until after his death to take me. Don't expect me to believe my cousin has been treated any differently." With a smirk, she pushed, "Tell me, Devon, did you have to teach the little thing or was she well practiced for you?" When she got no reaction, she tried again. "I didn't think you liked to bed virgins. Something such as that takes far too much reserve for a man like you to handle."

"I didn't have much choice in the matter where you were concerned."

Larissah never liked feeling as though she should regret her actions. "Tell me, Devon, does your charming innocent know that I had to satisfy you when she could not?"

"What Brianna and I share goes much deeper than physical touch," Devon ridiculed, avoiding the real question, but mocking her just the same.

She laughed shortly. "Obviously it does not *replace* it, since you came to me as soon as you arrived home."

Devon shrugged nonchalantly. "I could have been gratified by any of the local whores; you were merely the most convenient."

His cold words struck her harshly. Larissah had been unprepared for such an insult. Tears of true shame glimmered in her eyes, but as quickly as they had appeared, they were gone. Advancing on him purposefully, she slapped his cheek soundly. "Do not speak to me like that, Devon Elliott. You have sought me out many times and I have never denied you. Don't pretend that I was alone in our game. You owe me that much."

Going to the door, he looked back and simply stated, "Consider my debt paid. I no longer crave your services. It's over, Larissah."

To his retreating figure, she screeched, "That little Irish bitch could never please you as I have!"

He was in front of her in two strides. Devon held her upper arms so tightly that she had to grind her teeth to keep from crying out. Larissah's searing blue eyes widened a bit; she had never seen him so angry and as such heeded his words carefully. "Never again will you speak of Brianna in such a manner. I promise that you will rue the day if you do."

Larissah's body shook with rage, fear and indignation and her words were no different. "You don't know what you are giving up, Devon."

"Yes, Larissah, I do. I just don't know why it took me so long to do so."

"Have it your way Devon, but you may want to keep in touch. I *am* her only living blood relative and if I recall, Aunt Leila sent her here to be near *me*, not to satisfy *your* primal urges."

"Only because she didn't know you for the kind of woman you are," Devon countered.

"Be that as it may, her wishes were stated and I know that they will keep you near me. You always do the right thing, Devon."

He said nothing, just let go of her and turned to leave.

Larissah waited until his hand was on the doorknob and she was safely out of his reach before adding, "Soon enough, you will tire of Brianna's innocence and realize the extent of your foolishness." Leaning her rear against the desk, she warned, "With a little luck, I won't be involved elsewhere and *might* still be willing to take you as a lover."

Devon sneered. "Larissah, you've always had other lovers, even while you welcomed me into your bed. It was not well-kept secret. I simply never cared and I *still* don't. So, you see, there is no need for you to carry on with the pretense of waiting to find someone to fill your . . . *void* now that I no longer want the chore."

Before she could comment, Devon slammed out the door. Though her screech of anger followed him, Devon didn't care. All that mattered was that the scene and their affair had ended.

◊◊◊◊◊

Brianna was furious as she instructed Abram to take her home. If Devon found his driver gone and could not wait for him to return, then let him find his own way home. Besides, it hadn't appeared to Brianna that he would be ready to depart anytime soon.

He will never have the opportunity to embarrass or hurt me so completely again. I won't allow it. Even as her mind wailed its demands, she knew that it would be a difficult battle. How was she to stop her feelings? She did not need to speak the words aloud to make them any more real. There was no denying how she felt.

With time and space, Brianna would sort her muddled feelings, move on and forget how much she had come to love Devon Elliott.

Upon her arrival at Misty Heights, Brianna immediately penned a short note to Daniel, requesting the sanctuary she craved. If she went to Baltimore, it would not seem so much as she was running away or hiding. Daniel had certainly made it clear that she was welcome anytime she wished. He had plans to return to Misty Heights in the early fall. She could return with him then. It would provide her with an acceptable excuse for escaping and nearly two months away to heal and forget. The way she felt now, Brianna had no doubt that she would need at *least* that much time away before she was ready to talk to Devon again. Forgiving him seemed even farther in the future—if ever.

Sending Tansey off with directions to have the message wired from the train station, Brianna undressed and crawled into bed. They would leave in the morning. Tansey could act as her travelling companion—her freedom papers would stop anyone from claiming Tansey as a runaway or stolen property. Daniel had told Brianna many times that she was always welcome so she was confident he would not turn them away.

Devon wouldn't have a chance to try to stop Brianna with his wasted apologies and explanations.

Assuming he feels the need to offer any.

After tonight, she could no longer pretend that Devon returned her sentiments. All the more reason for Brianna to make haste. She would even forgo the lesser cost of a carriage ride from Ellicott's Mills to Baltimore and instead take the direct line from Harper's Ferry to Baltimore. It was more comfortable and—if he chose to follow—offered less chance that Devon could catch her before she had reached Daniel's home.

Unless something went terribly wrong, she would be settled in Baltimore almost before Devon even noticed her absence.

Tansey's hands shook as she pulled carried Brianna's carpetbag off the train and stepped into the crowded Mount Clare Station.

In truth, her hands had been shaking since the night before, when Brianna had woken her from a deep sleep and asked her to come to Baltimore with her—to *Daniel's.*

She could have said no. She had the right to say no—her freedom dictated as much. However, the friendship bond she had established with Brianna said otherwise. Her mistress friend's face had been tear streaked and sorrowful. Tansey had known so few friends during her life, the last thing she wanted to do was jeopardize the relationship she had with Brianna.

Looking through the crowd, Tansey saw Daniel a second before Brianna did. It was long enough for the lovers' eyes to meet. Averting his attention, Daniel welcomed Brianna before ushering her to his waiting cab and then turned to help Tansey inside the ride as well.

◊◊◊◊◊

There was little question in Daniel's mind that Devon had done something to make Brianna want to flee and therefore Daniel decided not to contact his brother about Brianna's request to spend the social season in Baltimore. Daniel figured it would serve his arrogant brother well to learn a lesson or two the hard way.

Unfortunately, by allowing Brianna the opportunity to educate his brother, Daniel might very well find himself in the dunce seat.

What would have once presented Daniel and Tansey with a thrilling opportunity now felt more like a strained inconvenience.

Daniel was determined to adjust, though. He liked Brianna greatly and wanted to make her comfortable in his home. He fully intended to give Brianna her space, ask no questions of her and offer her an enjoyable experience in the city.

In the meantime, he would do his best to make the most of an uncomfortable situation as far as his personal affairs were concerned. At least he could rest easy in the knowledge that Tansey knew nothing of his relationship with Meghan.

◊◊◊◊◊

Brianna was irritated. She hated Devon, she missed Devon, she wanted Devon, she couldn't stand the thought of Devon. The thought of Devon in Bolivar with Larissah was unacceptable. On top of that, Tansey was short tempered and Meghan was gloating with happiness. Daniel was dazed and confused or equally as annoyed as Brianna and Tansey.

The night before, Daniel had taken her to the theater with the Callear's. She enjoyed herself—more or less. She even managed to broach the subject of Daniel and Tansey, but unfortunately gained no more information from Daniel than she had Tansey.

Frustrated, but willing to drop the subject, she'd gone to bed with Daniel's other claim ringing in her ears—Devon was in love with her, not Larissah and would very likely be coming to Baltimore after her, soon. At least an hour of tossing and turning passed before Brianna finally fell asleep.

From the heavy feel of her eyelids, she'd hardly slept at all when a loud noise awakened her. Confused, Brianna called out to Tansey who stiffly reassured her mistress that it must have been the wind that caused her closet room door to slam closed.

Irritated anew at anyone bearing the name Elliott, Brianna flopped to her stomach and covered her head with her pillow. Reasoning that she would either fall asleep or suffocate before the morning, Brianna drifted back into dreams trying to decide which outcome she would prefer most.

◊◊◊◊◊

Over the next four weeks, Daniel ushered Meghan and Brianna from teas to gatherings, to galas, and dinners. The two young women were ecstatic and Daniel found their excitement invigorating and contagious.

The whirlwind of parties diverted Brianna's thoughts from Devon—most of the time.

Daniel was handed easy excuses for staying away from home and the varying degrees of temptation and irritation Tansey presented him there.

Meghan basked in the attention Daniel lavished upon her. She was not the only one who noticed his admiration, though, and rumors of a possible engagement began to circulate.

Currently, Meghan was being whirled around the floor in a lively dance with Daniel. Brianna was engaged in conversation with two young ladies, eager to hear of her far away homeland and the journey that brought her to Maryland. At the end of the song, Daniel swept Meghan from amid the circle of dancers.

"Enjoying yourself?" he asked, a bit out of breath from his exertions.

"The dancing is grand. Still I would much rather have you to myself." Meghan fanned herself, and then teasingly allowed the accessory to slide between the abundance of soft flesh pushing up from her lavender gown as she brought the fan to rest at her side.

Daniel laughed at her antics. "Patience, my sweet Meghan." The mood that he was in, Daniel was also reminding himself of propriety. He would have easily taken her up on the offer, delectable as she was this night, if not for his houseguest and her servant.

Meghan smiled sweetly at him and Daniel recalled just what it was that had attracted him to her originally—a vivacious attitude, mixed with the well-rounded curves of her body. "A lady must try, you do understand?"

Daniel chuckled. "Apparently you are not the only one who thinks so." Nodding toward the dance floor, Daniel pointed out Brianna who was now with a gentleman Daniel did not recognize. "Who is that? Do you know?"

"Mmm, he's Irish," Meghan began, as though the fact of his heritage explained why Daniel did not know him. "Mr. Mitchell, I believe, though I have only heard Caleb and Katherine speak of meeting him. Katherine pointed him out to me at a tea earlier in the week. I have wanted to introduce myself to him, but as yet have not had the opportunity."

Daniel could imagine that the striking young man had been kept quite busy with admirers at each function he attended. "Does he plan to return to Ireland?"

"From what I understand, he is visiting cousins and plans to return at the end of the month." Meghan drew her eyes away from the man in question and back to her companion. "Why is it that you are so interested?"

Smiling, and feeling genuinely happy for it, he answered, "Because it would appear that our dear Brianna is interested as well."

◊◊◊◊◊

"When will you be returning to Harper's Ferry?" Joseph Mitchell asked of his lovely dancing partner.

For the first time since coming to Baltimore, Brianna was having fun. This gentleman from her homeland, made excellent conversation and was a fine dancer—easily attested by the smooth way they now glided around the floor. "I'm not sure yet. I have come on an extended visit and will have to wait to see just how long I am enjoying myself."

Flirting openly, Joseph asked, "And are you enjoying yourself now?"

Brianna felt herself blush as she enjoyed the attention this man was giving her. "Very much so, Mr. Mitchell." Joseph's treatment was refreshing to her bruised ego. Though not as forthright as Devon's coquetry, Brianna found Joseph to be innocently beguiling with his attraction.

They continued several times around the floor without further comment, before he asked, "I realize that things are done differently here—"

"Not quite so much as one would think," Brianna interrupted with a light smile.

"True. Still, 'tis not home, is it?"

Brianna's longing for Ireland was stronger at that moment than it had been in months. "Nothing is ever quite the same as home." Shaking away the feeling of homesickness, she prompted, "Please forgive my interruption, Mr. Mitchell. Continue on with what you were about to say."

"I was simply wondering if I might call on you sometime before I return to Ireland."

"That would be fine, sir." Brianna smiled prettily and batting her lashes to match, inquired, "But I would like to know how long I can expect to enjoy your company before you return home and leave me behind."

For the first time that evening, Joseph's tone sounded unhappy. "Unfortunately, I will only be here for another two weeks."

"Why would you be findin' that unfortunate, Mr. Mitchell, when so soon, you'll be seein' our lovely homeland again?" Even Brianna could hear the thickening of her accent in the company of this fellow countryman. It felt good to let her heritage shine—not that she had been hiding it—time spent in her

new American home had simply dwindled some of her strongest brogue.

Joseph's smile was dashing, and he offered it to her without
shame. "Don't count me wrong, Miss McClaran. I was most
anxious to return home." His face was completely serious
when he spoke again, "Until I met you."

"You do flatter me well, Mr. Mitchell." Brianna flashed a
receptive smile and invited, "I shall certainly look forward to
your visits, no matter how long they are able to continue."

"Rest assured, Miss McClaran, that I don't intend to keep
you waiting long." Joseph promised, feeling certain that the
best of his trip was yet to come.

Chapter Twelve

Looking out over the portion of the Potomac River that bordered his property, Devon reeled in his fishing line once more. At the rate the fish were biting, he would be living off catfish and bass for the next year or more if he stayed any longer. Gathering his pole and the fish he had snared, he lazily began following the winding path that led home.

It seemed such a long time had passed since Brianna had gone to Baltimore and he missed her sorely. In the beginning, it had taken everything within him to keep from chasing after her. He had forced himself to remain behind, though, to give her some time to heal from the hurt he had caused her. Even if it was a misunderstanding, the fact remained that Brianna believed he had betrayed her. In time, after her temper cooled, Devon would go to her and help her see reason. He would clarify the entire truth of his past with Larissah and the reasons he had decided to end it. He would also explain the reality of what Brianna had witnessed the night before she had gone to Baltimore.

In order to help in his plight of remaining far from Brianna and keeping his mind off her, Devon had taken on some menial tasks around his land. The muscle-wrenching chores kept him busy through the day and he welcomed sleep greedily at night. Time passed much faster if he was unconscious—but even then, his mind was wide-open to visions of her.

His dreams were a mixture of pleasure and pain in which Devon could touch Brianna, love her freely in all the ways his heart and body desired.

When he woke though, she was achingly omitted from his life.

Even after Daniel had sent word that he would return her to Misty Heights by the middle of September, Devon's need for Brianna had not been eased.

This only served to bolster Devon's certainty that in the end he would have her as his own.

It would just take some time and caring on Devon's part, to resurrect her trust in him.

It would take the patience and honesty she had so bravely asked of him and now believed he had denied her.

Until she returned to Bolivar, he would rely upon Daniel to care for Brianna as Devon slowly counted the days that passed. He would last this separation—after all it was only two more weeks and most of her absence was behind him now.

Propping his fishing pole against the back porch wall, Devon entered the house through the kitchen. Just inside the door, Abram stopped him. "Mista Devon, this come fo' ya."

Thanking the man, Devon took the paper and walked into the main portion of Misty Heights.

Opening the note, Daniel's script was revealed.

Devon,

There has been a change of plans. The Osbornes have invited us to their home for a weekend gala. We will return directly to Misty Heights from Frederick at the beginning of next week. Meghan will be returning with us, as Brianna's guest.

I look forward to seeing you ~
Daniel

A broad smile of pure relief covered Devon's features and with it, a new plan formed in his mind—one that forgot all of his previous determinations and cautions to the contrary.

Why should I wait here for her to return?

If he used all haste, Devon could travel to Baltimore in time to meet them and go along to the home of their acquaintances. He might be able to right the wrongs he'd done and then they could enjoy the gala weekend together.

Calling behind him for Abram, Devon bounded up the stairs to begin preparations for leaving.

◊◊◊◊◊

Joseph Mitchell arrived promptly at one-thirty in the afternoon, just as he had every day after the first evening when he'd initially met Brianna. For this outing—since Meghan had committed to previous plans—Tansey was the next choice to act as their chaperone—an idea Daniel found particularly amusing, though he kept the fact to himself.

Promising to be back far before the evening meal, Brianna and Joseph—with Tansey in tow—set out for the Thames Street Park. The day was a bit windy but not brisk, the air still warm despite autumn's arrival.

Brianna took Joseph's arm and allowed him to promenade her proudly amid the other passersby.

During their time of blossoming friendship, Brianna shared stories about her time in America and the sights committed to her memory—Devon excluded as much as possible. Joseph's interest in Brianna made her feel special and their commonalities made conversation light and easy.

"Traveling to Maryland was just a way to reassure myself that the lifestyle I have planned out in Ireland is exactly what I want," Joseph explained.

"A wise choice, Mr. Mitchell, one I wish was offered to ladies."

Joseph eyed her a moment, then answered thoughtfully, "If you'll permit my saying so, isn't that exactly what your mother provided for *you*?"

Brianna had never seriously thought of her arrangement in that manner and the surprised look on her features proved as much. "I suppose you're right, Mr. Mitchell. I must thank you for bringing it to my attention since at sometimes I find myself questioning the sanity of my mother sending me so far away from all that is familiar to me."

"Mothers are rarely wrong—at least that is what mine continually tells me."

Brianna laughed, remembering her mother before her father's passing with a bittersweet smile.

"Besides," Joseph continued, "you seem to have adjusted well. Mr. Elliott is a fine man; one that I gather is a fair guardian."

Focusing on Devon's duty rather than his person, Brianna replied, "Yes, my guardian is a good man, though it is not the Mr. Elliott with whom you are acquainted. I have been placed in the care of Daniel's older brother, Captain Devon Elliott."

Trying to recall the name, Joseph did not notice the slight glance exchanged between his companion and her maid. "I do not think I have had the honor of making his acquaintance."

"Oh, you would surely remember if you had." Brianna spoke bluntly before taking the opportunity to survey her tone, and then veered quickly, "Tell me, Mr. Mitchell, what are your plans for returning home?"

"My family—father, uncle, and brother—have a law firm." He shrugged, unimpressed with the tradition. "I am expected to join them there."

"And what of a sweet lass? Do you have anyone who pines for your return?" Brianna questioned in pretty flirtation.

"No, not at present, which is a blessing since I don't seem to notice anyone except you these days." Brianna caught the gleam in his eye and realized that Joseph was far more serious than she was comfortable with. She sincerely did not wish to see him go, but she was still not ready to hear such overtures from any man.

Tugging his arm lightly, she smiled and advised, "Let us make the most of the time we have before you return home. That way when you've left me behind, we'll have happy moments to think on until some other lady turns your head and thoughts away from your friend here in America."

"A doubtful expectation at best," Joseph assured, and then jovially laughed away their teasing so that they might do as Brianna suggested and enjoy the rest of the day in the sunshine.

◊◊◊◊◊

Wasting no time, Devon arrived in Fells Point mid-morning the day after receiving Daniel's notice. To his disappointment the townhouse was empty of all occupants, save the regular household help. To his benefit, however, Devon learned that Daniel would be out until supper and Brianna intended to return in time for afternoon tea in the front parlor.

Giving strict orders not to inform Brianna of his arrival, Devon planned his surprise. Taking the seat in the front room that would afford him the advantage of seeing Brianna before she saw him, Devon waited.

Barely a quarter-hour passed before his patience was rewarded and he heard Brianna's entrance. When she walked into the room, her eyes were distant, lost in thought, giving Devon time to recover from the unexpected amount of pleasure seeing her again brought.

She wore a sapphire-blue tea dress—the under-sleeves and shirt contrasted bright white with the dark material. Her auburn hair was pulled back and wound into a thick roll, encircling her crown with thin blue and white ribbons wound becomingly through the twist.

Taking a seat in the ladies' chair, Brianna had just poured herself a cup of tea when she sensed him—*knew* that he was near even before she actually saw him. Brianna's eyes snapped up, the jade gaze landing on him instantly and she wondered that she hadn't felt his presence sooner.

Devon found her reaction extremely entertaining as well as insightful. He did not hear her speak, but read his name as it passed over her lips in little more than a breath.

His charm came out in full force. "May I join you, Miss McClaran?"

Any chance of a warm reception from her dissolved as quickly as the sugar cube she plopped into her teacup. "It seems to me that you already have."

"Indeed." Devon felt no need to say more, but studied her closely. Emotions flitted on her features like the winds of a hurricane—each stronger than the last and vying for an uncertain control.

Brianna's relaxed demeanor of moments before was gone, her pleasant morning ended. She had enjoyed her morning walk with Joseph—it was their final before his return to Ireland. She had bid him farewell at the door but now Brianna couldn't help but wonder what Devon's reaction would have been had she invited Joseph in to share tea with her.

Brianna knew better than to do that, though, since his plans to return home were permanent and his feelings for her obvious. The dear man wore his heart on his sleeve and Brianna would never want to give him false hope since she knew their relationship could never grow beyond friendship.

All mainly due to the insufferable man in front of her now, once more finding a way to turn her composure upside down.

Brianna's head was spinning and she didn't dare pick up the teacup she had just filled, for the shaking of her hands would be just the type of small victory Devon would revel in. Alongside a myriad of other reactions her body was having— her stomach had begun reeling with traitorous excitement.

Devon moved to take a new seat—this one directly across from hers. So close to her now, Devon was able to smell the sweetness of the tea leaves that she requested Hesper to blend with her soap. She made no offer to speak further or serve him, so he poured his own hot liquid and asked, "Have you enjoyed your time here in Baltimore?"

She sipped her tea tentatively. "Indeed." She mimicked not only his earlier word, but also its tone. "And you? Have you enjoyed *your* time of freedom?"

"No," he answered quickly. The single word startled her with its brutal honesty.

"Pity," she replied, biting into a dainty slice of jam covered toast and allowing him to grasp how little she actually cared.

Devon decided that he would give her one more chance. He would try to remain calm and offer her another opportunity at civil conversation. "Where were you this morning?"

"Out," she answered truthfully. Why did he care anyway? Why was he here? Things had just started to make some sense again and here he was, tormenting her as usual.

"Out *where*?" His tone became sharper, though he wore the same even smile plastered on his face.

"I went for a walk by the harbor with an acquaintance," she taunted, hoping the bite of her words stung. "Is there anything else you would care to know?"

"Yes," he began through clenched teeth. "I want to know *who* this friend is."

"He is no one you would know." Brianna smiled smugly, hoping that those words would cause him to feel something of the jealousy she had suffered during the weeks that had passed.

She was rewarded by Devon's new expression.

Devon's fists tightened—an argument he had been prepared for, but *not* arriving to find her out and about, cavorting with other men. "I have no wish to pull answers from you, Brianna. You will tell me now and fully, *who* is this man and *what* have you been doing with him?"

His tone was becoming demanding and Brianna set her chin against it, ready to do battle, but to Devon's amazement, rather than fire at him with anger, Brianna laughed. "What business is it of yours?" She read the look in his expression and with an unladylike roll of her eyes, answered for him. "Save your breath, I have not been away from you so long that I have forgotten that you are"—here she imitated his deep voice and authoritative tone to the best of her ability—"my guardian, with the unalienable right to know *every* move I make."

Brianna could tell that Devon failed to see the humor in her mocking comment. With a sigh, she yielded at last, "His name is Joseph Mitchell. He is from Ireland and I'm sorry to say he is returning there soon."

Devon's dark brows were still drawn. "Not soon *enough*, I'm sure."

"Early tomorrow morning, in fact." Brianna's tone was full of sincere sorrow. "And how, may I ask, is Larissah?"

Brianna was awarded a small victory with the jolt of guilt that passed over his features. Shaking off the emotion, Devon firmly informed her, "I am not here to discuss Larissah with you. I still want to know more about this Gerald or John or Judas . . . ."

"Joseph," she offered casually, and smiled at his fuming look.

"*Whomever*—what is he to *you*?" Devon didn't care if he appeared or sounded like a lovesick fool. He would have his answers.

"He is gone," Brianna answered simply.

Anything would be better than her cool manner. Devon wanted to hear her blame him outright for what had happened with Larissah. He wanted her to admit that she felt something for this other man. He would even be pleased to hear her scream or curse him—*anything* but this mild acceptance of his presence.

Devon slammed his fists against the armrests of his chair, causing her to look up sharply, amusement lacing her eyes. "Brianna, you will quit acting as though nothing has happened between us and give me the answers that I desire."

"I have given you answers; I tire of giving you *everything*, Devon." Her tone was still cool, though now she met his demanding gaze head on.

"I have yet to take *everything*, though I daresay if I'd been so inclined, it would have been offered easily."

Brianna's face flamed both in anger and in humiliation. She was embarrassed at the memories flooding her mind and furious that he would use her feelings as a form of attack. "Rest assured I will not make such a mistake again."

Devon laughed, the sound of it full of confidence. The look that came with it declared that they both knew how little truth those words held. "When next I am given the opportunity, the *last* description you will choose for my touch is *mistake*."

"I don't care how confident you are, Captain Elliott. I guarantee you now that *no* opportunity will be presented—you overbearing, pigheaded, unfaithful *ass*."

Devon smirked, one dark brow raised lazily over his seductive blue eyes. "What a becoming vocabulary you have acquired in my absence."

"If you find that impressive, keep on in my presence and I will fill your ears with insults that would make Drake blush."

Devon laughed. "I seriously doubt that, though I might be interested and—quite likely—a bit aroused to hear you try."

"I have *nothing* more to say to you, Captain." At that moment, Brianna actually believed that she hated him.

Devon shrugged her adolescent words aside. "Fine, don't talk. *Listen*."

"Devon I heard and saw *perfectly*."

"You've heard or seen nothing of truth, Brianna. You are so blinded by your childish jealousy that you won't even allow yourself the chance to believe in me."

"I believed in you once and look where *that* has gotten me."

"Yes, and at our first real obstacle, you run off and hide like a coward."

When her eyes rose again to meet his, Devon knew he had finally pushed her to the limit. "A coward, is it? Well, know this—I would much rather be a coward than a hypocrite and a liar."

Devon ground his teeth together and had to force himself from keeping them tightly clenched while he spoke. "I never lied to you, Brianna."

She sniffed disdainfully. "*Everything* was a lie."

Devon saw red. "You *ungracious* . . ." He let the remainder of his insult die before passing over his lips. Taking a controlling breath, he began anew. "You are one of the *few* people who actually *does* know each aspect of my life and with whom I have shared *everything* openly *and honestly*."

Brianna wanted to hurt him; he deserved to hurt. "Is my cousin one of the *others*?"

"*Larissah*—and anything else that occurred before I met you—is none of your concern."

"How very convenient," Brianna simpered.

His teeth did remain clamped together this time. "What is *that* supposed to mean?"

For an educated man, Devon was certainly acting idiotic. Rationally, Brianna explained, "Quite simply that when you thought you had the chance to seduce me, you kept your relationship with my cousin hidden. Then, as soon as she offered herself to you, it was more of a temptation than you could resist. Now that you think you might prosper by telling me the truth of what has been between the two of you, you are more than willing to offer that information." Shaking her head, she finished, "In the end, *neither* of us mean anything to you."

Smiling sweetly, she guaranteed, "And I for one no longer intend to be your easily won conquest."

"If you mean nothing to me, why would I have bothered following you when Larissah was so willing and close?"

She shrugged. "Variety."

"Does that explain Joseph?"

His point hit home. "Joseph is my friend. Larissah is your lover."

"*Was* my lover," he reminded forcefully.

"Either way, Joseph does not mean as much to me as . . . ."

Brianna wanted to crawl from the room. The look on Devon's face showed that he knew exactly what she had been about to say.

Victorious amusement apparent in his dancing blue eyes and his blatant smirk, Devon prodded, "Pray continue, Flame."

Now she was *positive* she hated him.

Stubbornly she altered her words, "As you mean to *Larissah*." Devon continued with that annoying expression on his face and Brianna pushed, needing to see his arrogance jarred. "Or as much as being away from *you* means to me." Her cruel statement—however dishonest—was enough to obtain her goal.

With a forced calm that Brianna was far from truly feeling, she set aside her cup and informed him in the coolest tone her wild emotions could manage, "You should not have come here, Devon. If I had wanted to see you or talk to you, I would have returned to Misty Heights."

He was as impassive in tone as she was. "Then keep your distance still, Miss McClaran. It will be amusing to see if you can, or at least for how long."

Standing in all of his arrogant glory, enough of Devon's anger remained that he was not so gentle when he replaced the china teacup to the tray between them. Without another word, he exited the room, leaving Brianna staring numbly at the dish he had been holding within his strong fingers moments before. The newly cracked cup mocked Brianna—symbolizing not just the rending of their relationship, but the breaking of her heart in the process.

She had run from him, just as he had accused, but instead of giving her a chance to heal, time had done nothing but fool her. Yes, she was still hurt and still angry at his betrayal, but Brianna was also still hopelessly in love with Devon Elliott. Intuitively knew that no amount of time or space was likely to ever change that fact.

Chapter Thirteen

Guests began to arrive at the Osborne home two days before the gala. All of the visitors were invited to stay for the entire weekend, though some would arrive for only the ball on Sunday evening.

The Elliotts made their appearance the day before the culminating event.

While Tansey hung gowns in the armoire, Brianna relaxed in a warm bath. She listened to the excitement of people arriving—the noise from the main entrance below floating up through the window of her guest rooms. The welcoming addresses and introductions along with the soothing feel of the water were almost able to relieve her of the meddlesome visage of Devon—but only *almost*.

Since their clash two days prior, Brianna and Devon had spoken to each other only when necessary and then in the coolest of manners. Yet even with her hurt and anger still raw, Brianna was weary of the battle. She would rather their dispute come to an end than to drag on endlessly. Lately her pride was proving to be a troublesome emotion; still she must pay it *some* attention. Even if she had reconciled within herself, it was still important to stand firm. If she backed down now, Devon would think that she was weak and willing to be thrown aside with little afterthought.

Tansey interrupted Brianna's plaguing thoughts. "Which gown you gonna wear to the gala, Miz Brianna?" Tansey rubbed her hands over the material of the yellow gown, smoothing the wrinkles of travel from the one that was her personal favorite.

A lazy smile covered Brianna's relaxed features. No matter how often she insisted that Tansey not address her so formally and drop the 'Miz,' Tansey continued to do so. "I believe it will be the emerald for the gala, the yellow for morning tea, the lavender for the barbecue and the blue for this evening's supper."

"You sure will look pretty in all these frills." Tansey's tone was wistful, but not blatantly envious.

"And not one bit of good they'll be doing me."

"Only 'cause you stubborn as he is."

Both of Brianna's light brows shot upward. "There's a great deal to be said for tending one's pride, Tansey."

With a soft laugh, Tansey agreed, "Yes'm, it go before a fall."

"You'll not be preaching to me, when you've got a few of your own stumbles to be wary of." Tansey was immediately tight-lipped, but something in her expression reminded Brianna of the intuition she'd been having—something was troubling her servant-friend—had been for the past few days. Considering that she needed a distraction from her own tribulations, Brianna urged, "Tansey, what *are* you holding back from me?"

Tansey felt nervous, dreading what she must tell her mistress. "There *is* something I got ta say ta ya." Her fidgeting increased as Tansey added, "I ain't told Mista Devon yet, so I need you ta keep this quiet."

Rolling her eyes, Brianna stood and wrapped a towel around her body. "Not to worry, since Devon and I have little enough to say to one another."

"That'll change."

For a moment, Brianna was stunned into silence. She and Tansey were close, but still, most times, Tansey tended to guard her words, not allowing her conversations to become to forward or unprofessional. Finally, Brianna managed a short laugh. "And what makes you sure?"

"Mista Devon ain't never act like this with a woman that I seen 'afore."

"Not meaning you any offense, Tansey, but I'm thinking there might be a few things Devon does or says with women that you haven't been witnessing."

Bolstered by her secret, Tansey contradicted, "I know'd he lay with Miz Larissah."

"You should have told me, Tansey."

"Ain't my place."

"Is *Daniel* your place, then?"

Tansey's dark eyes bored into Brianna's lighter ones. "You ain't from here; you don't understand."

Thinking of the social structure in her homeland, Brianna suggested, "Don't be so sure."

"I sure if I had your chance, I wouldn't be wastin' it."

Brianna laughed sharply. "It's not seeming to me that our chances are so very different, Tansey."

Tansey's face became guarded again, as she thought of the chance she was preparing to take. Noting the distant expression, Brianna urged, "Tell me your mind, Tansey. Your secret's safe with me."

For fear her courage would leave her as quickly as it had come, Tansey blurted out, "When ya'll go back home, I ain't goin'."

Brianna found that she could do no more than stare at the other woman dumbly, totally at a loss for words. "*What*?"

Now that her plan was revealed, Tansey's nerves were calm and sure. "You heard right, Miz Brianna. Don't try an' stop me neither. That be why I can't go back. Mama an' Pappy won't never let me go if I did." Tansey shook off the feeling of betrayal those words gave her and declared, "I free an' I want ta see the world while I still young enough ta go."

Brianna could understand that this woman would want to see and learn more. But since she also gathered that there was another motive, she asked, "Why *now*, Tansey?"

Tansey forced herself not to squirm under Brianna's scrutiny. "I got my reasons." Stubbornly, she crossed her arms over her chest and nodded her head, giving a look that reminded Brianna very much of Hesper.

Brianna would have none of it; this tightlipped answer would not do. Sliding into her dressing robe, Brianna took the other woman's hand in her own and led her to sit on the edge of the bed. "Are you truly expecting me to just let you walk out of our lives without a better explanation than the one you just gave me?" Seeing tears of fear and defiance well in her friend's dark pools, Brianna reassured her, "As I've said to you already, you have nothing to worry about from me. I'll not judge you and you can talk to Devon in your own good time. You have my word, but in return, I'll be wanting the truth."

Tansey still looked unsure as she contemplated the wisdom of confiding in Brianna. She trusted her mistress, but the woman was living in a white household; how could she *possibly* understand her plight?

Taking a deep breath, she decided to take the chance. If nothing else, she would be able to share some of her strain with another person. "I can't stay here an' watch him love *that woman.*" The tears flowed silently from her chestnut brown eyes and Brianna forced herself not to cry with her friend.

"Does Daniel know that you are planning to leave?"

"No." Tansey looked guilty. "He would be just as upset as Mama. I'm gonna tell him, I jus' don't want ta tell him too soon. He won't want me ta go, but he don't want me ta stay with him either."

Brianna could not get over the irony of this story and wondered if every relationship followed the same basic form. Obviously the ones involving the Elliott men did. "Tansey, maybe you are wrong. Daniel might be happy for your chance at finding true freedom."

Shaking her head, Tansey whispered with wisdom well beyond her years, "No, he don't want me bein' a slave, but he can't give me my full freedom either. He loves me, even if he can't say so."

"And just what are you wanting from him, Tansey? Daniel Elliott is a loving man. He would offer you any help that you need to live the way you're wanting to."

"What I want, he can't never give me. He can't never be *my* man. I can't never get his name or give him love so's everybody sees it." Sobs racked Tansey's body and Brianna wrapped her arms around her friend, her mind racing.

What could she do to help Tansey? There must be some way to give her a portion of what she so desired. Then it hit her. It was a dangerous plan, but one that would certainly work. Yes, it had to work. If it did, Tansey and Daniel were about to share the most glorious weekend of their lives.

Pulling slowly back, Brianna's emerald eyes dazzled with conniving excitement. "Tansey, wipe away those tears. If you're leaving me, then I'll see to it that you find a wee bit of happiness before you go."

Doing as requested, Tansey dragged her fingertips along her cheeks. Watching Brianna's animated movements while trying to decipher her thickly Irish-accented words of excitement, a small hope began growing in Tansey as her friend's tirade evolved.

◊◊◊◊◊

At the same time, Devon was on the rear verandah with his brother making some plans of his own. "Any luck?" Daniel asked, genuinely curious about where Devon and Brianna stood at the present.

Devon shot him a look that answered before his words did. "Not a bit. That woman is even more stubborn than I am, if you can imagine that."

Daniel laughed. "If I had not witnessed it myself, I would be hard pressed to believe such a statement, Dev. Still, I doubt things are quite so bad."

Eyeing his brother tersely, Devon snapped, "*You* should know better than anyone, considering the you allowed her to hid with you."

Daniel wasn't put out by Devon's accusing statement. "Would you rather I had turned her away?"

"No, but I *would* rather you had stopped her from spending time with another man."

Daniel laughed, this time at his brother's look of earnest betrayal. "Do you mean Joseph Mitchell?"

"Are there others she failed to inform me of?"

This only sent Daniel laughing harder. "No, there are *not*, and I daresay, Mitchell is nice enough, but no threat to you." Grinning childishly a moment, he further noted, "Still, it serves you right to feel the way you do."

"*Me?*" Devon questioned his hypocrite of a brother. "I will remember to be so sympathetic when it is your turn to pay for the deeds you have done."

"Thank you for the warning," Daniel replied, his laughter somewhat calmer with the thought of what Devon had just thrown his way.

"And on that note, since you seem to be quite the lover of late, baby brother, have you any suggestions what I might do to remedy *my* current predicament?" Devon was rewarded with an abrupt and thorough end to Daniel's laughter.

"*I* hardly qualify as a great source of knowledge on the subject of romance. It is shameful the way I am feeling. Since Brianna arrived, I have wanted nothing more than to push Meghan aside and spend all of my time with Tansey. Still, when Tansey is not around, I could want no other woman more than Meghan."

Devon felt sorry for his younger sibling as he whispered his next words confidentially. "Daniel, we discussed this all before. There is truly only one choice you can make. Though, since you have not yet proposed to Meghan, I would gather you have yet to fully decide."

Daniel smiled at his brother's snooping. "Oh, I've made my choice. I just haven't followed through with it yet, as *your* escapade and its resulting unexpected houseguests has made it a bit difficult. If you must know, I intend to ask Meghan to marry me sometime before we leave for Misty Heights. Caleb has already agreed—in so many words *demanded* it—before he would allow me to escort her and Brianna from the city."

Devon liked Daniel's future brother-in-law and his smile showed it. "He is a wise man." With a crooked grin, Devon provoked, "It should be entertaining, with both ladies in attendance this weekend. I will be anxious to see how you and your wits can remain intact. Then again, you *could* take advantage of the opportunity to say *goodbye* to one and *hello* to the other." Devon wiggled his eyebrows playfully at his brother.

With dry acceptance of Devon's comment, Daniel countered, "Thank you so much for that enlightening assessment. With such wisdom as that, it is no wonder that Brianna has you chasing your tail."

"I am not . . ."

Daniel laughed. "Save your words for someone who does not know you as I do. Speaking of which, I am anxious to have you returned to your former self, so would you please get on with it?"

"If only it were so simple," Devon intoned with slight frustration.

"It will be if you just figure some way to woo Brianna back."

"*Now* who is full of wisdom?"

Choosing to ignore that verbal jab, Daniel continued, "Explain what happened, don't allow her to walk away, make her hear you out, even if you must follow after her to the privy, don't let her escape."

"Now *that* would certainly be a unique approach to courting." Devon laughed at the prospect of such avid attentions. "Perhaps a more subtle gesture?" He slid the box from his breast pocket and extended his filled hand to Daniel.

Lifting the lid, Daniel whistled lightly through his teeth, reminding Devon of the man who had sold him the ring. "You've been holding back on me, Dev." Returning the box to his brother, he questioned, "You call *this* subtle?"

Devon shrugged, and then standing to move inside for supper, he stated, "It's definitely preferable to serenading outside the privy."

With a chuckle, Daniel clapped Devon on the back and encouraged, "Then by all means, man, don't hold back. The worst that will happen is she'll reject you."

"Thanks so much for your overwhelming confidence," Devon griped and then swept in front of his brother to meet Meghan at the bottom of the stairs. Offering his arm to her, Devon gained Daniel's attention, looked with pointed appreciation toward the rear view of Meghan's gently swaying hips and teasingly inquired to his brother, "Maybe another conquest would clear my mind?"

Leaning toward his brother so that only Devon heard his remark, Daniel offered, "Be my guest. It would certainly make *my* weekend less stressful; though I doubt I could say the same for you." Coming around to the opposite side of Meghan then,

Daniel took her other arm and together the Elliott brothers led the oblivious and extremely pleased young woman to the table.

◊◊◊◊◊

As planned, Brianna was suitably late entering the dining room. As anticipated, most eyes turned her way—though she was not so foolish or conceited as to think that all of those appreciative glances were for her alone, especially considering the vision of grace and loveliness her companion presented.

Her friend wore a pale yellow gown, heightening the similar tint of her flesh—producing an exotic quality that was undeniable. The powder Brianna had patted over her comrade's skin—ensuring a fairer tone—glistened with each move she made. Her waist was smaller than Brianna's was, but her hips were a bit wider and her daring décolletage offered more of a view than Brianna would have expected.

Silky dark hair was pulled up in a single twist to lie vertically along the back of her head and down her graceful neck. The glimmer in her golden-brown eyes matched the bronze of her dangling earbobs, both of which were enhanced by the shade of her buttercup gown.

At the far end of the table, Devon and Daniel—engrossed in conversation with Meghan—did not notice the initial hum of murmurs buzzing amid the guests at the table.

Who is that?
Where did she come from?
Do you know her family?
She hasn't been here long or we would know her.

Smiling at the scene they were causing, Brianna led the way to the empty seats directly across from Devon and Daniel.

At the same moment Devon saw Brianna, Daniel's eyes slid across the table and his expression of greeting froze— Daniel Elliott was not as easily fooled as the rest of the Osbornes' guests.

Daniel was amazed. The fact that Brianna and Tansey had conspired against him—or perhaps *for* him—was humorous and frustrating all at once. He could easily imagine the two of them scheming amid giggles and primping, all in anticipation of his initial reaction.

Daniel was sure he had not disappointed them.

Not only had they made Tansey a delectable sight for him—and every other man in attendance—they had also created a gloriously tempting opportunity for him. Still, he imagined that was their intent all along—at least, he desperately hoped so.

If her unexpected appearance and complete beauty had not been enough of a shock to Daniel's senses, the self-assured smile she granted him made his heart leap inside his chest. Never had he imagined her looking as she did now. He nearly shook with the urge to call her by name, bring her to his side and declare to her and the rest of the room that she was his and he was proud to have her.

Noticeably forgotten, Meghan fumed at his side. The glare she sent first to Daniel, and then Brianna showed them just how unhappy she was. However, it was the gaze that Meghan leveled on Tansey that instantly reminded Devon of Larissah and for the first time he reconsidered his fine opinion of his prospective sister-in-law.

Meghan's blue eyes shot daggers. Whether Daniel knew this woman or this was their first meeting, Meghan didn't know, but there was no denying the powerful and instantaneous attraction between them.

Leaning close to Daniel—a bit closer than necessary—Meghan whispered, "*Who* is this new friend of Brianna's? I've not met her yet. Is she someone you know?"

It took Daniel a moment longer than Meghan cared for to pull his eyes away from Tansey. Then, even as his gaze focused on her, Meghan felt she had yet to garner his full attention. "*Daniel?*" she pushed, her anger quickly fusing with humiliation.

Flustered that he had completely forgotten about Meghan sitting next to him, he stammered, "Hmm? Oh . . . . No, no," he cleared his throat. "No, I don't believe I've had the pleasure of making her acquaintance yet."

"Something tells me you would recall had you previously been so fortunate." Wanting to be through with this uncomfortable feeling, Meghan gathered her composure before prompting, "Don't be keeping us in suspense, dear Brianna. Who's this new friend of yours?"

On Daniel's opposite side, Devon teased just loud enough for Daniel's ears, "I believe my time to gloat is drawing near." The only returned reaction was a heated glare that promised Devon his brother failed to find humor in his current situation.

Tansey concentrated on her behavior. She was under intense scrutiny from Meghan and the quick lessons Brianna had added to her limited knowledge of etiquette would have to see her through. The last thing she wanted to do was make a fool of herself in front of Meghan or Daniel. Silently, she waited with the others for Brianna's answer. "This is Chloe Sarasin."

"French, is it?" Brianna could tell from Meghan's tone that each detail she learned of the beautiful lady was to be under great speculation.

Brianna was thinking as quickly as she could, but panic was closing in. They had not foreseen the need to create an entire history for the evening.

Without warning, blessed assistance came from an unlikely source. "Miss Sarasin's father was French. Her mother is . . . from Louisiana." Pausing to level his eyes on Brianna with a look that promised she would owe him greatly for his help, Devon finished, "*If* I recall *correctly*." His swift rescue of the women opposite him was greatly appreciated and Devon could see them each begin to breathe easier for it.

"That's true, Captain Elliott. I can't believe you'd remember such a thing, though." Both gentlemen were further stunned by the sultry sweet voice that emanated from Tansey.

Collecting himself, Devon replied smoothly, "Simply because one does not talk about a flower or its origin daily, does not mean that they forget a single detail of its loveliness."

It was Brianna's turn to eye Devon oddly and he caught her look. What was this dribble spouting from his lips? She was doing her best not to laugh in his face for it. Sardonically, Brianna intoned, "What a *charmer* you've become, Devon."

"The weekend has only begun, Flame." The use of her intimate name caused her face to flush deeply in front of their witnesses.

Turning back to Tansey/Chloe, Brianna finished the introductions. "Chloe, *clearly* you are already acquainted with my guardian, Captain Devon Elliott." Moving quickly on to the next individual, Brianna unnecessarily introduced, "This is his younger brother, Daniel, and our friend, Miss Meghan Callear."

Meghan's cheeks reddened noticeably—she would have preferred that Brianna had more accurately indicated her close relationship with Daniel. Making matters worse, the entire time that Brianna spoke, the French woman's eyes never left Daniel for more than a brief second. Meghan would have no more of this woman's boldness. "And *how* is it, Miss Sarasin, that you are acquainted with Devon?"

Sensing the brewing trouble, Devon's deep voice penetrated the air—a slight warning tone underlying the words. "Chloe's father and mine did business on a few occasions."

"In Louisiana?" Though she attempted to make her tone sweetly curious, Meghan was fooling no one in her jealousy. "I didn't realize you have offices there."

Daniel wanted no parts of the interrogation he could see developing. To Meghan's knowledge, he had only met Chloe moments before. Despite the fact that she was correct in her assumptions, Daniel expected her to trust his word. Sternly he informed, "There's a good deal about *my* business that you don't know, Meghan."

Knowing she had crossed the line of Daniel's patience, Meghan gulped her wine and promptly shut her mouth, face flaming with indignation as the conversation continued around her without pause.

"Mr. Elliott, Brianna tells me you live in Baltimore. Do you like the city life?" To the average observer, Tansey would have appeared the perfect lady, but since they knew her well, Devon, Daniel and Brianna could decipher the slight hesitation in her voice as she carefully chose each word and its pronunciation before she spoke it.

Daniel's mood soared as he interacted with Tansey in a manner he had never dreamed possible. "The city is lovely and exciting, but I often find it holds a brashness that disagrees with my temperament. I much prefer the relaxing fresh air of the country. When I am visiting Misty Heights, I can be myself with no demands or pressures put upon me." Sipping his wine lightly, Daniel's eyes met hers as he finished, "However, as in many of life's facets, I find I am unable to choose between the numerous luxuries both offer."

"Here, here," Devon joined, raising his glass to his lips not missing the cool look that Brianna sent his way and taking advantage of the chance to smirk at her in return.

Turning her attention graciously back to the woman who had so openly scorned her before, Tansey beckoned, "Tell me, Miss Callear, how do you feel about *your* city home?"

The other woman's tone was calm and kind and Meghan found she liked Chloe even less for her ability to hold her composure. "I agree with Daniel; the city is exhilarating. I think I'd find country life lacking the zeal I enjoy surrounding myself with."

With studied calm, Tansey returned, "To hear Brianna's great descriptions of Misty Heights, I think I would find country living full of warmth and comfort. Why else would she have come to *love* her life there so much?"

If ever there was a moment that Brianna wished to rethink assisting Tansey, it was then.

Devon was surprised by Tansey's declaration and choked on the bite of food he had just taken. Quickly, he downed a drink in an attempt to subside his coughing.

With a devilish gleam in her eyes, Brianna invited, "Perhaps you could return with us and visit our home, Chloe. That way, you could form your own opinion. 'Twould be grand having *two* friends with me for a time."

Tansey, Devon and Daniel simultaneously flashed Brianna glances indicating she was pushing too far.

"Maybe another time, Brianna," Tansey declined graciously.

"What a shame, I for one will certainly miss getting to know more about you," Meghan intruded her opinion, with noticeably lacking sincerity.

"Don't fret, Miss Callear. I promise to visit Misty Heights one day. Perhaps you'll *still* be a *friend* of the Elliotts then."

It was the most cutting remark Tansey had offered Meghan yet, but instead of watching for her reaction, she looked to Brianna to see that her meaning was clearly interpreted by her friend—her departure would not be permanent.

Meghan did not attempt conversation through the rest of the meal. By the time they finished and the final dishes were cleared away, she was engulfed by such a fierce anger and jealously that she was not lying when she pled a headache and excused herself from present company.

Watching her leave the room briskly, Devon commented softly to his brother, "Ouch."

Daniel cringed visibly. "Yes, I imagine I will be paying for this evening for quite a while."

"You have the rest of your life for that," Tansey pointed out bluntly.

Daniel watched her for a moment before deciding she had not meant her comment viciously—it was merely a statement of fact. "You are right, *Chloe*, which is why I intend to make the most of this night and the remainder of the weekend. You understand, I must be *certain* the crime is well worth the punishment?"

Tansey did not even bat a lash at Daniel's straightforward expectations or that he had been so blunt with Devon and Brianna listening—they had nothing to lose now. "I wouldn't have it any other way, Mr. Elliott."

Daniel came around the table. Glancing toward Brianna, he winked adorably and whispered, "I am in your debt." Without further hesitation, he then led Tansey out the front entrance of the dining room, leaving the greatly entertained Devon and Brianna behind without another glance.

Still smiling, Brianna turned back from the sight of her retreating friends to find Devon staring at her—not at the doorway as she had been. It took only seconds of being caught in his gaze for Brianna to realize that she was in severe danger.

Chapter Fourteen

Devon's eyes held a determination to be reckoned with.
If Brianna didn't flee soon, he would strip the remaining threads of her wavering opposition from her. His handsome features did nothing to aid Brianna's attempt to ignore his charms. He wore the common formal wear of a gentleman— black breeches and jacket with a white shirt beneath his overcoat. His soft waves of ebony hair were pulled into a small tail at the nape of his suntanned neck with a black ribbon; his endlessly blue eyes were warm as he regarded her.

Time was running out. She couldn't be alone with him; it would only result in her easily won forgiveness. Watching the romance spark between Tansey and Daniel had made her heart light and the urge for love strong in her—now was *not* the time to be tempted by Devon.

Striving to ignore his unsettling stare, Brianna stated, "I believe I too will retire early tonight."

She stood, but Devon's words halted her. "Not yet, Brianna."

Green eyes flashed with annoyance and defiance tinged her words. "I beg your pardon?"

With an unwavering gaze, Devon replied, "I said that I don't want you to leave yet."

"You have said a lot of things in the past that I should not have abided by."

"I had no idea that you are fluent in French."

His sudden twist of subject took Brianna by surprise. "*What?*"

"*Sarasin*?" He chuckled. "Your . . . *friend's* name—it means dark-skinned."

"It was the first thing that came to mind. In case you failed to notice, I did not have a lot to work with." Smirking, she informed, "I should have known *you* would figure that out. Do you always have to be so observant?"

"Yes. Especially when I enjoy what I am observing so much."

"Stop trying to charm me," she ground with clipped words.

Devon could tell she was ready for a battle. Still, he had seen the sidelong glances she had given him throughout the meal and hope abounded in him. He could not chance losing this opportunity. As though she had not made her wishes for escape known, Devon further requested, "Come, spend some time with me. We should talk."

Brianna jutted her chin forward stubbornly. "I have nothing to say to you."

"Brianna, I am tired of waiting until *you* are ready to listen." Devon's tone stayed light though his statement was filled with honest frustration.

She smirked, "And *I* am tired of *you* altogether."

Devon chuckled softly, "I have missed your quick wit."

"Surely there is not much difference in talking to one lady or her *cousin*." She grinned proudly at the execution of her cutting remark.

Devon did not fall for her antagonizing; he would have his way this night. "Oh, but you are wrong, Brianna. There is only *one* cousin I wish to spend my time with."

"*This* evening."

"For far longer than that, if truth be told." The unexpected jolt his words gave Brianna made her feel as though he had pushed her over the edge a cliff and now she was hurtling toward a jarring end. The victory would surely be his. There was no use fighting him.

Walking around the table, he offered his hand to her. "Come, walk with me, Brianna." With a devilish gleam in his eye, he assured, "I will do my best not to charm your further."

Though she had yet to take his offered hand, Brianna could not stop a humored grin from lighting her lips. Softening a bit more, she teased with mock offense, "Then I suppose I will get no sweetly offered comparisons to a flower such as the lovely Miss Sarasin did?"

Devon smiled; Brianna's sense of humor boded well for him. Readily he indulged her, "I believe that your beauty deserves greater praise than such mediocre overtures. You are far more exquisite than mere words could convey." Grasping her hand then, he turned it so that her wrist was bared to him and kissed it softly—his teeth nipping lightly at the tender skin there. When he felt her involuntary shiver, he offered, "Still, if it pleases you . . . have you not yet realized that you are the most alluring lady in attendance this evening?"

Brianna offered him a taste of her light laughter before pointing out, "I somehow believe that Daniel would argue that fact."

"And I would argue *him* to the grave."

No matter what Daniel thought, Devon was certain of his own opinion. Brianna was lovely—the epitome of perfection. She was undeniably ravishing. No matter how angry she made him or what she did to surprise him, he wanted her just the same.

Her copper hair was caught in an upsweep, held by a small sapphire and diamond clasp. Loose spirals were permitted to sway down, framing her flawless features perfectly. The shimmering cerulean gown she wore paled her light coloring gracefully. Her slender neck and rounded shoulders were creamy, begging to be tasted by his wanting lips. A glittering sapphire broach drew his attention downward to where it was attached—resting temptingly upon the valley that his eyes now greedily surveyed.

When his gaze returned to her eyes, Brianna raised an inquisitive red-tinted eyebrow, causing Devon to smile. "Perhaps when you have finished judging my appearance, you would care to chance another look around the room. I would like to give your indecisive taste the opportunity to critique *all* competitors, Captain."

"You are mistaken, my dear. The fact is I have known all along what it is that I want." His voice was determined and caused a shiver to run through her. "And I feel it is only fair to forewarn you that I intend to have it still."

Brianna allowed Devon to lead her from the room—she was *definitely* losing the battle.

Her mind raced to stall him. "Even *you* must falter, Captain. Has there not been just one time that a particular goal of yours has been found unobtainable?"

Brianna's face was like an open book and Devon could easily guess at the internal battle she was waging. Still, this was more than she had allowed in weeks, so Devon simply relaxed and enjoyed her endeavor to out-talk him. "No, I always have my way."

She was groping for stability now. "*Always*? Is that not a slight exaggeration?"

"Not in the least, Flame." Then, in a conversational tone, he temptingly offered, "Shall I tell you what it is that I want and then prove to you that I will have it? Or, would you rather I simply take my desire, allowing *you* to learn as *I* seize?"

Her throat went dry as bone and Brianna prayed her next words sounded normal. "You have a reoccurring habit of giving compliments while pushing the limits of propriety, Devon."

He leaned close. "I don't care much about propriety and if I may say so, I recall a time or two at our home when *you* didn't either."

"Take care, Devon. You are *not* forgiven yet, so don't be expecting any of . . . *that*." Her cheeks flamed darker than he had ever seen them.

Devon's blue eyes were dancing now and he laughed loudly at her comment. He was gaining control and they both knew it. He wholeheartedly enjoyed watching her squirm in the discomfort and indignation of the inevitable situation. "Do not fret, Flame. I will go slowly with you."

"As far as I'm concerned, Devon Elliott, there is precisely one place you can go and I care *not* how fast you get there. Rest assured," she promised in a determined tone, "that *I* don't intend to be going with you, either."

His hearty laughter heralded their presence to others in the walking garden. Cobblestone paths wound through patches of herbs and flowers, ending where the massive lawn fanned out before them. Here Devon came to a halt, letting go of Brianna's arm. He took her hand and wound their fingers together, reassured when she did not pull away from his touch.

If Brianna was at ease, she would be more likely to accept what he wanted to say to her. "Brianna, about Larissah—"

Brianna tensed. "That is a subject I do not care to discuss with you, or anyone else." She turned her head away but still grasped his hand tightly.

Taking a deep breath, Devon maneuvered so that Brianna faced him again. "Fine, then let's talk about home."

"What about it?" She was defensive; her tone dripped with tension.

"What will it be like when we return to Misty Heights?"

"Different." She was being stubborn and knew it.

What does he want of me, though? she pondered silently. *How can he expect me to instantly forget what happened? Does he believe that my mind can forgive him as quickly as my treacherous heart has?*

"It doesn't have to be different, Brianna. Things are not as you believe."

"I have found that things are *never* what they seem to be, Devon. Events in life are only what you make of them and I cannot allow myself to be made a fool again. I won't let it happen. Not now, not ever."

"Brianna, you are not the fool. I am. I should have told you about Larissah from the beginning."

"Then why didn't you?"

"Because I was afraid that you would think I wanted the same type of relationship with you."

"And don't you?"

"No, I want more."

How desperately she wanted to believe his words and let them sink into her soul without question. She needed proof before she could let that happen, though. "Let me see if I understand what you are saying. *You* want *me* therefore—simply because you order it—I should come to you willingly, without question or concern?"

"It's not like that. Why are you being so difficult? Can't you just listen to me?" His voice was raspy with emotion and the effort to remain discreet in the open night air of the garden.

"Fine!" She threw her arms up in exasperation. "Enlighten me, if you feel you must. I would rather hear you out now than have you badgering me the entire weekend."

"And will you listen?" He sounded like a child that wanted to share a secret but was afraid of being laughed at.

"Yes," she offered with annoyance.

Devon pushed, further inquiring, "And will you *believe* me?"

"Perhaps." When her remark produced nothing but a stubborn stare from him, she conceded, "*That* depends on how truthful your words sound are. After you hid your betrayal from me, I cannot offer you more than that."

Closing his eyes for a moment, he inhaled the night air, hoping and praying that he be granted the words that would make her see his way in this. Opening his eyes, he tilted her chin so that their eyes locked. "Yes, Larissah and I were lovers, but that began before I met you. I have no desire for her now. I ended my relationship with her the night of her party."

Brianna never took her eyes from him and her words were unfaltering. "You will have to do *much* better than that."

"What do you wish to hear?"

"Why didn't you marry her? Why do you treat her no better than a trollop?"

"Had I been the one to take her virtue, then I *would* have married her."

Brianna was somehow not surprised by this information. "I see. Tell me true, do you or *did* you love her?"

"Larissah means nothing to me."

Brianna considered his words for a moment. "And that is supposed to make all of my worries go away? The fact that you bed my cousin and then claim that it means *nothing* to you does not make me overly anxious to follow in her footsteps, Devon. I do hope you understand." Her final remark was spoken as though she was having the most pleasant of conversations with a friend.

"Yes, Brianna, I do understand. That is why I am here, telling you what I am. I don't want you to assume her role. Don't you see? You mean much more to me than she does. More than she ever could." He was desperate to make her believe him. The box containing her ring burned against his chest, but Devon kept it hidden. Now was not the time, she was still too unsure. "You will trust me again, Brianna. Soon you will see the truth of it and know what actually happened that night. Then we will be together again."

"How can you be so sure of that?"

"Because you saw Larissah kissing me, *not* the other way around."

"I saw no struggle from where I stood."

Narrowing his eyes at her, he said, "And if you had stayed but a moment longer, you would have seen me shoving her away." He pulled her against his chest then and she let her hands drop.

Clenching her fists, Brianna struggled to fight back the tears of frustration he was causing. *"Don't,"* she pleaded with him softly.

He did not obey. "Brianna, I never meant to make you feel like this. I swear to you that I ended my relationship with Larissah because I want to begin one with you." Devon felt as though a heavy load had been lifted from his shoulders, such honesty was wonderful. He loosened his hold on her and took a step back, ready for her reaction to his declaration.

Brianna could not breathe. He wanted her, *truly* wanted her.

But what does that mean? That I should forgive and forget all easily?

No, not easily, she decided. "You've had your say, Devon." Brianna turned and walked back toward the house.

She nearly made it to the doorway when he gained on her and turned back to face him. She was caught between the cold bricks of the house and the heat of his hard chest as he implored, "And?"

Brianna hesitated, would have done so longer had he not leaned closer. She spoke to keep him from kissing her—that would not help her situation at all. "Let's begin with testing your behavior through the weekend."

"And after that, what else might I do to prove the extent of my feelings for you? Shall I declare it to everyone I meet?"

"You just hold your tongue. *Words* are not great proof, especially since you seem to have a talent with them."

"Talented or not, my words *are* true." When she tried to slip past him, Devon didn't budge, but added softly, "And I so very much need you to believe them."

Brianna was desperate to run. "*I* need more time."

Devon leaned even closer. So close that Brianna felt the brush of his lips against hers when he spoke. "I've given you enough time. Consider this fair warning, my Flame—your time is finished. I'll have your trust again and I will have *you* with it."

Unable to speak, Brianna nodded her head slowly, her eyes wide with innocent trepidation and the frustrating, all-consuming *need* for his kiss. Her mind screamed for battle, but her heart and body called only for submission—for Devon—since, what he wanted, was in all actuality, her deepest desires too.

However, to Brianna's utter amazement, he didn't kiss her as her lips yearned for, as her skin craved. Instead, he pushed away from the wall and made his way into the house and toward his room without looking her way again.

◊◊◊◊◊

Larissah glared at the man across from her and offered him another bout of insults. "How could you be so idiotic as to forget a gala given by the Osbornes? They offer the finest arrangements for their guests, the most memorable parties within social seasons." She made a sound of complete irritation. "You must be even more stupid than I previously thought."

Robert was quickly tiring of this woman and her sharp tongue. "I don't believe I like your tone, Larissah."

"And I don't believe I care." Her blue eyes narrowed dangerously. "If you feel so strongly, by all means, do not force yourself to share my *company* any longer, Robert."

"But then, *who* would do your bidding, Rissah?"

With a cool glance in his direction, Larissah purred, "We may be arrive late, but it would take me little time at all to find a suitable replacement for you."

Robert's expression mirrored Larissah's. "Do not mistakenly look to Devon. I daresay he's otherwise occupied these days." Robert gained some satisfaction in the obvious sting his words caused her.

"Not for long," Larissah vowed.

"I count the days," Robert returned, not even trying to be civil toward the woman any longer. It was easier to block her out altogether. Leaning his head back on the seat, he closed his eyes.

Across from him, Larissah was having similar thoughts. She couldn't even recall what had attracted her to this simpering man to begin with—probably his money. He wasn't even man enough to leave after she had stopped giving herself to him nearly two months before.

Robert was useless to her now. The only reason she had even agreed to travel with him to the Osborne home for the weekend was that every instinct within her cried that Devon was there. And where Devon was, Larissah needed to be.

Smiling maliciously, Larissah closed her blue eyes and contemplated what her ex-lover's reaction would be when she revealed her secret to him.

Even better . . . . Brianna's devastation.

◊◊◊◊◊

The mid-afternoon barbecue was a busy social affair for which Devon had no use or patience. After drawing battle lines with Brianna the previous night, Devon could hardly wait to make his next move. Unfortunately, he had to endure the outdoor gathering until such an opportunity presented itself.

"Why in the world do you look so sullen?" Daniel asked, walking up beside his brother.

With a glance of irritation, Devon stated, "I'm tired. Something to do with a rutting ass locking me out of my bedchamber. I tossed and turned for hours on the sitting room furniture."

Daniel smiled. "I wish I could say I am sorry . . . . "

"I heard *precisely* how sorry you were throughout the night."

"It may appease you to know that my pleasure has not extended into the daylight hours."

"Oh?" Devon was about to inquire about his brother's comment, but Brianna and Meghan chose that moment to walk past and Devon lost all concern for his brother's problems.

When Brianna chanced a sidelong peek in his direction, Devon chuckled. She wasn't ready to give in to him yet, but he had every intention of enjoying the fight. With a smile of pure confidence, Devon wondered how long Brianna would be able to resist the charm he intended to ply her with that evening.

If Devon had his way, her resolve wouldn't last until morning.

"It does a heart good to witness such keen glances of innocent love." Devon turned toward the voice and was surprised to find his brother had vanished without his realizing it.

He was doubly disappointed to discover Larissah now stood in his vacated spot. "What do *you* know about innocence *or* love?"

Batting her lashes coquettishly, she replied, "Only *that* which *you* taught me, *dearest* guardian."

"With so many teachers, how do you remember what you learned from whom?"

She ran her fingertip over his sleeve familiarly and forced a sigh of resignation. "Alas, generosity *has* always been one of my greatest flaws."

"Generosity—another term I am astounded that you understand."

"Do not be too surprised, Devon. I *understand* far more than you realize."

Devon looked her over with disdain. He wanted to get to the reason for her bothersome presence. With Larissah, an ulterior motive was usually involved. "I had hoped to be spared the pleasure of your presence this weekend."

Her laughter was like warm velvet. "Devon, I would never want to deny you any kind of pleasure."

"Don't do me any favors, Rissah." The smile that graced his lips did not even begin to touch his suspicious blue eyes. "Why are you here?"

"You have never been one to waste time, have you, Devon?"

"When one is dealing with a poisonous viper, time is of the essence. Don't you agree?"

The slight narrowing of her icy blue eyes was the only evidence that he had riled her at all. "And you would do well to remember that aggravating such a creature could prove just as lethal. You'd best take care."

Rather than remark, he pushed irritably, "You still have not answered me. Why are you here, Larissah?"

Manipulation lined every syllable of her words. "I came to see you. Don't I have the right to see my guardian when I wish?"

Ignoring her inquiry, Devon cautioned, "Don't ruin this weekend for me, Larissah." His warning was intense despite the barely cordial tone he was forced to retain out of courtesy for those conversing around them—those oblivious to the building tension.

Larissah raised a single dainty brow. "Why? Are you planning something special?" Peering in the direction Brianna had walked, an absurd possibility occurred to her. Not striving to hide her disgust, Larissah blurted incredulously, "Don't tell me you are going to *propose* to my cousin."

When Devon said nothing, Larissah studied him silently, the potential reality of what she had jested taking hold. "*Please* tell me you are not going to propose to my cousin." This time her words were tinged more with demand than jest.

Instinct warned Devon to lie about her question and he did so smoothly. "I hadn't planned on it, but since you brought the idea to mind, I may give it some serious consideration."

In spite of Devon's words, Larissah gathered that her off-handed guess was very close to the truth. Obviously, Devon and Brianna were devoted to one another even more than she had considered. "She is no more than a child. How can you expect to be happy with her?"

Looking deeply into her blue eyes, Devon made certain that she understood his meaning. "I have no need to *expect* anything from her, Larissah. Brianna makes me very happy already."

"So, my little cousin has proved an easy conquest for you?"

Devon laughed in a demeaning manner, "You *would* think that, Larissah, but alas, Brianna is not as willing as you were."

"Pity for you," she spat in offense.

"On the contrary—I find the challenge of her innocence refreshing."

"You must forgive me for doubting such a claim. You forget, I know you well, Devon."

"Not so well that you haven't realized I am able to find joy with a woman in realms *other* than her body." With growing contempt and failing patience, Devon added, "Still, you are entitled to your opinion, Larissah. Now, if you have nothing of more importance to say, I suggest you run off and find Robert. I'm sure he is somewhere fluttering about, waiting for your beck and call as usual."

With that, Devon turned on his heel and went in search of Brianna. With Larissah around, he intended to keep her as close to his side as possible.

Chapter Fifteen

Devon found Brianna walking behind the house. At his call, she turned to him and—to his glad surprise—smiled in his direction. "A smile? Should I thank you or beware?"

Her eyes narrowed but held no threat. "You'd be wise to do a bit of both, yet."

"Thank you. How are you feeling today?"

A fresh grin graced her lips and she replied, "Better than yesterday."

"Might that have something to do with our conversation?"

"It might," Brianna hedged.

Devon would take whatever he could get and promptly offered Brianna his arm. "Dare I hope you'll walk with me again today?"

Brianna hesitated. It was so easy to give in to charming Devon. Her every instinct screamed that he would win this challenge, but she didn't want to surrender too easily. Tilting her head to the side, she narrowed her green gaze and agreed, "Yes, I'll walk with you." Ignoring his arm, Brianna stepped in the direction she'd been headed before he'd stopped her. Casually, she commented, "After seeing you with all those guests, I thought sure you would be caught in some gentlemanly conversation for hours."

Offering her his arm, he assured, "Had I not managed escape, I very likely would have been."

"How did you break free?"

Devon chose not to mention Larissah for now. "I merely reminded those around me that I must tend to my ward. It is very important to see that she is properly chaperoned and enjoying herself."

"A blatant abuse of privilege."

"Not entirely since both considerations were truly on my mind."

Brianna chose to pay no attention to his smooth talk. "Allow me to ease your wandering; your ward is doing well."

"I'm glad to hear it." Looking around at the distance they had put between the Osborne house and the guests congregated there, Devon asked, "Now, could you be so kind as to inform me *where* she is headed? The gathering—in case you have lost your way—is in the opposite direction."

Brianna bit her bottom lip, as though in serious distress, but her light-hearted mood was undeniable. "I don't know if I should say."

Devon decided to play along by doing his best to seem miffed by her denial. "And *why* is that?"

"You may disapprove." As one who has no wish of being overheard, she whispered, "It may seem rather disgraceful."

Watching his expression, Brianna half expected Devon to drool, reminding her of the fairy tale wolf she recalled from childhood stories. "In that case, you *must* tell me."

With a light laugh, Brianna conceded, "Tansey told me of a creek just on the other side of the evergreen row there." She pointed so Devon looked to the row of trees ahead. "I thought I might go adventuring and see if it is as peaceful as she claims."

Wiggling his brows, Devon teased, "You weren't thinking of taking a scandalous dip were you?"

"Yes," she whispered conspiratorially, "but only my toes."

Closing his eyes, he savored the thought. "Mmm, those scrumptious toes again."

"And isn't it odd that *you* always seem to be around when they make an appearance?"

"Which I suppose makes me a very fortunate man."

As they reached the barrier of trees, Brianna glanced back toward the house and squinting, was able to see the women beginning to dwindle from the remaining crowd. The time had come for them to seek rest inside, leaving the men to boast over their masculine power. With an amused shake of her head, Brianna thought that she was glad to have timed her little adventure to avoid both.

Stepping in front of her, Devon disappeared between the branches of the needled tree row and was amazed at the way the environment seemed to swallow him from existence. No one would know about this escapade except he and Brianna—a tantalizing thought that didn't falter his steps in the least.

Following Devon's lead, Brianna pushed through the shrubbery and immediately felt as though she had entered another world. Hidden from direct sunlight, the gathering of saplings and trees, weeds, fallen logs and fresh earth filled the surrounding air with the scent of moss and nature. Adding to the mystique of the secret Eden, Brianna half-expected to see some wood sprites or fairies dodging for cover after the rude human intrusion of their home.

Clearing a space on a large rock, Brianna sat and searched beneath the layers of her skirts for the side-lacing of her boots. While unfastening them, she listened to the silence around her and enjoyed the serenity of the woods. In a soft tone, as though she was afraid of breaking the spell, she said, "It amazes me that we can be so near to other people, yet seem miles from civilization." Wiggling her feet free of her boots, she yanked on the toe-seam of each of her gray, knee-high stockings, pulled them off and felt the coolness of the ground under her feet. "No one will know that we are here."

"I certainly hope not," Devon returned.

Brianna glanced up just in time to see Devon's completely nude person flop unceremoniously into the rippling water.

Stunned, Brianna failed to control her open-mouthed expression, looking quickly back and forth between his pile of neatly folded clothing and his mischievously beaming features in the water. How he had managed to completely disrobe, in the same amount of time it had taken her to remove her shoes and stockings, was baffling.

The creek was no more than four feet deep where he stood, yet to Brianna's way of thinking that was not deep enough. The water ran in a scintillating cascade—droplets from his wet hair traveled over his cheeks and off his sturdy chin, rolling over the muscles of his chest to disappear into the murky water at the exact level of his narrow hips.

Devon laughed, advising, "Close your mouth, Brianna. The mosquitoes will bite and swell your tongue."

"But you are . . . I mean . . . you don't have . . . Devon Elliott, *where* are your *drawers*?"

Nodding in the direction of the pile of clothing she had already noticed, he stated, "With my other belongings. You didn't expect me to get my things wet and return to the house drenched, did you?"

"No, but I didn't expect you to jump in, bearing all that God gave you, either." She was trying desperately not to study exactly *that* of which she spoke.

"What then? Did you think I would let you come down here and have all of the fun without me?"

"How much fun can ten toes be?"

"I could show you."

"Soon I hope to learn never to predict *anything* you might do or say, Devon Elliott." Still, she was not going to give him the satisfaction of scaring her off. He was free to make a fool of himself but she certainly would not join him. Progressing carefully to the edge of the water, Brianna let the mud squish through her toes before rinsing them in the coolness of the creek.

For a while, they were quiet.

Devon—gliding through the water gracefully, enjoying the feel of the current as it washed the heat of the day from his limbs.

Brianna—driven to distraction in her attempts *not* to imagine just what it would feel like to be pressed up against all that was now bared to her gaze.

Devon taunted her with trailing glimpses of the width of his shoulders, the muscles of his chest, the tightness of his abdomen, the bulk of his arms, the laughter in his devilish blue eyes and the assertive smile on his full lips.

Mortified, Brianna realized that she had been doing exactly that which she had determined not to—worse yet, he had caught her.

"Well?" Devon questioned, the smirk not leaving his dripping features.

"Well, *what*?" She averted her eyes and—too late—tried to find something else to focus her gaze on.

"Do you like the view?"

Brianna turned back to him; her face flushed to rival the vibrant locks of her auburn hair and declared weakly, "I was *not viewing anything.*"

Devon fought to hold in his laughter. "Perhaps a wee peek then?"

"No!" Her face darkened considerably.

Shrugging, Devon caused a muscle in his chest to jump. "View, peek, look, stare, ogle . . . it matters not how you choose to phrase it." Pointing a dripping finger in her direction, Devon accused, "The fact remains, Miss McClaran, that you *were* doing it."

Planting her hands firmly on her hips, Brianna declared through clenched teeth, "Well, if you don't want a person to see your . . . your . . . *attributes*, then I suggest that you don't flaunt them." Her tone was as indignant as she could manage in the current situation and it only encouraged Devon's teasing.

"Flaunt?" He indicated his position in the water with a slap of his hand. "This is not flaunting, my dear Brianna." Grinning at her handsomely, he confirmed, "*This* is flaunting."

He had taken two long strides in her direction before Brianna comprehended his intention. Thrusting her arms straight out, she closed her eyes so tightly that her nose scrunched up. "Don't you dare, Devon Elliott!"

Even as she made her demands, Brianna felt the wetness of his bare chest against her hands and knew that she had spoken too late—or more likely—he simply chose to ignore her plea.

When Devon spoke again, his voice was soft and sensual—his breath warm on her cheek. "Oh, but I do dare, Flame. Where you are concerned, I seem unable to resist it."

Brianna felt his hands on the hook and eye fastenings of her blouse. Emerald eyes flew open in shock and she swatted at his hands. "*What* do you think you are doing?"

Not removing his gaze or hands from his self-appointed task, he replied, "Viewing and peeking." With one quick jerk, her already opened top was pulled out from the waistband of her skirt, "and looking and staring and ogling."

For a moment, Brianna was so amazed by his deft handling of her clothing that she scarcely paid heed to the fact that she stood before him with only her corset and chemise to cover her heaving chest—but only for a moment.

Glancing at her discarded shirt, now hanging from Devon's tanned fingers, she returned to reality and holding one arm across her chest, reached for her shirt with the other. "Well, I suggest that you view, peek, look, stare and ogle at someone or something *else*."

"That could be a problem." Devon leaned carelessly on the tree beside him and Brianna was infinitely thankful of her hooped-skirts, since they kept a decent distance between his lower body and hers.

Still stretching toward the elusive shirt, Brianna cautiously inquired, "Why?"

The charming smile spread across his full lips again. "Because it is *you* whom I find so pleasing to the eye."

"Since you seem to have a similar opinion of your own person, why not search out its reflection elsewhere?" Brianna felt a minor victory in her impertinent comment.

"Because it does not give me nearly the pleasure you do."

Brianna's eyes narrowed. "I doubt that greatly."

Devon said nothing, but his eyes began to darken.

With far less steam than she intended, Brianna scolded his expression, "You ought to be ashamed of yourself."

"I have nothing to be ashamed of." Taking her hand in his he stated, "But then you've already seen *that* for yourself."

"You are unbearably arrogant."

He smiled. "Yet you continue to *bear* me so well."

"Stop doing that!" Brianna felt certain that she was on the verge of a childish tantrum.

"What?" Devon was sincerely baffled by her outburst.

"Turning my words around to suit your purpose. It is very distracting."

"Not as distracting as I'd like to be."

"To be sure, I've no doubt about that."

"May I show you?"

"No."

"Then let's not talk." Glancing toward the inviting water behind them, he suggested, "Swim with me."

"No."

"I want you to swim with me, Flame."

Her fear doubled. "Devon, I can't."

"Yes, you can." He pulled her closer and reached around her waist, fluidly undoing her skirt. He deftly pulled the loose drawstrings of her petticoats and hoop.

In a mocking tone, Brianna remarked, "You seem to have done this before."

Devon grinned at her token protest. "Swimming? Yes, it's always been a favorite pastime of mine."

Stomping her foot, Brianna accidentally caused the material around her waist to slither down her legs and pool around her feet. "I don't mean that." Pointing at the skirts on the ground she revised, "I mean undressing a lady so adeptly."

"Mmm, my *other* favorite pastime."

"I'm thinking it's not in your best interest to remind me of that right now."

Devon flashed a smile that made Brianna's heart melt and with the emphasis of his encouraging fingers, he called, "Come to me so that I might rid you of that burdensome corset."

Brianna's hands flew up to the clothing in question and she nearly stumbled over her skirts in an effort to dodge him. "Devon, you cannot see me . . . what I mean is . . . it is not proper for you to see me . . ."

"Do you mean naked?" he questioned, his lips trembling with mirth.

"Yes."

Appeasing them both Devon suggested, "Why not come in with me, but keep your undergarments on."

"And you won't try to swim me out of them?"

He hesitated in thought. "Not right away."

"Devon!" Brianna was indignant.

Holding his hands up, much the same way she had earlier, he agreed, "Fine, if I promise to keep your virtue intact, will you come in with me?"

Brianna's face flamed. No matter what had passed between them before, this situation was entirely different and entirely improper. He was naked, she was half naked and now he was openly speaking of her virginity. "Maybe I should dress and go back—"

"I promise you I will chase you down without taking the time to get dressed if you leave me here like this."

His voice was steady and his eyes calm. Brianna had no doubt he would do exactly as promised.

"There is no way I can win in this situation."

Sapphire eyes danced, full lips smiled and with a wink, Devon stated, "That was my plan all along."

"Cheater."

His voice softened. "No. Not at all."

Slowly, Brianna turned her back to Devon and allowed him to untie the back lacings of her corset. When she faced him again—arms tightly crossed over her chest—Devon offered his hand once more. "Shall we?"

Keeping her hands in place, Brianna scolded, "That seems a rather dangerous proposition coming from you, Captain."

"Brianna, you have no reason to doubt me. I've promised not to touch you."

Her eyes went wide. "But I need you to."

It was Devon's turn to stumble for words. "I beg your pardon?"

"I cannot swim. I never learned how." Eyeing the small creek as though it were King Triton's deepest fathoms, Brianna added, "You will have to hold on to me so that I don't slip under the water."

With great patience and mild laughter lacing his words, Devon pointed out, "Brianna, the creek is only five feet at its maximum depth. One can hardly consider that dangerous circumstances."

"Yes, but I am not overly tall." Biting her lower lip, she further admitted, "And I am frightened."

Devon was not used to this dependent side of her and found that he liked it—and the opportunity it presented him with—very much. "If it will make you feel better, I will hold you."

"Not too tightly," Brianna admonished, reading the distinct gleam in his eyes.

Nodding, Devon took her hand in his and led her toward the water. "No, not too tightly."

The creek was refreshing and so long as she stood no more than knee deep in it, Brianna only felt the need to hold on to Devon's hand. As distraction from her fear, she focused on keeping her eyes averted from his naked maleness. The foliage along the creek bank was especially enchanting, but it soon made her think of Adam and Eve and Brianna's curious gaze would drift back to Devon's bare body.

After several minutes had passed, Devon urged, "Brianna, this is hardly swimming."

"It is near enough for me." She gripped his hand tighter.

"Come, I will teach you some basic strokes."

"I just want to learn how *not* to drown."

Devon chuckled and continued to guide her slowly until she stood beside him, the water reaching mid-waist and thankfully covering him at last.

The cool brown pool reached a bit higher on Brianna and when she noticed Devon's uninhibited gaze following the line of the water, she immediately bent her knees and lowered her body another few inches. This action only caused him to laugh harder before commenting, "Have a care not to go too far under, Brianna. I cannot teach you if you are completely submerged."

"This should be sufficient so long as you don't decide to *ogle* my face the same way you were my . . . my . . . well, you know."

Smiling mischievously, he returned, "Yes, I know."

Devon tried to release her hand, but she panicked and gripped it even tighter than before. "What are you doing? You promised not to let go."

"Yes." Still trying to pry his hand free, he added, "but I want to swim around a bit, so that you can watch the way I move and get an idea of what you need to do." When she still stared at him uncertainly, he offered, "I will not be far, Brianna. I won't let anything happen to you. Trust me."

Brianna felt suddenly certain that he was talking about more than just her swimming lessons, but could only nod her head slowly and allow him to free his hand from her grip.

As she stood in slow moving water, Brianna watched him swim and was once again enthralled by his fluid motions and the realization that she could never deny him. Deep within her heart, she had realized it all along. It had simply taken this precise moment—watching him glide smoothly through the water—for her to understand and accept the fact fully.

Standing, Devon brushed the water away from his face with his hands before smoothing down his thick ebony hair. He was slightly breathless from the exercise and his voice was ragged due to it. "Do you think you can try now?"

Brianna moistened her dry lips with the tip of her tongue before she was able to speak. "I think." The problem was *what* she had been thinking and it had nothing at all to do with swimming lessons.

Devon caught the look and hid a knowing smile. Perhaps the afternoon spent in this hideaway would benefit him yet.

As he pulled her out to where the water was up to her shoulders, he kept her eyes locked with his—he wanted her to know she could trust him in all things.

"Devon?" Her voice trembled slightly.

"You are fine. I won't let you go."

She nodded and began to move slowly toward the spot where he stood waiting for her.

Something brushed her leg and she jumped.

It passed by again and she panicked.

Jerking away, Brianna lost her footing and their slippery hands unlocked. Before Devon could grab her, she slipped beneath the surface and flailed so wildly that Devon had trouble catching her without causing harm to some very sensitive places on his body.

Devon forced himself to think clearly rather than panic with her. He waited for her arms to emerge again, and then pulled her wrists together and up, bringing Brianna—sputtering, coughing and sobbing—to the surface for air.

She clung to him, no longer caring that he was unclothed and she nearly as bare. "You said you would not let go, Devon."

Rubbing her back in a soothing motion he answered, "I didn't; you did."

"Oh," was all she could say. She was shaking and frightened and she still didn't know what had brushed her leg—only that it was not around to do so again. "Something touched me."

Nodding, he guessed, "Probably a fish or a snake."

She looked up at him, her cheek still resting against his wet chest. "That's not the most consoling reply you could offer."

He grinned at her sharp retort. "Do you want to go back to the bank?"

"No!" She gripped him desperately. "I want to stand here for a bit before I try moving again."

"I take it our swimming lesson is over for the day?" She said nothing, only nodded, so Devon took the opportunity to ask, "How is it that the daughter of a sailor never learned to swim?"

She shrugged. "I guess Da never thought it would be necessary. Every time I was at sea, I was on one of his ships. He knew that he and his captains were capable. There *were* dinghies after all."

Devon tried to hold back, but her logic was hilarious. He began to laugh softly. "Luckily for you, he was right." When she looked up at him, he added, "And it seems to be my good fortune as well."

He knew without question that she would not fight him at that moment and he lowered his lips to hers. She sighed into him and held nothing back. Brianna had been tempted one too many times in the last twenty-four hours and despite her hurt and anger during past weeks, she had missed him and wanted only to give in to the sheer pleasure of Devon's kiss.

Sliding her arms around his neck, she pulled on him until the thinness of her chemise was apparent and it felt as though they were separated by nothing but water.

Devon groaned from the utter pain he felt within the slight gratification Brianna was giving him. If he had his way, he would not bother returning to the bank but have her here in the water.

With each caress he gave, Brianna matched it with one of her own. Devon felt a new freedom with Brianna's avid desire and so allowed his hands to roam over her without reservation. Delving beneath the water, he stroked the soft roundness of her hips and continued his movements until he felt her press against him willingly.

Brianna lowered her hands to rest on the muscles of his biceps and did not falter when she felt his hands on her buttocks. Instead, she deepened the kiss on her own and Devon pulled her to him so that she felt the entire length of his desire against her. He wanted Brianna to know exactly how she made him feel.

As her instincts took over, Brianna was overwhelmed with conflicting emotions. Everything felt good, his hands, his lips, his breath, the breeze, the water running over her skin. She wanted to feel more, she was afraid to feel more. Her pulse raced, her breathing was heavy and her conscience was in a state of panic.

Hoping to thin clearly, Brianna broke their kiss. It was no help as Devon immediately lowered his mouth to explore more of her. Brianna arched her back and her rich cry of pleasure deepened as it tore from her.

Devon did not pull her chemise away but tantalized her breasts through the thin material. Water-soaked, the white cover was translucent and Devon gloried at the sight of Brianna's body. When he raised his lips to hers again, she slid her hands lower, to rest on his hips and Devon knew desire as never before. Slowly opening his eyes, he sensed that she was feeling the same way and that she would give all to him now if he were to ask.

Devon kissed her deeply again and when he smoothed his hand over her wet auburn tresses and down the length of her arm, he felt her shudder with the anticipation of his touch. "My beautiful Flame." He brought his finger up, lifting her chin lightly so that their eyes met. "As much as I desire you now—what I feel goes deeper than any touch can ease."

She nodded, her eyes intense. "Even so, I cannot go on like this, Devon." She was so trusting. Her emerald-gold eyes were imploring him to help ease her distress, her kiss-swollen lips taunting him to continue his torture.

"We must wait until the time is right." Devon held tight to his dwindling control, "When you are ready."

She licked her lips and guaranteed, "I've never been more ready." Her reasoning was basic—giving herself to him could not possibly be wrong when it was the only prospect that felt right. Denying him or herself pleasure was utter turmoil and Brianna could stand it no longer.

Devon closed his eyes and forced himself to think rationally. "Flame, do you realize what you are saying?" When his eyes opened again, the shimmering sapphire gaze held her tighter than any embrace could. The passionate promise within their depths convinced Brianna completely of her choice.

Pressing closer in reply, Brianna felt the heat of his arousal and suddenly, she was not so bold. Easing slightly back, she asked, "Will it . . . does it . . . hurt?"

Devon's burning blue eyes were patient, his soft spoken words gentle. "For you—but only the first time will stress your innocence. Still, sometimes the pleasure is so unbearable it is likened to pain."

She shivered, not at all the reaction Devon had anticipated. "I want to know. I want you to teach me."

Devon was going to give in to her innocent desire.

"I *do* hope you are talking about swimming," stated the amused masculine voice from the bank.

Brianna was mortified.

Devon was angry.

Both were surprised by Daniel's intrusion.

Devon found his tongue first and he intended to flay his brother with it—to make him pay for this bold intrusion. Deciding that bluntness should set his younger sibling straight, maybe even embarrass him adequately, Devon informed him, "Actually—before you so *rudely* interrupted us—I was about to take my time thoroughly teaching Brianna everything about . . ."

"Fishing!" She supplied the word so suddenly that both men were momentarily speechless and looked her way with surprise.

Laughing, Daniel stated, "Well, then you've certainly come to the right man."

"*I* thought so," Devon grated.

Daniel surveyed his brother a moment before stating, "You are either out of practice or forgetting something."

"Doubtful on *both* counts."

"Really, then where is your rod?"

"Exactly where it should be. Or at least *nearly* so."

Brianna could not help her reaction and covered her face with both hands. She didn't know if she wanted to laugh, cry, or scream.

Kindly, Daniel ignored Devon's testy comment and continued his list of sportsman wrongdoings. "I was under the impression that one kept their clothes *on* while fishing." Daniel glanced in a questioning manner toward Brianna's belongings skewed around the bank and Devon's in a single pile. "Perhaps father forgot to mention something when tutoring *me* on the sport."

"We were looking for bait," Devon spat out, his dark brows drawn together in dangerous warning. "We couldn't very well drench our outerwear."

"Oh, well that explains everything, then. Don't let me stop your activity. Pray continue."

"With you *watching*?" Brianna's tone was incredulous and high-pitched with the emotion.

Daniel shrugged. "Brianna, I've seen people hunt for fishing worms and hellgrammites before. It's nothing new to me."

She smacked the water soundly. "Oh *really*?" To the amazement of both brothers, she then stomped—as forcefully as the squishy terrain would allow—from her murky liquid cover. The thin material of her chemise clung to her shapely form, adding to its transparency, and leaving nothing to the imagination for either of the Elliott men.

No more than a foot separated Brianna and Devon's amused brother when she warned, in no uncertain terms, "Daniel Elliott, *you* are exceedingly close to *becoming* our bait."

Devon was first to recover from his shock and whooped with laughter. The look on his brother's face was priceless and he could think of nothing Daniel deserved more. Following Brianna's lead, Devon walked uninhibited from the water to stand beside her.

Looking from Devon to Brianna, Daniel commented dryly, "Well, Dev, I can certainly see why you would want to give her *private* lessons." After offering a conspiratorial wink, the younger Elliott turned and passed through the row of evergreens, his sidesplitting laughter sounding in their ears as he disappeared back into the world from which he had come.

Chapter Sixteen

Devon twirled Brianna effortlessly over the dance floor as the myriad of colored gowns around them created a kaleidoscope for their spinning view.

The moment they had entered the ballroom, Brianna's gaze found Larissah. Even as heated anger and jealously coiled within her stomach, Brianna begrudgingly admitted that her cousin was gorgeous.

Her talent for keeping court was evident. Her beauty shone, her porcelain complexion perfectly complemented by the golden-brown gown she wore. The decorative tiger lily in her upsweep of golden curls and golden lavaliere with garnets that encircled a large pearl set her appearance off with perfection. The accented décolletage of her bodice was surprisingly tasteful, though still daring enough to give a hint of what lay beneath the material.

The only drawback to Larissah's façade was that she knew exactly how good she looked.

Brianna consoled her irritation with the woman by reminding herself that tonight it was Larissah's turn to watch from a distance—and she did. Envy was plain on Larissah's face while she scrutinized every move Brianna and Devon made. The fuming expression she currently wore caused a surge of victory to course through Brianna; it felt good to outdo her vindictive cousin.

Nodding toward the glass doors leading to the gardens, Brianna silently asked Devon to relieve her of the stifling air inside the house. As the strains of the next dance began, he obliged and whisked her outside in an instant.

◊◊◊◊◊

"You have to admit that they make a handsome pair," Robert expressed from his place beside Larissah. When she gave no response, other than continuing to glare at the doorway through which Devon and Brianna had disappeared moments before, Robert added pleasantly, "Brianna McClaran is a *lovely* woman."

Looking to him with insincere sweetness, Larissah pondered, "If you find her to your liking, then why don't *you* try for her? It would certainly make my life simpler in more ways than one."

Larissah's obsession for Devon Elliott surpassed annoying—it bordered dangerously on psychotic. It was evident that the man was in love with Brianna McClaran, a fact that Larissah refused to accept. Robert couldn't care less about Elliott—they had never shared any camaraderie—but he had begun to feel compassion for Brianna. The young Irish woman drew a person to genuinely like her—at least everyone but Larissah.

His limited patience evident, Robert chastised, "He will never have you back. When are you going to realize that?"

Continuing to nod politely to those passing by, Larissah returned, "As soon as you realize that you can never replace him in any aspect of my life."

Robert looked to her, sincerely stunned by her conceited assumptions. "I no longer want to try. I am tired of your scheming ways."

"Then go—I have no more need for you." She still did not look at him but perpetually worked the crowd with her smile.

"Then I *will* take my leave," Robert stated, relieving both of them with his decision. "However, before I go, I have a question that begs an answer."

At last Larissah turned his way, her face and words full of disdain. "Then ask it so that I might be rid of you."

Bluntly, Robert inquired, "Is the child mine?"

Larissah went so rigid that her facial muscles ached around her frozen smile. "*What* are you talking about?"

Impatiently, he stated, "Though I have not seen you un-clothed for quite a while, I know your body and there have been some definite changes." He glanced pointedly at her growing bosom and smiled broadly when she flicked her fan open and waved it vigorously in front of her chest.

"I doubt you are even man enough to sire a child."

Robert shrugged her insult off easily. "So says you, but just remember, had you played your cards right, I would have married you, bastard child and all, guaranteeing you the secure lifestyle which you so greedily desire and are ungratefully ac-customed to."

Larissah laughed shortly. "Marry *you*? I would never have agreed to spend my life with a man as weak as you, Robert." Sniffing contemptuously, she added, "I will only ever need Devon. No other man could ever compare to him and his abil-ity to adequately provide *all* that I desire."

Grabbing her hand quickly, he bent over it, kissing her wrist in a salute of farewell. Standing again, Robert clashed his eyes with hers and promised, "I will be sure to send your regards to Nate when I return home, then. I'm sure he will be glad to hear of your decision." With that, he was gone, leaving Larissah behind in a stunned state of humiliated silence.

◊◊◊◊◊

Osborne Hall's promenade gardens and the full moon above provided Brianna and Devon much needed respite from the noise and heat they'd left behind in the ballroom. Extreme-ly happy in the moment and more so in the direction their rela-tionship was once again headed, Devon asked, "Have you en-joyed your weekend here?"

"Yes, it has been wonderful." Offering him a bashful smile, Brianna added, "It would have been perfect if not for Daniel's interruption and Larissah's arrival."

Though she had had no interaction with her cousin, simply knowing that Larissah was near put a burden on Brianna's emotions. The encounter with Devon and Daniel earlier had been full of so many feelings that Brianna was still sorting through them all.

On one hand, today's interlude with Devon was worse than any she had allowed or instigated yet—much worse on so many levels. What had transpired between them should shock and embarrass her. Instead she felt vibrant and alive and . . . yearning. Even with the recent anger she had felt toward him, Devon continued to win her over with the way he looked, the way he smelled, the way he sounded, the memory of his arms around her, his hands on her, branding her with each caress—all of it was driving her mad.

Only partially guessing at the extent of her thoughts, Devon laughed at Brianna's chagrined tone and brought her back into the conversation. "I daresay there should be no further disturbances from my younger brother. Daniel is overly occupied now with his new fiancée."

"So he has proposed at last?" Brianna queried with surprise.

"Yes, though I marvel that she consented after the scene you caused during our first dinner here."

Blushing, Brianna defended herself. "Devon, I hope you understand my reasons and aren't too angry. It's just that Tansey was heartsick and with her leaving . . . ." She clamped her lips shut, her eyes widening; she couldn't seem to keep anything secret from Devon.

Smiling at her reaction, he consoled, "Don't worry. I already know about that, too. Daniel told me this morning after Tansey was gone."

Brianna looked at him uncertainly. "And you're not angry with me?"

Shaking his head, Devon explained, "I can't say that I am happy to see her go—Tansey is family. Still, I think that she made a wise and selfless choice and I respect her for it."

"Good." Her genuine smile warmed him as always. "Now, if we could only rid ourselves of Larissah as easily."

Devon laughed at the scheming timbre in her voice. "What did you have in mind?"

"Do you want the version that lands us on a chain gang or the safer, less time consuming one?"

"You decide," Devon offered playfully.

Brianna pondered for a dramatic moment. "Let's play it safe; she is my cousin, after all, and though I can't stand the sight of her, Mama and Da would be sorely ashamed of me if they knew what I was thinking."

Devon could not contain his grin. "I daresay you are right. So, what shall it be? How do you intend to rid us of Larissah for a while?"

"I want to go home . . . to Misty Heights."

"*Now*? But I thought you were enjoying yourself." The surprise her request triggered was evident in Devon's voice.

"With *you*, I am, but something is warning me that we cannot hold her at bay for much longer."

Devon nodded his agreement. If truth were told, he had endured the same feeling throughout the evening. "You are sure, then?"

"Yes, Devon. I want to spend some time with you." Looking boldly into his sapphire eyes, she added, "*Uninterrupted time.*"

He hesitated no longer. "I'll get your wrap and arrange shipment of our belongings. When I return, we'll say our goodbyes and return home." With a chaste peck on the lips, he left an amused Brianna awaiting his return.

◊◊◊◊◊

Devon had been gone for nearly a quarter-hour. Brianna was about to go inside and search for him when she was alerted to another presence by the sound of fast footsteps approaching from behind her. Turning toward the sound, she recognized the man immediately and the recollection did not ease her anxiety.

"Mr. Montgomery, is there something wrong?"

Robert shook his head, trying to regain his lost breath after the track he had just traversed.

He had been ready to leave the gala when guilt overrode his anger at Larissah. Robert felt the need to warn this kind woman of what her cousin had in store. Not wanting to draw Larissah's attention, he had walked around the outside of the host's home and waited behind the barricade of bushes until Devon had re-entered the house. Robert knew that he would not get far if he had confronted Devon.

Glancing around to be sure that they were alone, Robert quietly replied, "On the contrary, Miss McClaran, there is something that I wish to do for you."

"For me?" Brianna could not begin to fathom what he meant. "Have out with it, sir." Looking over her shoulder toward the open door through which lively music continued to flow, she added, "Captain Elliott will be returning soon and we will be taking our leave." Brianna supposed it could do no harm for this man to know Devon would be returning presently—it certainly eased her tension.

"Good, because what I have to say is about your cousin."

"Speak freely, Mr. Montgomery." To that permission, she added, "I suspected she was somehow involved."

"You're correct—though Larissah does not know I am here. I come of my own accord." Brianna said nothing, only waited for him to continue. "I presume you know of her . . . indiscretions?"

"Enough of them," Brianna responded, growing more and more curious as to what this confrontation was all about.

"She has a plan, a cruel ruse to—"

"Robert Montgomery, unhand this lady at once! You should be ashamed of yourself!"

Larissah's enraged outburst drew several inquisitive guests away from the gala, toward the scene she was causing. With vindictive eyes, Larissah further declared to Brianna, "And to think my cousin would permit such actions."

The two charged at the focus of the growing crowd stood in stunned silence. "Robert Montgomery, I demand that you do right by my family and propose to my cousin at once!"

"You *what*?" Two voices rang out in united indignation.

"You certainly cannot expect to behave in the manner in which I found you and *not* marry." Looking at the guests around her, Larissah added, "That would be positively shameful."

"You do not actually expect me to marry this man for conversing with him in the garden?" Brianna was dumbfounded. Larissah had gone too far this time.

"Conversing, indeed. Maybe in Ireland that's how a lady speaks to a man, but let me assure you that what I stumbled upon was far more than talk by American standards." Larissah was having no trouble with her deception. It could very well be her last opportunity to push Brianna away and make Devon her own.

Robert felt like a fly trapped in a spider's web and he had no plan of becoming Larissah's latest victim. "What you saw and what you are *claiming* are two entirely different matters, Miss Chase."

The older woman forced tears. "And to think I considered you a beau, Robert. I suppose I was wrong."

He grew more enraged with the sympathetic glances Larissah was receiving from the crowd of onlookers. "Stop this farce, Larissah. I will *not* marry her."

"You won't?" She tried to sound disgraced rather than angry.

"No," Brianna firmly stood up to her cousin alongside her unexpected ally.

Larissah needed to corner the twosome in front of the crowd. She had to use the situation she had come upon—and none too soon—to her advantage. "Why not? It is apparent that you are well acquainted."

"Because she is already betrothed to me," Devon stated calmly as he parted the crowd with his words and body. Walking to Brianna's side, he protectively slipped a possessive arm around her waist—movements that were like dry-tender to the fury-fire engulfing Larissah's features.

"Betrothed . . . she's *your* intended?" Larissah hated the fact that she was stumbling through this doubtful statement. Devon certainly enjoyed making her fumble.

Devon nodded with complete composure and confidence, "That's correct."

Now was Larissah's chance to spread doubt and she pounced upon it greedily. "If this is true, then why have the banns not been cried?" Amid agreeing murmurs, Larissah watched the glance that passed between Devon and Brianna and knew that she was losing.

"Because I asked her only this afternoon." Calling on the crowd around them with his eyes, he added, "I had no desire to take any of the celebration from our hosts or the congratulations from my brother who also became engaged this day."

"How thoughtful," Larissah grated though clenched teeth.

Devon bowed slightly as though accepting her compliment graciously. "My delay was certainly not because I did not want everyone to know that she has agreed to be my wife."

Filling her tone with as much sympathy as she could manage, Larissah addressed Devon, "And already she is behaving thus with another man."

He was frank. "Larissah, I think you are lying. I don't know what your intentions are for doing so, but I am warning you . . . ." Looking at each person encircling them, he continued speaking, "And any other person in attendance, that if they intend to cause harm to my fiancée, then they will have *me* to answer to."

Not waiting or interested in a reply, Devon placed Brianna's shawl over her shoulders, took her arm and escorted his staggered and newly appointed fiancée from the view of the equally stunned spectators.

◊◊◊◊◊

Four hours after the scene outside the gala, Devon gently placed Brianna's sleeping form on the comfort of her mattress. She had succumbed to exhaustion during the train ride to Harper's Ferry.

Quickly, Devon stripped her of everything but her chemise and drawers. Laying her clothing over the chair in her sitting room, he turned back toward her and saw that she was watching him.

"We're home," she stated with soft contentment.

Noticing the exhausted smile that graced her lips, Devon walked back to her bedside. "Yes."

Her eyes widened a bit as she slowly recalled all that had transpired. "Devon, I'm sorry."

Brushing a stray lock of hair from her forehead he questioned, "Sorry for what, Flame?"

"I should have been prepared for anything Larissah might try. I just never truly suspected she would go so far as to involve other people in her schemes."

Devon shook his head and continued smoothing the auburn waves on her crown, "I gathered from his expression that Robert was as innocent of the situation as you were."

"Perhaps, but he said that he wanted to tell me something."

"What was that?"

"He didn't get the opportunity before Larissah made her absurd accusations."

"Maybe he was just trying to tell us what we already knew, that Larissah was going to try something to separate us." Smiling down at her concerned features he added, "Do not fret; it was not your doing. Larissah has always been this way and I feel certain she will never change. It is merely something we will have to learn to live with."

"How is it possible that I am related to someone so nasty?"

Devon flicked the tip of her nose lightly. "I would say you simply used up all of the goodness, saving none for her."

Brianna laughed. "I would try to believe that pathetic compliment had she not been born *before* me."

Shrugging, he suggested, "Then consider it a matter of environment." Kissing her on the cheek he recommended, "Get some sleep. Tomorrow will be a busy day."

Brianna groaned and burrowed beneath her quilted blanket. "What do we have to do that cannot wait? I desperately want only to enjoy being home again."

Before replying, Devon smiled and enjoyed the sound of her admission, muffled from beneath the pile of covers around her. "You may enjoy your home and solitude again, *after* we initiate plans for our wedding."

Brianna shot straight out of bed to stand in front of him. "Our *what*?"

Devon chuckled at her reaction. "Our *wedding*. Surely you have not forgotten my rescuing declaration so soon."

"No, I simply hadn't realized that you intended to hold me *to* it."

"Well, I do."

"Why?"

"Mainly because I gave my word in front of many witnesses." When her stubborn expression remained unchanged, Devon questioned, "Would it be so terrible, Brianna?"

She couldn't speak, couldn't even think clearly enough to form a complete sentence. "I do not . . . I cannot say . . . ."
Huffing, she stomped her foot childishly in a way that was be-

coming amusingly commonplace with her. "You are missing the point, Devon."

"Brianna that is *precisely* the point. We can't continue tempting each other as we did this weekend and not act on it."

Without consideration she cried, "Does that call for *marriage*?"

Devon could not believe his ears. "As far as *you* are concerned it does."

"Again you are dictating the direction of my life. Shouldn't I have *some* say in this?"

"It seems to me that you are doing just that," Devon commented, still entertained by her frustrated comments.

"Yes, but *you* are not *listening* to me."

"I am hearing every word you say."

"Devon, for *you*, *hearing* and *listening* are two entirely different matters."

He laughed. "You are right, but that doesn't change the way of things."

"Just how are *things*?"

"Exactly as I want them."

"You can guess just how surprised I am about *that*," Brianna responded sarcastically.

Looking at her—hands on hips, flaming hair billowing over her shoulders, chest heaving and red-faced in anger—Devon knew he wanted her, just as much as he knew that she humored him even in battle. "Has anyone ever encouraged you to learn to control that Irish temper of yours?"

In as threatening a manner as she could maintain, Brianna countered, "My heritage has *nothing* to do with my anger."

"Then why do you sound more like a leprechaun every time you speak to me?"

She stepped closer to him, almost as though she expected her petite form to intimidate Devon's brawn. "Because you're bloody frustrating, that's why!"

He shrugged, clearly indifferent to her words or aggravation. "We will be wed, Brianna."

His authoritative tone, mingled with her already boiling temper, pushed Brianna over the edge, and she spoke without contemplation, "I don't *want* to marry you."

It took only a second for Brianna to realize that Devon had easily deciphered her words for the lie that they were. With a barely concealed smirk, he responded, "Truly?"

She said nothing but nodded while trying to swallow past the dryness in her throat. Her chin lifted a notch. "When I marry, it will be *my* choice, *not* because I am forced to be treated as a child you can bend to your commands."

His statement came clear and true. "You are my charge, there is little difference between that and any child I might father."

"Apparently you found a difference this weekend." She moved another step toward him, "And if—as you have so *boldly* decreed—I am to be your wife, I think all pretenses of a difference should cease."

Devon closed his eyes, took a deep breath and prayed for restraint. "Do not tempt me now, Brianna." He was tired and had little strength left to save her virginity for their wedding night.

"How is that possible Captain, since you *claim* I am no more than a child you are forced to raise?" Brianna's tone and line of reasoning mocked him.

"As you've so astutely pointed out, this weekend was proof of exactly *what* I wish to claim."

"*Including* the marriage declaration?" Doubt rang loudly through her question.

"Brianna, surely you know me well enough to realize that anything I do is either for my wishes or the welfare of those in my care or my family name."

"So then which was your reasoning for binding us?"

Carefully, Devon responded, "Don't you think it was beneficial to all of my reasonings that your reputation was saved by me?"

Disappointed by his smooth evasion of a direct answer, Brianna reminded him, "I didn't *ask* for your sacrifice."

Devon nodded. "Perhaps not, but if I hadn't given you aid, you would be planning a marriage with Robert Montgomery rather than me." He smiled with infuriating self-assurance. "And you leave me little doubt as to where your preference lies."

Brianna's eyes flashed—for a moment Devon thought they actually changed shades. "Allow me to erase the bit of doubt that you might have, then." Her hands rose to the buttons at the front of her chemise.

Devon had not expected her defiance to take this direction. Without comment, he assertively pointed a shaking finger toward the bed behind her, demanding without words that she obey his order.

Clearly ignoring his silent command, Brianna smiled, continuing to unfasten her clothing with deliberate slowness. She would not allow the possibility of rejection to enter her mind— he *must* want her the way she wanted him.

Keeping his eyes safely focused on Brianna's pink cheeks, Devon ordered in a menacing tone, "Brianna McClaran, if you do not get into your bed, *alone*, and leave me in peace, I will give you the thrashing you so dearly deserve."

"So long as you *claim* this." The last button opened, teasing Devon with a glimpse of creamy cleavage. Her eyes stabbed him with more bravado than she actually felt at the moment. "This body where something inside me has already been claimed by you."

Devon clenched his jaw tight, fought against the raging animal that wanted to swoop in on her like its unsuspecting prey and warned her, "Brianna, you tempt me dangerously. I am only a man and my resistance is wearing thin. I don't know how much longer I can listen to such confessions without acting." He shook his head, ran his fingers through his hair, leaving it somewhat disheveled, much as he was feeling. "I'm not sure I can hold back."

His admission brought Brianna to him without reservation and she slipped one perfectly rounded shoulder out from under its cotton covering.

Immediately she saw the error of her ways.

Devon took one small step toward her—his determination clear.

Suddenly the line between punishment and what Brianna thought she wanted blurred. In one bounding leap, she was in her bed and under the covers, every one of her doubts parading gleefully through her mind. She should have known better than to push him, to tempt him with what she didn't fully understand. She had, though, and his foreboding air seemed far more intimidating now that it was laced with his male passion.

As he turned to leave the room, Brianna halted him once more. "Other than the fact that you have demanded it, tell me *why* I *should* marry you Devon."

He did not face her. "What other reason do you need?"

Brianna's heart raced. She wanted him to want her, to care for her. She wanted him to tell her what she meant to him. "I want to hear you speak the words."

He turned toward her then and the answer was in his eyes. "For you, Flame. Always for you."

Though it was not exactly the answer that she desired, for now, it was enough to appease Brianna's pride. Sliding down beneath the covers once more, she closed her eyes and tried in vain to calm her racing thoughts.

◊◊◊◊◊

The emotion burning within Larissah Chase could not adequately be described as anger. The weekend had been a disaster. She had been insulted, shunned, exposed, humiliated and duped. Now she watched as her bags were packed and prepared for travel.

Following a candelabra-wielding slave down the dark staircase, the seething woman determined that she would have her revenge. As she left the Osborne home under the shield of night, Larissah consoled her fury with the knowledge that she still held the most damaging piece of evidence—one that would be clear to everyone within another month.

Chapter Seventeen

During the next several weeks, Brianna let go of her remaining reservations about her marriage arrangement with Devon. There was no point extending the battle since they both knew it was what she wanted and Devon had a continuously annoying way of seeing that anything he put his mind to became a reality.

Still, Brianna would have liked a more romantic gesture on Devon's part. There was no doubt in her mind that she loved him, but did he love her or was he acting solely out of duty? His physical desire for her had been made clear on several occasions, but Brianna realized there was quite a difference between love and lust.

In the end, Brianna admitted to herself that no matter what had occurred to bring them to this pass in life, she was unbelievably happy that it had. If Devon was willing to face their future together without qualm, than she most certainly would not burden him with any more unpleasantness on the matter. She certainly didn't want him to change his mind now.

As Brianna sat in the parlor working on a quilt with Hesper, she allowed her mind to wander even farther than it had already. With her inner voice, she tentatively tested her new name, *Brianna Elliott, Mrs. Devon Elliott.* The thought of it gave her chills and made her giddy with joy. Thinking positively, she decided, was not nearly as hard as she had anticipated. Just as married life with Devon—particularly the life he would introduce her to on their wedding night—made her wish away the days until their union.

◊◊◊◊◊

Devon was searching out his bride to be. He had a surprise for her and was anxious to get her approval on the matter.

Since the day they had begun planning for their marriage ceremony, Devon had decided that it had become Brianna's goal to run him ragged in search for what she deemed "the perfect gown." Upon receiving a short letter from his brother, he found that Daniel was not having the same difficulty with his intended bride. Not only had Meghan found the gown and arranged for the limited number of guests attending, but she had done it all within the time period allotted her.

When Devon had questioned Brianna about the fact that she was not able to plan a wedding as quickly as her soon-to-be sister-in-law, she sternly shushed him and told him not to concern himself with the ceremony. Brianna assured him she would see that everything would be ready for the wedding and she would take argument from him about it. Considering the turnabout she had made in her willingness for their union, Devon had simply determined to avoid such conversations.

At least that was the plan until he unexpectedly came upon the perfect gown for Brianna.

Finding his fiancée mulling over a quilt with some assistance from Hesper, Devon entered the parlor and greeted them each cheerfully. "Good afternoon, ladies."

Hessie regarded him oddly, immediately wary of his expression. "Wha'cha up to, lookin' all sly and happy like that?"

Devon laughed through his explanation, "In case you haven't heard, I am to marry a very lovely lady; doesn't that give me every right to be happy?"

Still unsure, Hesper studied Devon warily. "I seen that look in them dev'lish eyes afore. Only mischief come from it then, an' I 'spect won't be no different now."

Brianna enjoyed Hesper's teasing. Since Tansey had gone Hesper had become sullen and withdrawn. Only some special attention from Abram had begun to ease her mind and broken heart.

Returning her attention to Devon, Brianna could see just what Hesper had been leery of when he walked to her side—

blue eyes sparkling with an unspoken secret and his full lips curved in an inviting grin. As he bent at the waist to kiss her cheek, Brianna laughed lightly. "Dear me, Devon, you *do* look like the cat that took the cream. Should I run for cover or wait to see what surprise awaits me?"

Devon enjoyed her good humor. "I recommend waiting since my offering is the likes of which you have yet to see from me." When her brow raised and a slow smile spread across her lips, Devon laughed loudly.

Brianna's face flamed.

Despite her attempts to remain separate from their conversation, Hesper chuckled at the young couple but continued to concentrate on the fabric in hand without comment or glance in their direction.

Wielding an admonishing tone, Brianna ordered, "Stop your teasing and tell me what your mind is brewing now."

"Very well," he agreed, standing before her and watching as she attempted to handle the needle as deftly as Hessie. "It is about those never-ending plans for our wedding."

Her fingers halted their attempts and her gaze sought his. "Devon Joshua Elliott, I told you already that you are not to concern yourself with my plans. If I *must* marry you, I will do so the way that *I* want."

"Your outlook flatters me to no end," he stated with dry sarcasm.

As though trying to teach a child a lesson, Brianna inquired, "Now, how would *you* feel if *you* had to marry someone as stubborn as you?"

Devon smiled fully at her. "Do you think that is really so hard for me to imagine?"

"You *are* the Devil." Brianna laughed with him at her light insult. "Have out with it since I know I will have no rest until you do."

Solemnly, Devon assured her, "After this, I will say no more on the entire matter." Brianna eyed him skeptically, but waited silently for his announcement, which came with boyish excitement. "I have found the perfect gown for you to wear for our ceremony." Devon didn't allow a chance for comment, but smiled his most charming of smiles and offered, "I thought perhaps you would wear the gown my mother did the day she wed my father."

Nothing could have prepared Brianna for the emotion that his unexpected endeavor caused her. He was honoring her in a way that she had not expected and the tears shone brightly in her appreciative eyes. "I would love nothing more."

He smiled warmly and wiped a trailing tear from her cheek, while questioning in a baiting manner, "*Nothing*?"

"You're incorrigible."

"Since you've realized that, there *is* another matter I wish to discuss with you an—"

"Devon, you just gave me your word . . . ." Her interrupting voice and expression froze with his movement.

Sliding from his seat, he knelt before her. "We should do this properly, don't you agree?" Pulling the emerald ring from his jacket pocket, he asked, "Brianna, will you be my wife?"

Hesper was no longer concentrating on the quilt, her dark face beamed with a proud smile and appreciation that she had not been excused from the room and therefore, forced to miss this monumental occasion.

This was far more than she had expected him to do or say when he had entered the room. It was amazing that he had put so much thought into what she might want. "Devon, you astound me. We have barely been apart, *when* have you had the time to find me a ring?" Her emotion-filled voice was a testimony to her surprise and it pleased him, though not nearly as much as her expression did.

"This?" He slipped the ring over the knuckle of her left ring finger and informed her proudly, "*This* I have been carry- ing around since before you . . . ." His statement faded out, his eyes rose to hers and quickly shuffling the direction of his words, Devon revealed, "I purchased this ring for you, *weeks* before the Osborne's gala."

"Truly?" Brianna breathed in question.

Devon nodded. "I have simply been waiting for the right time to ask you to marry me. Which I might add, you have yet to agree to."

Brianna was dumbfounded as she looked from his beaming smile and sincere blue eyes to the shimmering stone that now adorned her hand. "All this time, you *knew* that you were going to ask me to marry you? Even before that night with Robert?"

His smile radiated happiness. "Yes, Flame, all along I knew." Leaning a bit closer, he petitioned, "Now about that answer?"

Tears spilled over her cheeks and she brushed them away impatiently. "Oh yes, Devon, I do want to be your wife." Relief filled her, as the words she had held back for so long, were set free.

"Thank the Heavens." He laughed when she threw her arms around his neck, nearly toppling them both to the floor in the process of her embrace. In a hushed tone he advised, "Take care, Hessie may come in to find us entangled."

"Then let's not disappoint her." She kissed him, tentative and sweet.

Pulling away at the end of their caress, Devon said, "And to think you tried to stop me from adding anything to our wedding."

"Now Devon," she teased with a broad smile, "you must never forget that a woman is entitled to change her mind. Especially," she added, drawing out her accent, "an Irish lassie."

"I will keep that in mind, Flame."

"Aye and ye should indeed," Brianna affirmed, her next kiss assuring Devon that timing was indeed everything.

◊◊◊◊◊

Larissah shoved the nearly full plate of food away and stood up from the table. She had no appetite and saw no need to force the food down when chances were good that it would come back up again within the hour.

Walking to the dining room window, she pressed her heated cheek against the cool glass and fought back tears. Tears were for the weak and she was certainly not that. She had made it through difficulties before; she could most assuredly make it through a pregnancy.

She had been haunted by Robert's gloating words since returning from Frederick. So he knew about her affair with Nate. To Larissah's way of thinking, his not confronting her and tossing Nate from his property the moment he learned of their affair, only made Robert less of a man. Still, she found some pleasure in the fantasy of how devastating such a blow must have been to his male ego. She was only sorry that she had not been the one to present him with the insult.

Lowering her hand to her growing abdomen, she thought of the baby's father. Though she had been stupid enough to fall in love, Larissah remained realistic. Nate Carter was all strength and power; he was also Robert Montgomery's stable hand and therefore had no station or money. The only thing Nate could do for Larissah, was compliment her passionate nature and give her immense pleasure.

Therefore, Larissah needed an acceptable alternative to act as the father of her child.

As she headed to her upper rooms, Larissah fought another bout of nausea. How she had ever been so foolish as to allow herself to become pregnant was beyond her.

Anyone who is fool enough to fall in love is fool enough to bear a child, her mind taunted viciously.

Halfway up the stairs, her manservant stopped her ascent. "Miz Rissah, a note come for you while you was at your meal."

Impatiently, she turned to the man. "Well . . . bring it up to me." Ripping the envelope from his fingers, she tore at the paper and read the script inside. "How respectful," she grumbled, and then turned to continue her ascent.

The invitation to Daniel and Meghan's wedding was certainly not sent out of kindness or the actual wish for her to be among the guests. It was just like the Elliott's to remain socially proper—and leaving Larissah off the invitation list was something even *they* couldn't manage without a few raised brows. They had already pushed propriety to the limit by waiting to send out the invitation until Larissah would have just two days to prepare and travel to the Baltimore event. Sardonically Larissah guessed that all of the other guests had known of the upcoming nuptials for weeks.

No matter, since Larissah didn't really want to go. But then again, she loved each opportunity she had to make Devon squirm and Brianna flinch—each of the entertaining in their attempts to hide said reactions to Larissah's presence. Maybe an opening would even present itself for her to let Devon know of the child that grew inside her.

Without turning to see if Jonas was still there, Larissah instructed, "Fetch Bess for me, I'm going to a wedding and there are plans to be made." A slow smile, filled with chilling vengeance covered her attractive face—the time for revenge was closing in.

◊◊◊◊◊

Daniel and Meghan were blessed with a glorious autumn day for their wedding. To the average observer their joining was the happiest of occasions for both the bride and groom. Only Devon and Brianna were able to sense Daniel's unease. Even as he cared for and married Meghan, his deepest love belonged to another woman.

Still, even Daniel was unable to hide the honest pleasure the first sight of his bride gave him that day.

On Caleb's proud arm, Meghan walked down the garden-path behind Daniel's Fells Point home. Dressed in a flattering gown of pale-pink satin, her face was flushed with excitement as she floated forward. Anticipation of becoming his wife brightened her graceful smile. Her blonde hair was pulled back softly from her face, thick ringlets bobbing over her creamy shoulders as she approached her future.

It was a vision Daniel would treasure when he remembered this day in years to come.

Katherine stood witness for Meghan and Devon for Daniel. The guests were few—limited to family and close friends. No more than fifteen attended in total. It took only minutes for the quietly spoken vows and words of prayer to unite the couple for life.

Several times during the service, Brianna felt Devon's eyes on her. She tried to avoid it, but could not help returning his intense stare. As his eyes caressed her, Brianna felt the ring burning upon her finger. Subconsciously, she glanced down and rubbed her fingertips over the set-stone.

Since the day that he had made their commitment official, Brianna was relieved to know that he had intended to propose before being forced into it. Her new home became more secure each day and nothing would alter that happy existence.

She was truly home at last.

◊◊◊◊◊

Let them have their temporary happiness, Larissah thought as she witnessed the tender glances Devon and Brianna exchanged. Though seeing them so happy made her feel ill, Larissah would allow their sweet fairy tale existence to progress a bit more before she devastated it for them. The longer they went uninterrupted, the greater her final revenge would be in sundering their romantic haven.

Larissah made sure Devon saw her today—though she didn't speak to him. If she left now, without a word, she would succeed in either making him believe that he had finally convinced her that they had no future, or he would wonder at her uncharacteristic behavior. Either way, she would have a small victory for it.

The introduction of Mr. and Mrs. Daniel Elliott was made, Daniel kissed his new bride chastely on the lips, and Larissah stood to make her exit without attempting to extend even the pretext of congratulations.

◊◊◊◊◊

Three weeks after their wedding, Daniel brought his wife to Misty Heights. He and Devon were departing to Boston, Massachusetts on business a few days later and Meghan and Brianna would stay together while the men were away. An added bonus for their early arrival was the extension of their honeymoon. Though Daniel and Meghan appeared a few days before the trip, few in the household saw the newlyweds unless the couple chose to attend one of the daily meals.

Devon decided that he would use his spare time before the trip to woo Brianna ever closer to him. Canceling all callers and appointments, he made plans for them to spend days riding in the sun and share pleasant secluded afternoons together.

As luck would have it, a downpour lasted throughout one of their last days, stranding Devon and Brianna to finding their own means of entertainment in the parlor.

By late evening, Brianna reached the end of her patience with the weather. "Devon, I cannot bear another moment inside."

Over the book they were sharing, Devon looked at her with amusement. "Wherever did that come from?"

"From being cooped up for hours on end."

"Is my company that appalling?" He teased.

"Stop fishing for compliments. This rain is driving me insane."

With a charming smile that warmed Brianna to her toes, he mocked, "I thought that you would be used to the rain. Ireland is well known for such weather."

Rolling her eyes at him, she admonished, "I was used to that *in* Ireland, but I have become spoiled by the varying weather in my new home."

He smiled and chose not to opinionate that she had become spoiled by more than just the weather. "Be that as it may, there is little we can do about the circumstances. Not only is it wet outside, but it is dark and the air is chilled."

Standing, she grinned at him impishly. "Are you afraid of the dark or getting wet, Devon?"

"Neither; I simply do not relish the idea of catching cold just so that you might get some fresh air. The weather should break by morning and then you can spend the entire day outdoors with Meghan."

Brianna pouted prettily, "But I don't want to be outside with Meghan, I want to be with you."

Devon gave her a look that a parent would offer their errant offspring. "Brianna, don't be childish."

As soon as the devilish light entered her eyes, Devon knew he was in trouble. "You haven't seen childish yet, Devon." Her laughter trailed behind, as she dashed toward the kitchen.

Before he could reach her, Brianna burst through the back entrance of the house to twirl with arms outstretched in the rain. Standing in the threshold, Devon demanded, "Brianna McClaran, you will come back in the house at once."

Stopping her movements, she pushed the already rain-soaked hair from her face and taunted, "Only if you come out and bring me back in."

Watching her, Devon did not know if he wanted to laugh or moan. She looked unbearably tempting as the falling rain plastered her clothing against her skin. "Brianna, please."

Smiling broadly, she crooked her finger and in the huskiest voice she had learned, invited, "Won't you come out and play in the rain, Devon?"

"Minx," he growled as he stepped from the shelter into the cold rain. "Now we shall both be sick from the cold."

Brianna allowed herself bold freedom. It seemed the closer their wedding day came, the more anxious she grew for the touch and knowledge Devon would give her. Those feelings mixed with the fresh air and the rain caused Brianna to overflow with exhilaration. Giddy-excitement overtaking her innocence she offered, "Then come to me so that I might warm you."

"A *persistent* minx at that." Grabbing her around the waist, Devon kissed her, the rain mingling with their lips.

Kissing had become second nature to them in the last weeks. Each day that passed, Devon sensed what little shyness Brianna had around him dissolving and her desire for his touch growing dangerously. Still, he clung tightly to his resolve. Evan now, when Brianna's hands began to roam boldly over his chest and shoulders, Devon drew back and sternly accused, "You truly do wish to be the death of me, don't you?"

"Oh no, Devon," Brianna reached her hands up and slowly unbound her hair, the tendrils tumbling down and soaking in the rain almost before they lay against her shoulders. All innocence and yearning, she promised, "I intend to keep you alive and well, for a very, *very* long time."

Before he realized her intent, Brianna swung the loose tendrils from side to side, drenching Devon's face and chest in the attack and dousing most of the desire-laden imaginings she had just presented him, in the process.

Devon clamped his arms around her in a stilling band. Brianna tried to wiggle out of his embrace, but succeeded only in slipping in the mud and pulling them both to the ground. Squealing with laughter, she almost missed the gleam in his eyes as he brought a handful of clay up from the ground around them.

"Now what are you thinking to do with that muck, Devon Elliott?" Her eyes narrowed as she watched closely for his next move.

Nonchalantly continuing to work the sludge through his

fingers, Devon replied, "Make a mud pie."

The wariness in her green eyes grew. "That doesn't sound very appetizing."

Looking from her face, to the clump of watery dirt in his hand, Devon agreed, "It's not, but considering your teasing, it's certainly a better choice for our recreation."

From their current position, Brianna had easy access to his lips and took advantage of it. She kissed him as he had taught her, her teeth nibbling his full lower lip, her tongue lightly—just barely—caressing his mouth in a pleasure much more intense than her complete invasion would have given.

Pulling away, Devon admitted, "Perhaps I was mistaken."

Brianna smiled. "I thought I'd never hear those treasured words from your sweet lips, Devon." Concentrating on her game, Brianna was unprepared for the handful of mud Devon squeezed between his palms and her cheeks. The sticky dirt instantly began sliding down her face to plop in the puddle their antics were creating.

Brianna's eyes—or what he could see of them amid the mud—went from wide-open orbs of surprise to narrowed slits of retaliation as she smeared Devon's face with the brown ooze, too.

Trying to avoid another onslaught from him, Brianna endeavored to move away, but succeeded only in squirming until the suction of the ground had her fully and tightly against the front of Devon. Her continuous attempts to stand created hot friction between their bodies until finally Devon growled between clenched teeth, "For the love of God, Brianna, *stop* moving."

Needing several tries as well, Devon finally accomplished breaking their contact. Standing above her, both of them covered in mud, he could only shake his head in amusement. With ease, Devon bent down, plucked Brianna from the ground and strode toward the house with her in his arms. "What I am surely *not* mistaken about is that you *must* learn patience.

"Why, when there are far more interesting things I wish to learn?" Brianna's satisfied smirk was quickly replaced with a shriek of sheer surprise when Devon dunked her—head and shoulders—into the rain barrel beside the kitchen entrance.

Pulling her back out of the cold water effortlessly, Devon

carried her sputtering mud-caked body through the door and closed it firmly behind them with a kick of his dirty boot.

Chapter Eighteen

The house was quiet; everyone had been asleep for hours when Brianna tucked the cheesecloth cover over Hesper's freshly baked apple pie—now containing one less slice. Hoping that the midnight snack she had just ingested would help her rest better, Brianna picked up her candle and headed toward her bedroom.

Over the last weeks, she had been having a wonderful time with Devon. Tonight their outdoor escapade was no exception. Life was so much easier since her true emotions for him were uninhibited and he no longer hid his feelings from her either. They would have a good marriage and happy life together.

At the top of the staircase, Brianna lifted the candle a bit higher to spread the circle of light. Tiptoeing along the corridor, she thought of her parents and how much they would have been pleased with the direction her life had taken. It was a sad irony that without the terrible loss of those beloved people, it was unlikely she would have ever had the opportunity to fall in love with Devon.

"I suppose all things truly do happen for a reason," she muttered to herself and—as though on cue—the door to Devon's bedchamber opened directly beside her.

◊◊◊◊◊

Devon wanted to sleep. However, rest was not *all* his body craved.

The memory of Brianna's playful teasing in the rain was

torturing him. Every time he closed his eyes, he could see her, drenched from head to toe, beckoning him—her rich laughter luring him. Burdening him further was the symphony of pleasures his energetic brother and sister-in-law were serenading him with. Apparently, *they* didn't feel the need for sleep.

There were simply too many factors working against his efforts to slumber, so when Devon's stomach grumbled a protest, he gave up the battle. If he recalled correctly, Hesper had just baked an apple pie. Perhaps a piece would calm his nerves enough for sleep.

It was late, so Devon only put on his breeches before opening his bedroom door.

He blinked two times before he realized that Brianna was *truly* standing in front of him.

Devon did not even consider why Brianna was wandering through their home at this hour—he didn't really care. The only thing he knew was *what* he wanted and that he no longer wanted to wait for it.

Without a word, he stretched his arm out and wrapped his fingers around her hand. Brianna made no protest as Devon pulled her back into the room he had been prepared to leave. There was no sound except that of their tense breathing. They focused only on the present. Neither wanted to think about what was proper; they allowed their souls to lead the way.

Devon remained silent. He would wait and see if her bravado of the last few days would hold out. He would let her lead the way and he would *not* force her, but he'd be *damned* before he would stop her any more either.

Brianna reached out, her fingers rubbing his cheek sweetly. "Devon?" The uncertainty was clear in her eyes as she searched Devon's face for answers—she feared being turned away again.

Devon would not disappoint her this time. "Flame?"

Her hand dropped to his chest, her intense jade gaze watching for his reaction. "Touch me," she whispered.

Her bold request ensnared Devon like a heady aphrodisiac. Nothing else mattered but the two of them. He held her to him like a lifeline, every inch of her molded against his body. "I must be dreaming again."

"Then I pray that you continue to sleep."

Gently, Devon lifted her in his arms and carried her across the room to his bed. Placing her upon the mattress, he moved in beside her and brought her head to rest on his shoulder. "Brianna, if you stay here with me, if we spend this night together, do you realize where it will lead?" He kissed her brow lightly. "Everything will change."

Brianna appreciated Devon's consideration and the opportunity for her to change her mind, but she wasn't about to take it. "I know, but we are to be married anyway. I no longer want to wonder what I am missing with you. I do not want to worry about what is right or wrong."

That was all the answer Devon needed.

Taking her lips with his once more, his fingers made fast work of the tiny bows holding Brianna's sleeping-gown closed. With her flesh bared, he took his mouth from hers and his hungry gaze blazed a path his hands and lips soon followed. His tongue trailed, his mouth pulled and Brianna thought she would never be able to breathe normally again.

She was not shy; she wanted to learn and therefore held nothing back. Shifting her body, she offered Devon total access to her aching form and felt her nerves come to life under the grazing of his hand, the warmth of his mouth, the way he seemed to be everywhere at once.

Devon moved his hands to deepen their intimacy and Brianna clutched at him in desperation. She had never known such pleasure. Every inch of her body seemed alight with a flame only Devon could control. The rhythm of his touch changed torturously and her body moved to him, answering his primitive call without hesitation.

Brianna wanted to weep with the ecstasy of his caress. Gripping his shoulders tightly, she allowed Devon's skilled touch to lift her into a world of swirling colors. Brianna closed her smoldering green eyes to savor the pleasure he gave her. With the awe-filled sounds she was sensuously whimpering, Devon knew that it would not be long before she plunged over the edge of passion.

"Open your eyes, Flame. Look at me." His tone was not harsh, but neither did it broach any argument.

Brianna looked into Devon's powerful stare and felt her world explode.

All control of her body dissolved in a liquid passion and she called out to Devon, his name mingling with her whimpers of absolute satisfaction. Thousands of colors flashed behind her closed lids. Devon claimed her lips, forcing a new surge of heat to sear to the very core of her, bringing with it a pinnacle mixture of pleasure and pain. When at last, the ultimate of her exclamations tore forth it was captured by Devon's ardent kiss.

Devon ground his teeth, forcing himself to restrain. His nostrils flared as he felt her release against his hand and every instinct in him cried out to be obeyed. However, in the deepest parts of his heart, despite what he had started, Devon knew it was not time. No matter how much both of their bodies wanted it, they would have to wait. He wanted to have Brianna when she was his wife, not before. He would not chance her lamenting such a momentous time in their lives.

When Devon took his hands away and held her against his body, Brianna hid her embarrassment from him by burying her face into his shoulder.

Devon would allow her no regrets.

Tilting her head so that she was forced to look into his endless blue eyes, Devon offered, "Do not hide from me, my Flame. You have nothing to be ashamed of."

She smiled timidly. "But the way I behaved . . ."

"Was wonderful." He kissed her lightly.

Brianna looked sincerely relieved. "I was afraid that you would be disgusted, that I was too loud and anxious and . . ."

Devon chuckled softly. "You were exactly how I wanted you to be. It gives me pleasure watching you."

Her lashes dropped and the embarrassment returned, but she snuggled closer. "Devon?"

He was enjoying the feel of her resting comfortably against him and muttered, "Mmm?"

"What do we do now?"

He smiled into the darkness. "We sleep."

"Oh." She sounded truly disheartened and Devon laughed at his newfound prize.

"Tonight was enough for now, Flame. When I return, we will be married and then I will show you more."

"Much more?" she asked, her voice incredulous, the innocence in her wide eyes blatant.

"Undeniably." Devon smiled at her curiosity; he was indeed marrying an eager pupil—a fact that did not disappoint him in the least.

Brianna realized now that she had apparently known only the basics before tonight and this was a far cry from the wanderings of her imagination. "If there is *more, how* will I ever be able to look at you again?"

Laughter rimmed his response. "Oh, I imagine you will find a way, love."

"And will I like that? The *others*, I mean?"

"I daresay you will enjoy that even more than tonight." Devon's tone had taken on a different effect, a masculine sound that gave her chills.

"Faith and Begora."

Her gasped exclamation made him roar with laughter.

"Devon, hush, we do not need *everyone* knowing that I am in here with you."

The truth of her words penetrated his amusement. "Very well, Flame. I will try to control myself."

"I should say it's a bit late for that." Devon considered explaining her mistaken belief, but before he could begin, Brianna questioned in a more serious tone, "Devon, was that wrong? What I . . . you . . . I mean, what *we* just did?"

He didn't laugh this time. He had known she might need this reassurance. "It may have been early, but since we will soon be married, I don't see it as wrong. There will be no more though until after the ceremony. What a man and his wife share together is to be special and I intend for it to be exactly that on our wedding night." Pulling away so that he could see her more clearly he questioned, "Did you mind it? Was my touch uncomfortable to you in any way?"

Her face flamed even redder than before. "What do *you* think?"

Kissing the tip of her nose, he returned, "I think, my Flame, you are going to enjoy married life very much."

Snuggling down beside him and closing her eyes, she agreed, "I think you are right, Devon."

◊◊◊◊◊

Devon woke to find the space beside him disappointingly empty. It was daylight, though, and he agreed that such discretion was wise. There was certainly no need for the entire household to know about their master and soon to be mistress' late night activities.

Rolling from his bed, Devon dressed for the day. Pulling on a clean pair of breeches, he walked to his washstand and splashed water on his face. A movement in the mirror caught his attention and through it he watched Daniel enter his room unannounced.

Scooping up a towel, he turned to his younger brother while dabbing droplets of water from his cheeks. "Good morning, Daniel. I would ask how you slept but considering the sounds coming through the wall it was quite evident that you *didn't*."

Smiling, Daniel sat on the edge of his brother's unmade bed. "You are just jealous that you were not enjoying the same situation."

"True enough," Devon replied with a mild twinge of regret. "And how fares your new wife this morning? Is she even out of bed yet?"

Daniel enjoyed his brother's good-natured ribbing. "Yes. I allowed her to find refuge with Brianna for the day."

"Brianna? Is she awake already?" Devon allowed his features to show nothing of what he was feeling.

"Mmm, she's been up for quite a while." Daniel watched his brother closely. "In fact, I thought for certain I heard her moving around long before dawn."

"I didn't notice," Devon answered honestly, while looking down at the buttons on his shirt as he fastened them.

"Must have been the wind," Daniel murmured. Though he gave in to Devon's words easily, Daniel still had his doubts about their truthfulness. Devon was conveniently forgetting that sound traveled both ways through the wall. However, now that they were engaged, it did not matter to Daniel what Devon and Brianna did behind closed doors. He was simply glad to see his brother so happy.

"Was there something other than nighttime noises that you wanted to discuss with me?"

Leaving his musings behind, Daniel replied, "Yes, I came to see if you were up to a morning ride. The ladies are busy with plans of their own and it has been far too long since I have traveled over our land on horseback."

Devon was instantly transported back to their younger years. "Will we be racing?"

Daniel stood and walked toward the door with his brother, "Only if you intend to lose."

"Never," Devon vowed, closing the door to his room after they passed into the hallway.

◊◊◊◊◊

The evening meal of blackened catfish, sweet potatoes and lima beans was rushed. Meghan yawned several times before claiming the need for rest—an excuse Devon had no doubt to be true.

Daniel managed to inform his company three different times that he still needed to prepare for his early departure. Devon said nothing, merely gave his brother an all-knowing smile. As soon as their plates were clean, the newlyweds left the room hand in hand.

"It is good to see him so happy," Brianna said, watching the scene with Devon. "I had worried that he would not be."

Devon studied Brianna a moment before commenting, "Daniel would not have married Meghan if he would not have been happy. Everything works out in the end."

"Even for Tansey?" Brianna's concern for her friend was clear in the worried tone of her whispered words.

"I am sure that she is making the most of her freedom. Do not fret. Remember, she promised to return home one day and I am sure she intends to uphold her word."

"I know. I'm just disappointed that she won't be here for our wedding."

Devon understood. The women had become dear friends and even with their cultural differences, Tansey was more of a younger sister to Devon than a servant. "Brianna, you know how difficult her being here would make Daniel's life, even if only for a short visit."

"Of course I do. That's partly why I didn't beg her to

stay."

"I thought you considered Meghan a friend, too."

His point hit home and Brianna blushed with her reply. "I do. She is a wonderful friend,"—an unintended look of frustration passed over her face—"when she is not moody or complaining." With a shrug, Brianna guessed, "She wasn't this difficult on the *Sea Enchantress*. Hopefully when she is feeling better, she will return to her old self."

Devon's concern and curiosity was immediate. "Daniel did not mention she was ill."

"Meghan assures me 'tis nothing serious; a headache and weak stomach."

With a roll of his eyes, Devon suggested, "Perhaps if she got some rest she would feel better."

Brianna's bewilderment lasted only a moment before her cheeks flamed bright red and Devon laughed at her reaction.

"You're nearly as unbearable as Meghan. At least once she's feeling better, I'll only have to deal with her lectures about my lack of excitement over what *she* believes is important in a ladies life."

Devon grinned, thoroughly entertained by Brianna's accurate description of his sister-in-law.

Uncertain as to what his expression meant, Brianna felt the need to clarify, "She *is* rather opinionated."

His words leading, Devon inquired, "Is that a quality you dislike?"

It was Brianna's turn to laugh. "I am marrying *you* aren't I?"

His blue eyes darkened with sheer pleasure. "Yes, you are."

Brianna tingled from head to toe. Deciding that was a far too dangerous feeling where Devon was concerned, she told him, "Which is why I feel so sorry for Tansey. I cannot imagine not being able to spend my life with you."

Thrilled with her declaration, Devon wanted to cling to some happiness during his trip and so turned the subject from Daniel's entangled love life. Leaning back in his chair, Devon ordered, "Enough of this depressing talk. Tell me; is everything ready for the wedding?"

Brianna smiled. "Yes, I just need the groom to return home

in *promptly* two weeks so we have a few days before our wedding to finish last-minute details."

Devon chuckled. "Wild horses couldn't keep me from returning in time for our wedding, Flame. However, I *am* afraid that I will not be very good company for the evening as—unlike my brother—I honestly *do* have much to prepare for my morning departure." Standing, he walked around the table and offered his hand. "Would you care to retire now, as well?"

Sheer disappointment washed over Brianna. With a sigh she offered, "I suppose I will walk up with you since I have no wish to stay down here alone."

They were each silent in their own thoughts as they walked hand in hand up the staircase. Devon led them to Brianna's door before letting go of her hand. "I will be gone before you wake in the morning, Flame."

She didn't want him to leave, but knew that he had no choice. "Then I shall miss you until you are returned to me, Devon." She wanted to say more, to ask him to spend the night with her again, but could not summon the courage.

Devon was fighting similar urges, but he too left them unvoiced. Leaning down, he kissed her softly. "I will be back as soon as I can."

"Promise it," Brianna urged, needed to prolong their separation.

"I swear it." Then he kissed her in a way that was sure to linger with her throughout the entirety of their separation.

◊◊◊◊◊

By the end of the first week of Devon's absence, Brianna missed him desperately. She longed to hear his laughter, to see the range of emotions that could light his startling blue eyes.

By the middle of the following week, she would even have been grateful to witness the disdainful and authoritative tone of his that made her cringe with anger.

Meghan was in worse shape than Brianna. The newly married woman would flit between humors of sheer delight when speaking about Daniel, to almost simultaneous tears. Lately, she was so moody that Brianna was never sure how or even *if* she wanted to approach her.

Still, considering that Brianna's only other option for company during the next week was Larissah, she had no problem choosing to overlook her soon-to-be sister-in-laws grumpiness. If Brianna were honest, she probably wasn't the best of company these days either.

Checking the air outside and finding it cool, but clear, Brianna thought that maybe a buggy ride would do Meghan some good. With a lighter step, Brianna headed toward Daniel and Meghan's rooms to extend the invitation.

◊◊◊◊◊

The illness Meghan had been fighting off was finally getting the best of her.

The sound of Hesper's throaty alto had awakened her.

The scent of frying ham sent her bolting from bed and toward her chamber pot.

Sometime later, she made her way weakly back to the bed and pulled the covers up over her quaking form. Whatever she had eaten was certainly wreaking havoc on her insides. Closing her eyes, she tried to sleep again, but the air around her was heavy and everything seemed to be spinning.

She mistook the sound of her closing door for her pounding head and was therefore unaware of Brianna's presence until the other woman spoke.

Seeing the condition of her friend, Brianna's jovial steps abruptly changed to a stride of concern. "Meghan, what is the matter with you? Are you sick?"

Meghan afforded a glance from beneath barely open lids and forced through clenched teeth, "What makes you think that there is something wrong?"

Brianna smiled and perched herself on the side of the bed.

The movement threw Meghan into action again and throwing the blankets aside, she dodged Brianna and barely made it to the hidden chamber pot before getting sick again.

Brianna waited for the bout of retching to end before peeking around the room divider. "Shall I help you back to bed?"

Pale faced and shaking, Meghan could only nod.

Helping Meghan stand, Brianna put a supportive arm around the weak woman and walked her slowly back to bed.

Once Meghan was snugly tucked beneath the quilts, Brianna worried, "I thought you would be feeling better by now."

Meghan's eyes remained closed. "I will be fine by midday."

Brianna's brow furrowed. "I'm going to get Hesper. I'm sure she will have something to help you."

Just as Brianna laid her hand on the doorknob, Meghan suggested, "Perhaps she could begin by *ceasing* to fry that infernal meat." Smiling at her friend's outburst, Brianna headed for the kitchen in search of assistance.

◊◊◊◊◊

Nearly an hour later, Meghan had been bathed, her hair dried and clothing changed. The bed linens had been stripped and replaced and Meghan's cheeks had regained some color, though she still looked uncomfortable beneath her haven of blankets.

"Well, what's her illness?" Brianna impatiently asked for the fifth time since Hesper had entered the room. Just as when she had inquired before, the older woman continued the task of cleaning the mess of Meghan's nausea, ignoring her mistress for the work at hand.

A sound from the bed finally brought an answer from the caregiver. "Hessie, *please* answer her so that she will leave and I might get some sleep. She is going to wear a hole through the floor with her nervous pacing."

Brianna looked only mildly offended. "Such thanks for getting you help. I will remember that in the future."

Rather than comment, Meghan simply turned and stuck her tongue out at Brianna.

"Oh, *that* certainly improves your appearance," Brianna mocked.

Hessie laughed at the girls. Understandably, the older woman had not been fond of Meghan initially. It had not taken her long to warm up to Daniel's new wife though. Meghan Elliott was a kind woman who dearly loved her husband. Even with her daughter fleeing from a broken heart, Hesper could not deny such loyalty as Meghan showed Daniel.

Smiling broadly, Hessie announced, "Miz Meghan goin' to

be fine. She jus' goin' to have a baby, that all."

Meghan attempted to sit up in bed, but the dizziness overwhelmed her again and she flopped back to the pillows. "That's *all*?" she echoed in complete surprise.

Brianna was momentarily stunned, but as Hessie's words sank in, she felt happiness engulf her entire body. "Oh, Meghan, Daniel will be so happy."

"A baby," Meghan stated dumbly. Brianna's words slowly registered, a smile of complete joy covered her sickly features and she murmured, "Yes, Daniel will be thrilled."

Chapter Nineteen

In Boston, Devon and Daniel were not having much suc-
cess and continuously haggled over the price for the warehouse
they wanted to purchase for Chase-Elliott-McClaran Shipping.

"The amount he is asking is outrageous, Daniel, and we
both know it."

Looking across the restaurant table at his older sibling,
Daniel concurred, "Yes, but it is as *low* as he is willing to go."
Downing an oyster from its half-shell, he followed it with a
healthy swill of ale and the remainder of his comment, "You
know as well as I do how much that piece of property will benefit us."

"Of course I do. Otherwise I would not have traveled to
this city at all." Devon looked around the establishment with a
frown. "You know my great dislike for the area." Cracking
into the orange-shelled lobster tail on his plate, Devon pulled a
clump of juicy white meat away. Pleased with the lobster's
flavor, Devon informed his brother, "After several attempts,
this establishment is the *only* pleasure I am able to find in a
town full of pretentious snobs."

Daniel did not share his brother's opinion of Boston; to him
it was a thriving metropolis, ripe for business and abounding in
opportunity for any that chose to call it home. Nervously, Daniel looked around the crowded room, reassured that no one else
patronizing the oyster house had overheard Devon's rude
comment.

"In all likelihood, once this particular venture is finished,
you will no longer find it necessary to return above the Mason-

Dixon Line again. I will gladly take care of all business trans-
actions here."

"You will find no argument from me," Devon agreed readily.

Looking at his brother doubtfully, Daniel admitted, "A fact
that is staggering to my mind."

Smiling in his self-assured way, Devon shrugged. "I would
be a fool to attempt my business in Boston. Certainly my
wisecracking brother would fare far better than I ever could,
especially amid all the other cunning businessmen around
here."

Looking only mildly unsure, Daniel laughed, remarking, "I
will try to interpret that as a compliment and consider it your
point that Boston is not your favorite place to be."

Honestly, Devon answered, "The only places I care to visit
less are Hell and Salem." Gulping his final bite of lobster, he
added with a smirk, "*Precisely* in *that* order."

"Mmm, and the fact that you have been kept so far and
long from Brianna does not add to your love of this trip in the
least, I'm certain."

"*You* are correct." Sighing, Devon veered the topic back to
its original track. "The price, as you know, is not beyond our
means. If you truly believe that this venture will benefit the
company, then I will agree to it."

"I do, Devon. We both know the other interested buyer is
the reason the price is so high. If not for that man, we could
have walked away nearly two hundred dollars wealthier."

Disgusted, Devon suggested, "Chances are great that in this
city the other buyer is a plant to urge us to buy."

"You may be right, but there is no way to prove it." Teasing then, he added, "And since your nightly company is nothing in comparison to that of my new bride, I long to be finished
here and return to her and all her charms." With mock shame,
he added, "Of course I mean no disrespect to your fine company."

"Of course." Devon rolled his eyes and wiped his fingers
on the linen napkin in his lap. "And were *you* an auburn-haired
creature with flashing green eyes, I would have enjoyed my
own trip far more—even *here*."

Throwing coins on the table to cover their meals, Devon

grabbed his over coat from the seat-rack and concluded, "Come along and we shall divest ourselves of a large sum of money, buy your building and return home to the women we long for."

Proof of Daniel's eager agreement was visible as he grabbed his own overcoat, slid it on and darted out the door ahead of Devon.

◊◊◊◊◊

So intent were they on their own conversation and departure, neither Devon nor Daniel noticed the woman seated at a nearby table. She had noticed them however and reveled silently in the sight of Daniel's face. Though it was hard for her to hear him talk about his new wife so adoringly, she was glad that he had found happiness with her.

From the beginning, that was all Tansey had wanted for him and her time away hadn't lessened that desire in the least.

◊◊◊◊◊

Three days after learning of her pregnancy, Meghan made her way downstairs. Brianna looked up to see her entering the dining room for breakfast. Taking the seat beside Brianna, Meghan gingerly pushed the empty plate away from its spot in front of her. "Brianna, I thought maybe we could do something today."

Eyeing her pale friend curiously, Brianna shoved a forkful of steaming sausage into her mouth and watched as Meghan's pasty-white skin shaded to a milky green hue. "Are you sure you are up to an outing? Quite honestly, you do not look your best."

Forcing a shaky smile, Meghan disregarded her words. "I will be fine by midmorning."

"If you are certain," Brianna faltered. "I *would* love to get out of the house, but I don't want Daniel returning to a sick wife. He and Devon would both blame me for not taking better care of you." After the look she gained from the previous bite of food, Brianna opted to end her meal—a choice that visibly relieved the ill woman. Standing, she asked, "What do you have in mind?"

Wobbling on her shaky legs, Meghan suggested, "Something with lots of fresh air."

Quickly thinking through her options, Brianna clapped her hands together and enthusiastically promised her friend, "I have just the thing."

◊◊◊◊◊

Larissah climbed the steps leading to the front door of Misty Heights. Her timing was perfect. Devon was away, leaving Brianna far more susceptible to the doubt Larissah was about to place in her mind.

When Larissah reached the door, she glanced down to recheck her appearance. The dress she had chosen left no question of her physical condition. She had rounded out quite nicely and just that morning had felt the first stirrings of movement within her swollen womb.

Raising her hand to the doorknocker, Larissah did not get the chance to lay her fingers upon it before the door opened in front of her.

Brianna's cheerful smile evaporated the moment she saw her cousin standing before her. Brianna knew that her displeasure was conveyed clearly when the satisfied gleam in Larissah's eyes glowed brighter.

"To what do I owe this honor?" Brianna asked with significantly false appreciation.

Larissah straightened an imaginary wrinkle from the skirt of her gown, forcing Brianna to wait for her reply. "I have news of Devon that I think you may be interested in, *dear* cousin."

Brianna's skin crawled with apprehension, her body tense with anticipation, but it was Meghan, coming up behind Brianna, who spoke next. "Is everything alright? Have you word from Daniel or Devon?"

Larissah's eyes flitted to Meghan as she came out the door to stand beside Brianna. "No, but what I have to say is really only a matter for family."

Brianna was quick to retaliate to this rude dismissal. "Meghan *is* my family."

Larissah looked on them with pity. "Oh, yes, I would suppose you Irish would accept one another, even if no one else will have you."

Meghan glared at Larissah and reminded her coldly, "Devon and Daniel chose *us* over you."

Larissah tilted her head to the side, "Which only proves there really *is* no accounting for taste."

Pointedly looking Meghan over, Larissah finished, "*Especially* considering the way *you* look. Are you ill, Meghan?"

"Little you care," Brianna spat.

Larissah offered an expression that suggested Brianna was exactly right.

Meghan smirked in return, while proudly announcing, "I can imagine your joy when I tell you that I'm not ill but expecting Daniel's child."

"Well, Meghan," Larissah began with a surprising smile, "even if I'm *not* thrilled that you and Daniel have procreated, I *am* in a position to sympathize with your physical discomfort." Pulling the material of her dark day-dress taut against her swelled stomach, Larissah forced her point home as she smiled triumphantly.

Brianna felt ill. There was no chance of concealing the effect Larissah's obvious condition had on her. Still, she managed to control her words enough to ask, "What has your bastard child to do with us?"

Looking sincerely sympathetic, Larissah answered, "Not *us*, Brianna; and mind you, this child is no bastard." She rested her hand over her swollen stomach. "Your fiancée is the babe's father."

The air closed in on her, but Brianna fought the feeling off. "You must truly think I am a fool. The child is not Devon's. He told me that he has not been with you since bringing me here from Ireland."

The soft sound of shock beside her, told Brianna that Daniel had obviously not shared the details of Devon's affairs with Meghan.

Larissah's short laugh was cruel and self-assured. "The fact that you are a *fool* is neither lessened or intensified by what I think."

"Your opinion doesn't matter to me, Larissah. Only your lies are of concern to me now."

"And what of *Devon's* lies?" The moment she had been waiting for these past four months had finally come. At last she would begin her ruse and make Devon hers for all time.

"We have no secrets, only honesty." The force that Brianna wanted to convey was lacking in her tone.

"Then surely he told you he came to see me the day you arrived from Ireland."

Brianna felt a slight victory. "As a matter of fact, he did."

Larissah raised a light brow. "But did he tell you *everything* that happened during our visit?" She smiled, her confidence building when Brianna paled, proving that her words were doing their job. "Was he devoted enough, *honest* enough to confide in you how, with my generous persuasion, he decided to extend his pleasurable visit with me before returning home to you?"

"You lie." Brianna's tone sounded uncertain even to her own ears.

With precision, Larissah slammed Brianna's doubt into full swing, "I could offer a detailed summary if you like, but somehow I doubt your innocent ears or loving heart could handle that incriminating information." With a nasty smile she concluded, "Brianna, there is no sense denying the truth. It will only prolong the inevitable and make your agony all the more unbearable."

"What a terrible, *hateful*, woman you are." Amazement filled Meghan's blaming words. "How could Devon have *ever* loved someone like you?"

Larissah's smug smile was fierce and she clucked her tongue in a correcting manner. "Meghan, having been in the bed of an Elliott man, *you* should know well that *love* has nothing to do with what Devon and I share."

During this exchange, Brianna stood in pain-filled shock. The overwhelming pleasure Larissah was receiving from the entire scene made the younger woman feel physically ill. How could a person enjoy causing another such pain? It was all entirely beyond Brianna's realm of understanding.

Suddenly, Brianna felt the need for something familiar to hold onto and grasped for something tangible that would make Devon seem less guilty of his part in this unfolding nightmare. Without thought of the consequences, she grasped out blindly.

"Since then? Have there been other times since that day?" Just as soon as they were spoken, Brianna regretted her words. Her panicked attempt to clear Devon of this treachery placed her at the mercy of her vindictive cousin.

"I don't see how that is any of *your* concern." Larissah sounded far more proper than she had a right to.

"He is *my* fiancée, Larissah. I want to know."

Larissah would let her languish in her curiosity. Rubbing her palms suggestively along the sides of her inflated abdomen, she gloated, "Does it really matter *if* or *when*, Brianna? It should be enough for you to know that the afternoon in question was enough to make him mine forever."

"No," Meghan intervened, seething as she felt Brianna faltering beside her. "It was enough to create a babe and make you a whore to anyone with sight."

Larissah narrowed her eyes as she declared, "Oh, no, you insolent Irish trash. What it has made me is an *Elliott*."

Brianna felt suddenly numb. It reminded her of the dreadful helplessness brought on by the death of a loved one. Weariness and tears filling her eyes, Brianna looked to her cousin and stated in distressed exhaustion, "Fine, Larissah. It is finished; you have won."

Larissah's smile was full of unwarranted pride. "As I have always known I would."

With all of Brianna's faith and dreams in Devon crumbling around her, Larissah turned away from the women and toward her waiting buggy.

The only thing that pleased Larissah more than Brianna's words and expression, was the horror filled sobs that sounded behind her just as the driver flicked the reins against the horses back and completed her departure.

Chapter Twenty

Devon and Daniel arrived home two days before Christmas. Meghan welcomed her husband home with a kiss that left no doubt to any witnessing it that she had missed him just as greatly as he had her.

Devon was sorely disappointed that Brianna had claimed a headache and missed his homecoming by remaining in her room. When Daniel and Meghan retired immediately following supper, Devon went to bed and warmed himself with dreams of how Brianna would welcome him when she felt better.

He prayed that she would not be ill for long.

◊◊◊◊◊

In her room, Brianna was not as content as Devon. She had missed him desperately and staying away from him was sheer torture. *If he wants a warm reception, let him find it with Larissah*, her mind ruthlessly advised.

Nevertheless, even those warnings didn't change the fact that she wanted to go to him, demand the truth from him. Brianna needed to hear it from him; she *deserved* to hear it from him.

Her internal battle continued; *He has had ample opportunity to be honest with you already, what would make this occasion any different?* Tears rolled down her cheeks and a soft sob escaped her heart-broken form. Brianna knew that the faster she accepted that truth, the better off she would be.

Snuggling down into the warmth of her blanketed bed, Brianna closed her eyes. She wanted to sleep, to clear her mind. There was so much she needed to sort out, so much to plan, that her thoughts could not find rest.

Each time she replayed Larissah's gloating tone and harmful words, Brianna tried to find some flaw, but could not. Everything Larissah had happily accused rang true. In the end, that made Devon the liar, not Larissah.

"How could he have done this? How could he have made such sweet promises to me, while she carried his child?" Yet even with all that she had learned, Brianna's love for Devon was a constant. With depressing certainty, she knew that if he came to her now, bared all and begged her forgiveness, her broken heart would not deny him.

These thoughts infuriated and disgusted her at the same time. She didn't want to love him anymore, but how does a person just stop loving?

Wiping the tears away, she forced her strength to the front and encouraged aloud, "Brianna, get yourself under control. Where's your dignity?" With a shaky breath, she thought of what she was worth and knew that Devon had failed her miserably.

Brianna decided then that she would fight her feelings—fight *Devon* every step of the way. She mentally braced herself to remain firm when he started to plead with his eyes, his handsome smile, his touch, and his empty words . . . .

Brianna was ready to cry again.

Just as sleep was mercifully upon her, Brianna heard Jonathan's voice clearly. *No matter how far or how long you are away, you always have a home and family with us.*

She would go home again. Home to love and safety and trust.

Home to Ireland.

◊◊◊◊◊

Brianna's eyes were heavy the next morning. She moved around her room slowly, taking her time dressing for the day. Just because she felt defeated and weary was no reason to look the part and her extended toilette gave her mind and body time to prepare for what was to come.

When she could stall no longer, Brianna walked toward her door, knowing that each step brought her closer to a dreaded confrontation with Devon and her broken heart.

In the parlor below, Devon awaited Brianna anxiously. As soon as he had come down that morning, he had made himself comfortable, determined that he would do nothing else before seeing her. He hoped that her delayed rising did not mean that she was still feeling ill. He had purchased a special gift for her and was as eager as a child to offer her the small prize.

When at last Brianna joined him, Devon thought she looked fresh. The color of her cheeks heightened by the deep green of her causal day-dress, insinuated that she was feeling better. Devon moved directly to her, wanting to pull her close to him and feel her weight against his chest. "Brianna, I have missed you greatly."

Deftly, she sidestepped and slid by him. Moving to take the chair closest to the door, Brianna sat, nervously arranging the folds of her skirt around her legs. "Have you?" Brianna found she was unable to say more while concentrating on avoiding his sultry blue eyes.

Unaware of her turmoil, Devon mistook her question for wavering emotions. Kneeling in front of her, he took each of her soft hands in his own and answered, "Desperately, Flame. In fact, Daniel and I returned early because we could not suffer the distance from our ladies for even one more day." He flashed a smile that made Brianna want to forget all that Larissah had claimed.

Brianna's heart was ready with its silent argument, *What if he is telling the truth? What if he actually feels this way for me and only me?*

Her rationale pushed her to remain focused. *If he truly loved you, then Larissah would not be carrying his child.*

Retracting her hands from his, Brianna coolly countered, "That's odd, Devon. I thought you might be *glad* for your time apart from me." Though she tried to avoid his gaze, Devon could easily see the pain and betrayal in her eyes and her comment filled his soul with apprehension.

"Brianna, what is bothering you? Has something changed your feelings? Are you having second thoughts?" He offered an uncertain grin, attempting to lighten the mood. "Are those precious feet of yours getting cold?"

Brianna ignored his sweet teasing. She was eager to move from him, but was trapped on the chair, each of his hands now resting on the arms of the seat she occupied. Since she couldn't escape, she faced him head-on, firmly locking her gaze with his sapphire-blue one. "Yes, *everything* has changed."

"Then maybe you should enlighten me as to why this alteration has occurred, considering when I left, I had no reason to think *anything* was amiss between us."

His eyes burned into her and Brianna flushed with his meaning and her anger. "Maybe *Larissah* should enlighten you."

The name spoken set his dark eyes on fire and Brianna wanted to be free of him and the danger therein, even more than before. "What has she done this time?" Inadvertently granting Brianna's wish, Devon pushed away from the chair and began pacing the room. "You have seen her ways." Stopping to face her, Devon threw his hands in the air with frustration. "I have warned you time and again that she is a deceitful woman. All that she says is for her own good; she will stop at nothing for gain. What *lies* has she spun to interfere with our lives now?"

Free from her prison, Brianna unfortunately felt no less trapped. "It would appear"—her voice shook, thick with emotion—"that she has undeniable proof this time."

"Proof of *what*, Brianna? How am I to battle this demon I don't understand?"

An oddly serene smile touched her features. "The thought of it leaves me bitter and I have no desire to taint my lips with its horrible certainty. Go to Larissah for the information you seek."

Devon was momentarily stunned that she would defy him on what was obviously such an important matter. From the look she offered, he realized that there would be no swaying her otherwise. His words were a mixture of pleading, confusion, pain and anger, "I'll do as you say but be sure that when I ferret out this lie, there will be Hell to pay."

"A debt I fear is yours to pay," she growled with contempt as she left him to his sad discovery.

◊◊◊◊◊

Larissah had just resigned herself to a day spent alone at home when Abram entered Reverie. Taking the missive from him, she felt her bravery falter a bit. Devon had returned early and reading the paper in hand—for the first time—Larissah questioned the sensibility of claiming Devon as the father of her child.

Since she could think of no way to put him off and no reason to delay the altercation to come, Larissah allowed Abram to help her into her cloak and out the door to the waiting buggy.

In the entranceway to her home, the piece of paper she had been holding lay haphazardly upon the table. Its scrawled message read simply: *Now!*

◊◊◊◊◊

Though well on the way to complete inebriation, Devon's senses were alert enough to recognize the sound of Larissah's arrival before she even entered Misty Heights. When she sashayed into his office, attempting to hide her fear behind a golden smile, Devon was neither fooled nor impressed.

Closing the door behind her, Larissah fussed with the cuffs of her lacy sleeves. "You wished to see me, Devon?"

Just the sound of her voice set his teeth on edge. "How disappointed I am in you, Rissah, I expected at least a foolish act of denial. You didn't even attempt to question if it was I who sent you the note or not."

Rolling her eyes and moving to stand before him, hands on hips, she insulted him, "I would recognize such atrocious script anywhere." Lifting the nearly empty decanter of brandy from the sideboard, she continued, "And I find it no surprise that you have not considered the fact that *Abram* came to fetch me. A near certain clue that you desired my company." Her final comment held a hint of offering that did not go unnoticed by its recipient.

"A choice of words I would not have made," he intoned scathingly.

Her smile wavered and Larissah set the container down with a thud. "Then whatever prompted you to send such a short and demanding note?"

Without further delay, Devon questioned, "What have you done to Brianna?"

Slowly, Larissah's smile turned brilliant and cunning. "So, she's turned cold on you, eh? And without telling you; perhaps there's more Chase in her blood than I've given her credit for."

"*You* are the exception to your family's characteristics, Larissah, *not* Brianna."

"Which only makes me wonder which of those qualities our child will inherit." Larissah turned, giving Devon the same effective view of her body that she had afforded Brianna and Meghan just days before.

The room fell silent as a tomb.

Devon looked stunned and then laughed. "You expect me to take responsibility for another man's babe? I will not play father to your bastard."

For a moment, a chilling fear settled in her blood. What were the chances that Devon would not take the child? She had been so sure of her ability to use this farce as a means to convince Brianna to leave Devon that the idea of him shirking his unwanted duty had never truly been considered.

Rather than dwell on that outcome, Larissah set her mind to making Devon see her way. Even if he did not believe that the child was his, he would at least accept the possibility. "What do you mean? Of course, the child is yours. You were the last man that I have been with."

"Correct me if I am wrong—"

"Gladly."

With a quieting glance, Devon continued, "But *we* have not done much of anything for some time now."

The frosty smile on her lips moved up to her eyes as she purred, "Yet it takes so little time." She caressed her rounded belly meaningfully.

Devon scoffed loudly. He did not even have to wonder if she was lying—he was positive. "And now I suppose you expect me to believe that you are so heartbroken by my recent denials that you have waited for me in celibacy?" He laughed blatantly. "Even *you* cannot be as audacious as that, Rissah."

Her tone was strong. "*Accept* it, Devon."

"Accept it? Accept it?" His temper was rising with each word he uttered. "You *truly* expect me to believe this farce, don't you?"

"And why would you doubt me? We have been together many times."

"You have also been with *many* other men, *many* other times."

"That is true, but I have only ever loved you."

He laughed again. Larissah's plea was convincing. However, Devon knew her and her schemes well. "The only thing you love about me is my money and my . . . well, let's suffice it to say, I don't believe you love me for anything aside from what I can provide for your financial or physical pleasure. As for you convincing Brianna of this lie, I will *never* forgive you. I have struggled to earn her trust and now you have destroyed that. Do not push this farce further, Larissah. Do not push *me* further."

She stood her ground, clinging boldly to what was likely her last chance. In a matter-of-fact tone she demanded, "It is already done. You have no other choice."

His face flushed with anger before she had finished speaking. "I most certainly *do* have a choice. I will deny all that you say. I am in love with Brianna. I could never and *will* never love you. *You* may accept *that*."

Larissah's clear eyes narrowed dangerously and she stepped to him, her words coming out in a soft hiss. "Perhaps you would see *my* reputation ruined, but would you do the same to hers? If you deny me, I promise that no one will accept her socially. Can you imagine what the little Catholic parish would think of her frolicking? It would not be hard to make them believe that the two of you have been lovers since your arrival."

"None of that circle would believe you. You hide your indiscretions well, but not perfectly."

"An ounce of doubt is all I need and it is human nature to believe the worst—even in church folk. Which, I think, takes care of hindering your business, too, and with it—Daniel, his Irish wife *and* their whelp." Poking her finger sharply into his chest, Larissah promised, "I will devastate *all* that you hold dear."

Devon could never allow Larissah to realize his disappointment in first learning of his future niece or nephew through her spiteful means—it would only add to her victory. "Have you nothing of your father's honor within you?"

Her reply came easily, "Honor is a weakness I will not allow myself to feel—it's entirely overrated."

With each damning syllable she spoke, Devon knew that he was trapped. Unlike Larissah, honor *was* all-important to him and just as she deemed it a weakness, she was using Devon's against him.

Though he was a man in a man's world and people would treat him well to his face, behind closed doors—where society and business really counted—he would be shunned. The damage to the Elliott name and company would be irreversible. Brianna would be hurt, Daniel and his family too and all that their parents had worked so hard to create and maintain would be ruined. And Brianna was suffering enough now that he would not risk hurting her in a way that even remotely involved her father or her cherished memory of him.

Along with this disgusting revelation came the understanding of Brianna's recent coldness. She must have felt so much pain when Larissah had declared her bastard to be his—it was no wonder she looked at him with such scorn and betrayal. With the damage done, he could think of no way to prove Larissah false to Brianna or his peers. Indeed, the woman finally had him exactly where she wanted him—trapped in her web of deception.

With fists clenched, Devon praised viciously, "You have planned well, Rissah." Her smile was maliciously accepting and she basked in the feeling of victory until Devon spoke again. "Make no mistake, though, if I *ever* have the *slightest* chance of proving this child you carry is not my own burden, you had best beware. The same is said for you being faithful to my name and me. You will pay dearly for what you are costing me, and those dues begin with your taking no other lovers except me, and believe me, those occasions will be *rare*. You will also learn to be obedient and respectful, just as the vows you are forcing me into dictate."

Larissah chuckled, "And you expect me to believe I will get the same treatment from you?"

Devon sneered. "Don't even bother considering such options. If I am angered by you and I choose to take a switch to your bared rump in the middle of High Street, I will."

"I don't suggest—"

Devon continued, ignoring her interruption. "Furthermore, if I choose to bed every lover I've ever had plus each whore Baltimore has to offer, I'll do so *with* you in the same room if I wish." Larissah opened her mouth to speak. "And you'll not say a *word* about it." She closed her mouth again.

Stepping to her, Devon caught Larissah's raised chin within the viselike grip of his fingers. "And then, *when* I am blessedly able to uncover this cruelty for the ruse that it is, the bastard's father will be dealing with you and the babe, not I." Devon released his hold on her with a force that threw Larissah off balance. "This is your *only* warning, Larissah. Heed it well."

By the time she was able to right her footing, Devon had mercifully left the room without causing her or the child any permanent damage—a fact that amazed Devon and Larissah equally.

◊◊◊◊◊

Thanks to recent events, Christmas was not the joyous occasion of years past.

Just days before, Brianna had demanded Devon send out notice of their cancelled engagement. It had taken a huge argument before his spite overrode his determination and Garrett sent handwritten notes to his closest neighbors.

Brianna had spent the rest of the day in her room and Devon had locked himself in his study.

Meghan and Daniel were trapped between holiday traditions, Brianna's angered sadness and Devon's constant sulking.

The entire change of events had been a shock to Daniel, but he could not openly question his older sibling. When the time was right, he would speak to him privately about his reasons for giving into Larissah. For now, all he could do was watch him fight to make the woman he loved realize that nothing had changed the way he felt for her.

Devon's demanding behavior only drove Brianna further away. Every time she entered a room to find him in it, she turned to leave. Even when he didn't speak to her, his gaze followed her with longing.

Their most recent argument had ensued as Daniel and Meghan opened their Christmas gifts from each other. Devon snapped at everyone; his heart mourned future Christmases he would be unable to share with Brianna.

When Brianna commented on how nice it was to see two people so in love and how happy she was about their impending parenthood, Devon scoffed, "Yet you throw aside your opportunity for the same."

Her sensitivities ever tender now, Brianna reminded him, "If you had not thrown your clothes aside as easily, then we would still be headed in that direction."

Her words could not be argued with and Devon was hurt by the truth and the blame held therein. He stormed from the house without another word and Brianna—embarrassed by her actions and hurting constantly in his presence—fled to her room and a new bout of tears.

That had been more than an hour earlier.

Daniel and Meghan now sat before the fire in the front parlor, enjoying the silence the current time of calm provided. Glancing worriedly out the window, Meghan noted that the snow was no longer holding off. "Do you think that you should go after him?"

Daniel's gaze followed hers to the window. "He will be fine, Meghan. Devon has been out in far worse weather than this." Daniel hugged her close and consoled, "If it makes you feel better though, if he is not back in another hour, I'll go after him then."

"It would serve him right to freeze every inch of his body."

Daniel laughed at Brianna's statement and watched her enter the room. "Somehow I don't believe you mean a word of that."

Smiling, she concurred, "Perhaps just his head; that way any foolish thoughts will go unvoiced since his tongue will be unable to wag. And maybe his"—she raised her brow meaningfully—"reason for our recent problems, too." Brianna and Daniel were alone in their laughter.

Meghan scolded them tersely, "I don't think this is a jesting matter. There is a man out in the cold and not at all dressed for such weather. You should be ashamed of yourselves."

"The only thing I am ashamed of is that I ever let that man weasel his way into my heart." Looking at Meghan, she offered humbly, "But the truth is, he left in such a fury and the sky is looking so fierce, that I came down to see if he had returned yet."

Trying to put the women at ease, Daniel said, "As you can see he has not returned, but there is nothing to worry about. Devon knows this land well and will not take any unnecessary risks."

"I hope that you are right," Meghan stated, still sounding mildly unsure.

"I know I am," Daniel finalized with the utmost confidence.

◊◊◊◊◊

Daniel Elliott could not have been further from correct at that moment. In such a state of anger, Devon had veered from his normal riding path in search of a new place of solitude—one *without* memories of time shared with Brianna.

Now, snow was falling around him at a steady pace, making the problem not that he *didn't* know where he was, but that he *did.*

As a boy, he had played here often and knew that the steep incline ended in the freezing waters of the river some hundred feet below. Though Leviathan kept his footing sure for the time, the ground beneath the stallion's hooves was becoming slick with mud and freezing ice. Devon knew that he did not have much time to get out of his precarious situation before it worsened.

Even out *of her presence, Brianna causes me trouble*, Devon thought, deciding that he would not be in this situation had she not angered him to the point she had. *Why can't she just listen to reason and believe what I tell her? Why must she lash out with cruel blame and reminders?*

Perhaps because you are going to marry another woman who claims she is carrying your child, the annoying side of his brain rationalized.

Stupidly lost in thought, Devon failed to notice the rock under Leviathan's hoof until the horse whinnied in pain and lost his footing. Devon attempted to grasp the branches of a nearby tree, but the ice-slick bark slipped through his hands, roughly tearing his riding gloves and scraping his palms open. He landed with a force that knocked the wind from him—a sound drowned out by the snapping of his leg.

When Devon's eyes widened in pain, he dimly saw Leviathan regain his footing and tear off through the woods to the top of the hill and away from danger.

The positive aspect of his animal's desertion was that within a short time, Leviathan would be at Misty Heights. Now all Devon could do was pray that someone there would notice and care enough that he was not astride the mount to search him out in this weather.

Another bout of anguish tore through his leg and the searing hot pain capitulated Devon into unconsciousness and away from any thoughts or worries.

◊◊◊◊◊

The threesome within the warmth of Misty Heights was enjoying Hessie's soulful rendition of *Silent Night*. In her seat across from Daniel and Meghan, Brianna noted the way the new Mrs. Elliott relaxed in her husband's arms with her head lying against his shoulder; her features were comfortable and content. Though still somewhat pale with her pregnancy illness, she was faring better since Daniel had returned from Boston.

Shifting her gaze to Daniel, the emotion in his eyes was more evident than Meghan's. Brianna wondered if Daniel was thinking of his wife, or if Hessie's voice made him think of Tansey. It had been months since they had last seen her and they had yet to receive any word from her. It pained Brianna to think that even after the vow he had made to Meghan, Daniel may still be longing for his lost love. Perhaps the holidays emphasized some bittersweet memories for him. In addition, no one had been able to mention Tansey and how she was missed for fear of arousing Meghan's suspicions—which, only made the loss of Tansey more prominent.

A sound at the window drew Brianna's attention. The snow had changed over to sleet and was landing against the panes with a light, repetitive tapping. What she saw beyond the glass set her in motion before words could even be formed and she bolted from her seat in horror.

Leviathan was crossing the front lawn toward the rear-stables, but Devon was not astride or leading the horse. An icy chill that rivaled the one outside settled into Brianna's blood and without further thought, she raced for the door.

In the same instant, Daniel realized what had startled her Brianna grabbed her cloak and threw the entranceway wide. Only steps behind Brianna, Daniel was still too late to stop her. Already she had reached Leviathan and jumped on his back. She gave rein to the mighty horse as they galloped away from the house.

At first she struggled with the bulk of her dress, but as Daniel watched, Brianna managed to right herself in the saddle even while spurring the mount faster and clinging desperately to the reins in hand.

Cursing the woman for her stubborn bravery, Daniel raced back into the house. God alone knew what might have happened to thwart Devon from returning home, so they would need to be prepared for the worst.

Shouting demands that all be readied for their return, Daniel quickly bundled his outerwear around him and dashed toward the stable. With each action, a silent prayer cadenced through his mind—*Dear God, help me to find them soon and keep us each safe until we are home again.*

◊◊◊◊◊

Brianna was frantic. In just seconds, she had gone from being warm and cozy to worried and miserably cold on Leviathan's back. In the minimal amount of time she had been outside, her ill-suited evening dress was torn and wet from her exertions. Again, she pulled her wool cloak tighter to her body, trying to block out some of the blustery wind.

Coming to an area she was unfamiliar with, Brianna leaned down against Leviathan's neck and soothingly gave him rein. "Come now, laddie, you must help us. Take me to him. You can do it, you know where he is."

Traveling a short distance deeper into the trees, Brianna knew that they were headed in the right direction. Leviathan became more skittish with each powerful step of his hooves. At last, Brianna realized that she would need to tether him—if she forced him any farther, his nervous steps on the slippery ground might cause more harm than good.

Dismounting, Brianna searched for a sturdy branch to tie the stallion to, almost losing her footing when a nearby moan startled her. Never in her life had she heard a sound of pain that made her so happy.

"Devon?" She gained no response.

Following the path carefully, she rounded a huge tree, its roots sticking up in spots from the ground.

When she saw him, relief flooded through Brianna even as she noticed the odd angle of his leg. Immediately, she allowed instinct to take over. Bunching her skirts tightly between her legs, Brianna dropped to her hands and knees and crawled to his side. There was no way she could lift him and she knew it. She would simply have to keep him comfortable and warm until Daniel found them—hopefully, that wouldn't be long.

Taking care not to bump his injured leg, Brianna placed her body partially on top of Devon's and wrapped them both in her warm cape. Relief flooded her when she felt the steady rise-and-fall pattern of his breathing. Even if he wasn't conscious, he was alive. Then, to her further relief, his blue eyes fluttered open.

"Flame," he whispered in strained recognition.

"Yes, my love." Snuggling closer to him, Brianna slipped her arm beneath his head in support and prompted, "Close your eyes and rest now, Daniel will be here soon."

For once, Devon did exactly as she ordered without argument.

Chapter Twenty-One

Glistening snowflakes began falling again in the early morning hours and lasted throughout the day. Devon rested peacefully now. The night had been difficult. Daniel and Abram had straightened Devon's leg and splinted it with a piece of barn-board. Wrapped in strips of old bed sheet-bandages, the appendage now rested upon a pile of pillows while he slept.

Brianna was more concerned about the terrible cough that had set into his lungs than his mending leg. She remained by his side, repeatedly covering his brow with cool cloths to keep a fever at bay. Ignoring her own fatigue, Brianna covered a yawn and rubbed the back of her neck with her free hand.

"You should not have come out there for me." Devon's voice sounded tired and his reprimand held little force.

"What would you have me do, leave you out in the cold to freeze?"

"Can you honestly say the thought didn't occur to you?"

Recalling her comment to Daniel and Meghan, Brianna felt a pang of guilt and sheepishly replied, "Perhaps briefly."

Devon tried to laugh but was cut short when the action brought a shot of pain to his head. "Am I going to survive?"

Removing the now tepid cloth from his forehead, Brianna dipped it in the cool water of the basin before replacing it again. "I daresay it will take far more to end your stubborn days than a bad cold and a broken leg, Devon Elliott."

Devon relaxed under the smooth touch of her hand on his brow and instigated softly, "Perhaps, but I also thought it would have taken a great deal *less* to get you into my private chambers again."

Brianna flicked the tip of his nose with her finger. "It is obvious you are well on the way to a full recovery."

"Want to speed it along?" He flashed his most tempting smile, and then cringed at its effect on his headache.

"What a rascal you are." She laughed despite her prudish attempt not to.

"And you love me for it," Devon baited.

Brianna gave him a sidelong glance but offered no remark.

Her silence was encouraging, so Devon suggested, "Maybe enough to forgive my wrongs and marry me as planned?" His tone was a bit more serious than a moment before.

"I think your fiancée may have a problem with that."

"Some fiancée she is. I believe she is duty-bound to be here, so where is she? Most likely too busy with someone else's *care* to tend to mine."

"Are you disappointed? If you're missing her, I can send Abram to fetch Larissah here."

Devon closed his eyes and groaned, his sudden bout of nausea not entirely due to the pain behind his eyes. "Please no, I merely thought it strange that she is not taking advantage of this perfect opportunity to bring me torment."

Reaching for the glass of water at his bedside, Brianna spoke nonchalantly, "She doesn't know of your injuries."

Devon's eyes squinted open and a knowing smile came to his lips. "And why is that?"

Brianna would not meet his smug gaze. "I didn't think it was necessary to have her here. She would only get in the way."

"Then I give thanks for such foresight and the sacrifice you've made by standing in her place."

Brianna looked at him then. "You needn't be so full of yourself, Devon. No one else wanted her here, either." When the twinkle in his eyes grew, she informed him haughtily, "Besides, the care I have given is nothing I would not have done for Daniel if he had been in the same situation as you."

"You mean you would have curled your body so intimately—and very nicely I might add—against my brother's as you did mine in the woods, if he too were stranded in the cold?"

"I suppose I would have left that part of the care to his . . ."

"Wife?" Devon finished for her.

"A role I would act far better if someone else were not already cast in the part."

Despite her harsh words, Devon saw right through her. Brianna might deny him with her last breath, but Devon was surer than ever that she still loved him. Her heroics the day before and throughout the night certified it.

"Now hush, I don't want you to waste any more energy talking." Brianna was very firm in her nurse-like scolding. "I'm going to get you some broth from the kitchen and I expect you to sleep until I return."

Despite her high and mighty decrees, Brianna could feel his mirth-filled, all-knowing expression burning into the back of her as she made her exit and he murmured, "Yes, Flame."

◊◊◊◊◊

When Brianna returned, Devon was not sleeping as promised, but propped up against his pillows. She set the bed-tray—complete with broth and bread on it—across his lap and mocked, "I'm so glad you rested."

"I don't need more rest than I'm getting already."

"Good, then you can use your energy to feed yourself."

"I can think of a better outlet."

"Of course you can, but that won't be happening either."

"Shirking your duties so soon?"

Brianna smirked, "Oh, but remember, they are not *my* duties."

"We could change that," Devon persisted stubbornly.

"No, we can't." Brianna sighed. "Devon, I don't want to continue this argument every time we are together."

"Then what *do* you want?"

Brianna braced herself for Devon's certain outrage. "I'm returning to Ireland in two weeks."

Devon amazed her with his calm. "No, you're not."

"I've contacted Jonathan and he's agreed to help me settle into my home again."

"Misty Heights *is* your home."

"No, Misty Heights is *your* home. It is Larissah's home."

His calm broke then. Devon slammed the back of his hand into the tray across his lap, throwing it over the other side of the bed to land on the floor with a clatter. "Damn it, Brianna, I will not allow you to go."

"You cannot stop me, Devon."

His determination was strong. "I have every right to stop you and I will use them all if need be."

"And force me to remain here, face the embarrassment of a broken engagement, then watch you and Larissah marry and raise a family. How very generous of you." Her sarcastic words out, Brianna stood and walked toward the door. "If I have to, I'll leave while you're still abed. But I will *not*, under any circumstances, remain here and subject my heart or mind to any more anguish brought by you or my cousin."

Brianna slammed the door on her way out of the room, not caring who heard the noise, what they thought or what else Devon might have to say.

◊◊◊◊◊

Throughout the remainder of the week, the entire household helped with Devon's care. Each person had a shift and when Daniel stepped into Devon's room for his current one, it was just in time to see his sibling foolishly attempt to stand from his bed for the third time.

"What are you doing?" Daniel asked with a mixture of amazement, amusement and exasperation.

Looking up as though he was doing nothing out of the ordinary, Devon replied, "I'm going to stop Brianna from leaving."

Lifting his older brother so that he was again perched on the edge of the bed, his bandaged leg sticking directly and stiffly out in front of him, Daniel advised, "I think that would be an impossible task, even for a healthy man."

True to stubborn Elliott form, Devon boasted, "Well, just watch and learn because I intend to do *just* that." His self-confident grin was wiped away with Daniel's next question.

"How?"

"What do you mean *how*?"

"I didn't realize the word had so many definitions."

"Don't be sharp with me, brat. You know exactly what I mean." Devon's head throbbed, his leg ached and his foot—which he could not begin to reach—was itching, he was in no mood to swap words with his brother.

Daniel merely laughed at Devon's discomfort. "What I mean is that you can't even roll over without assistance, let alone get out of bed, so *how* do you intend to stop Brianna from leaving?"

Devon failed to find the humor in Daniel's stream of comments, so he shut him up promptly. "That's where *you* come in."

Daniel watched his brother a moment and knew he was very determined. Trying to waylay his plans he indulged, "Let's just *say* that I agree to help you—which, by the way, has a very *slim* chance of occurring—exactly *what* do you plan to say to Brianna once you confront her? And then, when she walks away from you anyway, do you plan to hobble after her quickly?"

"I will do or say whatever I have to, but I will *not* lose Brianna."

Daniel felt a moment of pity and his soft words conveyed it. "You already have, Dev."

"She is mine until she sails away from America, and I plan to take every opportunity I have to stop *that* from happening." Starting to push himself up again, Devon added, "Now, are you going to help me or not?"

Daniel remained in his place, leaning against the doorjamb while his sibling struggled for balance. "Do you realize that my wife will have my hide for this, not to mention what Brianna and Hesper will do when they see that I've gotten you out of bed?"

"You aren't really afraid of three women, are you?" Devon asked, trying to ignore the pain in his leg.

"When it is *those* three women, I am."

"I would do it for you," Devon prompted as sweat began to bead his brow.

"And I'm glad of it."

Letting out a stressed breath, Devon flopped back on the bed again and asked, "Will you go and bring *her* to *me*, then?"

Daniel's resolve broke with the desperate tone of his brother's words. "I think it would be much easier to take *you* to *her*."

Devon smiled. "I'm sure you're right." Lifting his arm toward his brother for help, he asked, "So what are we waiting for?"

Daniel groaned and went to his brother's aid. "Why do I *know* I'm going to regret this?"

◊◊◊◊◊

Brianna was in her room with Hesper, packing the last of her belongings for departure. She wasn't in the mood to talk so the room was silent except for the rustle of clothing and the soft melody of Hesper's humming.

Tomorrow morning, Brianna—along with Daniel and Meghan—would board a train bound for Baltimore and in just three days more, she would be on her way to sea, and home to Ireland.

Frustration etched her soft features. It seemed that she had been trying to redirect her life for so long now, that she would never again be in a permanent place of contentment. It was ironic that for as much as she had hated leaving Ireland, Brianna didn't really want to return now. Just as before, she was losing everyone that she loved in this new home.

Without warning, the door to Brianna's private sitting room opened and Devon was toted in by his younger sibling. The stunned bystanders watched as Daniel half-drug Devon through the connecting door to her bedroom and carefully deposited his load on the edge of Brianna's bed. The younger man then took Hesper's arm and left the room without a word.

Hesper and Daniel were barely out of sight when Devon blurted, "Do not think that avoiding me until you go will make the leaving any easier."

Brianna sputtered through her shock and resentment—the resentment won out. "You think my taking the time to pack is *avoiding* you? As a ship captain I would think you understand that a trip takes some preparation."

"You have not been in to check on my welfare all morning." His pouting tone would have made Brianna laugh under other circumstances.

"That is because I left you just after midnight and you were fine then." In exasperation, she snapped, "I was not aware that my presence was so crucial to your recovery." Taking more clothing in hand, Brianna renewed her task.

"Your presence is crucial to every part of my life, Brianna."

"If that were true, I wouldn't have to leave at all, would I?"

"Don't be obstinate Brianna. I haven't the patience."

Brianna continued to fold her garments neatly. "Nor have I and since we have said all of this already, I am wondering why you are forcing the issue again. What we shared is over."

Devon felt his face flush with anger. "If it is over, then why did you care enough to race out in the freezing weather to help me? Why did you feel the need to spend hours at my bedside, if you do not care?"

"Again with this argument?" She sighed with exasperation and when he didn't answer, but continued to glare stubbornly at her, Brianna conceded, "Very well then, don't you think I owe you that much? That I would help you when I could? You brought me into your home to give me shelter. You feed me, shelter me—"

"I love you."

She said nothing, couldn't have if she tried. *Why did he have to choose* now *to say those words? He had been given so many opportunities during the last year, why did he wait until now?*

Devon felt her weakening and took advantage of it. "Can you say that you don't feel the same? Can you say that all we have shared means nothing to you? Can you really walk away from me? From *us*?"

"What other choice do I have? I've accepted what has happened, you should do the same." She didn't look up, but ran her fingers along the lace edge of the night-trail in her hand.

"I will do nothing of the kind. Larissah has no proof that the child is mine. Stay with me, I want you to stay, I *need* you to stay."

Brianna sighed and looked up at him. It would do her no good to demand that he leave, he wouldn't do it even if he were able and she certainly could not drag him from the room. "Devon, it may be true that Larissah has no proof, but she won't need it. A woman's cry of wrongdoing is much louder than that of a man's. All she need do is place a bit of doubt in the mind of your peers and your reputation will be ruined."

Devon hated that her reasoning was so similar and just as sound as Larissah's. "I don't care; I only want to be with you." He sounded lost and it broke Brianna's heart to hear this strong man expose himself to her.

Tears in her eyes, she turned and sat beside him. "What would you have me do, stay here and take what scraps of your life you can offer me?"

"We can leave. I can whisk you away to Mexico or California. Better yet, we will return to Ireland and be married there."

His suggestion held more appeal than Brianna should allow. Laughing lightly, she reminded, "Somehow I don't see you *whisking* me anywhere in your present condition."

"I would manage," he assured her with renewed determination.

Brianna shook her head. "And what about Daniel?"

"Daniel is a grown man with a wife to care for him. He can handle the company in Boston. We can offer Baltimore to Drake and I can reopen the Dublin office." The idea began to please him more by the second and Devon wondered why he hadn't thought of this solution before. "The plans can be made in a hurry and we can be gone within a month."

Devon sounded as anxious and carefree as Brianna wanted to be. "We can't."

"We *can*," he insisted. "I have the legal right to do with you whatever I find in your best interest." He smiled and leaned toward her, "And I definitely find *me* in your best interest."

Brianna forced herself to ignore his dancing blue eyes and full lips and think rationally. "What about Larissah? Isn't she also your legal responsibility? Do you really think it is in her best interest to leave *her* stranded with a child?"

"You seem to find every excuse to leave me." His words became harsh and angry. "Maybe you *are* more like your cousin than I believed."

His insult disgusted her. "You have a responsibility, Devon. Be a man and see to it."

"And you have so little trust in me that you believe Larissah's claim over my word."

Brianna stared him down in anger. How dare he place the blame on her? "You think I should trust you? Tell me, was Larissah lying when she said that you bedded her the same day we arrived?"

"No, she did not lie, but I didn't understand my feelings for you then. I have never loved a woman before; I was confused by how you made me feel."

"It would seem that you looked for your answers in the wrong place. How am I to believe that you loved me when you sought her love instead of mine?" Tears found their way down her cheeks. "Those times I foolishly offered myself to you, only to be turned away."

Her words trailed off and it was the first time Devon *truly* regretted sparing her virginity. Running shaky fingers through his hair, Devon concluded, "Brianna, I can do nothing more than tell you how I feel and why I made the mistakes I did."

Brianna wanted to take him into her arms and console him. She wanted to feel the strength of his arms envelop her and block the cruel truth of what must be. Instead, she stood in silence.

And it was that silence that finally convinced Devon that he could not sway Brianna—he had lost her love forever.

With as much dignity as he could muster, Devon stood. "Goodbye, Brianna." Then he limped from the room, the pain in his leg nowhere near the searing in his heart.

◊◊◊◊◊

Meghan and Daniel watched from the dock, as the ship christened *Voyager* carried Brianna toward Ireland. "How will she make it without him?" Meghan wondered aloud.

"Do not worry, Brianna is strong, she will do well." Wrapping his arm around his wife, Daniel turned and began leading them toward the waiting carriage.

"And what of Devon? Will he need you to be with him now?"

Daniel watched Meghan thoughtfully. She had come to know him well—far better than he had ever suspected she would during their courtship. Her gentle sympathy for Devon only added to the easy way she had begun burrowing into his heart, something else he hadn't planned.

"Not just yet. Devon will need some time alone to brood over his loss and I don't want to be anywhere around him while that happens. For now he has Hesper."

"Just the same, when you go back, I would like to go with you." She hesitated before informing, "In fact, I would like to have our child there."

"At Misty Heights?" He asked incredulously.

Meghan laughed lightly at his surprise. "Is that a problem?"

"No, not at all. I just thought you would like to remain in the city, close to Katherine and Caleb."

Meghan rolled her eyes. "So that they can dote over me constantly? No, thank you." With less aversion, she added, "Besides, they have baby Cordelia now and I don't want to interfere in their time as a family." She smiled serenely at him and offered, "This time is for *us* to share, Daniel."

Unexpected warmth filled Daniel. "You honor me, Meghan."

"It is easy when I love you so much."

And the space left by Tansey's departure closed inside Daniel a little more.

Chapter Twenty-Two

Larissah preened in the back of her carriage as it rumbled toward her fiancée's home. It was high time she made her presence and authority felt at Misty Heights. Through the gossip of her slaves, she had learned that Brianna was gone—none too soon as far as Larissah was concerned. Life would be much easier now that her younger cousin wasn't around to get in the way.

Rounding a curve in the road, the vehicle lurched, jarring Larissah as it came to a bouncing halt. Sticking her head out the side-window, she demanded, "Why have we stopped, Zeek?"

The Negro driver called back in his slow drawl, "That there stone in the road was a powerful big one, Miz Laa-rissah, an' awful hard to get 'round."

Rolling her eyes, Larissah insisted, "Well, we are certainly *around* it now." Her impatience was growing. "I have a schedule to keep, so let's move on."

Before she was back through the window again, the slave replied, "Cain't, Miz Laa-rissah."

She gripped the edge of the window for restraint and asked through clenched teeth, "What do you mean we *can't*?"

"The back wheel done busted when we rolled over dat rock."

"Then fix it, Zeek, and please do not make me instruct you on every move you make. I have too much to do today for my time to be wasted on your lack of sense."

"Yes'm." Zeek never really listened to his mistress when she got into one of her moods—which happened quite frequently. He just took her insults with a grain of salt and slowed his pace more—it was the one way her slaves could retaliate without being completely insubordinate and risking—quite literally—their hide.

Larissah watched in growing frustration as the man climbed from the cab and began shuffling in the opposite direction than they had been heading. Throwing the door wide open, Larissah clumsily disembarked the carriage. "Where in God's name do you think you are *going*, Zeek?"

The gray-haired man turned toward her with a surprised expression. "I goin' to git the stuff I needin' to fix dat wheel, Miz Laa-rissah."

"You have to walk all the way back to Reverie?"

Zeek was enjoying the nasty woman's frustration. "If you wantin' dat wheel fixed today, I does."

"Why do I even bother speaking?" Larissah wondered to no one in particular.

Zeek was ready with a lazy answer, though. "Cain't rightly say, Miz Laa-rissah."

"I'd guess it's because you like to hear the sound of your own voice." Both occupants of the road were startled by the unexpected male answer. "Go on, Zeek. I will stay with Miss Larissah and see to the horses until you are able to return with help."

The slave looked uncertainly from the man astride the horse to his now extremely pale owner. "That what you wantin', Miz Laa-rissah?"

She swallowed and tried to vocalize her assent but failed. She nodded instead.

The slave walked away and Larissah stood in silence as the very large, very handsome man dismounted, then walked around to gain a better view of the damage done to the carriage wheel.

To the average observer, Nate Carter could pass for the most dashing of gentleman—until they recognized him as Robert Montgomery's indentured stable hand.

Nate used his meager income to keep himself in style for opportunities like this one, when he was allowed time away from his duties at Montgomery's townhouse. His build was powerful, his height intimidating, his features—dark brown eyes and hair, full lips—were endlessly seductive.

Nate's demeanor was trained and his speech educated thanks to his mother's efforts. A laundress by trade, she had decided early to help her son rise above his legacy of being the bastard of a senator. She would have more for her son whose father had denied him from birth. However, even her carefully laid plans would get him nowhere if Nate didn't have the means to propel him upward in society.

Larissah also knew that those same needs were the primary reason she was in Nate's life. With her money, he could make his way in the acceptable—maybe even upper crust—world. Larissah only needed to willingly lose face and marry a lowly stable hand for his dreams to succeed.

A soft whistle slipped through his teeth and drew Larissah's attention from his firm body, now crouched in front of the broken wheel as he examined the extent of the damage. "This will take an entire replacement. Do you have the parts at Reverie?"

"What?" Larissah managed to croak out.

Turning toward her, the man repeated, "I asked if you—"

"I know *what* you said, but I thought perhaps you might have something of greater importance to discuss with me."

Standing slowly, Nate regained his full height before deliberately eyeing her swollen condition. "You look well."

"*Well*?" Larissah gasped.

"Don't force me to be rude, Rissah." Nate liked giving her the impression that he found her pregnancy unappealing, even though the opposite was true.

"Did you know?"

"Of the child, you mean?" When she nodded, he walked closer to her and replied, "I had my suspicions."

"Why haven't you come to me, then?" She tried to keep her voice from shaking. It would do no good to let this man know his effect on her or how much she had missed him.

"I never came to you without prompting before. Why should now be any different?" He didn't sound callous, just curious.

"Perhaps to see about my well-being," she snapped more than a little perturbed by his disinterest.

"Robert informed me that you had everything taken care of."

"How kind of him. And did you trade opinions on my favors while you were discussing me?"

Nate smiled broadly at her discomfort. "Not *this* time."

Larissah raised her chin in an attempt to snub him. "At any rate, Robert is right; I *do* have everything taken care of." Offering a slight, though unintentional pout, she questioned, "But what if I had been ill?"

"Are you suggesting that I would care?" His dark eyes dared her to delve further into this conversation.

Larissah obliged. "You don't?"

He chose to frustrate her more by not answering. Instead, he blatantly cornered, "Is the child mine?"

"What do *you* think?" Larissah demanded, angered by his doubt.

His tone finally took on a more heated timbre. "Considering the number of men you spread your legs for, I have no idea."

Blood fused her cheeks and for the first time, Larissah felt sincere shame for her past indiscretions. "How dare you speak to me in such a manner?"

Nate was forthright and defensive. "Because I am the true father of the child and you have denied me that right."

"What would you have me do? You can't really think I would take you into my home and become the laughing stock of the area." Larissah sounded as though she would be ill just from the mere suggestion.

"You nasty bitch, I'm good enough to fill your body but not your home?"

"Just as I am good enough to pay your way but not to receive pleasure as your lover."

His tone lowered and despite herself, Larissah felt a tremor at the sound of it. "Oh, you're *good* enough, Rissah. You just don't deserve it." Looking at her shapely body, he added, "Though you really don't look as though you've been denied any pleasure, considering the condition you're in."

"No thanks to you," she snapped.

"Really? From the way you were just pouting for my touch, I'd say you should thank me very much." Nate laughed at her annoyed expression and then asked, "What I am truly curious about, though, is why you didn't protect yourself during our affair?"

Larissah looked up at him in question. "What do you mean?"

Nate rolled his eyes. "Don't play innocent with me now, Larissah; it is far too late for that."

Reluctantly she informed him, "Because I chose not to."

"And for Montgomery and Elliott—what was your choice with them? Was it any child you craved, or just mine in particular?"

"*That* is none of *your* concern," she announced with pleasurable disdain.

Her moment was short-lived. Nate grabbed her arms with the speed of a striking serpent. "You are wrong. It *is* my business, for I aim to know if the child is *truly* mine."

Her eyes spit blue-fire sparks at him. "Unhand me, you brute. I will tell you nothing until you do."

Rather than comply, Nate mercilessly pulled her across the road and into the back of the broken carriage with him. Leaning over her, his presence was dominating. "You will tell me *now*."

"Go to Hell," she seethed.

Nate laughed, but there was no humor in the sound. "Soon enough, but for now, I will have my answer."

"Why? You already said that you don't care."

"I said that I do not care for *you*. I said nothing about how I feel for the child."

Feeling increased power with her understanding, Larissah taunted, "So the bastard wants to become the father he never had."

In a flash, he gripped her chin with the vise-like force of his fingers. "Tell me."

With a jerk of her head, Larissah shook his hand away and spat out, "Yes, damn you, the baby is yours. I know that the bastard is yours because I was with no one but you since my last cycle."

His words were quiet but determined. "I will not allow you to force Elliott to take you as his wife and the child—*my* child—as his own."

Larissah laughed maliciously. "*You* have no choice in the matter, Nate."

With equal malevolence he responded, "*Choice*, my dear, is not needed when one has the power that I do."

Apprehension caused the blood in her veins to run cold, but Larissah managed to mask most of the emotion with her haughty reply. "*Power*? What power could *you* possibly have?"

"Quite simply that *this* time, you will not have your way, Larissah." Leaning over her again, he stated, "It was far too easy for me to control you from the beginning. I have had experience with women like you in the past—surely you didn't think you were the first." Mocking her with his eyes, he added, "You *were* the first one to love me though."

"You are a greater fool than I thought if you believe that," she denied vehemently, all the while cursing herself for the truth of his words.

An all-knowing smile covered his sensual lips, and then he plundered her mouth with them. He kissed her with all of the brutality she deserved and when she went soft under him, her surrender imminent, he pulled back. With belittling laughter, Nate declared, "Your eyes and your touch give you away, Larissah. After so many years of playing your games, I would have thought you would have learned to mask them better."

"Get off of me," she demanded, trying in vain to push his muscular form away. When he didn't budge, she asked, "What do you plan to do?"

"About the child?"

"What else could I mean?"

"Considering the position I have you in now, I wanted clarification." Nate's hand rubbed her swollen breast lightly.

Larissah did her best to look down her nose at him—a difficult task in her current place. "Not likely."

Nate merely increased the pressure of his hand, his eyes watching the lazy motion with fascination as he spoke. "You will know my plans in due time. For now, though, I intend to use the knowledge I have to my advantage."

Larissah recognized the light in his eyes and could easily guess what he meant. "You *can't* be serious," she failed to sound as unwilling as she would have liked.

Blessedly, his distracting caress ended. "Serious enough to go to Elliott myself if you do not concede to each of my . . . desires at my whim."

"He won't believe you." Even as she spoke, Larissah knew how wrong her claim was. Devon Elliott would jump at the chance to deny her and the child his name.

Surprisingly, Nate agreed, "Perhaps not." Larissah's relief was short lived. "But *Robert* will and Devon would believe him."

Darting her eyes away, she nervously questioned, "How can you be certain of that?"

"Come, now," Nate patronized, "Robert may be a fool, but give him *some* credit. Surely he would love the opportunity to humiliate you publicly as you did him."

Larissah knew too well that Nate was right, but still she fought his control with a scathing comment of her own. "Perhaps, but would he want it enough to believe the nonsense of his worthless servant?"

Ignoring her attempted insult, Nate taunted, "Listen closely, Larissah, for this is where the plot thickens." He paused as though sharing an exciting fairy tale with an eager child. "Though neither Robert nor Devon respects the other, they are still on the same social level. As you so obviously understand *that* nonsense, you can comprehend that when Robert confronts Devon with the truth, Elliott will have to take his word as a gentleman, which will provide him with the perfect opportunity to leave you behind without a second thought. He would be off for that lovely auburn-haired cousin of yours in a flash." Raising his hand to lightly brush her cheek, Nate questioned, "Is that clear enough for you, sweet Rissah?"

Fierce anger filled Larissah; this man had bested her at her own game. "You unbelievable bastard."

Smiling, he agreed, "Just as my own son shall be." Then his lips plundered hers once more.

◊◊◊◊◊

Brianna was returned to Ireland for three full weeks now.

It had taken no more than three days for her to realize that nothing was the same as before or as simple to readjust to as she had expected.

She told herself that it was because of the stress she was feeling, but her honest heart understood the truth—it wasn't Ireland that had changed. It was Brianna.

From day one, Jonathan and Lauren had dutifully—and happily—taken over Brianna's welfare. While she appreciated their good intentions, Brianna had grown accustomed to a certain sense of independence, something they didn't seem to understand. Nearly every day or evening they dotingly offered their company.

Gracefully, Brianna had managed to decline tonight's invitation to dinner and theater by claiming fatigue. Truthfully, she just wanted to be alone and especially avoid the added frustration of her reuniting with the Gordon's daughter, Deirdre.

Just before Brianna's departure for Maryland, Dee had been away to finishing school. She'd only returned home three months before and Brianna could not see how the time away or money spent had benefited her friend. As far as Brianna could tell, Dee had used her opportunity to learn how to be a proper lady and homemaker to flutter her lashes and chase down a husband. A goal upon which she was intent, making it difficult for Dee to focus her energies on any other aspect of life— except perhaps gossip.

Brianna's recent experiences were vastly different than those Dee had been through. Where Dee had once seemed full of fun and laughter, Brianna now found her jokes and comments to be immature and flirtatious. The personality alterations were creating a wide chasm between the childhood playmates.

The loss of a close friend weighed on Brianna as she tried to erase Devon from her mind—a feat she was coming to believe might never be completed. Her time in America—painful or not—was too firmly impressed upon her soul. In addition, without Tansey or Meghan to talk to, Brianna felt lonely and abandoned. With a melancholy smile, Brianna thought of each of them and wished for Meghan and her understanding ear,

Hesper's caring advice or Tansey's complete empathy of Brianna's feelings.

She decided to connect with them the only way she possibly could now. Sitting at the writing desk in the upstairs family parlor, Brianna took quill in hand and began to write:

Dearest Meghan,

I sincerely pray that this letter finds each of you well. I must confess that I yearn for news of your progressing condition. I imagine that you are no longer able to conceal the growth of life within you. I wish so dearly that I could be there to experience your changes firsthand.

Does Daniel burst with masculine pride each time he lays his proud eyes upon you? I am certain he does.

All is well here, despite the horrible famine sweeping through the majority of our counties. I am, with the help of the Gordons' planning, assisting those in need any way I can. Perhaps there was some positive reason for my return, after all. If I am able to help but one family to rest better, then it will have all been worthwhile.

Send Hesper and Abram my best wishes and let them know I have inquired after them and tell Daniel that I miss him to distraction.

Please do not delay in your reply; I will await it daily.

All my love and prayers,
Brianna G. McClaran

Folding the letter, Brianna ignored the tears flowing freely from her eyes. The strain had finally taken its toll and she reckoned that there was no reason for her to hide its effects now—not even within the lines of her letter.

Meghan would be able to sense her longing to inquire more, but her fear of the answers and her pride had held Brianna back from putting such questions to paper. What Devon was doing in his life had nothing to do with Brianna now, anyway, and she was certainly far better off not knowing.

Placing the addressed letter on the desk corner, Brianna walked to her bedroom. There was no need to stay up longer— misery would certainly join her just as happily in her dreams as it did during her waking hours.

◊◊◊◊◊

Each day that passed without Brianna in it, Devon's mood grew blacker. His time was spent in either his study or his bedroom and his diet consisted of little more than brandy.

He passed the hours trying in vain to place the blame for his situation. Larissah and her selfishness were the first cause; Brianna followed with her unwillingness to listen to the truth, and finally Devon would place the blame on his weakness for beautiful women. He would then think of Larissah and the cycle would begin again.

Now—as he was telling himself that he was better off without Brianna's finicky love—he was taken off guard when Daniel barged into his study.

"What the Hell do you want?" Devon growled, his displeasure at the intrusion evident.

"For you to stop acting like a lovesick fool and get on with your life," Daniel demanded plainly.

"I don't recall asking you to come here and witness *or* judge my actions." Devon took another long swill of brandy before dismissing, "You can see yourself out."

"That's very charming of you, big brother, but I'm not leaving until you are sober again."

"Then you might miss the birth of your child."

"Not likely since my expecting wife is with me."

That answer brought forth thoughts of a loyal woman and sincere love and suddenly, Devon felt very tired. All of the heat left his eyes and when he looked at Daniel again, he gave in. "What am I going to do? Look at me, I can't even function through a normal day, let alone take care of business."

It pained Daniel to realize the full extent of what Devon was enduring. Not only his heart, but his pride, too, had been wounded when Brianna denied him. "The only thing you can do is go on with the life and family you are being forced into."

"I'm just glad to hear that you believe the truth of my situation."

Daniel shrugged. "I know Larissah. It's not a hard conclusion to make."

"Truth or not, I have to deal with it," Devon admitted, as much to himself as his brother.

"Maybe you should get away, go spend some time with Drake on the *Enchantress*," Daniel suggested.

"Have you forgotten that I am to be wed in a month?"

"This will give you plenty of time to relax and come to terms with what will be."

Somberly, Devon predicted, "I don't think my life will last that long."

Glancing toward the closed door, Daniel confided, "I know how you feel, Dev. Even with Meghan in my life, when Tansey first left, I couldn't think of anything except her. But I also know that lounging in grief for too long can kill a man."

"That doesn't sound like a terrible fate."

Daniel ignored that remark. "I won't stand by and watch you drink yourself into ruin." Taking the whiskey bottle from the edge of the desk, Daniel replaced it in the cabinet. "Come on, you will feel much better after you have some real food and fresh air."

Still looking unsure, Devon attempted to speak with a vigor he was far from feeling. "You are probably right, and though I still think it would be easier to wallow in myself pity, I appreciate the fact that you are here for me."

"It is my place."

Healing begun for one and continuing for the other, the brothers left the stuffy room arm-in-arm together.

◊◊◊◊◊

Larissah's aching feet were upon the footstool and her head rested against the chair-back when Devon unceremoniously invaded the sanctuary of her private sitting room.

"Don't slam the door," Larissah begged, jarring slightly when her request went either unheard or unheeded. With one eye barely open, she commented dryly, "Don't mind me, Devon. Please, make yourself at home."

Devon took in her entire appearance and laughed. Clad in no more than her shift, stockings and drawers, her stomach protruding noticeably, Larissah looked as uncomfortable as she felt. "I see the child is not a burden only to me," Devon mocked with evident mirth.

Using all the charm she could muster, Larissah preened, "Oh, my love, you will never know what good it does my heart to hear you speak so kindly of our child."

"And you shall never know just how glad I am to see you in such a natural state of motherhood."

All civility left Larissah as the pounding in her forehead became greater. "What do you want? I am in no mood to match wits with you today." Her eyes closed as though she was unable to concentrate on his comments and his movements at the same time.

"To think I have the rest of my life to look forward to such warm receptions," he mumbled with artificial happiness.

"If I were not feeling so utterly horrid, I would gladly tell you exactly *where* you could keep those warm receptions."

"If you were not feeling so utterly horrid, I would have no need to be here either to give *or* to endure receptions of any kind," Devon replied pointedly.

"Yet, by some misfortune you are dutifully here anyway," Larissah ground through teeth clenched in discomfort and aggravation.

Graciously, Devon offered, "Sweet Rissah, if that is truly how you feel or you are having second thoughts about your plans for our future, I'll gladly go now and rid you of my company."

Larissah managed a smile that made Devon's skin crawl. "Fear not, gallant sir, no matter my present mood, I still intend to have you as my husband just as much as I did before this headache *and* your presence ailed me."

"Your charm is overwhelming; I am such a lucky man." Devon muttered with thick sarcasm, before informing, "I came to tell you that I am going to Baltimore for the next two weeks."

"How dutiful," Larissah mumbled cynically.

"That is precisely why I am here, nothing more." Devon was anxious to be away from her. "Do you or the child need anything brought back?"

Larissah sniffed in a painful attempt at a mocking laugh. "The only thing I require is that you are sure to find your way back in time to marry me. Don't embarrass us by missing or messing up this *joyous* occasion."

Devon's cynicism matched her own. "Not for the world."

"It is not the *world* I am concerned with, Devon, just Ireland."

Larissah's comment struck Devon exactly as she had hoped, but he hid his reaction well. Walking toward the door, he chuckled, "Rissah, Ireland is not your worry; the *truth* is."

"And the truth is that you would be off to the land of Saint Patrick in the blink of a blarney eye if the opportunity presented itself."

Devon found her Irish puns only mildly entertaining. "At least you have grasped a clear understanding of my feelings for you and the relationship you are forcing us into."

With an impatient wave of her wrist and a throaty sound of aggravation, Larissah dismissed him, "Just go, I no longer care to be in your presence."

"Is this a sympathetic granting of the *opportunity* we were just discussing or are you merely freeing me temporarily?" Devon knew what her reply would be but couldn't give up the slightest chance of escape or tormenting Larissah.

"Poor, poor, Devon, the only sympathy you'll have from me is *that* for your simple-minded attempts to end our relationship. A lesser woman would be scarred by such treatment." Larissah smiled slowly. "Oh, that's right, a lesser woman already *was* scarred by your treatment."

Devon's hands balled into tight fists. "You callous bitch."

"A fact you'd be wise to remember." With a determination her aching head had difficulty presenting, Larissah finished, "Since it is precisely *that* which will return you to become my husband. You'd also do well to keep in mind that there is no way in the world—*including* Ireland—that I will ever let you go."

"Just as you should keep in mind that I will never give up trying," Devon supplied, mimicking her own false consideration perfectly.

"I understand that you are a clumsy oaf and nothing more."

Devon laughed as he left the room; it was an easy front to hide the misery Larissah's accusations brought him. True glee entered the sound only when the sound of her empty lunch tray and dishes collided with the backside of the door he had just walked through, giving him full credit for hiding the truth from her as deftly as she did him.

Chapter Twenty-Three

Brianna awoke feeling no more joy than she had during the days before, yet she was resigned to accept the hand fate had given her.

It was time to emerge from this mode of depression; it would help nothing and only push those who cared for her away in frustration. She would make the most of this situation, which would not be difficult to do if she merely put forth a bit of effort. If she took the time to stop being so selfish and look outward from her comparatively petty problems, she could certainly find people in far worse shape than she was—just one more reason for her to move her idle body out of her home and find a way to help those less fortunate than herself.

With that in mind, Brianna arrived at the Gordon's house just past noon. Being informed that they were taking mid-morning tea, Brianna headed toward the dining room. She forced a smile to her lips—she had lost weight during her ordeal and knew that the gaunt appearance did not look well on her. Perhaps today she would begin attempting to remedy that problem as well.

A burst of laughter emanated from the people around the table, welcoming Brianna into their presence. Jonathan caught her attention immediately and stood to welcome her. "Brianna, what a lovely surprise. Had we known you would be joining us, we would have waited."

Kissing her surrogate father on the cheek, she allowed, "If I had known before this morning that my travels would bring me here, I would have been polite enough to notify you. I am sorry to intrude."

"Nonsense, you are family and always welcome. You know that." Indicating an empty seat, Jonathan invited, "Come, join us now; there is more than enough."

Smiling she admitted, "Gladly, everything looks lovely."

Nodding toward the maid closest to the kitchen, Lauren offered, "We will have a place set for you right away, dear."

Taking a seat beside Deirdre, Brianna looked toward their non-family guest and gasped, "*Joseph*?" Her smile came easily as she inquired, "What on earth are you doing here?"

Joseph's already grin changed to laughter at her response to his presence. "My family's firm is trying to convince Mr. Gordon to join our firm and he has been kind enough to invite me into his home to meet his family and further discuss the merger." Raising his glass in her direction, Joseph added, "A fact for which I am doubly pleased at the moment."

Brianna blushed, but before she could comment, Deirdre intervened, "Have mercy, Bria, and how do you know our Mr. Mitchell?"

Joseph supplied the answer, addressing everyone present. "During my recent time abroad, it was my good fortune to meet and befriend Brianna." Looking to her in question, he further commented, "Though it had been my understanding that she was to remain on in America with her guardian and his family, not return home to Ireland."

"Plans have a way of changing, Joseph," she vaguely explained.

He nodded. "So you'll not be returning to America? It'll be home for you in Ireland?"

"For good and all," Brianna replied with a warm smile.

Joseph could not begin to hide his enthusiasm. He had been sincerely distressed to part from her company; the Saints were watching over him that they should come together again so easily.

Somehow, Lauren felt the need to break the silence; the looks passing between Brianna and Joseph were far warmer than the ones Dee was beginning to dart toward her friend. "And it's happy we are that she has returned to us safe and sound. We've missed her dearly."

"You see, Joseph," Jonathan began in explanation, "Brianna's father and I were longtime friends and likewise so were our daughters. Brianna is like family and though it pained us to let her go so far away, it had been the decision of her mother. I was therefore bound to the choice Mrs. McClaran had made for her child's future."

"And here I sit in the same city where I've dwelled my entire life, while all those around me travel the world and find adventure in foreign lands," Deirdre moaned with envy.

"How quickly you've forgotten the privilege of a French finishing school," Brianna pointed out, allowing her friend to hear how much her ungratefulness annoyed her.

"A Catholic school with nuns as chaperones hardly compares to travels across the sea with a handsome guardian." Deirdre smirked, "I daresay I would have stayed home, as well."

"And saved your parents the worry and expense. I couldn't agree more," Brianna stated.

"It is obvious that your guardian didn't attend to your manners as well as a finishing school did mine. Perhaps he should have sent you to the nuns instead of home."

"Ladies?" Lauren interjected, not entirely surprised by the squabble but equally embarrassed by it for both the young women and herself.

Brianna cleared her throat lightly and added, "At any rate, I daresay I would have much rather foregone the trip and stayed here where everything is familiar to me, Dee. Do not feel that you missed anything by your different experiences which kept you nearer to the ones who love you most."

"She is right, Miss Gordon," Joseph agreed, before inferring to Brianna, "Still, I hope that there was no great misfortune that caused your return. When last I visited the Elliotts in Baltimore, they made no mention of your departure. I merely assumed that you were in Virginia."

Brianna choked on the piece of jam-covered biscuit she had just taken a bite of and fought for composure. Eyes watering, she managed to sputter, "You were in Baltimore again so recently?"

Joseph looked chagrined. "Well, I never actually left to begin with."

"But I thought you were leaving the day after our last visit."

"Yes, that was my plan and by the time I was able to notify you that my stay would be extended, you had already returned to Captain Elliott's home."

A flood of memories washed over Brianna, as she recalled all that had happened during those weeks of which Joseph spoke. Setting her mind aright, Brianna firmly decided that she wouldn't think about that now. "When *did* you return to Ireland?"

"My great-aunt, with whom I'd been staying, took a turn for the worse and unfortunately passed away. There were arrangements to be made, legal matters to handle, and traditions to attend. I returned to Dublin just last week."

"I'm sorry for your family's loss," Brianna offered kindly.

Joseph nodded his acceptance and Brianna questioned, "And when was it that you saw Daniel and Meghan?" Brianna was starving for information, and though she tried not to be obvious, was failing miserably.

Joseph sipped his wine before answering. "The night before I departed Baltimore, actually. I had bumped into—quite literally I might add—Mrs. Elliott and she remembered the time we had shared while you were staying with them." Neither Brianna nor Joseph looked at anyone else at the table, but both felt the heavy heat of curious gazes boring into them at his offhanded comment. "That's when Mrs. Elliott was gracious enough to invite me to dine at her home along with Mr. Elliott's brother who was staying with them, as well."

All of Brianna's insides stopped functioning, started again, jumbled together, and then began operating at an accelerated speed. "Devon was there? Was he alone?" The words were out before Brianna thought them through and her impatiently demanding tone caught the witnesses by surprise.

"Yes," Joseph replied cautiously, watching her for another outburst. "Should he be expected to have company in his brother's home?"

Brianna spoke with disdain of the situation. "Perhaps his intended bride."

"Really?" Joseph sounded confused. "It strikes me odd that not only was he alone, but also neither the Captain nor his family mentioned his upcoming nuptials."

Brianna blurted her response. "If you knew his fiancée, you may also better understand their reasoning for secrecy." Cringing inwardly, Brianna scolded herself; *I really must gain control of this wagging tongue of mine.*

"Who is she?" Joseph inquired, intrigued by Brianna's obvious dislike for the woman.

"My cousin, Larissah Chase."

Joseph nodded, "Ah, well, I have met Miss Chase once or twice and I can say that she is certainly a lady one does not soon forget." Joseph found that he wasn't comfortable with the possibilities Brianna's reactions were placing in his mind. "I am surprised—considering your relation to both Miss Chase and Captain Elliott—that you didn't remain for the wedding."

Brianna thought she might actually gag at the prospect of witnessing that union. While she fought the urge, Lauren had the chance to note how deeply Joseph's comment affected the younger woman. In an instant, Brianna's face went from flushed to pale, her expression immediately closed off. Lauren could imagine a fortress wall sliding into place over her features, over her heart—over everything except her eyes. They were the windows to Brianna's soul and the one place where she had never been able to keep her feelings silent, especially from Lauren.

Pain, raw and clear, filled her green orbs entirely, so deeply that Lauren nearly gasped aloud with understanding.

With luck, Deirdre saved Brianna by interrupting, "How coincidental that the two of you should know so many of the same people, yet never once did you realize that you would meet again here, in Dublin."

Brianna breathed a silent sigh of relief for the change of subject, and then replied, "I think I can speak for both Joseph and myself when I say that neither of us would have guessed that our lives or the plans we had for them would change so drastically. We had no reason to think that our paths would cross again."

"Then you spent a great deal of time with Mr. Mitchell, did you, Bria?"

Even though Deirdre smiled, Brianna knew that the idea bothered her friend. As charming and handsome as Joseph was, with his boyishly sweet face, happy green eyes and curly blonde hair, it was not difficult to figure why Dee seemed so annoyed by their slight history. The fact was that it was hard to imagine anyone *not* liking Joseph.

Except Devon, Brianna pushed that thought quickly aside and replied honestly, "Not nearly as much time as we might have liked."

"And now that we are home again, Brianna, I hope to continue our friendship, if you are agreeable." Hope lit Joseph's eyes as he boldly put her on the spot in front of his new comrades.

Brianna did not disappoint him. "That would be nice. In fact, I look forward to it."

This time Deirdre hid her envy well; no one could realize how disheartened she felt by the rekindling of this relationship.

"However, it's only fair to warn you that I may not have a great deal of time for socializing, Joseph." Looking toward Jonathan, she continued, "Which brings 'round the original reason for my visit today." Brianna didn't wait for a response. "I've been thinking that there must be some way that we can help those suffering from the famine. They are virtually our neighbors and we have more than enough to sustain ourselves, should we not help those less fortunate?" Though Brianna had been specifically addressing Jonathan, each person around her nodded his or her head in affirmation.

"What a wonderful idea, Bria," Lauren complimented. "I am sure the convents are looking for help in serving food for those in need. There is also probably a great want for supplies and attendants to care for the sick."

Deirdre was ready with further assistance. "I'll write Sister Kathleen and ask how we might best put our services to use." Blushing, she added, "If you don't mind the company?"

Brianna laughed. "Of course not, Dee. Certainly the more help the better." Silently, Brianna prayed this act of kindness might bridge the gap between her and Deirdre.

"I will be passing by the convent on my way home this afternoon," Joseph informed them. "If you would care for an escort, I would be glad to see you there and home safely. That way your request will be delivered with haste."

"Yes, thank you, Mr. Mitchell," Deirdre accepted without pause.

"Indeed, your help is greatly appreciated, Joseph." Moreover, the smile Brianna offered proved to everyone in attendance that she was truly—and *finally*—ready to move forward with her life.

◊◊◊◊◊

At Devon's request, Daniel and Meghan returned to their Fell's Point home with him rather than stay on at Misty Heights. Even if Devon wanted to be as far from Larissah as he could be, his family was another matter. He needed them for moral support, but the truth of it was he did not trust himself to be alone.

Just as Larissah had accused, Devon too badly wanted to board the *Sea Enchantress* and sail for Ireland and Brianna. Making his yearning worse, Meghan had innocently invited Joseph Mitchell to dine with them one evening. Devon couldn't be rude in his brother's home, so he attended without complaint. However, when Joseph began asking about Brianna, Devon reached his limit. With barely contained silence, he waited for Daniel's polite explanation that Brianna had chosen to return to Ireland—too homesick to remain in America.

After that encounter, Devon spent a lot of his time at the docks tending to business, allowing his younger sibling the freedom of sharing time with his expecting wife. It also offered Devon the ability to avoid any more visiting reminders of his loss.

Just recently returning to Daniel's townhouse at the end of another workday, Devon walked past Daniel's bedchamber and the sound of laughter met him from behind the closed door.

For the first time since learning of Brianna's decisions to leave him happiness and hope filled Devon with the sound of the newlywed's bliss. He did not envy or begrudge Daniel his joy. Rather he clung to it, reasoning that if his younger brother could find happiness against all odds, then perhaps he could, too.

No matter how much he yearned for the sight, sound and scent of Brianna, he was determined to move on. Somehow, Devon would lead a happy life whether his ex-fiancée or future bride wanted him to or not.

◊◊◊◊◊

Lauren Gordon was beside herself with excited anticipation—she had been ever since Joseph Mitchell's visit and the obvious stir it caused between Deirdre and Brianna. Not for the first time recently, Jonathan walked into the room and caught his wife grinning with a girlishly dreamy expression on her attractive features.

Jon smiled; his wife was happy and kindhearted and wished the same feelings for everyone around her. "Day dreaming again?" he questioned, placing a light kiss on her cheek.

Lauren beamed, "You know me well."

Pulling his wife against his side, Jonathan queried, "Tell me then, is it Deirdre you have married off to Mr. Mitchell today or are you trying to rid us of our dear Brianna again so soon?" Taking a seat on the settee with her, he reminded, "If I recall correctly, you had Brianna betrothed to Devon Elliott *long* before they even reached America. We can all see how wrong that idea was. Perhaps your senses are beginning to fail you a bit."

Lauren ignored his pessimism. "Did you not notice the fuss Joseph sharing company in our home has made?"

"I saw no *fuss*, only two dutiful young women wanting to be charitable to unfortunates in their homeland and a young man willing to aid them."

"Mmm, that is because *you* are a man and not at all observant to such delicate matters as a woman is." Smiling confidently, Lauren suggested, "Do not be deceived by what you think you see, my love."

"I see only what my eyes show me—only a lovesick matchmaking meddler would believe that there could be more than that, Mrs. Gordon."

"A meddler is it?" Lauren asked in a bantering way. "Know this my fine husband; Brianna is more in love with the elusive Captain than even *I* had thought she would be."

Jon looked doubtful, "The Captain brought only arguments and tension. That is hardly a mixture for great romance—her return home is proof positive of that."

"True," Lauren nodded in certain agreement. Brianna will do her healing here—not as quickly or in the same direction as Joseph might like—but healing just the same."

"Certain, are you?"

"Entirely," Lauren pledged.

"Then tell me wise wife, what will happen next since the man you believe Brianna loves is an ocean away, preparing to wed another woman?"

Lauren bit at her bottom lip with obvious concern before admitting, "I cannot positively say, but I pray she'll accept Joseph's attention."

Jonathan guffawed. "First you claim Brianna loves Devon, next you want her to accept another man's calls," he leaned toward his wife to better see her scheming face, "explain that, if you will."

"Time."

"*Time* for *what*?"

"Time for Brianna to heal, decide to return to America and face her fears. Time for Joseph to accept her choice and time for Deirdre to convince him *she* is the woman he should be with."

Jonathan wavered between amusement and frustration, "Why not simply leave Brianna out of the mix altogether?"

"Because, Deirdre has some growing up to do yet."

Jon nodded in silent agreement to that observation, and then advised, "Let this one go, my sweet." Taking her face gently between his hand and looking into her kind eyes, he explained, "I long to see Brianna happy as much as you do, but I do not think that even you, with all of your powers and good intentions, can steer a union for her."

Lauren considered his words for a moment and then set her jaw against his negativity. "I can't do that, Jon. She needs to be happy."

Jonathan's persuasion was consistent. "And she will be, but on her own time and with the man she chooses."

"Joseph is not the man for her," Lauren stubbornly warned.

"Then why lead her toward him?"

Patting his clean-shaven face patiently, Lauren whispered, "Because he will help her heal."

Jonathan decided against arguing further, kissed her lips tenderly and accepted, "I'm sure you are right, my dear, completely right."

◊◊◊◊◊

Spring was coming early and the air within her home was warm as Larissah wiped the sweat from her brow. Three more days and the deed would be done. At long last Devon Elliott would be hers—name, money and passion.

Two more months and her womb would be free of its burden.

Larissah did little more these days than lie around and wait for the glorious time when the child would no longer kick at her sides and cause constant discomfort.

As though on cue, the babe moved and at the same time, the most recent reason for her anxiety strode into the parlor to join her. Stopping in his tracks to look her over from head to toe, Nate pondered, "Do you even realize how fetching you are sprawled out and relaxed like that?" A sincerely appreciative and sensual gleam came to his dark eyes as he offered the compliment.

In her present state, Larissah easily overlooked such attractions. Glaring in his direction, she declared, "No more than you realize what a tax your visits have become to my senses and my body."

Nate leaned over her and kissed her cheek lightly. "Am I to believe that you have tired of my attentions so soon, Larissah?"

"Yes," she replied with empty honesty.

"Doubtful at best," he countered, full of self-assurance.

Larissah's blue eyes narrowed at his arrogance. "You can believe that *and* the fact that despite the pleasure I found from you before, I detest you just as passionately now."

Nate laughed, still able to see her spiteful and hormonal lies for what they were. Enjoying the fun of tormenting her, he questioned, "And were it Devon Elliott who had come to you as I have now, would your arms and legs be open to him?"

In the haughtiest manner she could manage, Larissah reminded him, "In case you have forgotten, in a very short time I shall be his wife. Then Devon will have the right to liberties you will no longer possess."

Clicking his tongue at her misgivings, Nate corrected, "But our arrangement was not made to end with your nuptials, Ris." Mocking her with feigned concern and regret, he queried, "You *did* understand that, didn't you?"

"I understand *perfectly*," she gritted out in annoyance, eyes throwing icy sparks his way. "I understand that you are a cad who would force himself not only on a woman with child, but also one who is soon to be married to another man."

Patronizingly, he stated, "Come now, Larissah, I don't recall a time that force was ever necessary between us." Smiling with wicked charm, Nate offered his hand and prodded, "Shall I prove it to you now?"

"Do I really have a choice?"

"You've always had a choice," he stated practically.

Larissah felt her blood begin to boil. "Not one that I am willing to make."

Nate shrugged a single shoulder. "A choice is a choice. Whether or not both options are appealing is another matter altogether." His tone became annoyingly buoyant then. "Now, come and join me, Ris. I don't want to be rushed with you and I'm short on time already."

Faking concern, she suggested, "Then perhaps we should forgo our usual activities so that you are not held up from your servile duties."

Shaking his head with a smile, Nate presented, "That's not necessary; if need be, I am willing to inform my employer of my whereabouts. I am sure you would agree that Robert would well understand the temptations of such a body as yours, even bloated as it is with my child." Nate let his hand drop and began popping open the fastenings on the front of her bodice. "Since you seem to be so comfortable where you are and not willing to move at a pace more suitable to me or a place more private, I suppose I will simply have my way with you here."

Shoving his groping hands away, Larissah stood slowly, her stomach bulging out before her as she heaved her weight up from the chair. "Very well, I'll *move*; there is no reason to unsettle the slaves who might happen upon such a scene. They pray and chant around me far too much as it is, there is no need to cause them further lamentations. All that mumbling grates on one's nerves after a while." Offering him a sour smile, she added, "Much as you do."

"And with such gentle words from your loving lips, you continue to wonder why it is that I return for your favors." Nate then swept her into his arms and proceeded to carry Larissah up the stairs. Her waddling was taking far too long for his liking. "Let us go and see what I can do to restore your once high opinion of me, even if just for a short time."

◊◊◊◊◊

Devon rounded the bend that would lead him to Misty Heights and the comforts of home. It had been good to find some time away from life's pressures. That brief moment of freedom was over though, and he must now return to reality and all of the demands that he had managed to avoid these past few weeks.

As Devon rode, he contemplated his next move. He could return to Misty Heights immediately and spend the remainder of the day in the tranquility he would certainly find there or he could call on his bride-to-be and let her know he had returned. Now that the day was so near, Devon could see no way around this dreaded marriage. It was time to face his future no matter how distasteful he found it.

His decision made, Devon reined Leviathan in and turned the stead in a slightly different direction. Indeed, it was time to take hold of his responsibilities and embrace them and Larissah completely. Perhaps by doing so, in time, she would change and they could share some form of companionship—anything would be better than the rivalry they had been offering one another of late.

Until then, Devon guessed he could at least take advantage of the one thing they had always had in common, that which had continually returned them to each other—and turmoil— time and time again.

Devon's thoughts ceased their direction. There was a horse tethered in front of Larissah's home, a horse he recognized at a glance. It didn't take much thought to ponder exactly what Robert Montgomery was doing at Reverie. Even in her condition, Larissah could not remain faithful.

Moreover, she apparently hadn't expected Devon to return home early.

Now, her folly was Devon's luck, and with it, Larissah may have finally found a way to make Devon truly happy—she was offering him his freedom and didn't even know it yet.

Devon jumped down from Leviathan's saddle before the horse's hooves had a chance to stop. He strode purposefully through the front door, not bothering to close it behind him—time was of the essence and he would be passing through its opening again soon, anyway.

◊◊◊◊◊

Uncomfortable as the pregnancy made her, Larissah could not deny the expertise of Nate's lovemaking. She didn't even care that he knew how good he was; she simply allowed her senses to bask in the feel of him without inhibition.

In fact, Larissah was so enthralled by Nate's touch that she failed to hear the bedchamber door open and it took her desire-clouded wits several more moments to register the sound of laughter.

But when it did, terror struck Larissah's soul.

Devon stood in the doorway and absorbed the entire scene with amusement. Over her, Nate ceased his movements, joining in the jovial sound, their mixed mirth reminding Larissah of youths committing a great joke. This time, however, the laugh was at her expense.

Fighting back tears of humiliation and rage, Larissah waited with horrid anticipation. Her world was about to crumble around her and she had no doubt that Devon was eager for the demolition to commence.

Chapter Twenty-Four

Devon could hear the familiar sounds of Larissah's passion floating down the hall long before he reached her bedchamber door. Surprised to find the entry unlocked, he opened it before either occupant knew he was there.

The man was the first to take note of the new presence in the room and to his credit, continued to please the woman below him for several moments, daring Devon with his eyes to make him cease.

That bravado—as well as the revelation of exactly who Larissah's lover was—sent Devon over the edge. The sound of laughter, full of sincere happiness, exploded from his beaming features.

Not relinquishing his position, Nate questioned, "Is there something I can help you with, Captain?"

Devon's reply was cheerful. "Believe it or not, you already have." And at that moment, his gaze clashed with Larissah's unbelieving one.

Pushing against Nate's muscular chest to no avail, Larissah screeched, "Get off of me, you fool!"

Without budging, Nate countered, "Why? I seriously doubt that there is anything within view that Captain Elliott hasn't seen numerous times already." Grinning down at Larissah, he added, "And something tells me he doesn't care if I stop or not."

"You, Nate, are absolutely correct," Devon agreed with a smile.

Larissah fruitlessly attempted to free herself again. "I cannot believe the two of you are behaving as though we are having this conversation at a social gathering."

Devon smiled. "Rissah, I for one, have never in my life enjoyed a social gathering so much as I am this moment."

"Here, here," Nate inserted with a smirk that brought another bout of laughter roaring from the doorway.

Larissah was in shock and rather certain that Nate had planned for them to be caught. How he'd managed it, she wasn't sure, but the arrival of him and Devon so closely together had to be more than mere coincidence. With heavy sarcasm, she spat, "I am so glad that the two of you are so amiable."

"Why wouldn't we be? We are, after all, both getting exactly what we want from you." Devon's easy comment set Larissah on edge. The Devon Elliott she knew was nothing like the odd man who stood before her now. The boy she had watched grow into a man—had grown alongside—should be cursing her, ranting and raving about his precious honor and how she had humiliated him and smudged his family name.

Crystal blue eyes narrowed with suspicion, Larissah demanded, "What are you about, Devon? What is this game? Why are you so calm?"

When Devon leveled his gaze on her, Larissah saw what she had missed before—behind his good-natured smile, Devon's molten blue eyes were an inferno of hatred and the heat of it carried to his words. "Quite simply because I truly do not care what you do or with whom you do it, Larissah. In fact, you have made me happier today than ever before."

With more bravado than she felt, Larissah seethed, "You are more of an idiot than I imagined. How can you possibly find happiness in my bedding another man?"

Shaking his head at her in a mock-sympathetic manner, Devon asked, "Don't you recall that I explicitly advised you, if I were to catch you with any man, in any type of position I find to be compromising, he may have my blessing along with you and your child to contend with?"

Running his hand down Larissah's bare side, Nate replied, "I'd place a safe wager that this would qualify as compromising."

Devon's laughter erupted again.

Rather than scream, as she wanted to, Larissah offered a sultry laugh of her own. "Devon, we both know that you will not risk your family name by denying our child the right to his or her father."

Devon looked at her in amazement. "Larissah, I tire of your lies and I am certain that the child inside you is nearer his father now than he ever would be with me—even if I held him in my arms."

"What do you intend to do? Leave me stranded?"

Bluntly, Devon replied, "Fend for yourself, you always have, or perhaps Nate might be of some assistance to you."

"He is a *servant*," Larissah screeched out with contempt.

"Apparently he has served *you* well," Devon denounced, still somewhat astonished at the extent of Larissah's aristocratic attitude. "Bear in mind that he is *not* merely a servant. If you would pay further attention to the social ladder you scour so coarsely for pleasurable bedmates, then you would know that Nate Carter is an indentured servant, *not* a slave."

"Of course I know . . ."

"You would *also* know," Devon continued with a firm tutorial tone, "that thanks to his good work ethic, Robert Montgomery treats Nate more as a friend and a gentleman than a servant and has therefore assured him good standing socially, even going so far as to offer letters of reference to highly stationed families. Many of whom are currently searching out husbands for their fine young ladies and the considerable dowries that go with them."

Nate smirked. "And, *I* might add, their dowries are not the *only* considerable attributes some have offered me away from Papa's watchful eye."

"Oh, and I'm sure you declined gracefully," Larissah seethed.

Nate merely smiled; the truth was he hadn't touched any woman except Larissah in nearly a year. However, he greatly enjoyed watching her consider the possibility that he had.

Jealously coursing through every inch of her being, Larissah demanded, "Who is it that's caught your fancy?"

Nate made a sound of incredulity. "After watching you torture Captain Elliott and Miss McClaran, do you really think I'd be so stupid as to tell you *that*?"

Larissah's retort was punctual. "Yes."

Devon began to formulate a plan then, one that made him want to roar with laughter and preen with the genius of its revenge. Clearing his throat as an obvious and intentional interruption, he advised, "You would be wise to grasp this opportunity before it too evades you, Larissah."

"*What* possibility is that?" she seethed disdainfully.

Looking to Nate, Devon questioned, "Tell me, man, have you proposed or made promises to any of the ladies you've been spending time with?"

Nate shook his head negatively and rolled to his side, pulling the sheet up over his waist. He even took the time to aid Larissah when she scrambled to do the same, and then answered, "No, why do you ask?"

"Quite plainly, because if you are not otherwise intended and you wish to marry Larissah, raise what I assume to be your child and have this land to farm and the fortune that comes with it, I will give you my blessing and the legal means to do so."

Nate didn't have the chance to respond.

"Devon, you wouldn't." Larissah's tone was uncharacteristically soft and unsure as she inquired, "What will I tell people? Surely not the *truth*."

"Heavens no, Larissah," Nate gasped in mock horror. "How could you face anyone again with them knowing you had taken a lowly stable hand to your bed and were now unwed and carrying his bastard child?"

Looking up at the man who mocked her, Larissah could think of no suitable retort and so promptly spat in his face.

Nate was enraged. He had had quite enough of this woman and her ways—it was high time she learned a lesson in respect. Grabbing a handful of her blonde hair, he yanked her toward him and placed her face directly in front of his. "Count your blessings that my bastard child has just saved you from a beating you well deserve."

"And is long overdue," Devon added, drawing the couple's attention back to him.

Nate warned Larissah and informed Devon, "Once I am her husband and our child is delivered, I will not hold back from punishing her when she deserves it."

"I wouldn't expect otherwise," Devon agreed. "Is that your reply, then? You'll marry Larissah?"

Wiping the remainder of her recent insult from his cheek, Nate responded, "You can understand my hesitance even at *this* moment?"

Devon chuckled, "Man, I would understand your hesitance at *any* time." Pausing, Devon sighed. "Think on the long term of what I am offering you, though; consider it a wedding gift for each of us. Larissah can save face socially by claiming that I forced her to marry, as it was high time she did so. She can tell everyone that you had a private union months ago and, of course, she was so ashamed by its social ramifications, followed closely by impending motherhood, that she stayed away from public scrutiny until now."

A small sound of humor escaped Nate's full lips at the farce of a story and the fact that society could be so easily duped, so long as a bit of juicy gossip pushed a tale along.

Devon continued, uninterrupted, "You, Mr. Carter, will finally have the social standing you've so long strived for and I think it's safe to say that you'll *both* have the lovers you actually desire." Looking directly at Nate, Devon opinionated, "Which may be the best chance anyone will ever have at making Larissah Chase faithful to one man."

Already fairly sure of what the reply would be, Nate asked, "And what do *you* get out of all this generosity, Captain?"

Smiling in a way that made Larissah's stomach turn with trepidation, Devon declared, "I intend to make Brianna McClaran mine at last."

Larissah fumed. "Even after all the time you've been apart from her and the way she cowered at the first opposition for your affections, you want her? Even after the way she denied you all that I offered, you still want that Irish . . ."

Devon took a menacing step toward the bed, his smile instantly gone. "Take care, it is the woman I love you speak of."

"*Love*? How dare you preach to *me* of love when you throw mine aside so carelessly?" Larissah's voice strained to the point of cracking as she yelled at him.

Devon laughed again, though this time the sound was scathing. "You know *nothing* of love except that which you feel for yourself or the physical kind which you offer so freely that it means nothing to you or your lovers."

In a courteous fashion, Devon noted in Nate's direction, "Present company excepted."

Nodding his head graciously, Nate responded, "Not necessarily, but I thank you for saying so, anyway."

Larissah screeched. She was momentarily unable to form words, but her aggravation was so strong that she needed to vent it any way possible. Her loss of vocabulary was short-lived however and she ranted, "To Hell with the both of you! Just go, Devon! Leave me in peace and go! I have nothing more to say to you!"

"Not just yet, for I have something to say to you, Larissah." When she made no remark, Devon continued, "I will be off to Ireland as soon as humanly possible. Therefore, it would be in your best interest to begin circulating the story of your marriage to Nate. Add *nothing* that will harm my family, which shouldn't be difficult since I certainly didn't share the news of our farce betrothal with anyone except Daniel, Meghan and Brianna. Considering the fact that you have been cooped up here and unable to spread the lie outside of your home, I'd assume that not many people would have heard we were planning to marry, anyway."

Allowing the words he had spoken to sink into her manipulative mind, Devon then finished, "After I return, I expect the reputations of everyone involved in your scheme to still be properly intact."

Returning the attention to him, Nate inquired, "How soon can your offer be arranged?"

Devon smiled, feeling the rightness of his duty meld with the sweetness of revenge. "I'll be leaving for Ireland in no more than two days. If you bring me written permission or a note clearing you of servitude from Montgomery, I would be pleased to perform the ceremony on the spot, myself."

Nate nodded and promised, "I'll have it to you by tomorrow at noon."

"I can hardly wait," Devon assured him and left the room's occupants to their plans and pleasure as he departed with thoughts of the same for himself.

◊◊◊◊◊

Brianna slumped in the seat of the covered-buggy and watched Joseph's animated features as he laughed at her apparent misery. "You look plum whipped, Bria. I think you should be taking a day away from helping others so that you might help yourself instead."

Exhausted after the twelfth day in a row of mending clothing, cleaning and changing bedding and serving warm broth for the needy, Brianna somehow found the energy to laugh. "*Plum whipped?* Joseph, I think that's the funniest thing I've heard in weeks."

The sound of her mirth brought a smile to his face. "It's an American phrase I picked up while visiting."

"How cute. Were I to use any of the terms I learned during my stay, I *should* be plum whipped, *directly* over someone's knee."

Joseph roared with laughter as that amusing picture filled his mind. "Never the less, Brianna, you *should* be thinking of your health. I may be bold in saying so, but you look too pale and it won't help anyone if you come down with an ailment of your own."

Hoping to make him happy and as a result be able to enjoy the remainder of their ride home, Brianna conceded, "Fine, I will take tomorrow off for rest."

"You will not return until Monday," Joseph affirmed, his declaration stronger than Brianna was accustomed to from him.

In exasperation, she reminded him, "Joseph Mitchell, that is *four* days hence."

"And Sister Kathleen and the rest of the volunteers will get by just fine without you," he finished, not allowing her to argue further.

"Faith and Begora, soon you'll be telling me what I can and cannot wear and whom I can and cannot spend my time with." Not contemplating her words, she added with a huff, "You sound like an overbearing guardian or a demanding husband."

"Is that an invitation?" Joseph inquired, only teasing somewhat.

Brianna shook her head. "The last thing I need is another guardian, thank you very much."

"And what of a husband, do you need one of those?" Joseph was suddenly very serious.

Since renewing their friendship, Brianna and Joseph had scarcely allowed a day to pass that they were not together. It thrilled Joseph and recently—unbeknownst to Brianna—he had spoken to Jonathan about his intentions.

Joseph knew that by most social standards he was early with his plans, but he felt that he and Brianna were as close as any other courting couple he knew and she made him insanely happy. He wouldn't risk losing as fine a catch as Brianna by waiting too long to make his objectives known.

Joseph's only worry was that when Brianna looked at him, it was as a friend or a brother, not with the eyes of a lover. Perhaps if she understood his true feelings, hers would begin to change for him and the glances he dreamed of her bestowing upon him would begin.

Though the sincerity of his words caused Brianna to blush, she tried to lighten the air around them with an easy chuckle. "Joseph, I've had a guardian and quite nearly a husband already, and neither has worked out for me in the past."

It was the first time Brianna had opened up to anyone in Ireland even the slightest about what had occurred in Virginia. Joseph did not attempt to hide his surprise. "What? You've been engaged? When? To whom? When did it end? Why did it end?"

"If I answer *one* of your questions, can the others wait?"

"We'll see."

Brianna held her breath, almost reconsidered and then blurted out, "It was Devon."

Joseph was oddly validated; he had always known, always *felt* that there was more than just a platonic guardian/ward relationship between Brianna and Devon.

While he tried to hide the hurt and envy from his voice, Joseph was almost successful, but not entirely. "Why is it you never mentioned being engaged to him before?"

"Because you never asked before," she replied smartly, hoping that her perkiness would bring him around to smile again.

It didn't work. "Brianna McClaran, don't you be flip with me, girlie. Either you were engaged before we met, while we were sharing time together or quickly after our parting company in America. Which is it?"

Straightening herself in the seat beside him, she begged, "Another time please? After all, you *have* demanded that I take the next few days off. I am somehow certain that you won't deprive me of your company during that time."

"Don't be so sure of your powers over me," Joseph skulked. "Especially now."

"Next time, Joseph," she vowed with an emotion-filled sigh.

Skeptically he watched her, mildly pondering the validity of her vow. "You promise?"

"Only if you promise to keep my secret safe; I have no wish for the Gordons to know of my misfortunes.

Joseph nodded. "Done."

Her eyes met his and despite the topic, Brianna felt her heart open to Joseph just a little more. "Thank you, kind friend."

Clearing his throat, Joseph overlooked the chaste endearment and offered, "How about I make it a wee bit easier on you by taking you for lunch at Daugherty's?" He knew that of all the pubs available to females, this was Brianna's favorite.

In acceptance, Brianna closed her eyes, leaned back against the seat to rest her head and observed in a tired mumble, "A man after my own heart."

"You, my dear, have *no* idea." With that assurance, Joseph turned the buggy down D'Olier Street and toward Brianna's home there.

◊◊◊◊◊

Daniel and Meghan arrived at Misty Heights only a few hours after Devon and, with one glance at his brother's worried face and his sister-in-law's frail form, Devon knew that his intentions of leaving directly for Ireland must change.

Devon listened with intent sympathy as Daniel explained that some complications had arisen with the pregnancy and the doctor had insisted that Meghan be on bed rest until the child's birth.

Devon welcomed them to use Misty Heights for as long as they needed, even as he dreaded the realization that he could not possibly sail to Ireland while Meghan was ill and Daniel needed his support.

After seeing Larissah and Nate married, Devon was re-signed to waiting, and began assisting Hesper and Daniel in keeping vigil by Meghan's bedside. Now, as he sat watching the steady rise and fall of her chest as she breathed in sleep, Devon paid particular attention to the slight mound of the sheet where the babe lay beneath her skin.

The days had been long and during Meghan's waking hours, her frustration was evident. She despised being stuck in bed and she and Daniel argued a lot as a result. Meghan insist-ed that it would be no strain for her to have a leisurely walk around the grounds. Daniel would hear nothing of it and terse-ly reminded her that had she notified him of her condition sooner, she would likely not be abed as she was now.

On top of the expected annoyances, everyone knew that Devon was anxious to leave. His denied wishes only added to the level of tension in the household. It was as though he were a wild animal, caged from the freedom he so desperately craved.

A stirring at his side caught Devon's attention and for the first time since he had entered the room, Meghan opened her eyes. Forcing a weak grin, she observed with unintentional rudeness, "Devon, you are looking nearly as dreadful as your brother these days."

With a shrug of his shoulders, he returned, "A man must make certain sacrifices when someone he loves is unsafe."

With an unladylike roll of her eyes and failure to see the complement in his words, Meghan declared, "I am not unsafe, merely pregnant."

Devon took note of the aggravation in her voice and re-minded softly, "It is far better for you to endure this boredom and time in bed than to risk your health or the baby's." When she would have argued, Devon added, "Please don't fuss, Meghan. I need you and my niece or nephew to get well so that I might go and bring them an aunt from Ireland."

Chagrined by the reminder of Devon's forfeit for her, Meghan permitted, "How nice that will be for all of us."

"I couldn't agree more."

"Have you written her of your intentions?"

"No, I prefer the element of surprise." When Meghan prepared to voice her opinion, Devon shushed her, encouraging, "Rest now, so that you'll be strengthened and I will be able to return her to us all the sooner."

Snuggling down beneath her quilt, Meghan agreed, "I will try Devon, but I am so weary of all this relaxation and I can't imagine that such laziness is good for the baby, either."

Sympathetically, Devon replied, "We must heed Doctor Porter and Cobb's warnings. Do not fret, your child will get all of the exercise he or she needs. They will simply have to wait until *after* they are born to do so."

Meghan's soft blue eyes filled with frustration. "In the meantime, *I* am left to go mad."

"Hush, now," Devon consoled, tucking the blanket in close around her.

Noting the redness and strain around Devon's blue eyes, Meghan expressed, "This cannot possibly be good for you or Daniel, either. You both look worn, and Daniel worries constantly." Averting her eyes in thought, Meghan glanced back at her brother-in-law, suggesting, "Why don't the two of you go to town for supper? It would do you each good to get out."

Eyeing her skeptically, Devon replied, "Because even if I trusted you not to get out of bed, Daniel would never agree to it."

Rolling her eyes, Meghan huffed, "For Heaven's sake, Devon, Hesper will be here. Please go and allow me some peace from your infernal hovering. If you'll not leave for Ireland and Brianna, at least treat yourself and Daniel to a few hours away."

With light laughter, Devon contemplated her words before giving in. "Let me speak to Daniel and see if I can be as persuasive as you, my sweet sister."

◊◊◊◊◊

Three-quarters of an hour later, Daniel relaxed in the saddle and the familiar sensation of the animal beneath him. "I must admit that this has been refreshing for me already, Devon."

Laughing at the easy way of his brother, Devon anticipated, "If you think this is nice, just wait until you have some food in your gut."

"*That* will be pure bliss." Glancing aside at Devon, Daniel commented, "You know, I don't believe I have eaten an entire meal since we came to Misty Heights."

"You sound surprised. Don't forget that you've been rather preoccupied lately."

Daniel studied his brother before remarking, "I am not the only one whose priorities have changed during these past weeks."

Devon did not remark, but kept his eyes forward.

"Dev, I know what it must be taking for you to stay here and help us. I appreciate it more than words can convey."

"You are my brother, Daniel. You would do the same for me."

Guilt riddled the younger man. "That's just it. As much as you mean to me, I don't know if I *would* risk losing a woman like Brianna."

"Thanks for the support, Daniel," Devon replied, before sighing loudly. "You are right. It has not been easy, but the guilt I would feel if I left during this time isn't something I'm willing to live with. When the time is right for me to leave, then I will and not before."

"Fine, but then are you willing to risk Brianna's love?"

The direct question struck a nerve within Devon that he did not care to feel. "Are you saying that you want me to leave, Daniel? I thought you said you appreciate my being here."

"What I am saying is that *I* do not want to be the one blamed if you wait too long and lose Brianna. I am sure that Meghan shares my opinion, too. We do appreciate all that you've done, but we are fine now. Hesper and Abram can help; it is time for you to bring Brianna back home."

A mixture of relief, despair, excitement and guilt filled Devon. He wanted to forgo the dining plans with which he had enticed Daniel out of the house and immediately whisk away to

Baltimore. Yet at the same time, he still felt bound to remain where he was and protect his family.

Rather than argue the point further or give a rapid answer now, Devon nudged his stallion to a trot and asked, "May I at least eat first?" Not waiting for a reply, he left Daniel in the dust Leviathan kicked up as he tore off in response to his master's sharp kick in the side.

Quickly, the younger Elliott kneed his own mount, caught up to Devon and together the brothers raced for town.

Chapter Twenty-Five

Lauren Gordon was in her front parlor, awaiting Brianna's arrival to her home.

Since the discussion with her husband concerning Brianna's love life, Lauren could not shake the uncertainty his doubt had placed over her confidence in the direction Brianna's heart was leading her. Normally, Lauren's intuitions were unshakable, but as Joseph's feelings became stronger for Brianna, Lauren could see the young woman's resolve weakening—she was healing, but she was settling too. Lauren was determined to recalculate her matchmaking beliefs about Brianna and Devon before the evening was through.

As requested, Brianna arrived at the Gordons' home promptly at five o'clock in the evening. Her smile came easy when Lauren greeted her with a motherly-brazen comment. "I notice you have been spending a great deal of your time with Mr. Mitchell lately."

Handing her cape over to a bobbing young maid, Brianna didn't hesitate in her reply but allowed the comfort of Lauren's familiarity to envelop her like a loving embrace. "It seems to *me* that all of my time is being spent at the convent helping the sisters with their work."

Lauren kissed Brianna lightly on each cheek. "And when you're *not* at the convent? What of *that* time?"

Brianna conceded, "Perhaps I *am* spending a fair amount of time with Joseph, but why shouldn't I? I enjoy his company."

"I'd be willing to wager he enjoys yours even more," Lauren opinionated, leading the way into the parlor.

"Speaking of company," Brianna deftly changed the subject, "where are Jonathan and Dee?"

"Jonathan decided that it has been too long since he spoiled his daughter and is treating her to an evening out for supper and theater."

"So it's just the two of us tonight?" Brianna observed unnecessarily.

With a comforting smile, Lauren informed smoothly, "Yes, dear, I thought perhaps that would give us some time to talk."

Suddenly wary, Brianna watched Lauren closely. This woman was able to read her like a book. Often, friends had teased Lauren about having "The Gift" and sometimes Brianna wondered if it wasn't entirely a jest. Throughout her life, Lauren had been able to sense changes in Brianna when no one else could.

A sure suspicion came over Brianna that Lauren's gesture of invitation was not made merely for the pleasure of her company. Cautiously, Brianna inquired, "Is there a particular subject you're thinking of us talking *about*?"

Just as always, Lauren could sense her company's feelings and she knew that Brianna was on to her. Her next words came in a compassionate, reassuring tone. "It is only that you have taken quite a turn from the girl who left us, to the woman I see before me now. I am curious about your time away. What was it like? Did you make any friends? Did you an Devon finally move beyond your argumentative bantering?"

With a shaky chuckle, Brianna answered part of the question, while desperately avoiding the remainder. "Of course I had friends, Lauren. Why wouldn't I have?" Brianna could not control the weakness in her tone. She had been doing so well—or so she told herself—at avoiding thoughts of America and those remaining there. It had been over a month since she had written to Meghan and she had yet to gain a reply—maybe more had changed than she thought. Perhaps now that Brianna was out of sight, those she had counted as friends looked down on her, thinking her weak for running away.

Lauren said nothing, simply stared into Brianna's emerald eyes, watching as her mind raced. All of the answers this mother figure sought were apparent in Brianna's expression—

Lauren had only to sort them out. Clearly, she could see confusion, but there was also fear and possibly pain.

Gently, Lauren spoke, "You cannot hold such secrets in forever, my love. It is a woman's way to share her heart with a friend. Though it pains me, I can see the way you and Deirdre have grown apart." When Brianna would have interrupted and denied the truth of her accusations, Lauren held her hand up, warding off the words. "Do not argue it. I am very observant. I see not only this tension between you and Deirdre, but also the sorrow in you since your return. The first thing to brighten your mood was when Joseph Mitchell entered your life again. He has given you a glow that only the need of a mended heart can bring."

Entreating the younger woman with her kind tone and loving gaze, Lauren suggested, "Open up to me. Tell me what has been paining you."

Brianna looked everywhere in the room, seeming to search frantically for an exit from this conversation—finding none, she offered, "There is nothing I can say, Lauren. I promised myself not to look back and I cannot break that vow now. Too much is riding on my feelings."

Lauren recalled Jonathan telling her about his conversation with Joseph. If the man intended to propose to Brianna, then she would need to vent all of these feelings out before she could accept him fully. Even if that meant that for the first time in her life, Lauren would be wrong about the romance between two people, she knew that for Brianna's sake, there was no other way to handle this situation except with force.

Boldly Lauren demanded, "Tell me about Devon."

Brianna jolted visibly and knew that if Lauren had not seen the movement, then her close proximity to her on the settee would have allowed her to feel the action. Tears welled in Brianna's eyes. She was close to breaking and did not want to allow that to happen. Softly she replied, "I can't."

"You *must*," Lauren prodded.

"Why, Lauren? Why are you asking me this now, after I have healed and no longer want to think about my past?" Brianna's voice was shaking.

"How can you believe that your heart has healed if you cannot even talk about him without hurting? You can't even hear his name without it affecting you completely." The truth of those words bit into Brianna's innermost being and Lauren could sense it. She would not back off now—not when she was so close to learning what had elapsed between Brianna and her guardian.

Tears rolled freely as Brianna realized that Lauren was right. Brianna had not healed with Joseph's caring attention or her time away. She had simply put her emotions on hold and denied herself the right to mourn the love she had shared and lost.

"How is it that you know how I feel even when I do not?"

"It's a mother's job to know how her children feel, Brianna. Though you are not of my blood, you are the daughter of my heart." Hugging the girl gently, Lauren pulled away and informed her, "You'll also recall that I warned you when Devon first came that there would be no denying such passion."

"I remember." Brianna smiled with her memories. "I *also* remember that I could not stand him the first time I met him."

"True, but you certainly did enjoy looking at him and picking at him until he was as angry as any man could be."

"Trust me," Brianna remarked dryly, "he *could* be angrier."

Lauren laughed and urged with understanding, "You do not need to tell me all that transpired between you two. You are a lady and I know you would not have made wrong choices. I just want you to know that I realize the love you feel for him even now and I want you to remember that no matter what happened in your past, the future may still hold that chance for you again." She allowed those words to take root before adding, "In order to heal from Devon's love, you must first allow yourself to admit his love *and* yours. No one will begrudge you the time you need to do that, least of all me."

"And what about Joseph?"

"Joseph will wait. He has already and he knows the value of a lady such as you." Lauren was strong—certain beyond doubt—that her words were correct, even if the reason for them was selfish in wanting Brianna to feel desire again, so that she would regain the confidence to stand up for the man her heart truly wanted—Devon Elliott.

"You cannot love again until you have given Devon's memory time to heal. You will need the love and patience of a kind and good man to help you with that, Joseph is certainly that man."

"That is not fair to him. Why should Joseph wait for me to make up my mind?"

"Because that is what true love is all about and my dear, Joseph Mitchell truly loves you and will wait for you to truly love him in return." *Even if that never happens*, Lauren added to herself silently, feeling a mild pang of guilt for her slight deception.

Brianna sniffled, "I don't know if I'm ready, but I don't think I can wait any longer to talk about Devon either. If you believe that is what I need to do to move on, than let's get started."

"Take your time," Lauren offered. "We have the entire evening ahead of us." And the matchmaker settled in for the tale she had been longing to hear and knew it would, in fact, bring Brianna to think on the man of her heart *more* rather than less.

◊◊◊◊◊

Contrary to what he had coerced her into promising, Joseph did not broach the subject of Devon Elliott in the slightest during the following days. Not when they lunched at Brianna's favorite restaurant or when they spent time together on the promenade of Ha'Penny Bridge.

While Joseph's curiosity was aching to discover the truth and extent of Brianna's relationship with Devon, every other instinct within him cried out against it with the distinct and strong feeling that the truth was actually the *last* thing he wanted to hear.

In the end, Joseph decided he did *not* want to know what had occurred between the pair. What was in Brianna's past was best left there.

Brianna didn't mind Joseph's change of heart in the least. She had dreaded his questions, had even considered feigning illness to avoid his company. Instcad, she determined that Joseph was her friend and if he were sincere in his feelings for her, they would not change because of what she and Devon had shared. She would answer his questions as they came and accept the choices she had made.

Still, she felt tremendous relief in the fact that she didn't have to say anything about it at all.

The sun was beginning to fade on the horizon, signaling the end of their time at Ha'Penny Park. "It's time to return home," Brianna suggested, though she was enjoying the scenery immensely.

"The end of another lovely day, made even better by my sharing it with you," Joseph agreed sweetly, turning them toward the waiting coach as he spoke. Brianna smiled at his compliment—offering kind words seemed second nature to him.

Continuing to enjoy the sights and sounds of the other couples and families around them, Brianna noticed a group a short distance ahead of her and Joseph.

A woman, just about Brianna's age was holding an infant in her arms. At her side, a handsome man with dark hair held the hand of a wobbling toddler. From this distance, Brianna could almost imagine it was Devon. Even as she tried to push the thought away, the man turned toward her, offering her a clearer view of his face and the uncanny resemblance was so great that she almost thought that he would walk toward her in greeting at any moment now.

Catching the direction of her gaze and the objects of her attention, Joseph misinterpreted her look of affection for dreams of motherhood. Warmth, such as had become very familiar around Brianna, grew within him and without pause, Joseph asked, "Brianna, would you consider becoming my wife?"

She was not unpleasantly shocked by his question, only mildly surprised. More than anything, the way he proposed amused Brianna, reminding her of the way he requested she join him for any of their regular outings. Sincerely, she asked, "Are you being *serious*, Joseph?"

He took no offense at her reaction and stopping where they stood, Joseph turned her to face him, informing her softly, "Brianna, I am more serious about this than I have been about anything else in my life."

Brianna smiled, thinking of her recent time with Lauren and once more considered the possibility of perceptive powers within that woman. "This is rather sudden."

Nodding, Joseph agreed, "Yes, I know, but that does not change how I feel about you."

Tentatively she asked, "And just how is that, Joseph?"

Flicking her tenderly on the tip of her nose, he scolded, "Don't you know, Bria? I love you with all that I am." Joseph felt sure that Brianna was holding her breath. The color left her face and she wobbled slightly. "I do hope that this is a positive reaction to my declaration."

Holding tightly to his arm, Brianna thought of the advice Lauren had given her. *You cannot love again until you have given Devon's memory time to heal. You will need the love and patience of a kind and good man to help you with that. Joseph is certainly that man.*

That was Lauren's opinion, but was that really what Brianna thought? How could she not? Looking back to the very evening she had met Joseph, Brianna had always known he would do anything for her happiness. Gazing into his eyes now only affirmed Brianna's belief of that.

With a fresh smile lighting her lovely features, Brianna replied, "Yes, Joseph, I think I would like being your wife."

Hugging her tightly and drawing several interested looks from passersby, Joseph promised, "And I am going to make you very happy that you said so."

◇◇◇◇◇

Devon decided to give into his anxiety and Daniel's urgings and left for Baltimore and the *Sea Enchantress* immediately following their dinner out.

Now, it was the second week out of port and nothing was going as smoothly as the first had.

Without warning, a sudden squall overtook the schooner, sweeping the ship and causing the sail to fill aback, nearly turning them completely about. The forceful winds lasted for three days. With no place to find anchor the Captain did everything in his power to keep the course from being greatly waylaid. Had they been loaded down during the voyage, perhaps the distance they were pushed off course would not have been so vast, but in his haste to reach Brianna, Devon had foregone any business and therefore additional weight as well. Now he regretted that decision very much.

Having the sails doused and placed in the lazy jacks, Devon hoped to force the wind around the vessel instead of over it.

At last, on the end of the third day, the vane high above the deck went limp. No wind was offered for the sails and a new toil began—where the gale had been constant before, now no breeze stirred.

Anyone who had any sense steered clear of the Captain.

Devon cursed the sails, he cursed the schooner and he cursed the sea for playing such a trick on him. It had gotten so bad that he began looking for a smirking mermaid somewhere off the port of the ship, her siren song mesmerizing the wind like a sleepy lullaby.

It was five days before he was able to write in his logbook that they were once again underway. Calculating the distance the winds had driven them off course with the time Mother Nature had kept them at a standstill, Devon estimated the *Sea Enchantress* and her crew to be a full seven days behind schedule.

◊◊◊◊◊

Brianna stood on a footstool in the middle of her sitting room while the local seamstress pinned the hem of her wedding gown. Her head was beginning to throb and every time she looked at the giddy expression Deirdre wore, she wanted to scream.

Each day that passed since Joseph's proposal, Brianna felt like duty, guilt and sorrow were slowly suffocating her. He was kind and gentle, loving and giving. He was a dear friend and a valued confidant; Joseph was all that Brianna should want in a husband—except that he *wasn't* Devon.

"Finished, Miss McClaran," the seamstress interrupted with her cheerful announcement. "I should have the gown back to you before week's end." Rising slowly from the perch of her knees, the woman waited for the feeling to return to her feet before moving again.

That was enough of a pause to throw Deirdre into a near panic. "Is that the soonest you can have it returned to us, Mrs. Lynch? I don't know if I feel comfortable with that time frame. We'll only have one week to make any further alterations."

Brianna glared at Deirdre. The closer the wedding, the more of a burden this decision-making friend and her advice-giving mother became. Turning to the seamstress with a sympathetic expression, Brianna stated kindly, "Pay her no mind, Mrs. Lynch. One week will be fine." Deirdre said nothing more but lowered her eyes to the wristband of her day dress, pulling at its decorative trim.

Looking pointedly away from the younger of the two women and to her actual patron, Mrs. Lynch informed her, "After this session, no further alterations will be needed." Clearing the room of her belongings, the seamstress found her own way from Brianna's house.

Flopping unceremoniously onto the settee, Brianna decried, "I don't want to see another flower, seamstress or menu as long as I live."

Deirdre looked uncertainly at her friend. "Do you have any idea of how disappointing you are? A bride should be the picture of giddiness and *you* most defiantly are *not*."

"Then it's a good thing that *you* are happy enough for the both of us, Dee," Brianna teased before offering an off-handed explanation. "But never you mind, I imagine my nerves are just getting the best of me."

Calmly, Deirdre replied, "There is nothing for you to be nervous about, Bria. Joseph is a wonderful man and will make you very happy. I only wish I were so lucky as to find someone like him."

There was the briefest flash of an expression that caught Brianna's attention and caused her to study Dee a moment longer than she normally would have. Deciding that her guilt was playing on her again, Brianna shook the odd feeling away with the assurance, "I just don't want to make any mistakes."

Lauren laughed lightly and joined the advice giving. "There will be plenty of those in your future, my sweet, but I doubt that marrying Joseph is one of them. I cannot think of a man better suited to the job and *you* shouldn't, either." Lauren's eyes bored into Brianna's with meaning—perhaps a bit harsher than needed, but lately, Lauren was irritable over her mistaken matchmaking. It didn't help matters that Jonathan took every opportunity to smugly remind her that the wedding was drawing closer and with it, Lauren's necessary admission of error.

When Lauren was rewarded with a timid smile from Brianna, she surmised that her implication had been understood and relented somewhat. It wasn't entirely the young woman's fault that Lauren was failing—part of the blame certainly lay in Lauren's desire to see her own daughter bound to the kindhearted Joseph Mitchell.

Brianna returned all occupants of the room to the conversation at hand by commenting, "Just the same, I cannot begin to imagine how excited you will be to plan your own wedding, Dee."

Deirdre rolled her eyes skyward. "Humph, you mean *if* I plan my own wedding."

Brianna smiled impishly. "It is my understanding that you have been sharing a fair amount of time with Charles Flannery. Perhaps he will make his intentions known soon"

"Oh, he already has," Deirdre remarked nonchalantly.

Brianna shot up in her seat and Lauren turned her head sharply, both fixing their eyes impatiently on Dee, and crying out in unison, "*What*?"

Raising her hand to her head as though overcome with the possibility, Brianna demanded, "Dee, how dare you keep this from me?" But, Brianna's indigence was paled in comparison to the genuine happiness the news brought her.

"Do not overexert yourself, Brianna. It would seem that his only *true* intention is to bore me into agreeing to his marriage proposal or death, whichever comes first."

Brianna laughed. "It isn't all that bad, now is it?"

Speaking in the most nasal tone she could manage, Deirdre mimicked, "Miss Gordon, I would be the happiest lad alive if you would spend the afternoon riding with me. Miss Gordon, I would be the happiest lad alive if you would share mid-morning tea and a stroll in the park with me. Miss Gordon, I would be the happiest lad alive if you would spend your life with me." Rolling her eyes skyward, Deirdre admitted, "How can I be excited about someone who is so monotone in his requests, no matter what they are?" Shaking her head, she added, "Sometimes I think he is afraid of forgetting my name since he feels the need to say it at the beginning or end of each statement he mutters."

Brianna was a heap of giggles at her friend's wonderful sense of humor. "Well, at least *you* are able to tell the difference between a love interest and a friend."

"True, but it takes no great talent to know when a man makes me smile just thinking of him or if he bores me to tears."

"Come now, you must consider Mr. Flannery a friend. Else you would not agree to see him so regularly."

"I consider him a business associate of my father's. As there is no other available man calling, I have little choice than to agree to his company."

"Each of you ladies would do well to remember that *any* man can be a lover, but not all men have the gift of being your friend." Looking in Brianna's direction more than Dee's, she added, "And usually one is much better to have than the other."

"Yes, but which one, the lover or the friend?" Brianna asked sincerely.

Dee studied her mother and friend as they shared words. She was unable to decipher their exact meaning but guessed that the statements from Brianna were a slight toward Joseph in some way and that was something she could not manage to let pass.

Lightly touching and then sniffing the vase of colorful tulips Joseph had brought to Brianna earlier in the day, Dee stated with soft conviction, "Your decision to love Joseph should not be so difficult, Brianna. Whether you consider him a lover or a friend, the man obviously adores you and yet you question the passion you feel for him."

"That's just it, Dee. I feel *nothing* past friendship for him, no passion at all."

"Then perhaps you should leave him to someone who does." There was no disguising or mistaking *that* comment *or* its meaning.

Quietly, Lauren broke the silent tension that instantly built. "Brianna, you and I have been over this already. Dee is right in her words, even if her intentions are wrong." She gave her daughter a meaningful look of disappointment before continuing, "Joseph *is* a good man and unless you intend to give him his due, I would expect you to call this marriage off."

"You needn't lecture me further, Lauren. I am an adult and I know what must be done."

"Then I suggest you act like it. Come to terms with the fact that Devon Elliott is over, Joseph is your future and what you should look forward to."

"A fact I remind myself of daily," Brianna claimed with sadness in her voice. "Lauren, I know that you are only concerned for my well-being, but do not be. I will wed Joseph and be a good and faithful wife to him. Devon is married now and will soon be a father. I am resigned to all of this and so I beg of you, don't remind me of the painful fact every time we are together."

Sympathetic sorrow filled the older lady's voice. "I just want to be sure you understand that what you wanted before cannot be, no matter how desperately you hold onto or long for it."

"I know, Lauren, and by the time I am Joseph's wife, I will have grieved enough to rid my mind of Devon. Fear not, I have no intentions of hurting my future husband."

"Intentional or not, the pain would be the same to him."

Deirdre reentered the conversation with a sound of disapproving amazement. "Am I to understand that you are marrying Joseph even though you harbor feelings for another man? A man with whom you lived for the better part of a year." Her implication hung heavily in the air around them.

"Deirdre Gordon, there is no reason for you to be so insulting," Lauren reprimanded.

"Let us allow Brianna to decide that." Offering a look full of jealous insinuation, Dee pushed, "Are you even being the slightest bit fair to Joseph, or have you given more than just your heart to the fine Captain?"

Pain and anger fused as Brianna retorted, "How dare you question me like this?"

"How dare *you* betray *Joseph* like this?"

Brianna's fury raged, but she somehow managed to keep her words calm but pointedly fierce. "I gave Devon my *love* only and that was before I knew Joseph."

"Where is your Captain and that love now? Joseph is the one you *should* love now—none other."

Brianna nodded. "I am aware of that. What I'm not so sure of is why *you* feel such a need to act as Joseph's champion. Is there something stirring between the two of you that I need to know about? Is he playing *me* for the fool?"

Dee scoffed, "Do not turn this around on Joseph. Unfortunately for me, he is besotted with you far beyond the chances of infidelity."

"You sound rather disappointed by that."

"Only because you don't deserve his loyalty. You would discard it and his heart in an instant if Devon Elliott wanted you again."

"There you are wrong, Dee, for *I* don't care to be a man's second choice—unless of course you can convince me that it doesn't feel as unpleasant as I imagine." Brianna's insult cut deep and Deirdre said nothing. The room fell suddenly silent and only the labored breathing of the arguing women filled the tense air.

Glancing toward Lauren, Dee said, "I'm leaving, Mother. I'll send Matty back after you with the carriage once I'm home."

Lauren advised with an almost pleading tone, "Dee, you shouldn't leave this way. You and Brianna need to talk; you need to work this out."

She shook her head. "No, I think we've both said enough for now. I've already promised to stand up with her, so if she still wants me, I'll be back for the wedding. Perhaps we'll talk again after that." Dee left without looking in Brianna's direction again.

Lauren offered an unsure promise, "It will all work out, Brianna. Even friends need time apart."

Brianna raised a single brow. "Right now, there's little I want more." She strode out the door then, searching out sanctuary from *both* of the Gordon women.

◊◊◊◊◊

Brianna smiled back toward the man following her. She was happy in the moment and in the days since arguing with

Deirdre, she had been forcing herself to concentrate on those occasions more and more.

Dee had been right in her statements, even if her reasoning was wrong. If nothing else, Deirdre had opened Brianna's eyes to the blessing of Joseph. Guilt had handled the rest of the change in Brianna's dwindling resistance to the acceptance of Joseph Mitchell's love for her.

It was time for Brianna to let go and love the man she had chosen—albeit secondly—to spend the rest of her life with. It was time to be fair to the man who loved her and deserved her love in return.

Halting her thoughts, Brianna allowed the salty air of the cliffs overlooking the Irish Sea and the sounds of nature to surround her senses. Stretching her arms wide, she spun in slow circles, then faster and faster. She inhaled deeply, forcing her mind to capture this moment, which she desperately wanted to remember forever. Her skirts billowed out, whipping around her legs until they tangled, toppling her in a dizzy spiral.

Setting aside the basket of treats in his hand, Joseph pulled her into his arms, laughing with her as he stopped her fall. "I adore your sense of freedom, Brianna."

Catching her breath between giggles, she teased, "Is that *all* you adore?"

Joseph smiled. "Far from it." Pushing aside a stray wisp of hair dancing against her cheek, he assured her, "I cannot even begin to list all of the qualities I love about you, but know this—love you, I do, and with all of my heart."

Resting her hands on his shoulders, Brianna looked into his green eyes and believed every word he spoke. She was in the mood for fun, though, and so replied smartly, "Of course you do. Why else would you put up with me?"

"You mean besides the fact that you are so pleasing to my eyes?"

"Oh, how you do go on, sir," she intoned with the best southern-belle accent she could manage.

"I could, if you like," Joseph assured, taking her hand and walking to the edge of the cliff. When she would have stepped even closer, he squeezed her hand. "Not so close, Bria. It makes me uneasy."

Not wanting to upset him, she stepped back to where he was and closed her eyes. Releasing his hand, Brianna reached up and unbound the few still restrained curls of her previously pinned up hair. As the cinnamon strands whipped around her wildly, Brianna threw her head back and in an instant, she was unexpectedly transported to another time and place—to another memory.

The brushing sensation of the wind mixed with the scents in the air carried Brianna swiftly to the deck of the *Sea Enchantress*. Behind her closed lids, she could see each wave that carried her, each sail filled with wind above her and each delicious feature of the Captain guiding the ship at its helm.

Watching from beside her, Joseph distinguished from her expression that Brianna was lost somewhere in a memory. He had not pressured her to tell him about her past. To him it did not matter what had happened.

Still, at times like these, he couldn't help but wonder what it was that brought that serene smile to her full lips. What was it about a man who could make Brianna fall in love, then force her away across oceans, but move her so deeply that she loved him still? And with that, Joseph could not hold back the envy that coursed through him and the unmatched need to make her forget Elliott and think of him that same way.

Joseph pulled her close and lowered his lips to hers.

It was the first time he had kissed her and Brianna tensed in his arms. The unexpected kiss brought her crashing back to present reality and she pulled away suddenly. His touch wasn't distasteful, but she needed to reassure herself that the kiss was not merely another dimension of her vision—a fantasy that haunted her daily.

The look in Joseph's eyes was enough to convince Brianna not only of who was touching her, but also the passion with which he did so. Without another thought, she moved to offer her lips to him again. Now that he had begun this caress, Brianna wanted to experiment, to see if the pleasant sensations Joseph was causing in her were capable of taking her farther. She needed to know that he could heat her body the way it had been enlivened before.

The feel of his lips covering hers and the weight of his hands on her waist offered Brianna a sense of security she had not felt since returning to Dublin. She had never thought to feel this way with a man again, and though Joseph's touch was different—lighter and more patient—than Devon's, it was still good. When Joseph moved to deepen the kiss, Brianna opened herself willingly.

Joseph had dreamed of this moment and now knew that the reality of Brianna was even more intense for him than the imagining. She was soft as his lips moved boldly over hers and a force of passion stirred through Joseph. She melded her body to his and he forced away the passing thought that someone had taught her well to kiss in such a satisfying way.

This time when she broke away and opened her eyes slowly—languishingly—Brianna looked directly into eyes of green and felt a mild pang of disappointment that they were not blue. Softly, she suggested, "Let's not get carried away, Joseph."

He heard the catch in her voice and prayed that he had not pushed her too far. Moving her hands from his shoulders, Joseph took one in his and admitted, "That would be quite easy for me to do with you."

Brianna didn't comment at first and then, glancing away from him, forced herself to admit aloud, "I understand completely."

"Do you, Brianna? Do you *really* understand?'

Brianna wasn't sure what he meant, but knew the question made her nervous. "What do you mean, Joseph?"

"What I mean is, do you love me?"

Rather than supply an immediate answer, she implored, "We are to be married in just a matter of days, Joseph. Why would you ask such a question of me?" Subconsciously her eyes darted back toward the sea, a reply in itself for Joseph.

"Just know this, Brianna; I love you enough to work through whatever memories are keeping part of you from me. I know that Devon has hurt you and I will do everything in my power to erase that unease from your heart, but in return, I require that you are always honest with me. Especially when I ask, do you think you can ever truly love me?"

Brianna wasn't surprised that Joseph had guessed her secret. He watched her closely and read her well—hiding her feelings from him would be forever impossible. And this man who knew her well, had taken her into his heart and offered to spend the rest of his life with her, was asking for this promise—a promise of truthfulness, and that was the least she could give him. "I will always be honest with you." Contemplating her next words, she added, "I do love you, perhaps not as greatly or in the same way you do me, but you are without doubt my closest friend and I would not want to jeopardize that for anything." Brianna wanted to offer him something more, something good to hold onto and so said, "In time, I am sure that I will be able to forget those things which haunt me and my love for you will become all that you need it to be."

Kissing her lightly on the forehead, he guaranteed, "That is all I ask and I thank you for telling me so."

"Joseph?" She was tentative with her tone and he turned to her, waiting to hear what she had to say. "I will hold nothing back from you when we are married. I vow to be a wife to you in every sense of the word from the very beginning; still, it may take my heart more time to give in to you than it will my body." Brianna blushed deeply with her blatant words, but she had wanted to explain herself to him fully.

Joseph hugged her tightly. "My lovely, Bria we have forever."

In that moment, Brianna knew that she would indeed be able to love this man with all of her heart, just as soon as she could push the remainder of the other man in her memory away.

◊◊◊◊◊

Three days later, Drake informed the Captain of the *Sea Enchantress* that land had been spotted. They had finally reached the shore of Ireland. In high spirits, Devon anticipated the approaching time when he would go to Brianna's home. Once there, he would beg her to forgive him, to love him and to finally become his wife.

Chapter Twenty-Six

Tomorrow was her wedding day and Brianna had just returned home from an evening spent with her future husband at
the Gordons' house. They all enjoyed the time socializing
without any detailed wedding plans. Even Deirdre had joined
them and she and Brianna were at least civil, if not overly
warm to one another. Brianna had refrained from telling Joseph of their argument or the revelation of Dee's hidden feelings for him. She felt pity for Dee's situation but was not willing to give up her own chance at a happy life just so that Dee
could step into her place.

Deirdre would find someone eventually and hopefully, the
friendship the two had shared most of their lives would also
return to normal.

At the end of the night, Joseph dropped Brianna at home
and hurried on his way. He did not intend to jinx himself by
seeing his bride too near their wedding day.

Alone now in her family home, Brianna walked through
each room, nostalgia keeping her company. She wondered if
the chambers would appear different after she was married.
Even though such a thought seemed a bit silly, Brianna refused
to disregard it. Any major changes in one's life made them
look at all aspects of it differently. When she had lost her father, his study was somehow quieter. After her mother's death,
Leila and Patrick's private chambers had seemed more dismal
to Brianna than ever before. When she returned from America,
Brianna had felt as though the entire house was lonely, missing
some of the all-important laughter and overall gaiety that it had
reflected in each of her childhood memories. It was almost as

though the house mourned the McClarans' life changes just as much as its people did.

Entering her father's study, Brianna walked to the leather chair behind his desk and sat in it. Patrick had been a large man and the enormity of his seat swallowed Brianna's smaller form. She felt deserted with the realization that neither of her parents would be with her on such a big day in her life, but silently reinforced in her mind that they would be with her in spirit, if not in body.

Brianna sat in reminiscing silence until her maid came to inquire if there was anything more to be done for the night. Brianna declined, thanked the woman and dismissed her. Tomorrow would be busy for everyone; there was no need to keep her from bed any later.

Thinking to take her own advice, Brianna braced her hands against the top of the cherry wood desk and pushed herself up. A piece of paper stubbornly clung to the palm of her hand and so she shook her wrist lightly to dislodge it. The paper swirled the few inches back to the desktop and when Brianna glimpsed it, the breath lodged in her throat.

Unnecessarily, her eyes darted over the authoritative scrawl and down to the bold signature below. It was Devon's letter of reply to her mother, the one accepting the proffered role as her guardian and the responsibility of Brianna in his life.

As though it were a lifeline, Brianna grasped the page and carried it with her to her bedroom. Quickly readying herself for bed, she crawled beneath the covers and then read each word over and over again until she could nearly imagine Devon standing before her, his deep voice reciting the message to her verbatim.

By the third time she had completed the note, pain clenched tightly in her chest, so Brianna let the tears run free. Tonight would be the last time she could ever allow her forbidden feelings for Devon to fill her soul. It was important—no, it was *necessary*—that she give into one more night of sorrow. At this time tomorrow, she would belong to another man in every sense of the word and Devon Elliott would have to become no more than a memory in her life, a faded ideal of times best forgotten.

Blowing out the candle, Brianna slipped the sheet of paper under her pillow and closed her eyes. With little effort, she conjured his vision and allowed dreams of him to overtake her.

Tomorrow she would be Joseph's, but tonight she belonged to Devon.

◊◊◊◊◊

Jonathan, Lauren and Deirdre arrived early the next morning and ate breakfast with Brianna. Deirdre was pale and Brianna had large, dark half-circles beneath her eyes. There was not much conversation throughout the meal. Jonathan and Lauren continuously exchanged guarded looks of concern, each debating which of the women was more likely to pass out first—the bride or the maid of honor.

At the end of the morning meal, Jonathan remained below to oversee the decorative arrangements for the early afternoon events and Lauren and Deirdre went upstairs with Brianna so that they could begin preparations of their own.

Following up the stairs behind the slow moving wife-to-be, Lauren said a silent prayer and hoped that Brianna's appearance this morning did not foretell the way the rest of her day or life would go, while Jonathan mumbled some unintelligible remark about the cost of being right.

◊◊◊◊◊

Drake looked out over the busy Fleet Street wharf where the *Sea Enchantress* docked. Giving orders to put the schooner to anchor, the first mate turned with purpose and headed below—he had orders of his own to follow. It was blessedly time to notify the nerve-wrecked captain that they had reached their destination at last.

◊◊◊◊◊

Joseph had been up since the first signs of dawn and was now walking proudly toward the D'Olier Street home that by the end of the day would be his permanent address. Glancing down, he reassured himself that his feet were indeed touching the ground, for as far as Joseph Mitchell was concerned, this was the very best day of his life and nothing could put the slightest damper on his happy mood.

◊◊◊◊◊

Brianna stood in front of her full-length mirror, freshly dried and powdered from her bath; she wore nothing more than her stockings, shoes and chemise. In the process of having her corset added to the layers of clothing that would complete her outfit for the day, Brianna watched through the reflective glass, grimacing as the maid pulled tightly on the strings cinching in her waistline.

"For Heaven's sake, Brianna, breathe or the woman will have you bound so tightly that you won't be able to move," Lauren scolded. Brushing the maid aside with a swipe of her hands, she took over the task.

Brianna had not realized until Lauren spoke that she had been holding her breath. Her mind was still in a haze from the dreams she had experienced the night before. A blush crept up her neck and spread over her cheeks, her reflection allowing no shelter for the reaction. It was the first sign of color that had graced her features that day and Brianna was ashamed that it had taken a man other than her intended husband to make her glow so fiercely.

Having resigned herself to being wrong about Brianna and Joseph, Lauren's attention to her intuitions was jumbled and she misread Brianna's sudden glances toward her freshly made bed and coloring cheeks. Supposing that the younger woman was feeling the effects of wedding night jitters, Lauren finished with the corset ties and patted Brianna lightly on the arm, soothing, "Do not worry, dear; the intimacies of being a wife are not as bad as you are guessing."

This comment only caused Brianna to turn redder and Deirdre to utter a groan of disgust. "Mother, Brianna has enough to worry with now. Do not cause her further discomfort by making her think of the act to come."

Lauren laughed at the innocent reaction of the twosome, each of them vivid with cheeks of cherry red and trying desperately to act mature about the situation. "Fine, I will let it rest," Lauren conceded, "so long as neither of you fret about it anymore today. This should be a fun filled day, not one of testiness and anxiety."

Smiling anew, the two younger women agreed. While Brianna took her seat so that the rest of her preparations could happen, Lauren added teasingly, "Joseph will be a much more thorough teacher than my mere words could be anyway." Both women closed their eyes and inhaled deeply, each searching inward for control over their hearts' true longings and the guilt those desires brought forth.

Lauren mistook both reactions for fresh embarrassment and laughed loudly.

◊◊◊◊◊

Devon strode down the gangplank and through the smelly crowd of people with long strides. All of the crew except five still tending posts on board *Sea Enchantress* were dismissed for shore leave a half-hour before and already Devon saw no sign of them. Likely, they were finding food and fun within one of the bawdy establishments bordering the docks of Dublin.

The wind blew slightly and Devon could smell rain in the air. It would not hold off the entire day and he silently thanked God that he was not still at sea. Another storm could have set them back even farther than his already deterred schedule.

At the edge of Fleet Street, Devon hailed a cab—his first two attempts overlooked him for other visitors to the city. On his third try, he expected to be omitted again, but the lady stepping to the cab said something to her companion and the gentleman offered to share their vehicle with Devon. Gratefully, Devon thanked the man and climbed into the seat opposite the thoughtful lady.

Nodding his head in her direction, Devon voiced, "I thank you, ma'am; seems to me I could have been waiting quite a while for a cabby to notice me."

Smiling at Devon, she returned, "Not at all, sir. There is no reason to waste so much extra space." She indicated the spot where he now sat while her companion climbed in beside her.

Stretching across the open space between the seats, Devon offered his hand to the gentleman. "I am Captain Devon Elliott, sir. I am pleased to make your acquaintance as well as that of this lovely lady."

Shaking his hand in return, the man said, "Martin Doyle and this is my wife, Constance." Tapping the top of the cab with his knuckles, Martin notified the cabby that they were ready for the trip to commence. "I'm afraid we are in a bit of a hurry, Captain."

"Running *late*, actually," Constance put in with a glance at her husband that told Devon who was to blame for their tardiness.

Clearing his throat, Martin continued, "I hope you will not be too put out if we request you tell the cabby your destination after ours is reached."

Feeling mild frustration at this newest delay, Devon reminded himself that he could still be standing on the street side waiting for a ride if not for this couple's generosity and so pushed aside his selfishness and responded kindly, "I completely understand."

"You are American, Captain." The words were more of a statement than a question and Devon turned his eyes to Constance, who had spoken them. "Are you visiting family or here on business?"

"Though I do have business here in Dublin, at this time you could say that I am visiting family." Smiling broadly, he announced, "I am here to ask a certain lady to be my wife."

Constance's eyes sparkled and Devon knew he had won the woman's favor in an instant. "Love must be in the air today."

"Why do you say that, Mrs. Doyle?" Devon liked the way the young woman flushed prettily when speaking and thinking of fresh romance.

"We are on our way to a wedding now." Sighing wistfully, she added, "It is so special to be invited to witness vows of love."

Chuckling and sharing a glance of camaraderie with Martin, Devon informed them, "It has come to be my opinion that women like to witness love, no matter *what* occasion calls for it."

Taking her husband's hand in a natural reflex, Constance returned, "Let's hope your lady thinks so, too."

Devon met her sweetly romantic eyes with his hopeful ones and agreed, "I am counting on it, Mrs. Doyle."

◊◊◊◊◊

Brianna stood alone at the top of the staircase and watched as Deirdre descended before her. Reaching the bottom of the stairs, Dee rounded the banister and stole a glance up at her friend, offering an encouraging smile. Seconds later, Jonathan appeared in her place and nodded his head to cue Brianna—it was time. With little hesitation, Brianna moved down the staircase.

By the time she reached Jonathan's side, Brianna was trembling, so he reached out to take her arm, aiding her down the remaining two steps. Smiling at her with reassurance, he turned her toward the parlor and emotion overcame Brianna at the sight greeting her eyes. All of the planning that Deirdre and Lauren had forced upon her had been worthwhile.

To the left and right of Brianna were vases filled to over-flowing with a rainbow of tulips. Each hue matched the ones her shaking hands gripped. White ribbons hung in soft waves around the doorway, along the banister and mantle. As she moved through the open doors of the decorated rooms, all eyes of the small crowd rested on her. Some guests in attendance, Brianna had not seen for a long time and the fact that they had come to share this day with her meant more than she could begin to express.

Looking to the front of the room then, Brianna felt tears well in her eyes as she caught Joseph's proud stare resting on her. He was handsome in his dark brown suit and waited on her with a smile that spoke volumes of his love. Deirdre was crying softly and Brianna offered her a smile, even as she tried not to wonder too deeply exactly what emotion was prompting her tears.

When they reached Joseph's side, Jonathan kissed Brianna lightly on the cheek and moved to stand beside Lauren. Re-turning her eyes to the man who now held her hand, Brianna felt a moment of panic before his tender words reached her ears. "You are breathtaking, my love."

Brianna was radiant in white lace. The sleeves of her gown stopped at the middle of her arms, matching gloves covered the remainder to the tips of her fingers. Layer after layer of lace overlapped the bodice and full skirt, giving the impression that Brianna was floating on air. Her hair had been left down, up-swept at the sides and a veil reached the middle of her back.

Smiling, the couple turned to face one another, signaling that the ceremony binding them for life should begin.

◊◊◊◊◊

Many of the places they were passing began to look famil-iar to Devon until at last, he remarked, "I think perhaps our destinations are in the same direction, Mr. Doyle. I am certain that this is the way to D'Olier Street."

"You're correct; it's just ahead on the right," Martin con-firmed. "Is your lady friend there?"

Even as the question was voiced, they rounded the corner and began making their way past the houses neighboring Bri-anna's home. "Yes." Finding the coincidence striking, Devon inquired, "Do you know the McClaran house?"

Constance gave a short laugh and replied, "As a matter of fact, it's Brianna McClaran whose wedding we are attending. Is your lady a friend of hers?"

There was no need for Devon to voice his answer.

The carriage had barely stopped before he tore open the door and leaped from its confines.

The Doyles hurried after him, not wanting to miss the scene that Devon's mixed expression of horror, anguish and outrage guaranteed to come.

◊◊◊◊◊

". . . to love, honor and cherish . . ." Joseph's affectionate tone and caring eyes were overflowing with tenderness as the words flowed from his lips.

"Until death do us part."

"Until death do us part," Joseph repeated, squeezing Brianna's hand lightly.

Taking a deep breath, Brianna readied herself and as Joseph had done moments before, began to repeat after the officiator, "I, Brianna Grace McClaran . . ."

"Promise to love, honor and obey . . ."

"Promise to . . . ." Air was not filling her lungs; small gasps were all she could manage. Closing her eyes and mouth, Brianna inhaled slowly, deeply through her nose and then swallowed past the fear that threatened to consume her.

She began again. "Promise to love, honor and . . ."

"Like Hell you do!"

Shock surrounded her and Brianna didn't even have to turn—in that moment she couldn't have even if she had wanted to. All she managed was one soft word, "Devon."

Her statement was a whisper of disbelief, but Joseph had heard it like her loudest cry and whirled on the intruding man with vengeance. In the appearance of Devon Elliott, Joseph's worst fears were being realized. Though Brianna hadn't moved or uttered a word past the other man's name, though she remained by his side in the midst of their wedding ceremony, Joseph somehow still imagined that she was slowly slipping through his fingers.

"What is the meaning of this?" Joseph was enraged and sounded it, though Brianna heard a hint of uncertainty in his tone as well.

Dazed, Brianna was not sure if his inquiry was directed at her or not, so she weakly and honestly answered, "I don't know, Joseph, I don't understand."

Amid the murmurings of outraged and surprised guests, Devon noticed only one sound, the name of the man Brianna stood with now. "Joseph? Joseph Mitchell?" Too late, he noticed and recognized the groom. Devon felt like a fool and that was not a role that he played well. Throwing a scathing glance toward Brianna, he reminded her of a careless statement she'd made months before. "And you assured me that he was no one to concern myself with."

With her increasing outrage, Brianna's emerald eyes began to glow and she narrowed them in his direction, her shock and immobility switching to adrenaline and anger. "Only *you* could be so condescending and bold as to intrude upon *my* wedding and find a way to make it seem *I* have done *you* some grievous wrong."

Her words sent shards of infuriation through him. Before Devon could comment, however, Joseph's demand filled the room. "Captain Elliott, what is it that you mean by coming in-to Brianna's home and interrupting our marriage ceremony?"

Laughing in a cool way that belied his true feelings and set Brianna's nerves on edge, Devon replied, "What I *mean*, Mr. Mitchell is to return *my* fiancée to *my* home and make her *my* wife."

Brianna heard nothing more as her final attempt at con-trolled breathing was lost somewhere in the shocked gasp rip-pling through her wedding guests.

She crumpled to the floor at the feet of her equally stunned bridegroom.

Chapter Twenty-Seven

Brianna sat up in bed and looked around groggily. Relief washed over every limb of her body as she surveyed her surroundings. The copper tub sat empty in front of the fireplace, all of her belongings arranged neatly on top of the vanity. Through the open door to her sitting room, she could see her wedding gown draped over the back of a chair, her veil spread over the seat in front of it.

Everything had been a dream, a detailed, heart-stopping nightmare, which she had no wish to experience ever again.

Climbing from her bed, she stretched her arms high overhead and allowed herself the luxury of a very unladylike yawn. Walking to the washstand, she leaned over to splash water on her cheeks, refreshing herself and clearing her face of sleep. When she stood again, the sound of her grumbling stomach drew attention to the fact that she was extremely hungry.

Donning her heavy house robe, she exited her room and headed toward the kitchen. Before long, Deirdre and Lauren would arrive to help her get ready for the day and Brianna was certain that they would not allow her time for a meal the likes of which her body was requesting.

Moving down the staircase, the patter of her bare feet on the wood floor was barely audible amid the bustling sounds of the working servants. As she passed them, Brianna admired the colorful floral arrangements and other decorations, amazed at how detailed Lauren's descriptions had been. It was almost as though Brianna had seen them all before.

Her attention on the activities in the parlor, Brianna missed the opening study door and slammed directly into the person exiting it. Speaking before looking up, Brianna assumed, "Jonathan, I'm sorry, I didn't realize you were already here."

When her eyes connected with the face she addressed, her stomach flipped, her heart thumped erratically and the dream came flooding back, washing the possibility of mere imagination away in its current.

"You're really here." Her voice was barely above a whisper, but the sound of emotions rushing through it was easily heard by Devon.

"Flame," he returned just as softly, filling the air around them with an immediate charge.

The moment was broken when Jonathan and Joseph came out of the room behind Devon and met the twosome in the corridor. Brianna blushed, only now thinking to grasp the top of her robe tightly closed. The innocent reaction pleased Devon since it assured him that she had not been as intimate with her near-husband as she had been with him.

Disappointed amazement in her tone, Brianna stated, "Believe it or not, I woke and thought that perhaps all of this was a dream."

"If only it were so, Bria." Joseph's sweet voice was filled with as much contempt as Brianna had ever heard it carry. Walking to her side, he placed a possessive hand at the small of her back and offered Devon a glare, daring him to make any objections.

What he did was worse—Devon smiled—and in that simple look, Brianna and Joseph knew that he was patronizing them, allowing them to have their fun for now because he had no doubt that in the end, he would win this game. Leveling his eyes on Brianna, he demanded, "You have a choice to make and I want no time wasted in your doing so."

Feeling the pressure of the last weeks, months, and year wash over her at Devon's mandate, Brianna amazed them all by covering her face with her hands and sobbing. In instant unity, all three of the men stepped to her rescue, attempting to offer comfort and assistance.

Forcefully, she pushed all of their efforts away and looked up, her eyes more angered and pained than any recalled having seen them before. "I am sick to death of making decisions such as these. I don't want to choose between families I love, homes I love or men that I love." Looking directly at Devon and Joseph she added, "I am tempted to choose *neither* of you and move to Sister Kathleen's monastery for the rest of my life."

Devon chuckled; confidence and intimate awareness filled his mocking words. "You, my Flame, would not make a very good nun."

If a weapon had been within reach, Brianna would have murdered Devon on the spot.

Jonathan and Joseph looked appalled, Devon proud, and Brianna managed only a growl of frustration as she pushed the three men aside to enter the open door behind them. The air within the study was thick with masculinity; no doubt, they had been discussing her in the same way they had when previously making decisions about her life. Obviously, her consent or input was just as unnecessary this time as the last.

Turning on them, she watched as they entered the room cautiously. "This time, it is *I* who will make the demands, gentlemen. Is that understood?" When each nodded in assent— the third slower than the rest—Brianna looked uncertainly at him and stipulated, "Captain Elliott, are you *certain* I've made myself clear?"

Her tone astonished him, and the other men in the room, as well. Devon had never seen her so angry before, but the control that she was wielding over them was making his desire for her intensify by the second. He loved this woman, her strong and willful mind, all that she was, and all that she would come to be and even the way she stood boldly against him now. However, even with those feelings in the forefront of his mind, Devon would have his say. "Make your demands, but rest assured that I, too, will be heard, Brianna."

"I expected as much and *each* of you will have your say, but *not* before I ask for it. And then you will *not* interrupt each other and you will not argue." She punctuated that and her final statement with a straight look at Devon. "Whatever decision I make will be definite and I will broach *no* attempts to sway me otherwise."

Jonathan was worried. "Bria, you must think this through rationally, not in anger. A lot weighs on the choice you will make."

She nodded in agreement. "Jon, you are so like a father to me and I respect you greatly. Your advice has not fallen upon deaf ears, but I already know that whatever I decide will not be easy. However, I also know that it will be *my* decision and mine *alone*."

Jonathan's glance showed he was proud of her assertiveness. "Then I shall remain here with you as support only. I will not attempt to influence your choice, nor will I allow anyone else to."

For the next several moments, Brianna said nothing.

After what seemed a much longer time to the men than it did to her, Brianna looked at Joseph. She could sense his anger and dread. The weight of the world seemed to rest upon his shoulders and Brianna knew that only she had the power to lift that burden. It was apparent that he had immediately—and understandably—realized the intense competition this other man created for him.

Reading the trust he conveyed to her with his eyes, Brianna knew that he was counting on her to be fair, to think over her options evenly and make a final decision that would be best for everyone involved. The compassion Joseph sent her with his glances warmed her and made her feel a similar comfort to that she had always felt with Daniel—right now she wasn't sure if *that* realization was a help or a hindrance.

Turning her eyes toward Devon, her feelings changed in a flash. A tremor rushed through her body when he met her inquisitive gaze head-on, challenging her to deny him—to deny what they both wanted so badly. His blue eyes were searing into her, offering no quarter as they reminded her of what he had to offer and promised to give that and more the instant she requested it.

Brianna was suddenly very sorry she had looked in his direction at all.

A slow, sensual smile covered his face and Brianna knew that Devon was either remembering the passionate interludes they had already shared or was planning and anticipating those he was haughtily sure would come again. Whichever it was didn't make much difference as Brianna's face flamed, causing his devilish grin to broaden, summoning the dashing rogue within him, a total counterpart to Joseph's handsome gentlemanliness Brianna was torn anew.

Shifting her eyes quickly away, they collided with Joseph's and Brianna felt her heart begin to break. In that one look, Joseph had been able to express that it was becoming obvious that Brianna's selection was already made. All of the proof he needed was clear in the glowing look of her eyes, the casual movements of her body toward Devon, even without conscious thought. Words were not required for her to express this as yet unspoken but heartfelt choice. Nevertheless, Joseph's perceptive gaze had been watching it all unfold like a mesmerizing Greek tragedy.

Fumbling for words, Brianna muttered, "There are many things that I could say now. I could easily sit before you and list each attribute that I love about you both and each detail that I detest. That would get us nowhere, though." Glancing briefly at Devon and then lingeringly at Joseph, she added, "Know this, though, I *have* and *always will* love both of you. No matter my choice, that will not change." Swallowing over the lump in her throat, she forced herself to continue, "I would give anything to keep from hurting either of you, but such a wish is unrealistic at this point."

Taking a steadying breath, she offered, "Joseph, you who are kind and giving to all you come in contact with would surely find another woman with whom you could share your life. A lady who would complement you perfectly."

Turning to Devon, she kept her eyes from meeting his for long. "And you, my powerful sea captain, with the authority and dashing looks you possess, along with the traveling adventures and unending passion you promise—it would be easy for you to win the heart of *any* woman you desire."

His tone was soft. "Apparently not *any* woman, Flame."

Brianna mentally dodged the caress of his voice; the temptation hovering in its sultry timbre lulled Brianna, but now was not the time to listen to such overtures.

Knowing that this situation was difficult for everyone and ready to see it end so that all involved could move on with their lives, Jonathan prompted, "Brianna, is your decision made?"

She thought a moment before answering, "In my heart, yes, but not in my mind. I want to have some time to think this through and be sure that the result will be the best one."

"How long do you plan to ponder?" Devon asked, not attempting to hide his displeasure in being put off longer.

Brianna reacted staunchly to his question. "Do not act disgruntled with *me*, Devon Elliott. After all that I've suffered due to you—a suffering which we've yet to sort out—you'll wait until Hell freezes over if I want you to." Daring him with her eyes to deny her this power, Brianna continued after a moment's pause, "I'll need clear explanations from you before I am capable of making an appropriate choice."

"I am here. That is all the explanation you should need." Devon's tone was factual and proved to Brianna yet again that there actually were times that even *he* did not realize the depth of his own conceit.

"In *your* mind perhaps, but *I* would prefer to hear what enabled you to come in search of me. How is it that you freed yourself of my cousin and—*if* you truly have—why would you still *want* to come for me?" Stopping her flow of questions, Brianna put her hands up to hold off Devon's responses. "Never mind that now, we'll speak of it later, in private. This is not a matter I wish to suffer Joseph and Jonathan through; I barely want to endure it myself."

In his usual soft manner, Joseph interceded, his eyes conveying sympathy for Brianna and at the same time imploring her to end his suffering. "Brianna, I've no wish to add to your pressure, but seeing as it was *my* wedding that was interrupted today, too, I think I've a right to know how long you plan to keep us waiting for your answer."

Devon interjected with his commanding brashness, "You've no more rights here than I do, Joseph. It's only because *our* plans were postponed first that Brianna is not *my* wife already. You should never have had the chance to propose, let alone speak your vows."

To the amazement of the room's occupants, Joseph denounced with uncharacteristic authority, "And had *you* treated her with the caring and concern that she so greatly deserves, *Devon*, Brianna would not have been here to *accept* my proposal." Snubbing him further, Joseph added, "It galls me to think that any man would find it difficult to remain faithful to Brianna. To top it off, you have the audacity to return to Ireland and claim Brianna as though she would never think to look for love elsewhere. As if she would run to you without a second thought."

The haughtiness with which Devon replied stunned them all. "If not for your interference, she would have." With an infuriating sneer he further declared, "You may mark my words on this as well. It matters not if she must deliberate for one hour, one day or one month, in the end result will be the same. I'd be more than willing to wager on it."

Joseph did not back down. "Yes, but with what would you wager? Her heart? We've already seen at what standard you regard that precious gem." Devon didn't remark but instigated Joseph more by appearing to miss his insulting comment altogether as he carelessly brushed a piece of lint off the sleeve of his dark jacket before looking up as though forcing himself to pay attention to what was going on.

Sensing the direction Devon's blasé attitude was leading this heated discussion, Jonathan sternly dove into the conversation before Joseph could comment again. "Gentlemen, I gave Brianna my word and must remind you not to argue this subject in her home."

Like animals in the wild, the men continued preening over Brianna—Devon, perhaps the fiercest of all as he growled out territorially, "Her *home* is in Virginia, with me."

Brianna's words pushed in just as firmly. "My *home* is wherever I choose for it to be."

Jonathan ended the pointless bickering. "Enough of this Brianna has a lot to mull over. If she is to make her selection wisely, fairly and in a timely fashion, we must let her get to it." Pausing to gather his wits, Jonathan adjourned, "We will meet here tomorrow at nine o'clock in the morning, at which time Brianna will tell us her final choice." Leveling his gaze on the older of the two men in question, Jonathan ordered, "Captain Elliott, if it is Brianna's wish, you may have one hour to explain yourself to her after we leave. After that time, Brianna is not to be bothered by either of you until the morning. Is that understood?"

When each man nodded, Jonathan walked to Joseph's side and patted him on the back. "Come, Joseph, I will see you home and we shall return together in the morning."

With that minor gesture, Devon became achingly aware of exactly where he stood with Jonathan Gordon and it bothered him that this man was leaving with such a low regard for him where once he had thought enough of him to turn Brianna over to his care. When Devon stopped to think about what he had done today, no matter the reason, he knew that Jonathan was right in his opinions and that he should make his apologies to Joseph.

"Mr. Mitchell." Devon waited until both men had turned their attention on him before speaking again. "I am sincerely sorry that I ruined such a special day for you."

Joseph thought for a moment before replying in earnest, "Forgiveness is not something I am ready to give you, Captain, but I do accept your apology." He gave an ironic grin and then added, "Doing so is easy since I understand exactly what prompted your actions. I would have done the same thing were I in your position. Obviously, we both know that Brianna is not a woman easily forgotten."

◊◊◊◊◊

The door was scarcely closed behind Jonathan and Joseph when Devon spoke. "Brianna, let's get this over with. What is it you want to hear from me?"

Instead of arrogance as Brianna would have expected, Devon's voice was filled with sincerity and concern and that moved her deeply. Taking a second before looking toward him, she answered, "I want to know everything. From the beginning, I want to know when you first began to want me, to love me. I want to know when and how often you betrayed me and took Larissah to your bed—then I want to know what made you come back for me? How is it possible that you are here?"

"All in an hour?" he asked lightly, attempting to ease the tension with some humor.

Smiling with understanding, Brianna complimented loosely, "You seem to be under the impression that you can do anything else you put your mind to. Let's see if you can live up to your beliefs."

Devon nodded in acceptance. "I will do my best not to disappoint either of us." Watching her glide back to the seat she had previously occupied, Devon had to fight the urge to step to her. He wanted to pull her into his arms and show her with his touch rather than words why he had come back. But that was not what *she* wanted now and even though he knew he could change her mind, he wouldn't. He respected Brianna and her wishes and would prove as much to her now.

Clearing his throat, Devon began, "I think in some ways, I wanted you from the very first time I saw those tiny toes peeking from beneath the hem of your evening dress. Though you treated me terribly—you were obstinate and rude—you were undeniably beautiful and full of fire and I ached to touch you."

"Don't hold back, Devon. Say what you feel," she interjected sarcastically.

Devon ignored her taunting comment and continued, "I knew for *certain* that I wanted you the same night we dined here together, just the two of us. In fact, if I had allowed myself, I would have taken you that soon."

She laughed lightly, shaking her head in disbelief. "You are even worse than I imagined, Devon. We had barely met and you were already making plans to . . . to . . ."

He stopped her feeble search for an appropriate word. "*Seduce* you?"

Brianna blushed and nodded.

Devon smiled and scolded, "Don't act so innocent, Miss McClaran. I was not alone in such thoughts that night. If I recall correctly, you *threw* yourself at me and were mine for the taking."

"I *tumbled*," she haughtily defended, though the sound of it was false even to her own ears.

Devon raised a doubtful dark-brow and then continued, "At any rate, *that* is when I wanted you. And though it does my bachelor's pride some harm admitting it, I fell in love with you the night we danced on board the *Sea Enchantress*."

"That was awfully soon, Devon," she claimed skeptically.

He shrugged. "It was my heart's choice, not mine." Smoothly he questioned, "And if you really think that was soon, then tell me, Miss-Prim-and-Proper, when did *you* fall in love with *me*?"

He wasn't as smooth as he thought. "What makes you think I *did* fall in love with you?" Brianna smirked at Devon, quite proud of herself and her quick remark.

"Do you *really* want me to tell you all of the times that you've made me *exceedingly* aware of your love for me?"

Her face went crimson. "We are talking about *your* feelings right now, not mine, Devon, so please, continue to do so."

He laughed and decided to let her rest a while from his teasing. Walking around the desk, Devon leaned on its edge, placing himself directly in front of her. "Whether you think our homeward voyage too soon or not, that is truthfully when I first felt love for you."

"Yet you forgot those feelings when next you saw Larissah."

"She was a release," Devon paused for emphasis. "A *one-time* release—*you* are my love." Certain he had her attention now, Devon continued, "I love everything about you, Brianna. I love the way you smile, your Irish accent, the flash of anger in your eyes, the way you do not back down even from *my* horrible temper. I love the fact that even when you are blazing with anger, I can usually calm you quickly—and I do *so* love appeasing you." When she would have swatted his arm, Devon adjusted his position to avoid her assault. "I even love the substantial fits you sometimes have when trying to make a point."

"I do *not* have fits," Brianna declared, sitting forward in her chair and sounding as though she would have one then.

Devon simply smiled at her example. "I love the constant thoughts that flow through your mind and the laughter that inebriates my senses. I love the shy way you touch me even as your green eyes burn with the unending desire I have yet to fully awaken in you."

Brianna could say nothing. Her mouth was dry and her stomach flip-flopped convulsively. "Go . . . go on." She cleared her throat so that she didn't sound like a croaking frog.

"Is that not *enough*?" Devon sounded incredulous.

Blushing, Brianna stated, "I did not mean about *me*. I want to know how you were able to get away from Larissah. I want to know how you came to be entangled with her in the first place."

As was his tendency, Devon raked his fingers roughly though his ebony curls. "Must I go into detail about my affair with her? It is truly something I would rather forget and leave in the past."

Devon was as near to begging as ever, but Brianna denied him anyway. "No, I want to know when you went to her and why. After this, we need never speak of it again."

Unbeknownst to Brianna, she had given Devon hope with her words, insinuating that they would be together in the future to have such a discussion. He did not let on to his insight, though—it was *possible* that she had simply misspoken.

With resignation, Devon opened his memories to her. "I was twenty-one when I first became Larissah's lover."

"Four years?" Brianna was completely stunned by the length of time Devon and her cousin had been intimate.

He nodded. "More or less—though there were times that we tired of one another for different reasons, but always seemed to return to the comfort of what we knew. In the beginning, we were curious about taking our lifelong friendship further. Righteous as I was, I think to some degree I had always intended to make Larissah my bride. But when I discovered that she was no innocent, she laughed at my surprise . . . ."

"Devon," Brianna overflowed with pity. She considered releasing him from his painful oath to speak the truth about his past. Devon silently declined, however, suddenly feeling the need to tell Brianna of his past now that he had begun. "Larissah was heartless, finding power and pleasure from my shock and pain. Still, she was willing and I had wanted her for years, so I took what she offered without hesitation. Even when I knew she was unfaithful to me, I turned a blind eye and continued to accept Larissah as my lover. We used each other with understanding and without qualm."

"But you never married her? Why?"

"After that first time, she disgusted me. She is beautiful to look at and a woman any man could desire but on the inside she is cold and lonely and enjoys causing emotional pain."

Looking up at Brianna and away from his thoughts, Devon stated, "Then, there was you. When I kissed you, I was lost and knew that I would never want another woman so desperately as I wanted you. You, however, were undoubtedly innocent and I was determined nothing would change that. I had the best intentions of keeping our relationship exactly as it was meant to be. Then, when I realized that wasn't going to be possible, I vowed that I wouldn't take your innocence before you understood what you were offering me and that I loved you even without that sacrifice." Without thought, Brianna raised her hand to clasp her fingers with his.

"The very day we returned to Misty Heights, I went to tell Larissah that our affair was over. I am ashamed to admit it, but as you already know, she ensnared me. Considering the visions of you that floated through my mind and the frustrations my body had been feeling due to my restraint from you, it was no great feat, either. Still, I swear to you, Brianna, by all that is Holy, that is the last time I was with her." He paused, waiting for her to comment, but she said nothing. She was waiting for him to finish. "I have been with no one else."

Brianna nodded in acceptance of his honesty and then asked, "And what about the child? Have you proven that you are not the father?"

"I was away in Baltimore and returned early, so I went to let Larissah know I was back. She had her lover in her bed when I arrived; he told me that the child was his."

"Robert," Brianna stated, not expecting Devon to oppose or confirm her comment.

Devon chuckled. "No, Nate Carter."

"Robert's stable hand?" Brianna was sincerely stunned.

"One and the same, though now he happens to be master of Reverie *and* Larissah."

Laughter rolled over her lips. "I am sure she loves that."

"I believe she will get used to it." Devon pulled Brianna to her feet then so she was standing no more than an inch in front of him. "That is *how* I was able to return to you. *Why* should be evident."

Brianna was slipping. "Tell me anyway."

He smiled and leaned toward her, appeasing her happily. "Because I need you, I love you and I am determined to spend the rest of my life with you."

Then he kissed her.

Devon did not hold back, did not even begin the kiss softly, but plunged forward, whisking Brianna into a whirlwind of emotions with him. She felt the silky smooth touch of his tongue against the outside of her lips and her thoughts cried out to fight him off. Her body, however, dared her to decline his capable touch. For months, she had yearned for exactly this and so her surrender came easily. She ignored the ethical voice in her head and the fact that she was supposed to be sharing this night with another man. She didn't even care about her promise to make a fair choice.

Instead of thinking, she allowed her arms to slide around Devon's neck and pull him down closer. She gave in to his persistent persuasion and parted her tender lips to his needing touch. Brianna's heart seemed to beat a rhythm matching that of his kiss and a familiar burning rose within her. She wanted it to take her over, she wanted Devon to carry her away to that place she knew he could so easily lead her to, but then he ended the kiss.

Brianna's heart was pounding and her nerves jumbled with fresh desire. Devon held onto her while she steadied herself. Brianna's closed lids opened lazily and disappointment tinged in them with a flashing green color. But, most importantly, Devon was able to read the answer he so desperately desired hidden within their sentiment.

Not letting on to his discovery, Devon whispered, "I will leave you to your thoughts for the night, Flame."

He did not wait for her to comment, but left her alone, still trembling from his touch, and nothing but a steadying hand upon her father's desk to keep her standing upright.

Chapter Twenty-Eight

A knock sounded on her front door promptly at nine o'clock the next morning. Brianna took a deep breath, readying herself for the next few hours.

Last evening she had dismissed the staff early and used the complete privacy to think over her options and plan how she would present her decision to the people now waiting outside her entranceway. The easy part of this situation was over—the challenge would be facing the men who meant so much to her. Brianna had to use every ounce of her concentration to turn the knob and open the door to welcome them to an event that would affect each of their lives forever.

With a quick smile she greeted, "Jonathan, Joseph, please come in." Closing the door after them, she offered, "I thought perhaps this morning the parlor would be more comfortable than the stuffy air of the study, though I imagine to you gentlemen it makes little difference at all."

Both men realized that she was rambling nervously and smiled at her effort to politely entertain. Joseph saved her by responding, "Bria, I simply want to get this entire scene over with. It matters not to me where that happens."

Devon saved her from having to reply by knocking on the door then. Jonathan took the initiative to greet him and return with him to where Brianna and Joseph waited solemnly. As soon as everyone sat, Jonathan inquired, "Brianna, you have, I hope, had sufficient time to think the matter over and make your decision?"

Looking at no one but him, she nodded, "Incredibly difficult as it was, yes, I have come to my conclusion." She stopped speaking then, as her heart began to race nervously.

Gently, Jonathan prompted, "Go on, dear; it will do none of you any good to keep waiting. Nor will it make your situation any easier."

Nodding, she agreed, "You are right, Jon." And, so, with tear-filled eyes, she looked to Devon. "You, my dashing love, will never know what it means that you would risk so much to be with me. You have traveled halfway around the world to claim my hand as your wife. You honor me greatly and there are no other words I can offer to express how flattered I am by your gesture."

She turned to Joseph then and found it extremely challenging to look into his warm brown eyes, now lit with the slightest ray of hope. Walking to him, she took his hands in hers and whispered so lightly that Devon and Jonathan had to strain to hear her words. "My sweet, sweet Joseph, when there was no one, there was you. I have loved you with all of my heart and you are the dearest of my friends."

Joseph's heart sank then and Brianna could see its descent in his face. For a split second, Brianna wondered if she had made the right choice. She closed her eyes, feeling tears spill down her cheeks as she forced herself to continue as practiced. "There could never truly be a replacement for you in my life, for you are like a brother to me and I will always remember you and the honest love we shared." He tried to pull his hands away, but she held tight. Brianna needed to feel his touch while she said the last of what she wanted him to hear—but if she didn't hurry, her rolling tears would soon make it impossible for her to speak. "I beg of you to feel no ill will toward me and I wish you all of the best. Go and find someone worthy of your love, for I cannot give you what you deserve in a wife."

"Bria . . ." Joseph would have tried to sway her, and though it caused her great pain, she stopped him.

"No, Joseph, my choice is made."

In that moment, Brianna knew fully that she had indeed made the right decision. From the instant she had heard Devon's voice thundering across this very room during the wedding ceremony, fate had sealed her life—melded her to Devon at long last.

How she had ever thought she could possibly forget her love for him or move on to share her life with another man was ridiculous. Brianna loved Devon with everything in her soul and there was not a thing in the world that would change that. Time and trials had already tried and failed. Her love for him was everlasting.

Looking to Devon's blue eyes then, she announced, "My choice has always been the same. I will be Devon's wife."

Joseph did pull away from Brianna's touch then and she no longer tried to stop him.

To his credit, Devon did not show any emotion at all, though a wave of triumph flowed forcefully through his veins at her proud declaration. Furthermore, it stunned him that he felt a weight lift from his heart—a weight of worry he hadn't totally realized was there until it was gone. That feeling only solidified Devon's appreciation of Brianna as he became conscious of just how much credit he had given Joseph as competition against him. Devon admitted to himself that though he had confidently sensed he would be Brianna's ultimate choice, there had surely been moments during the night when she had wavered between the two of them. It was a fact that he could not deny no matter how much his incredible pride wished to do so.

Devon knew beyond all doubt that if he were the one left behind, he would have hoped Joseph would be a gentleman and not flaunt his victory, so, standing slowly, Devon walked out of the room, pausing at Brianna's side long enough to say, "I will leave you to say your farewells. Send for me at the *Enchantress* when you are ready for my return." Brianna nodded and watched him leave the room.

Without a word, Jonathan stood and kissed Brianna softly on the cheek. Patting Joseph on the shoulder, he then followed Devon's lead and left Joseph and Brianna alone.

Immediately, Joseph turned to go, but Brianna stopped him with her words. "Joseph, please understand that I am sor . . ."

With more strength than he felt, Joseph demanded gruffly, "Do not tell me you are sorry, Brianna. Whatever else you say if you say you're sorry then our love—*my* love for *you*—meant nothing."

Tears streamed over her cheeks unchecked and she begged, "Please don't think that, Joseph. Your love meant everything to me. You saved me when there was no one else."

His brown eyes held confusion, but his words held pain, anger and conviction. "No, I filled a space when *Devon* was not there."

The truth-filled words were hard for Brianna to hear, but she took them without argument. She knew that she deserved every scathing remark he threw her way. "I thought he would never be free to love me," she excused weakly.

"And so that made it right for you to offer what was left of your heart to me?" Shaking his head, Joseph admitted, "I would rather have never loved you than to feel the pain this separation is bringing."

"Joseph, you knew that it was difficult for me to let go. We talked about it just a few days ago."

He nodded his affirmation. "Difficult, yes, but not impossible. I knew you were always thinking of him and I was a fool to believe I could make you forget him. The love you felt for him was always there in your eyes. Even those times when you looked at me with affection, Devon was always there, haunting you and taunting me. I thought that maybe in time . . . ." Joseph stopped—there was no reason to say more, nothing would change because of it.

He walked away from her and looked out the window to the street. "It doesn't matter now at any rate, does it, Brianna?"

When he looked back at her with a contemptuous expression, Brianna was desperate to find some comfort for him. "I want you to know that I am not sorry that I loved you, Joseph, but I *am* sorry that I hurt you."

Smiling weakly, the look barely reaching his eyes, he returned to her side and leaned down to kiss her softly on the lips. "It will take a long time, Brianna, but one day that hurt will fade and then I will love again." Standing straight, he allowed his fingers to trace the same course his lips had just made and added, "But a piece of my heart will always be left to you." Brianna could say nothing in reply. "I don't suppose I'll be seeing you again." He cleared his throat of the thickness accumulating there and finished, "So I wish you all the best."

"And I you, Joseph," she returned and before she could move to see him out, the dearest man she knew walked heart-broken from her home and her life.

◊◊◊◊◊

Brianna sent for Devon late in the afternoon, requesting that he join her in time for supper. Then they could spend the evening talking and deciding what their next step would be. It also gave her time to rest and freshen up after the very emotional twenty-four hours she had just endured.

Devon arrived as requested and they shared a companionable meal before retiring to the parlor. "Did you have an easy journey during your return?" Brianna asked curiously, curling into the crook of the davenport as was her custom.

Devon enjoyed the familiarity of her perch and taking the chair closest to the fire, answered with complete curiosity, "Has there been a time when something between you and me was *ever* simple?"

Scrunching up her nose, she remarked, "That difficult, was it?"

He smiled and amended, "I have been on worse voyages, but this one was so important that even the slightest delay seemed far longer than it actually was."

"Poor Drake."

Devon looked offended. "Drake? What about *me*?"

"You, my love, will never truly understand exactly *how* insufferable you can be. In a situation aboard the *Sea Enchantress*, Drake will always deserve and receive the most of my sympathy."

Chuckling softly at what he knew to be a well-earned truth, Devon admitted, "Near to a quarter of my crew has yet to speak to me. I fear I was a harsh commander during the entire trip."

Feigning surprise, she teased, "Come now, Devon, surely you must be exaggerating, for I have never known a gentler man than you." Immediately Joseph's face sprang to her mind and a pang of guilt entered her eyes.

Devon read and understood it. Soothingly, he suggested, "Brianna, you can talk about what happened if you think it will make you feel better."

Shaking her head, she answered, "No, I must put it behind me. With you is where I want to be and I cannot feel guilty over that for the rest of our lives."

"Thank you," he said, taking her completely off guard.

Brianna was not at all accustomed to hearing those words from Devon and at this moment was unsure as to why he spoke them. "I beg your pardon?"

"I said, thank you."

"I know *what* you said; I'm just not sure *why* you said it."

He shrugged. "I want to thank you for giving me another chance to prove my love for you, for being the woman that you are and for honoring me with your love. But most especially, I want to thank you for choosing me." His tone was deep and sincere and she dared not look at him for fear of where his bewitching eyes would lead her. Instead, she gazed into the fireplace and the flames burning there and answered truthfully, "The choice was an easy one. It was hurting Joseph that was difficult."

They were silent for a time, lost in their private thoughts, until Brianna asked, "How is everything at home?"

The way she automatically referred to his home as her own pleased Devon, but he was sorry that he must bear worrisome news. "Meghan has had some complications with her pregnancy and was on bed rest at Misty Heights when I left."

Brianna's eyes widened. "She must be going mad."

"If the babe hasn't arrived yet, I'd say yes, at least one of its parents has lost their sanity by now."

"And you say they are at Misty Heights, so everyone knows you've come for me?"

Devon grinned. "They *demanded* it."

Brianna felt comfortable warmth, like the feeling of family and belonging, slide into place. Still, she tried to sound miffed but came off more chagrined as she asked, "Did *no* one doubt that I would return with you?"

Smugly, Devon reminded her, "Well, they *have* witnessed the earth shattering effect I have on you."

"Perhaps they just know that I would be unable to resist the chance to meet Daniel's child first hand."

Pretending to contemplate her words, Devon corrected, "No, I think we *all* knew that your return has more to do with creating some Elliotts of your *own* than spoiling the one already in existence."

Even as she blushed, Brianna couldn't stop her laugh from bubbling forth and it felt good to set it free. "Well, knowing how you stop my advances at every opportunity, I imagine we'll be waiting a while longer for *that* happy occasion. Plus, since we've made it this long without actually *trying* to behave ourselves, it would be a shame to give in to our temptations before we're married now."

Devon mixed a stern glance with dry words, "Perhaps *you* were not trying, but *I* most definitely *was*. As for *waiting . . .*." He offered Brianna an all-knowing grin. ". . . Not even through the night."

Heat and longing filled every inch of Brianna.

With perfect timing, her emotions were interrupted as the Gordons were announced. Drake entered with them and the same priest that would have married Brianna to Joseph the day before brought up the end of the unexpected trail of visitors.

"Devon?"

With complete practicality he explained, "I thought that Father Beale would most understand our desire for haste. We both want some friends and witnesses in attendance." Lowering his voice as he moved to take her hand and pull her to her feet beside him, Devon assured softly, "And I have *no* intention of crossing the sea with you and not being able to partake of your body at every opportunity presented me."

When his words brought no comment, Devon looked down to see that he had shocked her speechless. Brianna was as red as her auburn hair. Color stained over her face and neck and Devon could scarcely wait to see if it spread all the way down to her lovely little toes.

◊◊◊◊◊

Brianna cried softly, though she felt no sadness. The fact was she could not recall a time that she had ever been happier.

With their hands clasped tightly together, Brianna was in the midst of becoming Devon's wife and the emotion of it all was remarkable.

She listened as he proudly declared her to be his one love for all his life and promised to keep her by his side through all trials and triumphs. Then, with softly spoken assurance, Brianna offered the same to Devon. In what seemed like seconds, she felt the gentle glide of a gold band being placed on her steady hand.

Devon's piercing blue eyes filled with unmatched elation. Though only a few witnesses attended to begin with, even they seemed to melt away until no one existed except he and Brianna.

As she returned each of his gestures, sealing them together forever, Devon felt tears welling in his eyes. It wasn't until Brianna's fingertips brushed the evidence of his joy from his cheek that Devon realized they had begun to fall.

Then the clergyman pronounced them man and wife.

Before the uniting words were fully uttered, Devon pulled her against him and just before their lips joined, he declared softly to his bride, "At long last." Then their lips met and with a kiss of tender claiming, he proved to everyone in witness that he intended to keep her as his for far longer than even their lives would last.

◊◊◊◊◊

Those invited to hear their vows lingered only a short time after the evening ceremony. Wishing the newlyweds well, the guests gracefully began taking their leave. Now, as she stood in the entrance hall at her new husband's side, Brianna suddenly felt very nervous. She tried desperately to avoid looking at Devon, surely he would take one look at her and know in what direction her thoughts had strayed.

The man in question had no need to see his wife's eyes to know what she was trying to keep from him. In fact, he found it somewhat amusing that she continued to stare toward the closed doorway almost as though their guests still stood there.

Rather than tease her about her trepidation, though, Devon wanted to be entirely sympathetic to her feelings and stood in the silence. He used the time to gather his thoughts so that he could be sure of what he would say and how he could tactfully handle their present situation. Everything needed to be perfect for Brianna and he would make sure that it was.

Touching her no more than to pull her snugly against his side, Devon offered, "Do you know how happy you have made me this evening, Mrs. Elliott?"

If anything could garner her attention quickly, hearing her new name spoken aloud could. Brianna's head snapped around girlishly and she insisted, "Say that again."

Smiling, Devon smoothly slid his other arm around her so that she was standing within the circle of them both. "Mrs. Elliott."

Brianna beamed and felt a bit of her anxiety slip away. "I can only hope that I have made you at least half as happy as you have made me." With a serene smile, Brianna added, "And our parents are surely pleased as they look down upon us."

Devon smiled. "Of course they are."

"Did you know they considered arranging this marriage?" Brianna questioned, smiling at his instantaneous look of surprise.

"No, I never heard that." He smiled again at his new wife. "Though I'm not surprised, our parents were wise people. They knew how perfect I would be for you."

Brianna laughed. "Perhaps they knew my mild manner would tame your overflowing ego."

"Yes, I'm sure that was their plan," Devon mocked with an arch of his brow. Leaning toward her, Devon kissed her lips lightly. "I suppose we could stand here all night and discuss our parents' achieved plans, what initiated them and who in this new union is the happiest." Kissing her in a more lingering manner, he finished, "But I have *far* better ways in mind to prove my love and happiness to you than mere words."

Brianna's face colored, but she did not want to disappoint Devon and so asked with provocative innocence, "And will these overtures of yours be to my liking?"

"I guarantee it." Devon's voice was huskier than he had anticipated, but rather than scare her off, the sound seemed to have a much more positive effect on his bride.

Devon's confidence made Brianna's excitement grow, but she was enjoying their banter too much to give in yet and her laughter tickled his senses. "During our time apart, I had nearly forgotten how arrogant you could be."

"Well, we won't have that problem again."

"Good."

"And, in case you are not aware of it," he began, his tone becoming informative, "there is a great deal of difference between *arrogant* bragging and *certain* promise." The familiar light began to gleam in his sapphire eyes and Brianna knew that their game was in full swing now.

"Yes, well, I can safely say *that* is something you taught me long ago, my dear husband."

Smiling, Devon stated proudly, "There, *that* is *precisely* why I married you."

His sudden change of attitude surprised Brianna and she questioned, "Exactly *what* reason is that?"

Looking at her as though he was flabbergasted that she needed an explanation, Devon declared, "Because you are so accepting and aware of my unending wealth of knowledge on all matters."

An unladylike hoot of laughter erupted from her and Brianna corrected, "Oh, my love, even on our wedding day, I cannot allow you to exaggerate so greatly."

Looking fully abashed, Devon defended himself. "On which part did I exaggerate?"

Still in the midst of her full-blown laughter, Brianna answered, "I believe it was the part about your perfection and *unending* knowledge."

"Is that so?" Devon raised an eyebrow and waited for her reply. Brianna nodded affirmatively and he took the moment to point out, "*You* are the one who used the adjective *perfect*, not I." Smirking, he questioned, "Need I say more?"

"No, you *needn't*, but I am somehow *certain* you will, anyway."

When she offered more giggles, Devon reprimanded, "Why, you ungrateful whelp, are you actually claiming that I have not taught you *anything* since you have known me?"

Looking up to him, her laughter ceased and Brianna began to tease him in another manner. "Not *nearly* enough, Captain."

Pressing her body against his in a gesture that could have only one meaning—only one result—Brianna made her bold offering and comfortable willingness completely understood to Devon.

His reply was instantaneous; sweeping Brianna off her feet, Devon captured her lips in a tender kiss that promised far more than she had known to this point. Bounding up the stairs and into her room, Devon kicked the door closed behind him and stood Brianna on her feet again.

Without a word, he began to unfasten the closure of her light-blue dress and in only a matter of seconds, Devon had stripped Brianna so that all she wore were her stockings, slippers and chemise.

Holding her gaze with his searing one, Devon knelt before her and slid off first one slipper and then the other. Casually, he slid his hands up the length of her calf and around to the back of her thighs until he reached the tantalizing point where her stocking ended and flesh began.

With precision, he rolled each stocking down and over her feet in a caressing way that caused Brianna to tingle. Then with unexpected speed, he moved his hands upward, beneath the material of her chemise and pulled the slip over her head so that she stood before him with nothing to cover her. Brianna was totally at Devon's mercy—exactly where they both wanted her to be.

Though innocence made her mildly hesitant, Brianna did not look away from Devon's heated gaze. She instinctively knew that if she did, it would ruin the moment for her husband; so instead, she reached forward and began undressing him, too.

Brianna's movements were far more awkward than Devon's had been. Still, he did not help her. He was aching with the need to be free of his binding clothing. Still, he would give her the opportunity to touch him openly and at her own pace. Devon would not make her feel inadequate in any way.

Since he had divested his jacket somewhere downstairs, she began with the buttons on his vest, sliding them one-by-one from their slots. When that task was complete, she did the same to the buttons of his white shirt beneath and slowly pulled the tail from the waistline of his breeches. Brianna then pushed the fabric from his shoulders and watched it glide smoothly over his muscled arms and hands to fall on the floor behind him.

Tentatively, Brianna rubbed her palms over the front of his bronze shoulders. Her movements grazed over his chest and the muscles there rippled beneath her touch. When she reached the taut plane of his abdomen, Brianna ceased her movements and looked into Devon's understanding eyes. There was no teasing laughter there. He realized this was as far as Brianna could go on her own and the flush of her cheeks that began as embarrassment, deepened to desire when he took her hands in his and together they finished ridding him of the rest of his clothing.

Devon moved slowly, sliding his hands up the length of Brianna's bare back. His fingers stopped and grasped hold of the full auburn curls spilling against her skin. Gently, he pulled her to his heady kiss and in the process pressed against her body with his. Carefully urging her back, Devon closed the few inches between them and the bed. When her legs brushed against the covering, Brianna had nowhere to go but back and did so willingly.

She was achingly aware of each inch of Devon's body against her own and Brianna's entire form came alive with chills of eager anticipation. Reaching up, she braced her hands against his shoulders and ended their kiss. "Devon, I love you." Her soft declaration was clear with the need to at last be free. "I think I started loving you the night we first kissed."

"Aye? And when did you know it for certain, Flame?"

Brianna thought a moment and answered, "Many times, but the first I had no doubt of my love was the same day Hessie told me how you had made preparations for my homecoming."

He pretended insult. "What? Not when I taught you to swim?"

"I did say *many* times, didn't I?"

He smiled—a devilishness that was purely his entering his eyes. "You did, Flame. Now, allow me to add another certainty to your list of memories."

Devon kissed her again and Brianna felt the change in his touch; he was becoming more passionate and she followed his lead blindly. The air around her grew heavy and she closed her eyes. His mouth and hands covered her body with pleasures and tender whispers of his adoration for her and the way she was making him feel.

Brianna's hands moved of their own accord now and each caress that Devon showered upon her, she mimicked in her own way. The gratification way of his touch was quickly returned to him with the purest need to arouse.

When Devon moved to feel her more intimately, Brianna did the same and felt Devon's entire body shake with the sensation. Once she had driven him past restraint and he could wait no longer, Devon carefully moved over her so that she cradled him with her body. Kissing her slowly—sensuously—he pulled back to declare, "You are my life, Brianna. Without you, I am nothing." Her eyes glistened with unshed tears and rather than answer him with words, Brianna moved her body toward him, her unspoken invitation satisfied by him in the following instant.

Devon moved slowly, easing the way for her pleasure as much as he possibly could. The burning sensation of her tearing skin caused Brianna to tense, but Devon's comforting words and soothing caresses made the uncomfortable twinge pass almost as quickly as it had come.

Soon they were moving as one. Together they soared, sensations washing over them that neither felt capable of—or the want of—controlling.

Neither one commanded their lovemaking any more than the other. They shared everything—their touches, their pleasure filled sounds, their whispered endearments, their hearts and souls.

Brianna's world exploded around her and all feeling left her body, only to return full force in the next instant. The sensations continuously fluctuated on and off, ultimately leaving Brianna shaking and breathless, her entire form tingling.

Devon followed her lead and within moments, they were lying together, wrapped in the warmth and security of each other's loving embrace. They drifted slowly to sleep, each of them comfortable, content and thoroughly satisfied in the love that they freely shared.

Finally, they were together, as had been ordained from the start.

Epilogue

1846 ~ Misty Heights ~ Bolivar, Virginia

Brianna watched the flashing colors of the fireflies filling the late summer landscape as she walked hand-in-hand through the back garden with her husband. The silence was comfortable between them, but Brianna's stomach fluttered. She had lured Devon outside for privacy.

Their sweet son, Joshua, was only three months past his first birthday, but Brianna's suspicions had been building of late. She had not said a word to anyone but waited patiently and allowed the now familiar sensations of new motherhood to overtake her until she was certain of her condition. Though she knew Devon loved their son, she was nervous about his reaction to the idea of a new child so soon.

Turning with his arm around her, Devon would have led his wife back into the house when Brianna halted him. "Joshua is sleeping. Let's not hurry back inside. I want to take advantage of this quiet time together."

Immediately, Devon knew that Brianna had something on her mind. She always preferred to talk to him during a walk when she was unsure of his reaction. Rather than rush her into giving the information, he casually asked, "Have you heard from Deirdre recently?"

Rounding the corner of the house, they headed toward the shelter of nearby tress, keeping their backs to the soft light of the sunset. Brianna smiled. "Yes, and you will be happy to know that he has *finally* asked her to be his wife."

Laughing softly, he remarked, "It certainly took the man long enough." Looking down at his wife, he admitted, "Though I can understand his hesitancy. It would certainly take any man a great deal of time to get over you."

"Joseph will be a wonderful husband for Dee. I had known before that she was interested in Joseph, but I'm surprised I didn't figure him returning those feelings."

"Perhaps that's because you were too busy entrapping him for yourself," Devon scolded and Brianna swatted his arm—neither meaning any harm in their words or actions. "Still, everything is working out just as I knew it would—perfectly."

Rolling her eyes, Brianna inquired, "Are you *ever* wrong?"

Offering his familiar smirk, Devon replied smartly, "You have known me long enough to answer that question for yourself, Mrs. Elliott."

They walked without speaking for a time and the air began to fill with the night sounds of crickets and other nocturnal animals. "It will be quiet without Sarah here," Brianna remarked, knowing that her nervous referral to Daniel and Meghan's daughter was just a means to lead Devon carefully toward the necessary conversation.

"It was time for Daniel's family to move on. Besides, if they stayed, in time the cackling of women's chatter would deafen the remaining men."

Playfully, Brianna demanded, "And what will happen when *you* have a daughter who cackles along with them?"

A sense of something to come was creeping over Devon, but he reigned in his excitement. "Then I will teach her to have something of interest to say." Stopping their pace, he turned to Brianna, "As perhaps *you* do now?"

Brianna merely smiled, choosing to keep her womanly secret a bit longer. Devon allowed it and quizzed, "Tell me, what you will give her, My Flame?"

"Besides a wonderful father?" she asked and when he granted her a heart-stopping smile in appreciation of her compliment, Brianna finished, "Something to argue with him about."

Kissing her lightly, Devon laughed and then rested his hands on her still-flat abdomen. "Exactly how long do I have to prepare for this feminine onslaught?"

Relief flooded through Brianna. "No more than seven months."

Hugging her tightly, he promised, "Then I shall do my best to make you proud and give our daughter proper competition."

"I have the utmost faith that you will," Brianna assured him, allowing Devon to lead her back toward their home full of warmth, love and acceptance.

◊◊◊◊◊

Brianna woke to find the space in bed beside her empty. Climbing from beneath the cozy haven of covers, she walked to the adjoining room and found the door ajar. Remaining unseen, she stood in the doorway and spied the touching scene before her.

Warmth flooded Brianna as she watched her husband holding their son tenderly in his powerful arms. Slowly, Devon worked the rocking chair back and forth while snuggling the child close to him. It constantly amazed Brianna that she could love two people so very much. At times like this, the feeling totally consumed her.

The boy in Devon's arms murmured and his father looked up to watch Brianna enter the room with them. "I wonder if a time will come when I tire of looking at him, Flame. He is perfect."

Resting one hand on Devon's shoulder, and smoothing the dark curls from Joshua's forehead with the other, she leaned closer to whisper, "Would you expect anything less? He *is* an Elliott, after all."

Looking toward her with love and pride abounding, Devon kissed his wife's lips. "Do you know how much I love you?"

Taking their son from Devon's arms, Brianna placed him gently back into the cradle. Turning back toward her husband, she teased, "I think I could venture a guess."

His rocking stopped instantly and Devon scolded, "You *think*?"

Smiling sensuously, she walked close enough that the soft cotton of her nightgown brushed his fingertips resting on the arms of the chair. Continuing past, she stopped in the doorway leading to their room and suggested, "Perhaps you would care to show me so that I might be certain?"

Glancing once more at his sleeping son, Devon rose from the chair, quickly divested himself of his unbuttoned breeches and stalked her in all of his naked glory. "Gladly."

Following her across the room to the bed she had so recently vacated, he deftly pulled her sleeping gown from her body. Bared to his gaze, Devon looked down at her, braced himself with bent arms, so that his full weight was not on the child growing within her, and lowered his head to kiss her neck.

Teasing her pulse with his teeth, Devon inquired, "Am I to forever be put to this task, demanding wife?" Continuing with the mock tone of a man set to an undertaking he was weary of, he finished, "Or is it possible that some day you will be able to fully comprehend my love for you without these arduous reminders?"

When his mouth lowered to begin kissing her more intimately, Brianna moaned and guaranteed him, "I most certainly hope not."

Devon's laugh was sensual in the caress of his mouth and he stopped once more to ponder, "At least tell me that you know how happy you have made me."

Pushing aside her passionate frustration to enjoy another of their bantering conversations, which she held so dear, Brianna murmured, "I recall another day that you asked me that same question."

"As do I. Now I find myself wondering if you realize that my happiness has grown, even since then."

Moving her hand lower to the exact spot, Brianna responded, "Yes, I am completely aware of how happy you are with me, Devon." He nipped at her bare skin playfully and she squealed in delight.

"Minx," he growled, as her hand began to move slowly against him.

Stopping her motions, Brianna asked, "Would you care to rephrase that, Captain?"

His blue eyes opened lazily and he captured her lips with his own full ones. "Forgive me, Flame?" he whispered in his most seductive tone, his lips holding just a breath away from hers.

Delicious chills of expectation raced over every inch of Brianna's bare body. "Always," she returned and then gave herself to him and the feelings that they provoked in each other.

All of the passion that they had felt for so long and been forced to hold back was released each time they joined and this occasion was no different.

With the future in sight and their family growing, nothing held them back from their dreams now. They climbed closer toward the heavens in the love of each other's arms and knew that together they could endure all things—nothing would ever change that.

In all areas of their lives their souls were united as one— Devon always her protector and Brianna his brightly burning Emerald Flame.

Author's Note . . .

While researching for the *Treasured Love Series*, I discovered several interesting bits of historical information, which allowed me to add depth to my story.

In the 1840's, pedal-powered sewing machines were introduced to the United States. Just as my *Emerald Flame* character, Ruth Donnellson, did, many local seamstress' or tailors commonly used the machines in their shops to speed up production. However, many items were still hand-sewn at home since—like anything new—machine-sewn garments were relatively expensive.

Like Ruth Donnellson, her dry goods store is also a figment of my imagination. The earliest documentation found of a similar business in Harper's Ferry was Gilbert Brothers, located on Shenandoah Street during the 1880's.

The original structure of St. Peter's Catholic Church on High Street in Harper's Ferry burned during the Civil War; therefore, the description used within Emerald Flame is based on the current church, reconstructed after the war ended.

Finally, the correct spelling for Harper's Ferry (Harpers Ferry) is in constant question. It appears that the contemporary choice has no apostrophe. The earlier spelling follows the possessive form, mostly likely because in 1761 the town founder—Robert Harper—ran a ferryboat across the Potomac River. This area became a starting point for settlers moving west and in 1763, the Virginia General Assembly officially established the town as *Shenandoah Falls at Mr. Harper's Ferry*.

In the interest of historical accuracy, I have chosen to use the spelling most likely used during the 1800's, though both spellings are correct.

June 2009

Katrina "Kat" Shelley lives in rural Maryland where she and her husband, Michael, have three beautiful children together. In addition to her love of reading and writing, Katrina enjoys teaching, singing, walking outdoors, and visiting historical areas.

Katrina has also released books under the author names: Kat Shelley and Shelley Nakopoulos.

Contact Katrina Shelley:

Email
authorkatrinashelley@yahoo.com

Webpage
www.katrinashelley.webs.com

Twitter/@KatShelley

Facebook
"Like" Katrina Shelley

Dear Readers,

The Elliotts have been a part of my imagination for so
long that I am thrilled to share them with you.

Please continue to follow this family, with me, throughout
the entire *Treasured Love Series*.

Book One ~ Emerald Flame

Book Two ~ Forbidden Amber

Book Three ~ Golden Confessions

Book Four ~ Sapphire Storm

Book Five ~ Cherished Ruby

(Contemporary)
Book Six ~ Precious Pearls

Timeless Melody
A time travel romance connected to the Elliott's
through business and friendship.

Happy Reading,

Katrina Shelley

Treasured Love Series ~ Book Two
Forbidden Amber

Tansey has loved Daniel Elliott for as long as she can remember. Very likely, since the day his father bought her parents from a passing slave trader and gave them their beloved freedom.

Even with Daniel loving Tansey in return, the end of their young romance is inevitable--it is forbidden.

Desperate to flee the certain heartache of watching Daniel marry the proper woman for his social station, Tansey leaves behind all that is safe and familiar. Creating a network of new and unexpected friends, Tansey learns to enhance her strengths, deny her weaknesses, and face her greatest fears; until one man's evil-doing and the charge of a murder she did not commit, force her home again.

Arriving at Misty Heights, Tansey finds her haven as changed as she, and realizes that her greatest challenge since leaving Daniel Elliott behind, may be thwarting the temptation to once more become his Forbidden Amber.

Read on to enjoy a preview . . .

Prologue

A buckboard carriage stopped in front of the large manor house known as Misty Heights and its driver helped an attractive young woman down from her wooden perch. After placing her luggage on the steps in front of the house, the man accepted her thanks with a nod and went on his way.

Suddenly feeling very alone, the woman readjusted the hold she had on her belongings, took a deep breath and silently reminded herself that she belonged here. Front door or not, she was coming home. Familiar scents overwhelmed her, bringing with them a flood of memories that were mixed with pleasure and pain. A great deal had changed in her life since the last day she was in this house and, as she stood before its welcoming entrance again, she wondered if it had been long enough.

No one inside knew that she was coming. She had no idea what she would find behind the door or how the homes occupants would react to her reappearance.

Still, nothing was being accomplished by her standing outside like a coward. Squaring her shoulders, she pushed her reservations aside and moved forward. Her hand shook slightly as she dropped the brass knocker against the heavy whitewashed door.

For a time, she heard nothing from within. Just as she would have knocked again, the click of footfalls reached her ears, and the door opened. Neither of the entryway occupants uttered a sound, though their astounded gazes spoke volumes. In the seconds it took the first wave of emotional shock to subside, they were transported back in time through a myriad of memories each had tried in vain to forget.

After all the time she had been gone, nothing had really changed; not even Daniel and Tansey's broken hearts

Look MOM, something for the little ones . . .

Written by Katrina Shelley *as* Shelley Nakopoulos
Illustrations by Emma Nakopoulos

The love between a mother and her child is as endless as their imaginations! Explore the wonder of HOW BIG that can be!

http://www.createspace.com/3397685

Soar through the year with monthly rhymes and artwork showing what the months look like to a child illustrator.
Allow your budding artist to create his or her own illustrations on the blank pages within the book.

https://www.createspace.com/3431604

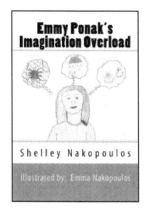

Psst! Hey, You! It's Emmy Ponak. The girl inside this book . . .

Ever since Emmy's parents told her they were moving into a new house, she was against the whole plan. A new house meant a new school, new neighbors and new creepy noises!

(Young Reader Chapter Book)
https://www.createspace.com/3524664

Read on for and EXCERPT:

↑
That's Me!

Emmaleigh Ruth Ponak

I am Emmy Ponak.

Well, my real name is Emmaleigh Ruth Ponak

because Mom and Dad named me after some

people in my family from the old days. My hair is brownish and wavy. My eyes are kind of green and kind of brown (I think that's called hazel) and my face is sprinkled with freckles.

What's sprinkled?

That just means some here and some there, like those colored candy thingys on top of a yummy ice cream cone or the quick thoughts and pictures that jump around in my brain all day. My grown-ups say that's 'cause of some letters. I think it's AD something, but I never really hear all of that messed up alphabet, 'cause I'd rather think about what I want to draw the very second I get home.

Anyway, though, Mom and Dad and Dr. Riddlin say that even with those letters, I'm a normalish kind of nine-year-old girl, living in the United States of America.

Did you stand up and stick your chest out real proud or salute?

I always try to do that whenever anybody says something about the good ole U.S. of A. 'cause a long time ago, before I was born, my daddy used to be a Marine and now it's his job to make other people want to be a Marine, too. I'm pretty sure that makes standing tall and proud for the country we live in a supposed-to.

What's a supposed-to?

That's those things grownups are always saying over and over again, like Emmy, you're supposed-to put your clothes in the hamper. Sometimes it sounds like, Emmy, you're supposed-to put your dishes in the sink, or, Emmy, you're supposed-to turn the light off when you leave the room.

Most the time I try to think hard about my supposed-to's, but keeping up with them all the time just makes me super, extra-big, tired and when that happens, sometimes my head gets to hurting and watch out, 'cause . . .

Well . . . never mind that, since we're just getting to know each other. Let's just take it slow. It'll be fun to see how we might be the same and how I'll do, making it through ANOTHER week of all my supposed-to's . . .

Chapter One New Home, Creepy Home

From the first day Emmy's mom and dad told her that they were moving into a new house, she was against the whole plan. A new house meant a new school, new neighbors, new friends to make, and new noises to get used to.

"Mom, just tell me *one last time*, why, oh, why do I have to share a room with Gracie? She still cries in the middle of the night and she's going to keep me awake and you know how I need my sleep or the niceness stays away from my heart."

Emmy's mom sighed and set down what seemed like the three-hundredth box she had brought into the new house that day. "Emmy, will you *please* stop complaining? I told you *and* your father told you that you only have to share a room with Gracie until we get the attic fixed up for your bedroom."

Emmy watched her mom take some blue dishes out of a box, rinse and dry them and then stack them all neatly in a cupboard.

Thinking she had watched and waited long enough, Emmy asked, "What's the rest of that hit line, mom?"

Mom kept stacking plates. "What's a hit line?"

"You know, the funny part of a joke."

Mom smiled a little. "You mean a punch line, *not* a hit line and, there isn't one."

Sounding a little frustrated, Emmy said, "Mom, *every* joke has a punch line."

Emmy's Mom nodded her head. "You are right about that, but *this* isn't a joke."

"What do you mean, it's *not* a joke?"

Stopping her work, Mom looked away from the dishes and at Emmy. "Sweetie, I promise the attic is going to make a super-cool bedroom for you."

Emmy huffed real loud, crossed her arms, and looked at her mom with eyes that said they didn't believe her words. "Mom, it doesn't matter how fun you *try* to make it sound, I just *can't* sleep in that place."

Mom looked confused. "Why not?"

Emmy couldn't believe her mom even needed to ask that question. "Mother, do you *know* what lives in attics?"

"Yes . . . *you* do."

Emmy tried to understand her mother's crazy talk. "Mom, are you *really* going to make your first-born daughter sleep up there with ghosts and spiders and bats and creaky noises?"

"Emmaleigh," Mom said in the way she did when she was getting aggravated. "*How* many times do I have to tell you that there is *no* such thing as ghosts?"

That was a super-duper easy question for Emmy to answer. "About a-hundred times for every *Creepy Kid Caper* movie I watch or book I read."

"Well, we can fix that. You just won't watch anymore of those scary shows until you're big enough to remember that they are only pretend," Mom said serious-like.

Emmy's eyes popped big and her voice went squeaky-high. "But, Mom-*uh*! Just give me one more chance. I *have* to watch them, they're my favorite and I'll be brave of those things now that you reminded me they are pretend."

Whatever Mom could have replied stopped because Emmy's little sister, Gracie, ran into the room and whooshed right past them with her long, little legs flying. Before Gracie could stop her quick feet, she bounced off the screen door and flopped smack-dab on her bottom.

The very next thing, she fell over and started laughing loud from her belly.

Mom closed the cupboard door slow and kept her eyes shut while she talked in a dangerous-quiet way. "Emmy, take Gracie out back and keep an eye on her for me."

Forgetting all about her promise to be brave, Emmy asked, "Mom, have you heard a word I've been sayin' to you?"

Mom's eyebrows got real close together. "*Now*," she said, pointing her finger like Emmy might have forgotten where the backdoor was.

Now, just let me tell you, I love that four-year-old Lillian Grace, especially when she pretends to be a cat named Fee-Fee. But, right now, even THAT fun wasn't about to keep me off the thin ice Nana (Dad's Mom) says I tread on a lot, especially since one side of my brain was tellin' me to be smart and drag Gracie into the backyard to play and the other side of my brain was screamin' that I'd pro'bly be a whole lot smarter to stay right where my body was.

Trying to decide which side of her brain to listen to, Emmy walked toward the back door and looked out to the place her mom was trying to send her and Gracie.

(Prob'ly to our DOOM!)

Made in the USA
Charleston, SC
05 December 2013